HER BROTHER'S KEEPER

BAEN BOOKS by MIKE KUPARI

Dead Six (with Larry Correia)
Swords of Exodus (with Larry Correia)

Her Brother's Keeper

HER BROTHER'S KEEPER

MIKE KUPARI

HER BROTHER'S KEEPER

A Baen Books Original

Baen Publishing Enterprises
P.O. Box 1403
Riverdale, NY 10471
www.baen.com

ISBN: 978-1-4767-8090-0

Cover art by Alan Pollack

First printing, November 2015

Distributed by Simon & Schuster
1230 Avenue of the Americas
New York, NY 10020

Library of Congress Cataloging-in-Publication Data

Kupari, Mike.
  Her brother's keeper / Mike Kupari.
      pages cm
  ISBN 978-1-4767-8090-0 (paperback)
1. Science fiction. I. Title.
  PS3611.U6H47 2015
  813'.6—dc23

                                                        2015030759

10 9 8 7 6 5 4 3 2 1

Pages by Joy Freeman (www.pagesbyjoy.com)
Printed in the United States of America

"All I ask is a tall ship and a star to steer her by."

—John Masefield

HER BROTHER'S KEEPER

Avalon
Arthurian System
Aberdeen Province, Northern Hemisphere

A cold ocean wind buffeted the elegant ground car as it made its way up the hill. Catherine Blackwood sat in the plush back seat, brooding in contemplative silence. The car's quiet hydrogen engine offered little more than a hum in the background, nothing to interrupt her thoughts. She peered out of the window, to her palatial home at the top of the hill. Blackwood Manor, ancestral home of Clan Blackwood. Catherine's family had owned this estate for centuries.

It hasn't changed at all. An elegant mansion stood like a monolith at the crest of the hill, flanked by groves of genetically enhanced oak and evergreen trees. The trees swayed in the same icy winds that rushed in to greet Catherine as the car door opened. She stepped onto the polished cobblestone drive, shoved her hands into the pockets of her flight jacket, and headed for the door.

With such history looming over her, Catherine felt uneasy being there. As she approached the ornate front doors, she felt like an interloper sneaking into someplace she didn't belong. She's grown up in that house, but it had been fifteen years since she'd laid eyes on it. It was fall in the highlands of the Aberdeen Province, and snow swirled in the salty ocean wind. Winter would be upon the Blackwood Estate soon, and Catherine was glad she wouldn't be there to see it.

Avalon was a cool world, and Aberdeen Province was the northernmost inhabited province. The winters were long, dark, and brutally cold. The ocean would freeze over all the way to the horizon, and two meters of snow would fall at the higher elevations. Catherine had had her fill of such winters growing up; just thinking about them darkened her mood. The sooner she lifted off from this miserable rock the happier she'd be.

Her anxiety worsened as she was led into the house by a gracious and courteous servant. She knew the way, of course, but politely let the young housemaid guide her to the manor's library. The maid's high-heeled shoes clicked on a polished floor made of native hardwood as they entered the room. Shelves of actual paper-and-binding books lined the walls beneath a vaulted ceiling. Warm light flickered from a cozy fireplace against one wall. Blackwood Manor was equipped with every modern convenience, but was built with an eye for old-world, prespace aesthetics. Wooden floors and paper books were luxuries on a world that had no native trees when it was first colonized. Forests were seeded during the terraforming process, but even after eight centuries of development, having wood furnishings was considered a luxury on Avalon.

A conservatively dressed male servant, as unfamiliar to her as the maid, quietly entered the room. The housemaid bowed and excused herself. He addressed Catherine formally, his hands folded behind his back. "Lady Blackwood, your father will be in to see you momentarily. If I may be so bold, my lady, welcome home."

Lady Blackwood. Catherine's heart sunk. That had been her mother's title, before she died. Now, as the eldest and only daughter of Clan Blackwood, that title was hers. Her father had never remarried. Dismissing the sad memories, Catherine thanked the man, and he too departed with a bow. She felt a slight twist in her stomach; the anticipation was getting to her. *Get a hold of yourself,* she thought bitterly. *It's only your father.*

It wasn't fear, so much. Catherine's father was a stern man, but he wasn't a monster. Perhaps it was the atmosphere, perhaps it was how long she'd been away. Being back in her ancestral home, so steeped in history as it was, made her feel small. She hadn't felt so unsure of herself in a long time. Once again, Catherine found herself wishing she was already on her way back to the spaceport, to leave Blackwood Manor and Avalon itself safely behind her.

The veteran spacer steeled herself as the door to her father's study quietly slid open. Catherine's last encounter with her father hadn't been pleasant, and she wasn't about to let him see her discomfort. He approved of neither her profession nor her lifestyle, and like the hot-tempered young woman who had stormed out all those years ago, she now quietly reveled in her rebelliousness. At the same time, she couldn't help but wonder why her father had asked her to come home. Tracking her down couldn't have been easy. It was this curiosity, she told herself, that had driven her to accept the invitation home.

Catherine squared her shoulders and folded her hands behind her back as her father entered the library. Even with the miracles of modern medicine, the years had taken their toll on him. His hair had gone completely gray and had thinned. He was far too practical a man to bother with silly cosmetic improvements like hair replacement.

"Father," Catherine said carefully.

Augustus Blackwood wasn't as imposing as Catherine remembered, but his eyes still burned with the fire of a man who never let anything stand in his way. He surprised his daughter by actually smiling. "My dear Catherine," he said, still speaking with the ancient, prespace Scottish accent that Avalon was known for. "My God, you look just like your mother now. My heart skipped a beat when I saw you. I'm so glad you came."

He didn't go so far as to embrace his estranged daughter, but Catherine was nonetheless taken aback by her father's candor. Commodore (retired) Councilman Augustus Blackwood was the most reserved man Catherine had ever known. He was the personification of a stereotypical Avalonian: stern, notoriously stubborn, proud to a fault, and so conservative as to be considered backward by those on other civilized worlds. Catherine had rarely seen this side of her father, and hardly at all after her mother died.

"I . . . it's good to see you too, Father," Catherine managed. "It *has* been a long time."

Her father nodded. "Indeed. Fifteen years now, is it?"

"Something like that. You, ah, look well."

Augustus chuckled sardonically. "I'm a few pounds heavier and a great deal balder than when I last saw you, but I get by. But you, my dear, you take my breath away. If only your mother could see you now!"

Catherine very much doubted her mother would approve of her drab spacer's flight suit. It's not how a proper lady from Clan

Blackwood should be seen, after all. Catherine wondered if any of the traditional Avalonian garb she'd had when she left home would still fit.

"I don't know what Mother would think of me," Catherine admitted honestly. "She always wanted me to be happy, but she expected...she expected a different outcome."

The old man's demeanor subtly darkened. This was not a pleasant topic of discussion. "As did I," he said flatly. Seeing the anger in his daughter's eyes, Augustus raised a hand before an argument could begin. "That's in the past now. I didn't call you home across God-only-knows how far to argue with you about your chosen profession."

"God isn't the only one who knows how far I traveled to get here. I was in Concordiat space, dropping off some VIP passengers on New Peking. That's over seven hundred hours of travel time, quite a bit of my ship's stores consumed, and a lot of remass burned. This is not even accounting for the money lost by running a personal errand and not taking on a contract. Fortunately, I was still in the Outer Colonies."

Augustus was a stubborn old goat, but he was an entrepreneur who had made his fortune expanding the family business, the Blackwood and Associates Trading Company. Catherine could see a twinkle of pride in his eye at her no-nonsense business sense, even if her "business" was something as uncouth as *privateering*.

Before saying anything, Augustus walked over to the wet bar near the fireplace. It was an old-fashioned fixture, built by hand out of polished wood and stocked with the finest Avalonian and off-world liquors money could buy. He chose an ornate bottle of twenty-year-old brandy, placed two small glasses on the bar, and poured.

Offering one of the drinks to his daughter, Augustus appeared to ponder his in silence for a few seconds before speaking. He was obviously troubled.

"I know it was a great deal of trouble for you to get home. It was a great deal of trouble for me to *find* you. I've had every ship in our fleet under orders to locate you, as well as every courier I could hire. I had them scouring registered flight plans, trying to figure out where you had gotten off to. Believe me when I say that I wouldn't have tracked you down and asked you to come all this way if the situation weren't so dire. You will be reimbursed for your expenses. But...your family is in trouble, Catherine. We..." He paused, taking a contemplative sip of alcohol. "I need your help."

Catherine was concerned, but intrigued. Her father had a fleet of interstellar-capable ships at his disposal. What sort of help could he need from a privateer? Catherine's ship, the *Andromeda*, was a capable vessel, but it couldn't move goods or people like one of the Company's freighters. Moreover, she'd never, in her entire life, actually heard her father *ask for help*.

"Father, what's going on?"

"Things have been going poorly for the business over the last few years. I've been lobbying my more protectionist compatriots on the Council to loosen some of our trade regulations and reduce tariffs, but the stubborn fools are worried about protecting in-system mining. I've tried to tell them that Avalon can't compete economically on domestic resource extraction alone, not when there's an entire galaxy full of unclaimed raw materials. The Miners' Guild may as well have a seat on the Council, though. Their hands are in enough bloody pockets."

Catherine had no love for Avalon's Byzantine politics. The skullduggery, the alliances, the rivalries, all of it seemed so petty to her. Before she could ask what any of this had to do with her, her father spoke again.

"Aberdeen has been hit hard by this recession. Many of our citizens have left for other provinces, or even emigrated off-world. The bloody Concordiat is stealing some of our best and brightest spacers! There are entire markets we could break into if the fools on the Council would only let us!"

Avalon was an old, long-established colony world, dating back to the waning days of the Second Federation. Some of its laws were archaic, including those regarding trade, and had been written centuries prior, with little amendment since. They reflected a much more dangerous, unstable time in inhabited space, when Avalon struggled for survival. The galactic map had changed, and so had the interstellar political and economic situation. Unfortunately, it seemed that the law hadn't changed with the times.

Catherine took a moment to sip her drink, choosing her words carefully. Her father was obviously deeply concerned, but he still had the notorious Blackwood temper. The last thing Catherine wanted was to have spent weeks in transit only to have an argument with him.

"I'm sorry to hear of your troubles, Father. What is it, exactly, that I can do for you?"

Augustus' eyes narrowed. "*My* troubles? Might I remind you that you are still Lady Blackwood of Clan Blackwood? Aberdeen is your home. Avalon is your home. Do you care nothing for your family name? Have you been in space so long that you've forgotten where you came from?"

As an experienced captain, Catherine knew the importance of being calm under pressure. Letting your temper get the better of you led to poor decisions which, in the unforgiving darkness of space, often had fatal consequences. Yet she struggled to maintain her reserve after her father's self-righteous comments. She, too, had the famous Blackwood temper, and had to resist the temptation to let him prod her into an outburst.

"No, I haven't forgotten," she said levelly. "How *is* Cecil, by the way? I seem to recall a conversation wherein you explained to me how he was the more suitable heir, being that he was fortunate enough to have been born with a penis and all."

Augustus' eye twitched involuntarily as Catherine named her younger brother. "Catherine, your brother—"

"And then," she interrupted. Her temper *had* gotten the best of her, she reflected. "I recall another conversation where it was made perfectly clear to me that a proper lady had no business in the Space Forces, despite graduating at the top of her class at the Academy. So yes, Father, I remember where I come from. I come from a narrow-minded, backward planet where a woman isn't good enough to do anything of note! Where I come from is the cultural laughingstock of civilized space!" That wasn't true, exactly. There were plenty of far-flung colonies that were known to be less enlightened than stodgy Avalon.

The room seemed to darken as Augustus' own famous temper rumbled. "Laughingstock? You impudent child! *I* was the laughingstock! My son and heir is a mercurial fool who couldn't manage a vending machine without cocking it up, and my daughter and eldest is a stubborn, self-righteous *Sapphic* who cares more about chasing her own wild impulses as a bloody *pirate* than she does the good of her family and her people! No, my dear, it was I who was laughed at. Those damned arrogant fools on the Council have had a grand old time at the expense of my name, and have managed to all but marginalize the Seat of Aberdeen in the process!"

Catherine gave her father an icy stare. Her hands unconsciously balled into fists. Beyond her father's prejudices, beyond his chauvinist impulses, even beyond the fact that he had sabotaged her career in the Space Forces, Catherine was aghast at being referred to as a *pirate*.

"Is that what this is about, then?" she asked, quietly seething. Her own Scottish-Avalonian accent became more pronounced with her anger. "I scarcely hear from you in years, and now you call me across space to insult my ship? Are you quite finished, then? Because I'll admit that I didn't turn out how you wanted, but I am *damned* good at what I do. I didn't go from being a junior flight officer on board the *Andromeda* to owning and commanding her because of my family name! *Nothing* was handed to me! I bloody well *earned* everything I have, Father, including the respect of my crew. My services are in high demand, and my reputation is impeccable! If you want to know about pirates, I can tell you about the nine confirmed pirate kills my ship has. But that will have to wait, because my time is very valuable. So if you're quite finished berating me and taking out your frustration with Cecil on me, I'll be on my way back to the spaceport. Perhaps we can do this again in another fifteen years."

Augustus Blackwood was red faced, and looked ready to explode. His daughter ignored his anger and turned to leave. "Catherine, wait," he said, before she left the library. She paused, turned slightly, and looked at him over her shoulder.

"Please," he continued, seemingly deflated. "Forgive an old man his pride. I didn't have you come all this way just to start an argument. I really do need your help, child. Surely you wouldn't see your family ruined just to spite me."

Catherine turned to face her father once again, and took a deep breath. "It hurt, Father. Not so much that you didn't name me as your heir. I understand how that would've been fought by the others on the Council. But when I decided to pursue my military career? Despite all the biases against me, despite everything, I *made* it. When I was assigned to the Fleet it was the proudest day of my life. I . . . thought you would have been proud of me. Clan Blackwood has such a history of military service. I was honoring the family."

The cheery fire snapped and popped as Augustus poured himself another, larger drink. He took a long sip from his glass before speaking again. "I was proud, Catherine. I wished so badly that your mother could have been alive to see it. I didn't want to end your career that way."

Before Catherine could complete her midshipman cruise on a Space Forces ship, the Avalonian High Council rescinded a ruling that allowed women to serve on board combat vessels. That ruling had been a desperate wartime expedient dating back over a hundred years, to the Second Interstellar War, but it had never been reversed.

Much to her own surprise, Catherine struggled to maintain composure. "Then why?"

"I was pressured by the Council. I wasn't the only seat holder with an unmarried daughter, you know. There was concern that you would start some sort of revolution. At the time, the Women's Legal Reform Coalition was pushing the Council to change the laws of primogeniture." For centuries, women could not legally inherit titles or lands under Avalonian law. After the war, the laws were changed so that a first-born daughter could inherit if there were no suitable male heirs, since so many had died in the Maggot onslaught. "The Reformers wanted equal inheritance rights for sons and daughters."

"How dreadful," Catherine commented dryly.

"Yes, well, at the time, the Reformers were quite popular with the commoners. Once the press caught wind of you graduating at the top of your Academy class, you were on your way to becoming a folk hero."

"Really?"

Augustus chuckled. "Indeed. You were too busy with your training and your studies to pay any attention to the media, but my people were being bombarded with requests for interviews with you. I...well, I'm afraid I suddenly found myself under a great deal of scrutiny from the Council, and a great deal of pressure. They were worried about the precedent you were setting."

"I was hardly the first Avalonian woman to serve on a military vessel."

"Indeed you weren't, but you were the only female officer in living memory serving not in the Women's Auxiliary but in the actual armed forces. The old fools on the Council, including *this* old fool, allowed too many activists and lobbyists to whisper into our ears. They told us of the social unrest that would inevitably occur if this sort of thing was allowed to continue. They warned us that first, women would be serving on combat ships, then daughters would be inheriting Council seats, and after that, a movement to institute elections would begin. Avalon, they said, would fall to the same social unrest that has plagued so many other colonies, and it would all start with you."

Catherine raised an eyebrow. "Elections? I was hardly intent on starting some ill-conceived democracy movement. I've studied history, I know where that sort of thing leads. I was never a political crusader."

Augustus took another sip. "I know, my dear, but I was under such pressure. The other Council Families were plotting alliances behind my back, threatening to marginalize me, to undermine the authority of the Blackwood name."

"Since when does Augustus Blackwood bow to such pressure?" Catherine asked.

Her father winced as if the words had physically wounded him. "I...I was wrong, Catherine. I was wrong to let those bloody dinosaurs sway me. I was compromising, I told myself, just like a responsible councilman should. All my so-called compromise did was embolden the vultures the next time they wanted something from me. It caused me no end of grief." Augustus looked contemplatively into the brandy in his glass. "And cost me a daughter. Forgive me, child. Forgive me my shortsighted pride."

Catherine's practiced command presence was the only thing that kept the tears back. This was the first time she'd heard her father apologize for anything since her mother had died. She took another sip of her own drink to keep her composure.

"Yes, well...what's done is done, I suppose. I like to think that I did well enough for myself regardless. At any rate we've gotten rather off topic, haven't we? What is it I can do for you, Father?"

Augustus' demeanor darkened again. "It's Cecil."

A pang of concern went through Catherine's chest. She wasn't close to her brother anymore, but he had been all she'd had after their mother died and their father became withdrawn and distant. "What's wrong?"

"He's been off-world for two years, and now he's being held for ransom. I need you to go find him, get him back, and bring him home."

"*Ransom?* Where is he?"

"As far as I know," Augustus said, "he is on Zanzibar."

Catherine closed her eyes and pinched the bridge of her nose between her finger and thumb. *Zanzibar.* A lawless, strife-torn, failed colony world near the raggedy edge of inhabited space. "What in God's name is Cecil doing there?"

New Austin
Lone Star System
Las Cruces Spaceport, Laredo Territory
Southern Hemisphere

"Marshal," the deputy sheriff complained, "are you sure about this? Everything looks normal to me."

Colonial Marshal Marcus Winchester ignored the deputy and continued to study the ship parked on the ramp through multifunction binoculars. With the optics zoomed in and gyro-stabilized, he was able to read the registration number on the hull of the ship. He turned to the bewildered-looking spaceport traffic controller and asked him if he'd run the ship's number when it set down.

"Of course," the controller said nervously. He was a short, sweaty man with a bad comb-over. "It checked out. That's the *Luxor*, an independent free trader. She comes through here two or three times a year."

Marcus frowned, lifting the binoculars to his eyes again. The *Luxor* had a fat, cylindrical hull capped with a blunt, rounded nose. Her unpainted gunmetal hull was covered with scorch marks, dents, and fabricated repairs. She stood a hair over fifty-three meters tall on her landing jacks. Stubby, aerodynamic radiators and small airfoils jutted out of her hull. The *Luxor* was presently the only ship on the parking apron at the so-called Las Cruces Spaceport, and was connected to the service tower at the port's only fully functional launch pad. The bridge from the tower was locked into the ship's open cargo bay, and a retractable umbilical refilled her reaction mass tanks. The spaceport terminal where Marcus found himself was maintained by robots and was in pristine condition, despite being practically deserted.

Marcus' partner, Deputy Marshal Wade Bishop, tapped the screen of his handheld. "She checks out, Boss," he said without looking up. "She's an old tub, currently registered to Captain Bartleby Oleander out of the Llewellyn Freehold. That comes from their transponder download from when they arrived in-system. Everything else I can pull up on the ship is from more than a year ago."

"The Freeholders ain't exactly known for their deep and abiding respect for customs law," Marcus said with a grin. "The only reason they bother to register in Concordiat space at all is so they can trade with the Inner Colonies. There's a very good chance that info is out of date or an outright lie."

The Llewellyn Freeholders were considered to be a bunch of belligerent anarchists by most civilized societies. Their colony had a barely functioning central government with almost no actual authority. The Freehold was notorious for its easy access to every imaginable vice and the stubborn, individualistic independence of its small permanent population. What existed on Freehold couldn't exactly be called a "black market"; as long as you weren't killing people or trafficking in slaves, you could buy or sell just about anything you could want on the open market. There were no taxes to speak of, precious few actual laws, and no police. Unscrupulous traders and smugglers would often register their ships as out of the Freehold to give themselves political cover.

None of that constituted suitable probable cause to detain the ship. If its registration information was outdated or forged, that was a job for the Colonial Customs Service, not the marshals.

This has to be the ship, Marcus thought to himself. *Why else would a free trader land way the hell out here?* With only two million total inhabitants, Las Cruces Spaceport was remote even by the standards of a frontier colony world. It was a former Concordiat Defense Force auxiliary landing field, built a century prior during the height of the Second Interstellar War. It wasn't used much then, and was effectively abandoned after the Concordiat achieved its hard-fought victory against the Maggots. It was run by one of the big mining firms on New Austin, who let non-company ships use it for a fee to pay for the cost of maintenance.

Private spaceports were supposed to have their personnel make sure that customs regulations were adhered to, but there wasn't much oversight. Las Cruces was a good place to get stolen goods off-world.

The perspiring traffic controller was one of a handful who manned the spaceport full-time. Most of its operations were automated and didn't require much oversight. "Marshal, please," he said. "The *Luxor* has come through here numerous times. I've met with Captain Oleander and have inspected his manifests. Everything is in order."

"Is that right?" Marcus asked. "When are they due to depart?"

The controller glanced at the transparent eyepiece over his right eye, as if he really needed to check the schedule to know when the only ship at the port was supposed to leave. "They're, ah, due to depart in two hours, sir."

"I see. Have they finished loading their cargo, then?"

"Yes sir, they have. I can send you their manifest."

"Please do. Is the crew all back on board?"

The controller looked around. "I'm not sure. It's not my job to keep track of spacers once they land."

Wade raised an eyebrow. "This spaceport is a controlled facility, isn't it? We went through a gate and were checked by security when we came in. I know you don't let whoever happens to show up come onto private property as they please."

A slightly overweight man wearing the gray and orange uniform of the Sierra Nevada Mining Concern's security patrol had been standing in the corner and hadn't said much so far. He piped up when Wade asked about security.

"No sir, we do not," he said, his voice filled with pride. "Company security protocols require all visitors to identify themselves, and we keep a log of when they come and go from the facility. Their movements while at the spaceport are monitored by our security system. As of right now, every individual who left the *Luxor* is back on board. The manifest lists the ship's complement at twelve."

Marcus nodded. The security guard had a ridiculous mustache and could stand to get more exercise, but at least he knew his business. The marshal also noticed that the spaceport controller had tensed up even more. Marcus and Wade exchanged a knowing glance. There was definitely something unusual going on here, but it didn't yet constitute probable cause. Marcus could probably bully his way onto the *Luxor* if he wanted to, but the Sierra Nevada Mining Concern and the owner of the *Luxor* would both have grounds for a lawsuit if he didn't find anything, and that would be the end of his career. Wade had sent the local judge a request for a warrant to detain the ship, but it had been declined.

Marcus shifted tactics, softened his tone, and addressed the controller again. "Listen, Mister...uh..."

"G-Greely," the controller stammered. "Odin Greely."

Odin? "Right. Mr. Greely. Here's the situation. Thirty-one hours ago, an unknown group of individuals executed a daylight robbery of a Sierra Nevada cargo train. They cut the tracks, knowing full well that the train's systems would automatically bring it to a halt. They had some pretty sophisticated communications jammers with them, and apparently knew what frequencies the trains transmit on, because no one realized the train had been stopped until it was all over. The company called the marshals and sent their own security team to investigate. Do you know what they found?"

"I, uh, how would I know that?"

"Millions of credits worth of refined platinum, rhodium, and iridium were taken. A literal truckload. The robbers, whoever they were, obviously knew what security measures were in place, because they were able to counteract them." Marcus glanced at the company security guard. "They also shot and killed the two security officers who were escorting the shipment. They were the only two people on the train."

Greely's face went pale. *Gotcha,* Marcus thought. "This isn't just an old-fashioned train heist. We're looking at a double homicide and armed robbery. Since there's likely no place on New Austin they could fence that much stolen metal, we suspect that they're going to try to get it off-world, which is smuggling. They'd need a remote spaceport, far from the eyes of the Customs Service, and a ship willing to take stolen property. They also had to know how to disable the security devices sent with the shipment, because we haven't been able to track it."

Wade spoke up. "What we're saying, Mr. Greely, is that this *had* to be an inside job. Someone with access to Sierra Nevada's systems had to be in on this. Someone with the authority to access security protocols."

"W-what are you trying to say?" Greely protested. "I don't have that kind of access! I'm just the spaceport controller!" His eyes darted to the door of the room. The two sheriff's deputies accompanying the pair of colonial marshals noticed his distress and quietly positioned themselves between Greely and the exit.

"Hey now, Mr. Greely," Marcus said, "calm down. I'm not making any accusations. I'm just bringing you up to speed on the situation. But now that you mention it, you've been awfully nervous since we got here. Do you know something about this? Have you heard something?"

Greely flustered. "Of course not. This is ridiculous! I've had enough of you two, I think. You don't have a warrant, and I haven't done anything wrong. I'm afraid I'm going to have to insist that you leave."

Marcus shrugged. "Fair enough. Bear in mind, though, that we're not just talking about the theft of some metal from the company. This is a murder investigation now. Two innocent men, peers of your security officer here, were shot down in cold blood. Both men had families, you know."

"That's...that's tragic," Greely managed, "but I've had enough of your accusations and veiled threats! I've done nothing wrong. If you want to talk to me again, you can get a warrant and talk to my lawyer!" He turned to the security guard, "Lazlo, escort these men to the gate."

Lazlo folded his arms across his chest and glared at Greely. He didn't move.

"Suit yourself," Wade stated. "But again, this is a murder investigation. We'll get a warrant, and we'll be back. If it's found out that a person was lying to a peace officer to cover up a murder...well, that's not good. Even if that person had nothing to do with the murder, that makes him an accomplice. That person would be looking at a very long stay in the Purgatory Correctional Facility. That's not a nice place to be, Mr. Greely."

The two sheriff's deputies glanced at each other. "Hey, Tam," the tall, thin man said to his female partner, "remember that child molester we hauled in a few months ago?"

The female deputy, a stocky woman with reddish hair, nodded. "Yeah. Chester Nightingale. Chester the Molester. He got sent to Purgatory, didn't he?"

Marcus smiled. The deputies were playing their parts perfectly.

"He sure did," the tall one said. "They were planning on moving him to the isolation block, for his own protection. But I guess there was a mix-up. He ended up in the general population."

"Oh hell," the female deputy said, feigning surprise. "That probably ended badly for him."

"You know it, partner. Cho-mos aren't too popular on the inside. He got involved in a fight. Another inmate ripped his jaw off. Like, clean *off*."

"Ouch!"

"Yeah. It happened so fast it was over before the corrections officers could pull him off the guy. He bled to death right there in the shower room."

"Well," the woman said with a shrug, "that's Purgatory. The worst of the worst go in there. And it's the only supermax prison on New Austin, so that's probably where anyone involved in this case will end up."

Greely finally cracked. "Okay! Okay. Look, I was just supposed to look the other way when a cargo haul came through, alright? I didn't know what they were hauling, who was hauling it, or where it came from. I certainly didn't know it would turn violent! I didn't even know that the attack on the train was related!"

"Oh, come on," Lazlo, the security officer, said.

"No, I swear!" Greely insisted. "I was just supposed to look the other way, and they were going to slip me a bribe. It's not like this sort of thing doesn't go on all the time!"

"Not on my watch, it doesn't!" Lazlo said, stepping toward Greely.

Marcus help up a hand. "Hold on there. This is a law enforcement matter now. The deputies here will take Mr. Greely into custody. I'm sure that the court will look favorably on his cooperation with the investigation."

"I will!" Greely squealed. "I'll tell you everything you want to know!"

"All I want to know is, what haul were you supposed to wave through?"

"It's supposed to arrive any time now. One truck. Don't know what it was carrying. I was just supposed to make sure it got let in. It was going to load its cargo onto the service tower lift, then leave. The ship was supposed to launch as soon as it was loaded. That's all I know, I swear!"

"Thank you for your cooperation, Mr. Greely," Marcus said. He turned to the deputies. "Take him into custody. The people that pulled off this heist are dangerous. Police custody is the safest place for him. Hurry—don't want our truck to see you leaving and get spooked. Thank you for your help, deputies. Excellent work."

"Sure thing, Marshal," the tall deputy said. "We'll send you a copy of his statement as soon as he gives it. But, hey, you want us to send you some backup? We're stretched kinda thin right now, but we could get a couple of other deputies out here."

"We've got it taken care of," Wade said. "I'm sending a request for them to airlift in a tac team, and get us a warrant to detain that ship."

Marcus patted the security guard on the shoulder. "And we've got Mr. Lazlo here to assist us."

The guard's eyes lit up, and his back straightened. His hand moved to the butt of the pistol on his hip. "I'm ready to render assistance, Marshal!"

Wade looked back down at his handheld. "The judge signed the warrant. Mr. Greely, before you go, can you lock down that service tower so the *Luxor* can't leave?"

"Y-yes, of course," Greely managed. He crossed the room to his control panel. A 3D image of the *Luxor* was displayed in the holotank, with all pertinent information available. When a ship was docked with a service tower, control of the ship's engine was typically given over to the spaceport traffic controller, with the crew locked out. This was a safety protocol that was observed across most of inhabited space. It prevented ships from taking off without clearance, destroying the service tower and killing ground crews with their exhaust. It also prevented damage to the ship itself. Most service towers were stout structures, enabling the transfer of heavy cargo and personnel into the ship. They were generally sturdy enough to stabilize the ship, even in high winds. Launching with one still attached to an open cargo bay would likely be catastrophic for the ship involved.

With the launch controls locked down, the two sheriff's deputies restrained Greely and escorted him out of the room. Marcus turned to Lazlo. "How many guards are on site right now?"

"I'm the shift supervisor. I've got two patrol officers here during the day, plus some security robots. We're pretty much out in the middle of nowhere. Not a lot of risk of theft or vandalism out here, usually."

"Alright," Marcus said. "I'm deputizing you and your officers. Let's get ready. Our guests will be here soon."

Lazlo's voice sounded in Marcus' earpiece. "Marshal! The security system just alerted me to a vehicle approaching the gate. It's a ten-ton, eight-by-eight wheeled cargo truck with five people in it. Its registration plate is covered with dirt, and it doesn't have a broadcasting transponder. We don't have any shipments on the schedule for today, and this truck isn't from one of the shipping companies."

"That's probably our mark then," Marcus replied. "Where are they at?"

"They're approaching the truck gate on the south end. What do you want me to do?"

"Let them in, but don't do anything to spook them. Just open the gate. If we're right about this we'll have our train robbers and some smugglers too. Tell your officers not to make any moves until I say so."

"Understood. Opening the gate."

The two colonial marshals watched on one of the security feeds as the big truck rumbled into the spaceport. It made a beeline for the *Luxor*, not adhering to the posted directions regarding driving on the flightline. It kept its distance from the terminal building as it approached the service tower. Swinging around, the truck backed up the ramp to the loading gate of the massive structure.

"Okay, it's happening," Marcus said into his transmitter. "Stand by." On the security feeds, the marshals watched the men climb out of the truck and remove the soft cover from the cargo container on the back. The container matched the size and volume of the missing Sierra Nevada Mining Concern property, but had been painted over. Its registration transmitters had all been disabled as well. It wasn't proof, but it *was* probable cause.

The suspect container was then lowered from the back of the truck onto a large wheeled dolly. The dolly and two of the men proceeded into the lift. The other three stayed at ground level, standing watch while their compatriots ascended.

The suspects were separated. Only two of them could get into the truck and attempt to flee. *Perfect.* Marcus keyed his transmitter. "Execute, execute, execute!" He then looked to his partner, behind the wheel of their vehicle. "Punch it!"

Wade nodded and stepped on the accelerator. Their patrol vehicle sped from where it had been hidden in a utility garage, across the flightline, toward the launch pad. The two marshals had access to every security feed at the spaceport, as well as real-time footage from a small aerial drone they had deployed. On cue, Lazlo initiated a security lock on the launch tower, freezing the lift halfway up.

As the marshals rolled across the vast, deserted tarmac, they were joined by a spaceport security patrol vehicle. The other security patrol was approaching the launch pad from a different direction. Two hundred meters out, Wade flipped on their lights and sirens. Right on top of the huge truck, the marshals' vehicle screeched to a halt. The two lawmen were out in a flash, guns up. Marcus used the armored police vehicle as cover. Wade had his big revolver drawn and was covering one of the suspects, a wiry man covered in tattoos. He reached for a gun hidden under his vest. Wade's revolver roared, and the tattooed man was dead before his body hit the tarmac.

"Colonial marshals!" Marcus shouted. "You two, get down on the ground!"

"Get down or I'll put you down!" Wade ordered, shifting his aim to the next closest suspect. "Now!" The two security vehicles arrived, and the three guards, dressed in orange and gray, piled out with sidearms drawn.

The suspect closest to Wade, a stocky man with a wild shock of orange hair, looked down at the body of his deceased compatriot before slowly lowering himself to the tarmac. The deputy marshal and one of the security officers moved in to restrain him. The other suspect, covered by Marcus' carbine, lifted his hands over his head, but didn't move. He stood near the driver's side door of the truck, staring Marcus down. He was a large, bald man with obvious bionic augmentations. His arms were black and rippled with synthetic sinews. His eyes had been replaced with ugly bionic implants, which made him look like he was wearing goggles. His long, sleeveless duster flapped in the breeze as he stood in silence. Marcus had a bad feeling about this one. The other suspects looked like a bunch of yokels, but the cyborg in the duster had the presence of a leader and the look of a hard-ened criminal.

He also didn't get down on the ground as he'd been told. "Last chance, tin-man, get down on the ground, face down, right now!" Marcus ordered. The cyborg smirked, but didn't move.

"Suit yourself," Marcus said. He flipped off the safety of the less-lethal launcher mounted under his stubby carbine, and squeezed the second trigger. With a muffled pop, a 30mm com-pliance round launched from his weapon, struck the stubborn cyborg in the chest, and initiated.

The big man grunted in agony as his body was shocked with a tremendous jolt of electricity. Spittle shot through gritted teeth as every muscle, natural and artificial, locked up. He fell to his knees, then unceremoniously flopped to the tarmac.

Marcus exhaled slowly, relieved. "I wasn't sure that was going to work," he said to Lazlo. He then approached the incapacitated suspect, slinging his carbine behind his back. "Cover me. You," he said, pointing to the other security guard, "keep your weapon on the guys in the lift." He moved toward the incapacitated suspect with a pair of restraints in hand.

The cyborg lurched upward just as Marcus stepped over him. An augmented arm backhanded the marshal, knocking him clean off his feet. In a flash the cyborg lunged forward, grabbing the closest security guard by his gun hand. He wrenched the guard's arm upward, snapping bone like sticks, and *threw* him at Lazlo. The two security officers tumbled to the pavement in a heap.

Realizing what was happening, Wade and the remaining security officer appeared from the other side of the truck just as the bionic criminal jumped back into the driver's seat. The truck's hydrogen engine whined as he hit the accelerator. The two injured guards were barely able to jump clear as the truck roared past, smashing aside their small electric patrol car without slowing down.

Wade's revolver roared as he rapidly fired off all seven shots at the fleeing truck. The big 12mm explosive rounds punched fist-sized holes in the back of the vehicle, but it didn't slow down. "Marshal, he's getting away!" he said. The empty cylinder ejected vertically from his weapon, and he slapped a fresh one into place before helping Marcus to his feet. "Come on! Are you alright?"

Marcus shook his head and blinked hard. "Yeah, I think so. I might have a cracked rib. Go go go! You drive!" Marcus shouted to Lazlo as he climbed into the vehicle. "Secure the scene until we get back! The tac team will be en route. We're going after him!" The colonial marshals didn't wait for Lazlo's response before speeding away after the fleeing criminal.

Wade drove as Marcus got on the radio and explained what was going on. The tactical team was on its way, but even traveling via VTOL aircraft, it would take them almost an hour to arrive. Marcus instructed the special response team commander to secure the launch pad. He didn't want to leave three security guards, one of whom was injured, and a few old security robots with the remainder of the cyborg's gang and the crew of the *Luxor*. With the marshals gone, they might try something.

Marcus next contacted the local sheriff's office and explained what was happening. The spaceport was in a very remote location, and the local sheriff only had a handful of deputies. It would be a while before they could set up a roadblock. On the other hand, there weren't that many roads in the outback. There really wasn't anyplace for the truck to hide.

"Where the hell does he think he's gonna go?" Wade asked, as if reading Marcus' mind.

"Damned if I know," Marcus said. "Unless..."

"Unless what, Boss?"

"Unless he's just trying to lure us out so he can kill us both. Have you figured out who this guy is?"

Without taking his eyes off the road, Wade turned the dash screen toward Marcus. "No match, Marshal. No criminal record, no record at all. Not even a name or address. Probably from off-world."

"Probably," Marcus agreed. "There are a few salty types out in the desert that like to stay off the grid, but this guy doesn't match that profile. He's got serious tech on him. You don't see that kind of augmentation out here that much."

Technological wonders like heavy bionic augmentation were hard to come by so far out from the Inner Colonies, the long-established technology and economic base of the Concordiat. Not only was it rare, but it wasn't cheap, either. The odds of a local criminal coming up with the funds to pay for that kind of augmentation weren't good. Just to be sure, though, Marcus told HQ to crosscheck the suspect with the augmentation clinics on New Austin.

"So what's the plan, Boss? We can't just chase him 'til we run out of fuel."

"The sheriff is trying to get a roadblock together, but that'll take too long. I want to stop this asshole before he hurts anybody else."

"I tried disabling his truck," Wade said. "It didn't work."

Marcus wasn't surprised. Any two-bit criminal worth a damn knew to disable the safety cutoffs and lockouts on their vehicles. A lot of regular people did it too, just on principle. Most vehicles were sold with them, but they weren't mandatory. "Let me see if I can get the surveillance bot in close enough to do something," the marshal said. He tapped his handheld and directed the small aerial drone to fly close, alongside the truck. "I want to try something before we just start shooting."

"Agreed," Wade said. "The Freeholder ship, the train heist, bribing mining company people, and now a dangerous cyborg. This could be something big."

Marcus watched the feed as the little drone barely managed to catch up with the speeding truck. The little bot had a less-lethal launcher mounted to it. It maneuvered into position, trying to get a shot through the driver's side window. It fired, but the round failed to penetrate the truck's industrial-grade safety-transparency window on the first shot. The driver didn't intend to give them another chance. He smashed a bionic elbow into the window, punching it out with the second blow. Before the drone could line up another shot, the fleeing criminal stuck a machine pistol out the window and fired.

"Shots fired!" Wade said, pointing out the obvious for the record. On the second burst, the cyborg managed to wing the little drone, damaging its control surfaces. The criminal pulled his weapon back inside to reload.

"Shit," Marcus snarled. "It's not stable enough to get a shot now."

"Ram him!" Wade said.

"What?"

"Ram him!"

Marcus grinned and told the drone to do just that. Using every bit of power it could muster, the little robot flew into the driver's side window as fast as it could. The video feeds went dead as it smashed right into the cyborg's head. Marcus looked up from his handheld just in time to see the truck swerve, then cut sharply to the left. Wade hit the brakes as the ten-ton vehicle, which had been barreling along at a hundred and twenty kilometers per hour, came off its wheels and flipped over. The massive truck rolled off the road and down a small hill, ripping a swath through the desert vegetation and kicking up a huge cloud of dust that obscured the wreck from view.

Wade pulled the marshals' vehicle to a stop at the edge of the road. "God *damn*," he said, still grinning.

Marcus was talking rapidly into his headset, requesting backup and medical support. The office was undoubtedly already vectoring those things to his position, having witnessed the crash in real time through the on-board cameras of the marshals' vehicle. "Let's go," Marcus said to Wade, retrieving his carbine from its mount in the cabin. "Grab your rifle, he's armed." Wade nodded and followed him out of their vehicle.

Weapons shouldered, the marshals cautiously made their way down the hill toward the wrecked truck. There was no cover on the approach, so they went in guns up and ready to fire. Marcus used a hand signal to tell Wade to swing wide to the left, spreading out while still being able to see each other. The suspect was dangerous and they weren't going to give him any more advantages.

"Colonial marshals!" Marcus announced. "Come out of the vehicle with your hands in the air or we will open fire!" The truck was on its side. Marcus could see the battered undercarriage, but had no visibility on the cabin. He moved to the right, hoping to get eyes on the suspect. Wade circled to the left, around the truck. They were coming at the suspect from two directions.

"Marshal, you see anything?" Wade asked.

Marcus advanced through the cloud of dust, trying to see into the truck's cabin through the windshield. "I see him! He's not moving! Wasn't wearing his restraints!"

"Be careful, Boss!" Wade warned. The cyborg had fooled them once before.

"Hey, tin-man!" Marcus said. "Dead or alive, you're coming with me!" No response. He looked up at Wade and shook his head.

"Medical support is inbound," Wade said. "We have to disarm him before they get here."

Marcus nodded. "Okay, I'm going to—" He was cut off as the safety transparency windshield smashed into him, knocking him into the dirt. The augmented suspect had kicked it out with both feet. Before the marshal knew what was happening, the murderous cyborg was on top of him. Marcus tried to bring his carbine up, struggling under the transparent sheet, but his attacker was too fast. The cyborg stepped on the weapon just as Marcus got it out from under the windshield, pinning it to the ground. He picked up the dislodged window, spun around, and hurled it like a discus. It spun through the air and smacked into Wade, knocking him off his feet. Turning back to Marcus, the cyborg clamped a massive synthetic hand onto Marshal's throat and hoisted him off the ground with one arm. The emergency release on Marcus' carbine sling gave way, leaving the rifle out of reach under the criminal's boot.

A steely hand wrapped around his neck, Marcus was eye-to-artificial-eye with the cyborg. The cyborg's eye lenses irised as he spoke. "Well, well, well," the he said, a metallic tang in his voice. "Not how you expected this to turn out, neh?" He let out a rumbling chuckle and squeezed Marcus' neck even tighter.

Marcus tried to speak, but couldn't get the words out.

"What's that? You got words for me, you backwater colony pig?" The cyborg relaxed his grip slightly.

Marcus gasped for air. "You...are...under arrest..."

An evil grin split the cyborg's face. Even his teeth were artificial, glinting silver in the afternoon sun. "Haw. How you—*HURK!*" *BLAM BLAM BLAM BLAM BLAM BLAM BLAM BLAM!* Marcus had pulled his 10mm automatic, stuck it into the cyborg's side, and rocked the trigger over and over. Whatever armor the cyborg was wearing, or had built in, didn't stop him from dropping Marcus. The marshal fell to the dirt, coughing, hacking, gasping for air. When he fired the cyborg reflexively squeezed so hard his throat had nearly been crushed.

Marcus was out of time. The cyborg was on top of him again, before he could bring his pistol to bear. The criminal's augmented face was purple with rage. Then his face exploded in a mass of blood, brains, and artificial structures. The top of his head pulped, the cyborg toppled over, crushing Marcus back into the dust. The marshal, still struggling to breathe, coughed and wheezed under the bulk of the augmented corpse. Blood and brains leaked onto his armored vest, but he didn't care. He lay on his back, staring up at the intensely blue sky, and tried to get some air.

"Marshal!" It was Wade. "You okay? Marshal!"

Unable to shout to his partner, Marcus simply raised a hand and waved.

"Holy shit," Wade said, appearing next to his partner. "I thought I got you." He held his powerful 8mm rifle at the low ready.

Marcus coughed. "Nice shot," he managed weakly. The armor-piercing explosive bullet was easily powerful enough to go clean through a human head. Wade had to have angled the shot so the bullet didn't also hit Marcus, while firing from the shoulder, and the cyborg and the marshal weren't holding still. "Damned nice shot."

"Thanks, Boss," Wade grinned. He grunted as he rolled the heavy corpse off of his partner, then helped Marcus to his feet.

Marcus holstered his sidearm and retrieved his carbine. "You ready to call it a day?"

Wade nodded, looking tired. "I've had enough fun for today."

Marcus shook his head, and forced himself to smile. "Call back to the spaceport and see how they're doing."

The eastern sky was on fire as the sun called Lone Star slowly sank beneath the jagged peaks of the distant Redemption Mountains. The patchy carpet of clouds exploded in shades of gold, red, and purple, and the first stars of the evening twinkled far above. The pale glow of New Austin's twin moons, rising into the night sky, took over as the last red rays of the sun disappeared below the horizon.

Annabelle Winchester sat on a weather-beaten boulder and sighed. "That was a really pretty sunset, Sparkles." Sparkles paid Annabelle no mind. The Laredo buckskin mare focused her attention on the desert floor, rooting through the shrubbery for things to eat.

As the blanket of night rolled across New Austin, the already scattered clouds cleared up, revealing the shining tapestry of stars that Annabelle never got tired of looking at. Laredo Territory was sparsely populated; there were no big, lit-up cities to hide the stars. The Izanami Nebula, only a few light-years away, filled part of the sky with its electric blue splendor. Twinkling dots, satellites and ships in orbit, zoomed silently across the sky. Annie's eyepiece, connected to the colonial network via her handheld, displayed information on the different stars and constellations.

Annie gazed up into the night sky with the oddest sense of longing. She devoured every text and media on space travel that she could find. It wasn't that she'd never been to space before. She had been six years old when the Winchester family made the long voyage to New Austin, but that hardly counted. Annie could barely remember it, and they spent most of the months-long journey in cold sleep anyway.

No, Annie wanted to *really* go to space. To see firsthand the engineering marvel and controlled chaos that was a spaceship. To experience freefall, to see New Austin from above, and to experience the exhilarating, mind-bending terror of translating between transit points. She longed to set foot on unexplored worlds and see for herself the incredibly ancient ruins of one of the long-vanished Antecessor Species. In her sixteen standard years, Annie had lived on two worlds and traversed the incredibly vast gulf between them via an interstellar-capable ship. She knew it was silly to pine for space travel when, for the vast majority of all of human history, such things had been impossible and unknown.

Yet, as silly as it was, in her heart Annie wanted to go back to space. She didn't know when or how, exactly, but she knew she would find a way. As if to confirm her desire, far to the north she saw the unmistakable glow and fiery plume of a ship lifting off, ascending into the night sky and the endless depths of space beyond. Her eyepiece told her the ship was the *MV Atago Maru,* registered on the Concordiat colony of Nippon. A diagram of the ship appeared before her right eye. It was a fat, blunt monster with airfoils symmetrically poking out of its hull, and stood eighty-three meters tall on its landing jacks. Annie didn't know where it was going, but she found herself wishing she was aboard it.

An electronic chirp interrupted Annie's wistful pondering. Her mom was calling. She accepted the call, and a small video image of her mother appeared on her eyepiece. "Hi Mom," Annie said.

"Hi honey. Where are you?"

"I'm up on the south ridge with Sparkles. I was just watching the sunset. Is Dad home yet?"

"He just called. He's on his way. I guess he had kind of a rough day, so I'm going to make a nice dinner. How's meatloaf sound?"

Annie's stomach growled. As she often did, she lost track of time while out on the lone prairie with Sparkles. It had been hours since she'd eaten lunch. "I'll come straight home, Mom. I'll be there in about an hour."

"Okay, dear. Be careful."

Annie smiled at her mother's doting, as if she couldn't handle herself out on the range. "See you later, Mom. Love you." Ending the call, Annie stood up, dusted off her jeans, and took one last, long gaze into the sky full of stars.

Sparkles lifted her head in concern at a chorus of yipping, crying, and yelping from off in the darkness somewhere. *Coyotes.*

"I hear 'em, girl," Annie said, grabbing her varmint carbine. The coyotes in Laredo Territory could be aggressive sometimes, especially to a lone horse with a lonely girl on her back. "Come on, we'd better get home." Annie stuck a foot into a stirrup and pulled herself up into the saddle.

Sparkles whinnied in agreement, and the two turned for home at a quick trot.

Annie's eyepiece had rudimentary night vision capability, but she didn't need it on such a clear night, even to keep watch for critters. The open desert was brightly lit by the twin moons, and Annie was able to ride Sparkles home using her own two eyes. As she crested the last ridge, the Winchester family ranch came into view below. Their single-story, prefabricated home was efficient and modern. Her parents had added onto it over the years, including a shade for her father's armored police vehicle (which was too tall to fit into the garage) and her mother's workshop. The roof was covered with solar panels and a backup radioisotope thermoelectric generator provided extra power if needed. There was no electrical grid in this part of Laredo Territory.

Next to the house stood a prefabricated barn where the Winchesters kept their few livestock. Annie guided Sparkles down the ridge, and led her into the barn. Once she had gotten the mare unsaddled, fed, and put in her stall, she slung her carbine over her shoulder and headed into the house.

Annie's stomach growled as the wonderful smell of her mother's cooking filled her nose. The whole house smelled of meatloaf, potatoes, and baking bread. Her mom didn't cook often, but when she did, she went all out. "I'm home, Mom!" she announced, unloading the 4.5mm caseless carbine she carried.

"Your father will be home soon, honey," her mom said. "Put your rifle away and get cleaned up for dinner. It's almost ready." Famished, Annie locked her weapon in its storage cabinet and headed to the washroom to shower. She'd been out riding all day and was eager to wash off the grit and change into some clean clothes.

When Annie walked into the kitchen, showered and changed, her father had just walked in the door and kissed her mom.

"Dad!" she said, giving her father a big hug.

"Hey darlin'," he said. "How are you?"

"I'm . . ." Annie noticed then the bruises on her father's face and neck. "Dad, holy shit."

"Language, young lady!" her mom corrected.

"Uh, sorry. What happened to you? Are you okay?"

Her father gave her a lopsided grin, hand on her shoulder. "I'm fine, baby. Just a rough day is all."

Annie noticed her mother giving her dad a worried look. They obviously didn't want to tell her what had actually happened. He'd probably had to shoot somebody or something. They always tried to hide stuff like that from her, as if she were a little kid who didn't know what was going on. She decided to drop it, for now. She was daddy's little girl, she thought, grinning. She'd get the truth out of him eventually.

Annie didn't talk much during dinner. She was too busy devouring her mother's homemade meatloaf. The potatoes and vegetables came from their own garden, and the bread was fresh and warm. It was much better than the prepackaged meals she usually ate when her mom was absorbed in her work or off at one of her claims.

Taking a sip of water, her father looked over at her mother. "How was business today, Ellie?"

"I spent all day in my workshop analyzing core samples. I'm pulling good ore out of the West Range site, but the Rocky Slope site just isn't producing. I'm probably going to cut my losses and shut it down. We're losing money on it just keeping it open, and putting a lot of wear and tear on my equipment."

Annie never had the love for rocks that her mom did. Eleanor Winchester was a geologist and miner by trade. She had several claims filed with the colonial government, and most of the family's income came from her mining business.

Annie's father had a worried look on his face. "So…are you thinking about opening up the Jerome Mountain site then? You've been sitting on it for almost two years."

"I know. It's just so remote, and the terrain out there is really rugged. Getting the equipment out there would be a nightmare. I'd have to rent some all-terrain vehicles, and I'd probably have to camp there during the season. The rock is dense, too. The drilling equipment I have probably won't last too long. I may have to use explosives."

"Wade could do the demo work for you. He was an explosives technician in the Defense Force."

"I'd need to pay him, and buy the explosives, and get some heavier equipment. I'd need a small crew, too. My bots couldn't handle that kind of work unsupervised, and it costs a lot of money to get a technician that far out if one of them breaks down."

"Ellie, you know I support you if that's what you want to do."

"It is, Marcus. It's just…I don't know. We don't have the money to invest in the kind of equipment I need. It'd be a lot."

"I could see about picking up some extra assignments," Annie's father suggested.

Her mom shook her head. "No. We're both gone too much as it is. I don't want to leave Annabelle alone all the time."

"I'm okay, Mom," Annie protested. "I can take care of myself."

"I know you can, sweetie," her father said. "That isn't the question. It's just not good for the family if we're gone all the time." He looked back over at her mother. "Could we borrow the money, maybe?"

"I don't think so. Especially now that Rocky Slope was a bust. The bank is going to question my judgment on possible mineral sites. Everything else we have is tied up in the property, the house, paying off debt, or Annie's university fund."

"You can use that," Annie interjected. "I don't want to go to university."

Her mother furrowed her brow. "Annabelle, don't be silly. You're not just going to live out here and be a ranch hand. You're going to university if I have to scrub floors to put you there."

Annie rolled her eyes and continued chewing her food. Her mom was being ridiculous. Why would anyone pay someone to scrub floors when there were robots that did that? Anyway, she just wouldn't listen. Going to a real university, with an actual campus, classes that assembled in person, and professors that you actually met with face-to-face was prestigious, a luxury, and one that Annie didn't see the point of. She'd been educated by remote access learning her entire life. She didn't understand the appeal of some old-fashioned university where everyone wore strange square hats and sat around in lecture halls or got drunk at parties. It all seemed so pretentious.

No, what Annie really wanted was to go to the New Austin Spaceflight Academy and become a spacer. But that cost even more money than the university, if you couldn't get a scholarship, and her mom never seemed to listen anyway. She was strongly considering just running off and joining the Concordiat Defense Force as soon as she turned eighteen, or maybe trying to get into the Survey Fleet or even the Courier Service. Anything to get out into space.

"I don't know what we're going to do, Marcus. If I can't up our revenue stream we're going to have a very hard time making the payments on the ranch."

"I guess we could always try to sell the place and move back to the city. Aterrizaje isn't anything like the arcologies back on Hayden."

Hayden was where Annie had been born. She didn't remember much of it, except that she and her family lived in a massive, two-hundred-level arcology outside of a huge Concordiat Defense Force Base. Hayden's small habitable landmass was very crowded. Pollution and crime were both high, as was the cost of living. The Winchesters decided that their daughter shouldn't have to grow up in such a place, and emigrated to New Austin when Annie was little. Her father was correct, though; Aterrizaje, the capital city of the New Austin Colony, wasn't anything like the congested urban wastelands of Hayden.

Annie's mother didn't seem consoled by that fact. She hated living in the city, and preferred making her living in the wide open spaces of New Austin's frontier. "I'll probably have to close up shop completely if we do that. Aterrizaje is just too far from my claims, and there isn't much good mining ground unclaimed anywhere close to the city. Either that or I'd have to be gone for weeks at a time."

"Well, don't stress too much, Ellie," Annie's father said reassuringly. "This is just a bump in the road. We'll figure it out. We always do."

As they were finishing up their meal, Annie idly thumbed the touch screen of her handheld, checking social media to see what her friends were doing. Her mom normally hated it when she used it at the table, but she'd waited long enough this time that all she got from her mother was a frown.

"Hey," she said, reading a posting on the small screen. "I almost forgot. The Aterrizaje Stampede is coming up soon. I've been practicing barrel racing with Sparkles all season. You guys are going to be able to take me, right?"

The Aterrizaje Stampede was an annual rodeo held in New Austin's capital city. It was a huge annual attraction, and Annie had been training hard for months to qualify for the junior division. "I don't know, honey," her mother said. "I need to get back out to my mines."

Annie looked pleadingly to her father. He gave her an apologetic look. "Honey, there was an, uh, incident at work today. There's gonna be an investigation. I don't know if I can get away."

"But..." she said, trailing off. Exhaling heavily, she set her handheld down and looked at her plate.

"This is important to her, Marcus," she heard her mom say. "It's the only time she really gets to see her friends."

"I know, baby, but I told you what happened today. Can you take her?"

"We're losing money every day my bots sit at Rocky Slope not doing anything."

"Well... what if she went by herself? She's old enough."

Annie's head shot up. "Can I, Mom?"

Her mother looked pensive. "I don't know, Marcus. There are other teenagers, and boys, and who knows what all goes on?"

"Mom! Don't you trust me?"

"It's not that I don't trust you, sweetie, I don't trust boys."

"But Mom!"

Marcus put his hand on his wife's shoulder. "Ellie, she's growing up. We let her go out on the range by herself. If she can handle the varmints out there I think she can handle a few teenagers."

"I can, Mom! You know I'm responsible!"

"Annie, hush," Marcus said, before turning back to Annie's mother. "We've got to let her out of the nest eventually. We raised her right. I'm not worried." He gave Annabelle a stern look. "Do I need to be worried?"

"Dad, no! You know me! I don't give a shit about boys!"

"Language!" Eleanor snapped. She stood up from the table, sighed, and told the kitchen appliances to pour her a glass of wine. "Fine, but we're going to establish some ground rules. You'll check in every night. No overnight parties, no boys in your room, and so help me God, young lady, if I find out you were drinking I'll lock you in a tower until you're eighteen!"

"Mom, I'm not gonna drink! I'm not stupid!"

"Sweetie, believe it or not, I was sixteen once. I know what kind of trouble a girl can get into." Eleanor shot a scowl at Marcus, who was obviously trying not to laugh. "What is so funny?"

"I know what kind of trouble you can get into too," he said. "Hell, you were trouble when we met. Nothing but trouble." He shook his head, smiling from ear to ear. "I used to have to stop you from starting fights at the club when we were dating."

"That...was a long time ago. And on another planet! And entirely beside the point! You," she said, pointing at Annie, "will not get into any fights!"

"Oh my God, Mom, I'm not going to get into fights! Will you give me some credit?"

Marcus' expression became more serious. "You know what I taught you about that," he said.

"Of course I do, Dad. You never start a fight, but you always damn well finish one."

He nodded in approval. "That's my girl. See, honey? She'll be fine."

The Privateer Ship *Andromeda*
Deep Space, nine hundred hours out from Avalon

Space travel is not an endeavor for the impatient. The miracle of the transit drive allows seemingly instantaneous travel between connected star systems, and this technological marvel is the foundation upon which interstellar civilization is built. But even with that kind of technology, there is no shortcut across space once a ship arrives in a star system. There's nothing to do but slog across the void between transit points, burning up reaction mass, trying to keep busy, and hoping nothing goes wrong.

Fortunately for Catherine, patience was something she had in abundance. She sat quietly in her chair on the *Andromeda*'s command deck, studying the various displays available to her. She didn't like using the heads-up display eyepieces that many preferred; they always seemed to give her headaches.

On her main screen was a projection of two possible routes to Zanzibar, and she didn't like either of them. Zanzibar wasn't the farthest-flung rock that humanity clung to, but coming all the way from the Arthurian System it might as well have been. Catherine blinked hard for a moment; she'd been staring at her displays for far too long. There was nothing for it. Looking at the screen more intently wasn't going to change the geometry of space-time. Even following the fastest route, it would take the *Andromeda* months to arrive at her destination. Unfortunately, the fastest route also meant going through some places that Catherine would rather avoid. Worse, that route was *still* the best option—the next-fastest route would add weeks to her transit time, and Catherine was in something of a hurry. Well, she thought, as much as one *can* be in a hurry when crossing interstellar distances.

One of her screens displayed a warning: T-minus 120 seconds to thrust. A moment later a voice piped up on the intercom throughout the ship. It was Colin, the *Andromeda*'s junior pilot. "Standby for turnover. Sixty seconds."

Catherine smiled. Colin was young, only twenty-six standard years old, and full of youthful exuberance. He was always cheerful and was genuinely excited about his duties. The warning gave everyone on board who wasn't strapped down time to grab onto something. A minute later, the *Andromeda* vibrated with the momentary firing of her maneuvering thrusters. In the blackness of space, the ship silently and gracefully flipped a hundred and eighty degrees, so that she was sailing tail-first toward her destination. "Turnover complete," Colin announced. "Stand by for burn. One gravity, thirty seconds."

Right on the mark, the ship rumbled as her four primary magneto-inertial fusion rockets lit up, blue-white exhaust flares lancing out into the void. Catherine felt the weight returning to her body as the ship accelerated, leveling off at what was close enough to one standard gravity as to make no difference. The vibrating and rumbling of the hull stabilized as the ship settled into her burn.

"One gravity," Colin announced cheerfully. "Burn time is one hour. Enjoy it while it lasts."

The intercom fell silent and Catherine unbuckled her harness. Standing up on the command deck, she stretched and brushed the wrinkles out of her flight suit. "I have a meeting in Astrogation," she announced to the two junior officers on deck. "Mister Azevedo, you have the ship. *Herr* von Spandau will take command once the meeting is over."

Luis Azevedo was another junior officer, and had been on board for less than a year. He hailed from Novo Brasil and had served in the merchant fleet there before being recruited onto the *Andromeda*. "Understood, Captain!" he said, standing up. He stepped across the command deck and stood by the captain's chair. He wouldn't sit until after Catherine had left, which was apparently tradition on Novo Brasil. There wasn't really a whole lot for him to do anyway, even during a burn, other than to stand watch and monitor systems. Still, it was good experience for him, especially for when his captain ran emergency training drills on him.

Catherine took one last look around the command deck. Luis stood with his hands folded behind his back next to her chair, his sage green flight suit crisp and presentable. There wasn't any reason he had to sit in her chair when assuming command. All of her displays could be brought up at his station. It was simply a spacefaring tradition, one that went back centuries. The other junior officer, Nattaya Tantirangsi, stayed at her console and focused on her duties. The captain nodded at Azevedo, turned, and left the compartment.

After a more rigorous stretching routine outside the hatch, where no one could see her, Catherine descended down one deck to Astrogation. A gruff voice with a thick Germanic accent announced, "Attention on deck!" when Catherine appeared in the compartment. It was Wolfram von Spandau, her First Officer and second-in-command of the *Andromeda*.

"Wolfram, please," she said, smiling. "Such formality is not necessary."

"Understood, *Kapitänin*," he replied dutifully. Catherine knew full well he wasn't going to change his ways. The stern spacer was a veteran of the Concordiat Defense Force and ran a very tight ship. The more relaxed atmosphere of a civilian privateer seemed to make him uncomfortable. Catherine had to force herself not giggle at him sometimes.

There was no reason she had to come down to Astrogation for this meeting. There was no real reason they even had to *have* a "meeting" in the first place. The *Andromeda* was almost seventy meters long, big for a ship in her class, but she still made for cramped quarters. Catherine could have just as easily had this discussion with her officers over the ship's network, but the captain liked to do things the old-fashioned way. She preferred face-to-face sit-downs with her officers and to talk in person. Some of her crew considered this habit an Avalonian quirk, and maybe it was. In any case, Astrogation had the new ultra-high-resolution holotank installed. That piece of equipment hadn't been cheap, and Catherine was determined to get as much use out of it as she could.

"Everyone relax," Catherine said to her assembled officers, who were crowded onto the Astrogation Deck. "I need your input on this. First, I apologize for waiting so long to fully brief everyone on the mission we are currently undertaking. It was for security reasons, and to protect client confidentiality. Has everyone gone over the information I sent them?" The room nodded in agreement. "Good. As you've probably ascertained, our destination is not actually Columbia. Astrogation, show us the way."

Kel Morrow, the *Andromeda*'s third officer and chief astrogator, nodded. "Yes ma'am." His fingers rapidly tapped at the controls for the holotank. The display started with a close-in 3D image of the ship, thrusting tail-first along a projected line of trajectory. The image zoomed outward, showing the trajectory from the jump point through which the *Andromeda* had entered the system to the one through which it would leave. "We're forty-four hours from docking with this resupply station," he said. The holotank portrayed a 3D image of an automated orbital platform from which the *Andromeda* would purchase reaction mass and supplies. "From there, we've got another hundred and eighteen hours until we translate to Lambert-1267. That's where we have to make our choice of route."

"Explain," the captain ordered. She knew the details, but she wanted to have things laid out plainly so her officers could offer useful input. She hadn't gotten into the details of their destination in the briefing.

"It's very simple," Morrow said. "Lambert-1267 has three known transit points, including the one through which we'll be translating into the system." The holotank projected an image of the *Andromeda* flashing through the transit point into the Lambert-1276 system, which consisted of only a red dwarf star. "One route will take us about four thousand hours to navigate, going through these systems." The holographic display zoomed out even further, showing a three-dimensional map of the local section of the galaxy. Glowing lines delineated stars connected by naturally occurring transit points. The route the ship was to take was displayed in red, with an alternate in blue, connecting the dots of stars, threading through the quantum maze of spacetime from their present location all the way to Zanzibar.

Wolfram von Spandau and Kel Morrow had both known the ultimate destination. The rest of her officers had only been told that they were going to go pick up a VIP, her brother, from the Llewellyn Freehold. There were noticeable reactions from her crew when they realized the terminus of their route.

Catherine raised an eyebrow. "Thoughts?"

Chief Engineer Indira Nair, the Second Officer, was the first to speak up. "Captain, your brother is on Zanzibar? Why is he there?"

"Another time, please. It's something of a long story. Give me your assessment of the routes."

The engineer looked back at the holotank, squinting a little. "These are the only two routes we can take?"

"For all practical purposes," Morrow said, "yes. We can vary either route through different systems, but none of those variations shortens the transit time. The routes chosen require the least amount of remass."

"*Madarchod*," she cursed. "The red route takes us there by way of Orlov's Star. I would rather not go through Combine space."

"Agreed," grunted Wolfram. "*Kapitänin,* it would be better if we could avoid the Orlov Combine altogether."

"Indeed," the captain agreed. "I think I speak for all of us when I say that none of us want to risk traversing their system. However, the alternate route is much further."

"The blue route adds another thousand hours of travel time to our journey," Astrogator Morrow explained, "assuming no complications. There are a lot of empty systems along the blue route, and it takes us a lot further out of our way. That's where the frontier was during the Second Interstellar War. There's not much out there these days."

"I . . . see," Indira admitted. She was a dark-skinned, dark-haired woman of Indian descent, with a razor-sharp mind and a blunt, upfront demeanor that Catherine found refreshing. "We will need to resupply. The ship was not designed for an unsupported patrol of that duration. We must be cautious." She didn't need to say what everyone was thinking. Running out of food, water, or reaction mass and being stranded in a remote star system was most spacers' worst nightmare.

"Precisely," Catherine agreed. "I've run the numbers. We can make it on that route. But we've got a thin margin of error, thinner than I'm comfortable with, and it assumes successful resupply in places that we don't have any up to date information on. This is a rescue mission. We're somewhat pressed for time."

Wolfram spoke up again. "With careful planning and execution, we could take the longer route and make up some of the lost time. It would require maximum efficiency in our flight operations.

There is more risk, yes, but surely that risk is no greater than going through Orlov's Star? The Combine is as likely as not to simply confiscate our ship and imprison us all for being spies."

Catherine didn't think it was as dire as that; independent courier ships traversed that system semi-regularly. There was experience behind her first officer's words, however. The Orlov Combine was a paranoid, xenophobic, total surveillance state. Its militant collectivist government put on a big show about being open to trade, and in fact many independent systems traded with them to get raw materials at low prices. But a single independent ship, with most of its crew hailing from the colonies of the Interstellar Concordiat? It was risky. The Orlov Combine considered the Concordiat the great imperialist oppressor and the reason for all of the suffering and poverty in their own system.

The *Andromeda* was a licensed privateer in Concordiat space, but was actually registered out of the small, independent colony of Heinlein. Theoretically, Catherine thought, there shouldn't be any legal hassles so long as they made sure they did everything correctly (including the paying of bribes).

Theoretically.

Wolfram von Spandau frowned at the holotank for a moment before speaking. "Could we not go *around* Orlov's Star?" Stepping forward, he tapped the holotank controls rapidly. The red route was altered, going several star systems out of its way to avoid Combine space.

"That route is technically possible, but logistically not so much. Our route depends on us being able to resupply at Orlov's Star. There aren't enough resupply points along that route that would allow us to simply circumvent Combine space. By the time we get close to Orlov's Star, we'll need to resupply there or else we will not make it to Zanzibar."

"Agreed," Indira Nair said. She studied the route for a moment, then sighed. "I hope you were paid up front, Captain."

"Uh, Cap'n, may I?" The question came from Mordecai Chang, the ship's purser, bookkeeper, and quartermaster. Unlike the rest of her officers, he wasn't present in person. His image appeared on a screen, as he was broadcasting from his workstation deep within the bowels of the ship. Catherine nodded at the screen, and Mordecai addressed the assembled officers. "Our contract with Blackwood & Associates stipulates that we are to find and recover one Cecil Ray Blackwood from the planet Zanzibar whether he is alive or dead." The screen split, showing Mordecai's image on one side and highlighted text from the contract on the other. "Our information is, obviously, months out of date, but he is being held for ransom. The client has paid half up front, given the distance we need to travel and the possibility that our subject may have expired long before we get there. The client agreed to a stipulation providing for a rather large emergency fund for the paying of ransoms, bribes, or otherwise greasing the proverbial wheels of commerce as necessary. If we get Mr. Blackwood home alive, we get not only the other half of the agreed payment but an additional twenty percent bonus, to be divided up equally amongst the crew, with the exception of the captain."

"This is personal for me. I don't require a bonus for saving my brother," Catherine stated.

Mordecai continued, looking at something off-screen. "If Mr. Blackwood is dead, we lose the twenty percent bonus but are still paid the rest of our contract price. That's unusual for a rescue mission, as is the amount they're paying us. Cap'n, it's none of my business, but I think it'd be more cost-effective for your father to just have another son."

Coming from anyone but her eccentric purser, that statement might have been insulting, but Mordecai was a wizard with money and tended to do a cost-benefit analysis on everything, almost compulsively. Catherine smiled lopsidedly. He was good enough at his job that she accommodated his severe social anxiety issues. "Aye, but we Avalonians are a clannish lot," she said, laying on her accent. "It would'na do for a man in me father's position to simply abandon his eldest son and heir."

"Understood, Cap'n," Mordecai replied, though Catherine very much doubted that he did. He had been raised and educated remotely, by machines. He was brilliant, but had difficulty relating to people. He rarely came out of his workstation. "I'm not complaining, merely pointing out the obvious." Such things were rarely obvious to anyone but Mordecai. "This endeavor is costing your father tens of millions of credits."

"Indeed," the captain said with a slight nod, "and in this case we owe it to the client to make every effort to accomplish the task. As I said, this is personal for me, a matter of blood and honor. That said, I wouldn't ask you all to go along with this if I thought it was going to get you killed. The mission will be risky, but it won't be the craziest thing we've ever done. The payment for this one should be enough for us to get the reactor refurbished and the propulsion system overhauled, for starters."

Indira's eyes lit up, though she maintained her reserve. "We'll finally be able to get the reactor upgrades I've been asking for?"

Catherine nodded with a slight smile.

"Very good, then," she said simply, actually smiling.

Well, Catherine thought. *That seems to have won them over.* She knew her crew harbored unvoiced concerns that Catherine's family was manipulating her into taking on a fool's errand that could get them killed or leave them financially ruined. (Unvoiced by all but Wolfram; he had asked Catherine bluntly when she returned from her meeting with her father, like a good exec should.) Finding out just how lucrative this job could be seemed to have assuaged their concerns. *But still,* Catherine wondered. *Mordecai isn't wrong. It* would *be easier for Father to have another son. He'd have to marry again, and his new bride would likely be younger than me, but such things are hardly unheard of.*

Something about it bothered her. He had practically thrown the money at her, barely concerning himself with the details of her expenses and fees. This, coming from Augustus Blackwood, the notorious, penny-pinching tightwad who was even more obsessive-compulsive about managing his money than Mordecai was. (There was an unflattering rumor that her father kept a large bin of hard currency somewhere, simply so he could swim in it. That one wasn't true, so far as Catherine knew.) Catherine couldn't put her finger on it, but something felt off about the whole thing. Her father had told her that Cecil had been on some kind of treasure hunt, but that he wasn't sure on the specifics. He said that he'd warned Cecil that he was going to get himself killed. Why risk so much to go get him when there was a goodly chance he was already dead? Why go through all the trouble to track Catherine down? It would've been faster and likely less expensive to hire a different privateer, after all.

Cecil, what are you doing out there? Collecting her thoughts, Catherine returned her attention to her assembled officers. "There is another, unfortunately pressing reason to take the shorter of the two routes. It offers more places to resupply, rearm, and recruit."

The crewmembers looked at each other. Wolfram was silent. He already knew the plan.

"Recruit *who*, Captain?" Kel Morrow asked.

Cargomaster Kimball, a diminutive man with curly hair and a goatee, was the ship's fourth officer. "We have fifteen open berths right now," he said, "but we'll need to take on additional supplies if we're going to have more bodies on board." The *Andromeda* had something of an unusual interior layout for a ship in her class. She was designed around a small crew and, in the gravest extreme, could successfully be piloted for a time by a single crewmember. She carried a complement of sixteen at present, and that was enough for Catherine's purposes. She had berthing for a up to thirty personnel plus the captain, which was large for a patrol ship. This design quirk allowed Catherine to carry extra passengers without the risks inherent in putting them into cold sleep.

"I'm aware, Mr. Kimball," she said calmingly. "I have thought this through, you know. You all must understand: my brother is being held for ransom. We don't have a lot of details, but the people holding him are not necessarily reasonable, nor inclined toward diplomacy. We may have to rescue him by force of arms. I have complete faith in my crew and I would take the *Andromeda* into battle anywhere, but most of you are career spacers, not trained commandos. We're going to need a few subject matter experts, as it were."

Kel looked at the holotank again, and slowly nodded. "I see. You mean to hire some mercenaries. New Austin, probably?" He tapped the controls and the route map zoomed into the Lone Star System, focusing on its sole habitable planet, New Austin.

"Makes sense, Skipper," came a deep voice from the group. It was Mazer Broadbent, the *Andromeda*'s security officer. He was an experienced veteran of the Concordiat Defense Force Military Police Corps. He was a quiet man with a dark complexion, black hair buzzed short, and a cybernetic right eye which reflected the soft glow of the holotank. "A lot of Concordiat veterans use their discharge bonuses to emigrate to New Austin. The Colonial government actively encourages and promotes it. It's a good place to find the kind of people you're looking for."

"It's also the *last* place you're likely to find the kind of people you're looking for, Captain," Kel said. "New Austin is on the

Concordiat frontier. They have no colonies beyond that, not out that way."

"Exactly," Catherine agreed. "This is the primary reason I wish to take the shorter route, even if it means risking transit through the Orlov's Star system. It's our best bet to recruit a team to accomplish our mission, and a good place to resupply and rearm. We're not licensed to operate as privateers in the Arthurian system. We couldn't purchase ordnance there. We will arm up on New Austin, recruit the ground team, and give the crew a little leave dirtside. It'll be the last real break they get before the long trip to Zanzibar, and it's going to add a couple of weeks to our journey. We'll be making up for lost time after that, so there'll be no time for delays."

"At least New Austin will be warm," Indira said. "I mean no offense, Captain, but your homeworld is cold. At least the part of it I saw was."

Catherine smiled. "Indeed. That's all I have for you. If there's nothing else, I'll be in my rack. Wolfram, the ship is yours. Dismissed."

New Austin
Lone Star System
Winchester Ranch, Laredo Territory
Southern Hemisphere

Chief Warrant Officer Marcus Winchester couldn't hear anything over the ringing of his ears. He was confused, his brain in a fog. His helmet visor was cracked and covered with dirt, its internal heads-up display flickering and garbled. He was on his back, on the ground. There was gunfire all around, and the sound of men shouting. Bringing his hands up, Marcus struggled to yank the faceplate from his helmet, but something was wrong with his hands. He could barely feel anything from his left hand, and he had lost all dexterity. He couldn't find the quick-release button. He tried to call for help, but the wind had been knocked out of him. Marcus couldn't speak.

Hands pressed against his chest, though he could barely feel them through his armored vest. Someone was talking to him, but he couldn't make out what they were saying through the fog in his brain. Moments later piercing white light blinded him as his helmet was pulled off his head.

"Chief!" the young Espatier said. "Hold on, we got you. Medic!"

Squinting against the piercing, bluish daylight of an alien sky, Marcus turned his head. He saw her then, the young girl he'd been talking to when the device detonated. She was face down in the mud, her lavender scarf stained with blood. She wasn't moving. Marcus reached out for her, extending his left arm, only to realize how badly mangled his hand was. Bone protruded from a gory wound, and two of his fingers were hanging on only by strings of tissue. There was no blood, just his fingers dangling from sinew like fruit on a tree limb.

Sitting up abruptly, Marcus reflexively checked his left hand. His heart raced and he was sweating heavily. *Where am I?* After a moment, he realized he was in his bedroom. It was dark. He carefully rubbed his left hand with his right. He could just barely feel the scar from the reconstructive surgery where his hand had been repaired. His fingers were all attached. Of course they were. His fingers were still there because he wasn't on war-torn Mildenhall anymore, and hadn't been for years.

Taking a deep breath, hoping his heart rate would slow, Marcus rubbed his face with his hands. In his career with the Concordiat Espatier Corps, he'd seen a great deal, but nothing haunted him like Mildenhall. He'd killed men, lost friends in battle, even uncovered a mass grave of massacred civilians once, but the dead girl with the lavender scarf would never let go of him.

Although the pounding of his heart slowly receded, Marcus knew he wouldn't be getting back to sleep. Next to him, Ellie was snoring peacefully, her hair splayed out over her pillow. At least he hadn't woken her up this time. It worried her terribly when he had that dream. Marcus shook his head. There was nothing for it—might as well get up. He quietly slipped out of bed and dressed without turning on the light.

A while later, Marcus was focused on nothing but the slowly lightening horizon in front of him. Lone Star would appear over the western mountains in an hour or so. In the meantime, the twin crescent moons hanging in the sky provided plenty of illumination for him as he jogged down the lonely highway at a steady pace. He was five kilometers from the ranch and wasn't even breathing hard; the physiological treatments and enhancements he'd received in the military helped him stay fit with minimal effort, even after all these years. Marcus wasn't out running because he needed to. Running just helped him clear his head. He focused on the horizon and tried to shake the memories that haunted him.

Five klicks out was a good turnaround point. Jogging through a U-turn on the faded ceramicrete highway, Marcus found himself reflecting on his military career. He missed the Espatier Corps sometimes, despite the inanity the Green Machine was capable of. The Special Operations Groups were different anyway. His friends and comrades from the 22nd SOG were some of the finest people that Marcus had ever known.

A lot of them were dead. The Concordiat Defense Force hadn't had to fight much in the way of large, conventional wars in the last century, not since the defeat of the Maggots and the end of the Second Interstellar War. There had been fleet actions here and skirmishes there, but nothing like the conflagration that had left millions and millions dead. There were wars, though—bloody, often protracted conflicts, insurgencies, and uprisings. Dirty little wars that didn't let the Concordiat bring the full weight of its space forces to bear, wars that were fought by the man on the ground. Much like the ancient, barbaric conflicts of pre-Space Age Earth, these wars were largely fought by soldiers with muddy boots, grim faces, and weapons in their hands.

Marcus often quietly wondered if it was worth it. A lot of brave young Concordiat citizens died in those campaigns, and some of them didn't accomplish much in the end. It was policy, though, handed down from the distant, aloof political leadership back on Earth. One of the articles of the Interstellar Concord was that the Concordiat would be there to defend not only its members, but to whatever extent possible, the entirety of the human race from oppression, tyranny, and war. Wherever human hearts yearned for freedom, the philosophers waxed, the Concordiat would answer their call.

It sounded good in theory. In reality, it meant getting involved in—often choosing sides in—ugly conflicts across inhabited space. Sometimes a new group of settlers would land on a colony world and conflict would arise with those that were already there. Sometimes two colonies on the same world would go to war with each other. Other times, like on Mildenhall, a fanatical group of infected, mutated militants would commit whatever atrocity, engage in whatever violence they deemed necessary to achieve their goals. In most cases, political leadership didn't let the Fleet simply blast the hostiles from orbit. They wanted to limit collateral damage, or minimize civilian casualties, or even win hearts and minds (Marcus winced at the recollection of how many times he'd heard *that* irritating platitude). Without fail, these stipulations meant boots on the ground. They meant that the Espatier Corps was going in, either *en masse* or as special operations units. These conflicts were always unique, but they all shared one thing in common: they afforded the least capable of enemies the opportunity to kill Concordiat personnel.

After Mildenhall, Marcus knew he was done with the military. He'd missed Annie's first steps while on one deployment, and had very nearly died while on another. Enough was enough. After that, he had decided to focus on his family. He left the Espatiers and used his discharge bonus to get his family a homestead on New Austin. Aside from the occasional violent criminal that needed shooting, his life had been very peaceful since settling on the frontier. He was home every night, Annie could ride her horse to her heart's content, and Eleanor was free to pursue her passion for rocks.

There was only the issue of paying for it all. Interstellar travel wasn't prohibitively expensive, but it wasn't cheap, either. Neither was purchasing a homestead and having a home built on it. Nonetheless, between his thoroughly mediocre colonial marshal's pay and Ellie's mining profits, they were on track to pay off their loans on time and still have some money to send Annie to a good school, provided nothing unforeseen happened. Marcus worried still. If his military career had taught him anything, it was that unforeseen shit liked to happen at the worst possible time.

His brooding was interrupted by an electronic chirp from his earpiece. Who would be calling so early? Without his eyepiece on he couldn't see the caller identifier. "Marshal Winchester," he said professionally, slowing to a walk.

"Dad!" It was Annie. "Where are you?" She sounded upset.

"I went for a run, honey," Marcus said, suddenly worried. "What's wrong? Are you okay?"

"Yeah, I'm fine. It's Mom. I think she's sick."

"Sick how?"

"Sick like she's in the washroom throwing up. I can hear her."

"Well, go see if she needs help. She might just have a bug. I'll come straight home."

"Okay, Dad. I just wanted to tell you."

"Annie, what in the hell are you doing up at this hour?"

Marcus' daughter laughed nervously. "I, uh, haven't been to bed yet, Dad. Liam and Sandra were running a space combat sim, so I joined their session."

Marcus chuckled to himself. Eleanor worried when Annie would get so absorbed in her machines, but at least in a multiplayer game she was interacting with her friends. Winchester Ranch was a long way from the nearest real town. Annie was home-schooled through a distance learning program. The few friends she had were scattered all over the Terraformed Zone. "Okay, honey. Just unplug for a while and see if your mom needs anything. I'll be back shortly."

"Okay, Dad. Love you, bye." Annie disconnected before Marcus could say anything else. Concerned for his wife, he headed for home at a brisk pace.

Hot and sweating, Marcus quickly strode through the front door of his home. Annie was sitting in the dimly lit kitchen, absentmindedly eating cereal as she focused on whatever was displayed on her headset. She was so absorbed in it she didn't notice her father until Marcus tapped her on the shoulder.

"Oh shit!" she said, dropping her spoon in a splash of milk. She pulled off the headset. "Dad! You scared the hell out of me."

Marcus laughed and shook his head. "I thought you were going to help your mom?"

"I did!" she protested. "All she wanted was water. She said she just has an upset stomach."

"I see," Marcus said. "I'll go talk to her."

"Dad . . . I think she's upset about something. I don't know what, but she looked really worried."

"Okay. Thank you, honey. Maybe get some sleep, hey?"

"I have to feed Sparkles first. She gets grouchy and kicks her stall door if I don't bring her breakfast at the crack of dawn."

"Sure. Where's your mom?"

"She's in your room."

Kissing his daughter on the top of the head, Marcus made his way to his bedroom. He gently knocked on the door before opening it. The lights were on, but dimmed. His wife was sitting on the bed, nursing a cup of water. Annie had been right; she really *did* look upset.

"Ellie?" Marcus asked softly. "What's wrong, baby? Annie said you were sick."

Eleanor Winchester sniffled and quickly wiped her eyes with a tissue. She was a proud woman who didn't like to be seen crying. She took a deep breath, and looked Marcus in the eyes. "I'm pregnant."

It took a moment for her words to register with her husband. "You're what?" he asked.

"Marcus, I'm pregnant. We're going to have a baby."

Marcus couldn't suppress the wide grin that appeared on his face. He crossed the room in a hurry, sat on the bed, and hugged his wife tightly. "Baby, that's great! Have you told Annie yet? Holy hell, I thought the doctor said you couldn't have any more kids!"

"He said I probably couldn't get pregnant again," Ellie corrected. "There was always a chance. I just gave up."

Both Marcus and Eleanor had wanted another child. Living so far removed from civilization, they worried about Annie growing up hardly ever seeing other kids in person. Marcus wouldn't admit it, but he'd really been hoping for a son. He never dared mention it for fear of hurting his wife's feelings. After all, it wasn't her fault.

"Why are you crying, baby?" he asked, holding his wife. "This is a good thing, right?"

Ellie nodded shakily. "I'm happy...I just...I just...Marcus, now I'm going to need to take it easy. I can't go out on weeks-long prospecting expeditions in the Outback. I can't be around the chemicals, confined spaces, the noise from blasting and machinery." She was right. Frontier mining with a small crew was no job for a pregnant woman. It was hard, occasionally dangerous work, even with modern equipment. Ellie was a conscientious enough woman that she'd be unwilling to risk anything happening. They'd tried to have a second child once, years before, and it had resulted in a miscarriage. Ellie had been devastated, and had fallen into depression for weeks. That's when the doctor had explained to her that she likely wouldn't be able to get pregnant again. Even with the miracles of Space Age medicine, some things were just out of human hands.

Marcus could see the concern on his wife's face. She was afraid it was going to happen again. He couldn't bear the thought of going through that kind of heartache again. He held her tightly and tried to sound comforting. "It's going to be okay, baby. We'll get you regular checkups, and you can stay home. I'll pick up more assignments if I have to."

"But what about our loans? Marcus, we can't afford to lose the money I take in."

"Relax, okay? We're not going to lose all of it. We'll just have to forget about Jerome Mountain until later. We have savings."

"That's for Annie's education!" Ellie protested, "and our

retirement. I don't want to be out there digging up rocks when I'm old and gray."

Marcus smiled at her. "Number one, that's bullshit. What else are you going to do, sit on the porch and knit? You'd go crazy staying at home, even if you were a hundred years old. You'll be out there in the desert until the day you croak. Number two, don't stress over it. I know how you get about money, but there's nothing for it right now. Let's just be thankful we have the savings to be able to get by with the cut in income. Even if we're just scraping by, it's only temporary, and we'll get through it. We got through everything else. This is no different. Okay?"

Ellie nodded, giving Marcus a faint smile. He leaned over, kissed her passionately, and put his hand on her belly.

"We're having a baby!" he said, grinning like a fool. He grabbed his handheld and sent Annie a message, telling her to come into their room.

A few moments later, their daughter appeared in their doorway looking confused. "Am I in trouble? What's going on? Mom, why were you crying?"

Ellie smiled at her daughter. "I'm pregnant. We're having a baby."

Annie's eyes lit up, her hands moved to her mouth, and she all but squealed, jumping up and down. She ran across the room, sat next to her mom, and hugged her tightly, almost in tears.

Marcus had rarely been so happy as he was just then. In the back of his mind, though, there was concern. He was going to have to raise another child to adulthood. He and his wife couldn't be gone as much as they often were. Annie was old enough to look after herself, and was mature enough to babysit, but Marcus knew his wife. She was a doting, dedicated mom and wouldn't settle for being an absentee parent. She wasn't going to be able to work full time like she had, and they were going to need money to provide for both of their children's futures now.

Annie was smart enough to get a scholarship to the university if she'd just apply herself, but she was bored with school and Marcus knew it. She took after him in that regard, and wasn't as studious and patient as her mother. She didn't want to go to the university anyway. Ellie didn't want to hear it, but he knew she wanted to go to the Spaceflight Academy. A few more years of saving and he probably could have sent her, but now?

Marcus held his family tightly, and resolved to find a way.

New Austin
Lone Star System

It took the *Andromeda* two hundred and twenty hours to complete the trajectory from the transit point through which she had entered the system to the orbit of New Austin. The dusty, dry planet was far from the heart of the Concordiat, but was slowly growing into a trading hub and center of frontier commerce. *Andromeda*'s sensors were tracking twenty-two other ships in the system. Lone Star had four transit points, and all were relatively close to the star itself. This was a huge benefit, economically speaking, and was one of the factors that enabled the system to get so much traffic. Transit points that were weeks' or even months' travel from each other or inhabited planets tended to not get as much traffic, since even the biggest ships could carry only so much reaction mass. In systems with enough traffic to make such things cost-effective, automated space tugs would help haul ships on long, in-system journeys, but New Austin had no such infrastructure in place yet.

The *Andromeda* approached New Austin at a comparatively high relative velocity. Tail first, she sailed into a low orbit, descending into the upper reaches of the planet's atmosphere. Her thermally shielded tail section heated up as she skimmed the atmosphere, bleeding off velocity and using far less propellant to decelerate than she would have otherwise. A single orbital rotation was enough to slow her to descent speed. The trajectory plotted by the flight computer had the ship begin her descent far above Aterrizaje, the colonial capital and home to the planet's largest spaceport.

Guided by spaceport traffic control, her systems synced with those on the ground to prevent a collision with other ships, the *Andromeda* descended through New Austin's atmosphere. Riding on her engines in a spectacular plume of smoke and fire, she gracefully slowed to almost a hover a few hundred meters over her designated landing pad. Sturdy landing jacks extended from the thick wingroots of her four large airfoils. The heavy ship set down on the landing pad amidst the roar of her engines and the smoke created by her exhaust. The landing gear hydraulics compressed as engine power was cut, and the stout craft curtsied politely as she settled onto *terra firma*. The ship's engines were locked out and the landing pad's service tower automatically aligned itself with the now-open ventral cargo bay. It adjusted itself to the correct height and length as it craned outward, like some kind of massive mechanical snake, and coupled with the cargo bay.

Inside, the *Andromeda*'s crew was quickly but carefully running through their postflight checklists and procedures. Even experienced spacers tended to move awkwardly after a months-long journey, most of which was spent in freefall, but the crew hustled as best they could. The captain had announced that they'd be dirtside for several local weeks, and that this was the last chance they'd get to stretch their legs and have some fun before the long haul to Zanzibar. The sooner the crew finished their assigned tasks, the sooner they could be out blowing their accumulated pay in the bars and brothels that had inevitably sprung up around every port since mankind had first taken to the sea, thousands of years before.

Catherine's officers and crew were busily making sure everything that she'd wanted done was seen to. Food stores were ordered from local suppliers, planetside maintenance was scheduled, and a refill for the ship's huge reaction mass tank was ordered. The liberty rotation had already been planned. The *Andromeda* was docked at a major spaceport with professional security, so there was little need for a standard watch rotation. Most of her crew would be heading out to have some fun.

Catherine had a lot of business to attend to during their stay, so she allowed herself the luxury of a few minutes to herself while she could. In the confines of her tiny cabin (the only such on the ship—being the captain had its privileges), she stripped out of her flight suit and entered her extremely cramped personal bathing unit, enjoying a gloriously long, hot shower. It felt good to be on a planet, with real gravity, the way human beings were meant to.

Stepping out of her bathing unit, she dried herself off with an utterly decadent fluffy towel, made of genuine, organic Egyptian cotton. She brushed her long, dark hair out thoroughly before rubbing the last of her body lotion onto her skin. The recycled air and artificial environment of the ship dried her skin out terribly. She would have to remember to stock up on her lotions and various other indulgences while she had the chance.

Catherine's wardrobe locker didn't have a lot of clothing in it. She had more flight suits than she did normal clothes. In her travels over the years, she had been to countless colony worlds, and each had its own fashions. What's more, different areas, sub-cultures, and cities often had their own unique styles as well. For a well-traveled spacer, it was nearly impossible to blend in with the locals in most. There simply wasn't enough space on the average ship for a large enough collection of clothes. As such, many spacers simply wore their crew uniforms when out and about.

Catherine was tired of her sage green flight suits, though, and found a nondescript pair of slacks and a purple, collared blouse to wear. From what she'd read about New Austin, this wouldn't draw any odd looks from the locals. Their style of dress wasn't particularly interesting or much different from hers. There was an old joke across civilized space that if a person walks in dressed like a hick but acting like he owned the place, he was a spacer. The origins of the saying and of the pejorative "hick" were a mystery, but in Catherine's experience it was mostly true.

For this reason, she normally didn't worry about appealing to the local aesthetic sensibilities. Around spaceports, it was simply expected and accepted that there would be people from other places, bringing with them different cultures, languages, and modes of dress. But given the nature of her present mission, Catherine felt the need to keep a low profile. Swaggering around Aterrizaje in her flight suit and leather flight jacket wasn't how one kept a *low profile*.

An electronic chirp told her someone was at the door just as she finished pulling on her boots. "It's open," she said, standing up and smoothing her blouse.

"*Kapitänin*," Wolfram von Spandau said, with a polite nod.

Her security officer, Mazer Broadbent, simply said, "Skipper."

Catherine smiled at her two dour officers as she punched a code into a small secure storage locker. "Mazer, what are the local regulations regarding the carrying of weapons?"

"Legal so long as you're on peaceable business," the broad-shouldered security man said. "The city has an ordinance against carrying weapons while intoxicated. The spaceport frowns on the open carrying of arms on its property. It draws attention."

"Very well," Catherine said. From the locker she picked the smaller of the two weapons there, a compact pulse laser with an abbreviated grip. It wasn't particularly powerful, but it was easy to conceal. The holster for it attached to her belt, just behind her right hip, and kept the butt of the weapon up high and tight against her side. A slight bulge was visible under her purple blouse, but after Catherine threw on a light jacket it disappeared completely.

Satisfied, the captain turned to her men. "Alright then. I don't know about you gentlemen, but they raise cattle on New Austin and I intend to have myself a steak." Catherine's officers fell in behind her as she made her way down to the cargo bay and out into the spaceport itself. Planning was best done over a hearty meal.

Capitol Starport, as it was known, was a sprawling complex a dozen kilometers outside of the city of Aterrizaje. In addition to long runways for spaceplanes and traditional aircraft, it boasted twenty landing pads, several of which were rated for some of the heaviest ships and the highest exhaust velocities. Railways carried ore and materials from distant refineries, and automated passenger trains brought travelers to and from the city. Aterrizaje was very near New Austin's equator, improving launch ballistics. Routine shuttle traffic from the Starport offered service to a space dock in geostationary orbit thirty-five thousand kilometers above it, allowing planetary access for very large and other nonatomospheric ships.

Despite having a small population, New Austin was growing. It was the last Concordiat colony along the *Andromeda*'s planned route, but the system enjoyed multiple transit points to other stars and was strategically located along popular trade routes. This was one of the reasons for the colony's founding; before the Second Interstellar War, the planet was home to only a few thousand prospectors, and was little more than an outpost. As the hostile aliens pushed deeper and deeper into Concordiat space, a desperate program of rapid colonization, decentralization, and strategic positioning was undertaken. The Concordiat very nearly lost the war and it was feared that even Earth itself would fall to the alien onslaught. The human race was determined to spread out as far and wide as possible as a bulwark against extinction.

The tide of the war turned. The aliens, Maggots as they were colloquially known, were frighteningly advanced but few in number. They were believed to be the last dwindling remnants of an ancient and once-mighty empire. As Concordiat and allied forces began to counter their tactics and push back, the aliens proved unable to adapt. It was believed that they didn't have thousands of years of vicious warfare in their recent racial memory, the way humans did. Whatever the reason, when humanity regrouped, the Concordiat and its allies put together the largest space armada in human history. They rolled through Maggot systems with a genocidal vengeance, destroying every enclave of the aliens that was found.

With the war won and the Maggots believed to be extinct, the Concordiat Contingency Colonization Initiative was defunded. New Austin had been supplied with a generous amount of starter infrastructure, and had been spared the horrors and destruction of the war. Without the C3I in place, though, its population and output expanded only slowly, at a natural pace. A century after the war, the growing colony was making peaceful, lucrative use of its strategic location along the interstellar trade lanes. In another two or three generations it would have the population and economic base to qualify for full Concordiat membership.

Catherine and her two crewmen found themselves in one of the starport's many restaurants. They were noticeably more expensive than what you'd find in town, but it saved a trip to the city and back. This particular establishment was called Buffalo Bill's Roadhouse and Steakery. Catherine didn't know who Buffalo Bill was, and she doubted that "steakery" was actually a word, but her cut of real beef was grilled to perfection and she attacked it greedily. Meals like this were a rare treat for spacers; typical rations, even if they claimed to be beef, rarely tasted like it. It seemed to Catherine that no matter whether the package claimed it was beef, chicken, pork, or something else, the ration meat always tasted the same and smelled like cat food.

The décor of the Steakery was modeled after stereotypical, romanticized notions of the ancient American West. The tables, floors, and walls all looked like they were made of wood. Spools of rope, horseshoes, and other equestrian accessories hung on the walls, as did more than one pair of steer horns. The staff wore denim blue jeans, wide-brimmed hats, and spoke with a typical New Austin drawl that was as much a product of the colony's marketing efforts as it was normal linguistic evolution. Being a higher-priced establishment, the Steakery used human servers and chefs, instead of automating it all for efficiency. Twangy acoustic guitar music played over the sound system as the three spacers finished their meals and their table was cleared.

Catherine laid her tablet on the table and looked over at her security officer. "Mazer, this is your area of expertise. What would you say is the preferred way to go about recruiting the sort of people we need? Shall we contact the local security companies?"

Mazer Broadbent took a long swig from the mug of dark beer in front of him. "I wouldn't say so, Skipper. I've checked out the local companies. They're small-timers; security guards, bodyguards, things like that. A lot of them employ former military, but not necessarily the caliber of person we're looking for. Also, these companies may not be prepared to support an operation like this contractually. In my opinion, our best bet is to recruit the same way we'd recruit crewmembers: post ads on the local network and interview prospects that reply. I uploaded an ad to that effect once we got close enough to New Austin to connect to its network."

"Very good," the captain said. "Any replies as of yet?"

"Several, Skipper," Mazer answered. "I'll begin the vetting process after this meeting."

The XO spoke up. "Perhaps it would be advisable to take the initiative, check the local job boards, and contact those prospects who might be qualified. We are pressed for time."

"Indeed we are, Wolfram," Catherine agreed. "Very well. Mazer, get someone to help you with the vetting if you need it. See about purchasing the necessary small arms, ammunition, and personal equipment for our team. We're trying to plan for unknown contingencies, so do the best you can with what we do know. Just stay within the budget." She sipped her wine and turned to her XO. "Wolfram, contact spaceport services and oversee a rapid refurbishment of the impact energy absorbers and thermal shielding. Get the radiators serviced and the remass tanks refilled. Pull crew off of liberty to assist if need be. I also want the ship cleaned, spotless, nose to tail, before we lift off."

"Understood, *Kapitänin*. I have already assigned a cleaning rotation. I will inspect the ship well in advance of our departure."

Catherine nodded, trying not to smile at the image of her exec conducting a white glove inspection of the *Andromeda*. "Excellent. I'll see to the recharging of the ship's magazines with whatever ordnance I can get my hands on. I'm not taking any chances on this one. Also, there is a courier ship in the system preparing to leave, and it's headed out toward Zanzibar. I'm going to upload a message to it and send word to Cecil's captors that we're coming to negotiate. The message will get there weeks before we do. Hopefully he's still alive." Catherine sipped her wine again, the concern obvious on her face. No word had been received from the people holding her brother for months.

There was no way to transmit messages through the naturally occurring transit corridors that connected stars. While in a star system, messages could be sent at the speed of light. Across interstellar distances, the only practical way to deliver messages was to upload them to a ship. Courier ships were therefore common across inhabited space. These stripped-down, high-speed vessels were designed specifically for receiving and rapidly delivering information. They had a minimal crew, powerful engines, and huge reaction mass tanks.

Couriers were so fundamental to interstellar communication that the ships themselves were afforded something akin to diplomatic immunity. Interfering with a courier ship, regardless of what colony it hailed from, was outlawed by custom and treaty, backed up by the threat of force from most spacefaring societies. Even oppressive regimes like the Orlov Combine generally left the couriers alone, as they themselves relied on them for communications and trade.

After a moment, Catherine's tone lightened. She smiled at her crewmen. "I think that's everything, then. For God's sake, both of you, try to get some R and R while we're here. I for one am going shopping. I know you're both married to the *Andromeda*, but you're not cheating on her if you take a couple of days for yourselves. Go to a brothel or a nightclub and find yourselves some companionship. You both need it."

Mazer Broadbent cracked a smile. Wolfram von Spandau only grunted and complained about the weak local beer. Catherine couldn't help herself this time; she giggled.

Zanzibar
Danzig-5012 Solar System
Equatorial Region

I hate this place.

Cecil Blackwood thought this to himself, the same as he did every day when he first woke up. It was worse when he'd been dreaming that he was back home on Avalon, and that his ill-fated expedition to Zanzibar had all been a bad dream. There was nothing worse than waking up to discover it was the other way around. He sat up in bed and swung his feet over the side, moving slowly so as not to wake up Bianca. On the stand next to his bed were a bottle and a small cup. As he did every morning, he poured himself a large shot of the ghastly local booze and knocked it back in one gulp. It tasted like some kind of cleaning solvent and burned all the way down, but the alcohol helped him hang on. It kept him sane.

Yeah, that's it. It keeps me sane.

Standing up, Cecil poured himself a cup of coffee from the machine in his room. Like the booze, the coffee was strong and coarse, but it, too, helped him get through the day. Cup in hand and naked as the day he was born, he stood in front of the large bay window, sipped his coffee, and studied the dusty, desolate street four stories below him. The local sun, Danzig, was low in the sky, bathing the town in its characteristic pale orange light. The locals were already out and about, milling through the streets, doing whatever it was these people did every day. Even after a year on Zanzibar, Cecil still wasn't sure. He couldn't remember how long it had been since he'd cared.

The dusty town below him was called Lang's Burg. That wasn't its original name. If the town even *had* a name, it had been forgotten. Much about Zanzibar had been forgotten, Cecil mused. So much so, that if he'd have known the awful truth about this place, he'd have stayed home.

Before the Second Interstellar War, Zanzibar had been a remote, but thriving, independent colony. The planet itself was a lifeless rock; even its core had long since cooled. There were no plate tectonics on Zanzibar, no seismic activity of any kind. Once, the planet had been volcanically active. Once, they said, it had oceans. At one point this world had been alive. It had supported life. Now the only life on Zanzibar was what mankind brought with it.

The funny thing was, planetary scientists and geologists still couldn't figure out what had happened, what had killed Zanzibar. There were numerous theories and none of them could be proven. What was known was that about four million years before humanity set foot on the planet, something happened that had scoured it barren. Now, the air was thin and unbelievably dry. The oxygen-nitrogen atmosphere was nominally breathable to people, but the atmospheric pressure was so low that it was like being high up in the mountains. Some stout locals had adapted to the thin air, but off-worlders like Cecil relied on respirators. They also filtered out the Zanzibaran dust, which in many areas was so fine you could put it in a cup and swirl it around like water. It played hell with the respiratory system, too. Cecil imagined he had a rock of dirt in his lungs at this point.

There was ice on Zanzibar, which created a supply of water. Before the war, a stubborn group of colonists had been determined to live on this Godforsaken rock. They pressurized their buildings or lived underground. They grew crops in hydroponic greenhouses and not only survived, but thrived. Off-world investment money poured into Zanzibar for a time. The planet was seen as a launching pad for colonial expeditions far beyond it. Numerous potential colony worlds had been identified back then, when the Concordiat was at the height of its expansion. Soon, the philosophers promised, a second Diaspora would begin, and humanity would spread even further across the galaxy. Zanzibar, they said, would be a critical logistics hub for this envisioned age of exploration.

So they said, Cecil mused. He'd read everything there was to read about Zanzibar before he'd begun this expedition. That was before those outward-bound expeditions had discovered the Maggots. When the war began, humanity was unprepared. Never before had a sentient, spacefaring species been encountered, and the encounters soon turned violent. When the alien invaders reached the Danzig-5012 system, they wiped out the small defensive fleet protecting it and blasted the scattered colonial settlements from orbit. They were remarkably precise in their targeting, only hitting human settlements with enough force to destroy them. Later in the war, on other worlds, they would use mass orbital bombardment techniques, but on Zanzibar they were very careful.

There were many theories about that as well, but Cecil fancied that he had that one figured out. There *was* something of value on Zanzibar, and it wasn't the usual natural resources that attracted human settlement. This world had once been alive. It had once, long, long ago, supported an alien civilization. Whatever had killed Zanzibar didn't leave many traces of these aliens, and little was known about them. If you wanted to find traces of them, you had to know where to look, and you had to dig. Cecil figured that even the Maggots valued that kind of knowledge.

Before the war, the colonial government had strictly controlled information about the long-dead alien civilization, referred to as the native *Zanzibari*. Even simple artifacts were extremely valuable, and some of the artifacts that had been found weren't so simple. It was feared that if the archaeological/paleontological expeditions weren't conducted in a controlled manner, outside interests would swarm Zanzibar and loot it of its invaluable alien treasures.

Much of that knowledge was lost in the war. Zanzibar's infrastructure was destroyed, and the shattered colony was all but abandoned as the war raged on. The Maggots never came back, but very little help arrived. The survivors of the onslaught banded into tribes, based around whoever could control the precious resources needed to produce food and water, and keep the necessary machinery running. And so it went, for over a hundred standard years. Even today, the small population of Zanzibar was fractured, divided, and usually under the thumb of one warlord or another.

Warlords like Aristotle Lang, who had been holding Cecil captive for the better part of Zanzibar's four-hundred-and-eighty-day year. The fact that those days were only nineteen and a half hours long hadn't helped much.

There you go again, Cecil, thinking too much. Just get through the day. One day at a time. Depressed, he walked back to his bed and poured a shot of the awful booze into his awful coffee. The combination was surprisingly good, and he finished the cup quickly.

Bianca stirred then. She sat up, yawning and stretching. Long, black hair cascaded over her shoulders and complimented her smooth, walnut-colored skin. She looked up at Cecil with dark, playful eyes and smiled. "Good day, Mista Ceecil," she said, with the gruff accent the inhabitants of the Zanzibaran wastes all seemed to have. Her ample, bare breasts bounced as she planted her feet on the floor and hugged him. Bianca was a concubine, given to Cecil by his captor many months ago. It would help him focus on his work, the old warlord promised, and would take his mind off foolishly trying to escape.

Old Aristotle Lang liked Cecil, he insisted. He really didn't want to have to kill him. For her part, Bianca insisted that she wanted to be with Cecil, and that she was "his" woman now. She didn't just screw him (though she did that eagerly and often, Cecil thought with a grin, and had none of the cultural inhibitions Avalonian women were saddled with); she cooked for him, cleaned their flat, washed his clothes, took care of him when he was sick, and rubbed his temples when he was hung over. She made for a better, proper Avalonian wife than half the Avalonian women he'd known ever would have. He couldn't imagine being apart from his sweet Bianca, and hated himself for it.

It was another one of Old Man Lang's methods, giving him something to care about. He knew that if he ran, not only would he probably die, but the bastards would probably kill Bianca too. Cecil couldn't bear that thought, he just couldn't bear it.

Bianca's skin was warm against Cecil's. He stood by the bed as she sat on it, arms wrapped around him, her head resting against his belly. She began to kiss him all over, her hands caressing his back and butt.

"I need to get to the work site soon," he managed weakly.

She grinned devilishly. "Mista Ceecil says he hasta go, but Little Ceecil says he wansta stay." Bianca did that thing she liked to do, and Cecil lost what little willpower he possessed.

Old Man Lang can wait a little longer. It's not like I'm going anywhere anyway.

✧ ✧ ✧

"Zak! My main man! How are you this fine day?"

Zak Mesa, historian and amateur archaeologist, rolled his eyes behind his gaudy, gold-rimmed smart glasses. "Not as good as you, Cecil," he said, not looking up from what he was doing. "You're late."

Cecil beamed stupidly. "Yes, well, a man has business he needs to take care of, as it were. At any rate, where are we at?"

Annoyed, Zak took off his glasses and rubbed his eyes. "Same place we were yesterday, Cecil. We're being held hostage on Zanzibar."

"True enough, my friend, but not what I meant. Have you uncovered any more possible dig sites? Lang is getting impatient."

"Impatient? I'm trying to make sense of what's left of records that were kept secret before the Maggots bombed this planet back to the stone age. It takes *time*."

Cecil looked around conspiratorially, then leaned in close to his unfortunate partner. "That's the idea, man. Give Lang enough to keep him happy, but not so much that we outlive our usefulness, yeah?"

"That's what I've been doing, Cecil. We're still alive, aren't we? Well, you're still alive because you said your rich family would pay for you. I only get to live as long as I come in handy."

"Zak," Cecil said, trying to sound reassuring, but coming across as condescending, "it's not like that. I hired you. You're my responsibility, you and your assistant both. I've been bargaining for all of our lives. I wouldn't abandon you two just to save my own skin. You may think I'm a blue-blooded rich man's son, but I'm not a coward."

We'll see when the time comes, the frustrated historian thought bitterly. He scratched his bald head and showed Cecil his tablet. "I've found more references to a vault where the prewar colonial government kept a lot of the more interesting artifacts. I just haven't found one yet listing where it is. I figure there's about a fifty-fifty chance it was blasted in the Maggot bombardment."

"I don't think they would've done that," Cecil insisted. "I think the Maggots knew about the species that had been here. I think the reason they were so careful in their attack on this world is that they didn't want to destroy any of the artifacts."

"I actually agree with you," Zak replied, "but they had no way of knowing about a secret government vault. It might've gotten destroyed by them, unknowingly."

Cecil furled his brow. "Wouldn't it make more sense to have the vault out in the wastes, closer to dig sites and away from the cities?"

"Yes and no. Less prying eyes in the immediate area, but construction out in the middle of nowhere would've been more suspicious. People would've gotten curious, thought something was up. An underground construction project in the city wouldn't have drawn that much attention, and they could've just hauled the artifacts in nondescript trucks."

"Bloody hell," Cecil muttered with resignation.

"Honestly though, it's not like we've had a bad run here. The stuff we have found is probably worth millions on the open market. Like this," Zak said, holding up a strangely smooth, angular stone, and handing it to Cecil. It was twelve centimeters tall, and had seven sides. Each side was engraved with a glyph that seemed to shine or even glow if it caught the light just right. Whatever it was made out of, it wasn't stone. It was perfectly smooth and weighed so little that it felt like it was made of aluminum.

"What is this?" Cecil said, examining the piece in awe. He'd seen them before, of course, but Zak hadn't shown him *this* fine specimen before.

"I have no idea," the historian admitted. "Neither did the Zanzibaran archaeologists. My spectrometer can't even identify what it's made out of. I don't want to risk damaging it by doing a more invasive procedure. I found it cataloged in the original dig site archives. *They* had no idea what it was either, but judging from where they found it, they estimated it to be about four million years old."

"Four million years," Cecil repeated. "That's about when they estimated that Zanzibar lost its magnetosphere, isn't it? My God. It just boggles the mind, Zak. What happened here? Who made this thing? What purpose did it serve?"

Zak raised his eyebrows. "I'd be curious to know how it sat unused for four million years and still looks new. It said that when they found it, after they cleaned the dirt off, they thought it was much more recent at first, or that it was an anomaly."

"Most of what we've found on this planet is anomalous," Cecil said. "So ... not to be crass, but how much is this thing worth?"

"Well, there isn't much of a network on Zanzibar, and it doesn't get updated very often, but according to the latest information, a generic alien artifact of this size and condition from just about any extinct species could fetch up to one-point-five million credits on the market, potentially more if it was auctioned off. And that's generic. Stuff from Zanzibar is exceedingly rare out there. We're definitely sitting on a fortune, Cecil. I just hope that Lang doesn't end up selling all this stuff off for the money. These are priceless relics from an unknown civilization. They need to be studied." He took the object back from Cecil, holding it delicately. "This belongs in a museum."

Cecil patted Zak on the shoulder. "I admire your passion, mate, but I'll be happy enough if we manage to get off of this rock alive."

Zak nodded in agreement. It was something they tried not to dwell on. Aristotle Lang appeared to be a jovial man, and he had, truth be told, taken very good care of his captives. They were never physically abused, they had plenty of food, and could do whatever they wanted as long as they didn't try to flee. But for all his pretenses of being a gentleman rogue, Lang was a stone cold killer and they both knew it. You didn't rise to the top of that particular dung heap without being willing to slit a few throats.

"Come on then. Speaking of the devil, we've got to go give Lang an update. The guards said he's in a good mood today, so this should be painless." As the two men left the historian's tiny, cluttered office, Zak found himself hoping to God, or whoever was listening, that Cecil's father had sent someone.

New Austin
Lone Star System
Laredo Territory
Southern Hemisphere

The proprietor of the establishment was quietly reading his tablet, feet up on the desk, when Marcus and Wade walked in. The door quietly hissed open, sending a warm draft into the shop. Elliot Landrieu, the owner of Laredo Armament and Supply, smiled at the two colonial marshals as they came into his shop. "Good afternoon, boys," he said, setting the tablet down and standing up. "What can I do ya for?"

"Ah, we're just killing time, Elliot," Marcus said, looking around. "Kinda slow today." The marshal liked visiting with Elliot. He was an old veteran of the Espatier Corps, always had good inventory at fair prices, and was a hell of a gunsmith on top of it. His shop was well-lit, with a friendly atmosphere despite the fact that Elliot looked like a crusty prospector, right down to the shaggy beard and denim overalls.

The blue and silver flag of the Interstellar Concordiat hung on the wall. Next to it was the rampant stallion on burnt orange banner that represented New Austin. Next to that was the red and silver Eagle, Globe, and Rocket flag of the Espatier Corps. Daylight poured in from large windows, and the walls were stocked with firearms of every sort. His wife, Meg, handcrafted leather holsters and gun belts, just like you'd have found on ancient Earth.

"I heard about that tussle you had with that cyborg fella," Elliot said. "Glad to see you're okay, Marshal. The news said he was a pretty bad hombre."

"Yeah, well, I owe Wade here for that one," Marcus answered, patting his partner on the shoulder. "He saved my ass with one well-placed shot."

Wade shrugged nonchalantly. "It was the ADR-808 you built for me," he said, referencing the powerful 8mm rifle he kept in their truck. "I couldn't have missed with that optic on there."

"Bull-*shit* you couldn't have missed," Marcus said with a grin. "You miss all the time. A fancy automatic optical gunsight can't make up for the fact that my daughter shoots better than you."

"Says the guy whose ass was saved by my amazing marksmanship!" Wade retorted. "Get this, Elliot: perfect headshot, standing position, forty meters. The perp's head was wobbling all over the place and he was choking Marcus here out. I had to line up the shot through a cloud of dust and make it without hitting *this* clown, who decided to try and go hug the dangerous felon."

Elliot let out a hard, raspy laugh and slapped the counter.

Wade pointed a finger at his partner. "And for the record, Boss, your daughter is an unnaturally good shot, and that's not a fair comparison."

Elliot laughed again, then gestured toward the selection of firearms on the wall. "Anything you boys wanna see? I've been playing with different configurations of the ADR-808 and the CAR90, since those are two of my best sellers."

"You got more lasers in stock than usual," Wade observed.

"Believe it or not, there's been more demand for them lately. I guess the economy is picking up. Take a look at this." After checking to make sure there was no power cell inserted, Elliot handed the stubby weapon to Wade. "It's an update to the LAS-5 design, the new J-model. I bought the schematics and manufacturing rights as soon as they became available."

"Wow, this is light for a laser carbine," Wade noted.

"Yep. More efficient cooling, too. It's the first real update to the LAS-5 in a generation. I paid a pretty penny for the rights to build them but they've been selling well. Improved optics on the six-centimeter lens, improved throughput on the power cell, and it's even a little more powerful. Four-point-eight kilojoules per shot now. Not too bad, hey?"

"Not bad at all," Wade agreed. "But I'll stick with my rifle. You got any more 12mm APHE in stock?"

Marcus absentmindedly browsed the store while his partner

bought ammunition for his revolver. It was an odd weapon, based on the earliest repeating handguns from ancient Earth, but it was modern all the same. It fired 12mm rounds from a disposable, seven-shot cylinder that vigorously ejected upward away from the gun when empty, allowing for a rapid reload. Marcus stuck with his regular 10mm automatic, but the Marshals Service was pretty lax on duty weapon specifications. After a run-in with a psychotic cyborg with built-in armor plating, Marcus could certainly see the value of armor piercing, high explosive 12mm rounds.

Wade himself was an odd sort, a former Nuclear/Explosive Ordnance Disposal technician from the Concordiat Defense Force. He was a couple centimeters taller and a few years younger than Marcus, but was the best partner the marshal had ever had. He had a screwed-up sense of humor and a penchant for dry wit that made him tolerable on ten-hour shifts. Two of the fingers on his right hand had to be reattached, he once admitted, after an accident while making homemade explosives. He'd been thirteen years old at the time.

While Wade and Elliot talked guns, Marcus retrieved his handheld and browsed through its applications. There was a response to the profile he had posted on a professional networking job board. *Interesting.* He opened the message and read it quietly.

Mr. Winchester:

The Privateer Ship Andromeda *is recruiting highly qualified and skilled personnel for an expedition to a remote system. We are looking for people of the highest caliber with extensive military experience. Unquestionable accountability, integrity and discretion is a must. Experience in the full spectrum of ground warfare operations is desired. The assignment will include protecting the ship's crew while conducting business in an austere, potentially hazardous environment.*

From your verified professional credentials, we believe you to be an outstanding candidate for this expedition. We are offering a generous pay package that we believe you will find to be more than competitive. This expedition is departing in a matter of weeks, so this offer is time-sensitive. If interested, please respond to this query and we will schedule an interview with you as soon as possible. Thank you.

Marcus looked up from his device and blinked hard. *Is this for real?* When he'd updated his portfolio on the professional networking board, he was hoping to be offered side-gigs as a personal bodyguard or some such, just to bring in extra money. He didn't expect an off-world expedition to try to recruit him. He wondered if it was a hoax, that someone was playing a joke on him, but the network site screened and vetted its job postings. *How generous is generous? Off-world. Holy hell, Ellie won't like that.*

"Hey, Wade," Marcus said. "Come here. You're going to love this."

Marcus nodded to the man on the screen of his handheld. Broadbent, he said his name was. He was an imposing man with a dark complexion and a cybernetic ocular implant. Marcus couldn't tell where his accent was from, exactly, but he was former Concordiat military.

"Do you have any further questions, Mr. Winchester? How about you, Mr. Bishop?"

Wade shook his head slightly. "No, I think that's all I have. Thank you for your time."

"No, thank you both, gentlemen," Mr. Broadbent replied. "Given both of your backgrounds, I believe you would make for valuable members of our team."

"I'm flattered, Mr. Broadbent," Marcus said, "and I *am* interested. I need to discuss this with my family before I can give you a solid answer."

"I understand. What about you, Mr. Bishop? Shall I send you a contract?"

"I'll be in touch," Wade said noncommittally. "I need to see to some things myself."

"Very well. Gentlemen, I'll be waiting for your call. Be advised, however, that we lift off in nineteen local days, one way or another. I urge you both to consider this opportunity carefully."

"We will. Thank you for your time."

"Good day," the spacer said, and the connection was severed.

Marcus lowered his handheld. He'd been holding it so both he and his partner could see the screen. The two colonial marshals were sitting inside their armored patrol vehicle. "What do you think, Wade?"

"I think that's some goddamn good money, Boss. Half up front, too. I'll take a year's sabbatical from the marshals for that kind of scratch."

"So you're all for this, huh? Why didn't you have him send you a contract?"

Wade smiled. "And leave you alone? No offense, but you wouldn't last a month out here on your own, and Ellie would kill me if I let you run around with some other jackass."

"Better to stick with the jackass you know," Marcus agreed.

"Exactly," Wade said. "And I don't want to go on something like this without someone I'm sure I can trust, especially when the thing is being cobbled together on such short notice."

"It would be better if we could watch each other's backs. You're not wrong, either; that *is* really good money. The half they're offering up front would be enough for Ellie to get another one of her claims up and running, with plenty left over to pay down debt. Damn."

"She's not going to be happy when you tell her you're thinking of leaving, even if it's for a job. They said we could be gone for over a year."

"We get paid extra if it runs longer than that. It could be a win-win."

"Assuming we come back alive," Wade mused.

"Mm," Marcus agreed. "There is that. You know what? What the hell, I'll talk to Ellie when I get home."

"Why not just call her?"

"That would be safer in case she wants to slug me," Marcus grinned. "But I can take my lumps. I owe it to her."

"Let me know what she says, Boss."

Zanzibar
Danzig-5012 Solar System
Equatorial Region

"Gentlemen! I'm so pleased to hear of your progress!" Aristotle Lang was beaming as he strode into the underground dig site. As usual, his entourage of bodyguards, flunkies, toadies, and female eye candy were in tow. "I had to come see it for myself!" Lang's bodyguards fanned out around the chamber and glowered at the captives. They all wore face masks with oxygen condensers and filters and long gray coats with matching skull caps. The goons carried a mishmash of guns and knives, and wore body armor and load bearing equipment if they had it. In the dig site, most of them had their trademark goggles either dangling around their necks or up on their foreheads.

Cecil Blackwood and Zak Mesa exchanged a knowing glance. This was the sort of thing that kept them employed and, by extension, kept them alive. Zak especially hated turning over priceless ancient alien artifacts to a warlord like Lang, but there was nothing he could do.

The warlord didn't look like much—a heavy-set, middle-aged bald man, broad and squat with a noticeable belly. Nonetheless Lang was cunning, ruthless, and a shrewd negotiator. A man didn't keep his position as being the post powerful warlord on Zanzibar without being intelligent and being able to think on his feet.

"Mr. Lang," Cecil began. It was always better when Cecil did the talking. "Thanks to the untiring efforts of Mr. Mesa, we were able to confirm that this site was worth excavating. It's not the vault we've been hunting for, but it may still prove to be a good find."

"Ah, Mr. Blackwood," Lang began, "I've heard that sweet Bianca is being very nice to you?" Cecil nodded nervously. He knew that the old warlord did things like this to remind him he was essentially a house pet. "Good, good. I could give your counterpart a concubine as well; I have many, but he has refused. Pity. In any case," Lang continued, trying to sound intellectual, "please explain what you have found."

"This was a storage site for artifacts when the Maggots hit this system over a century ago. It was, at the time, a closely guarded secret. Before the orbital bombardment began, they used explosives to blast the entryway and seal it before fleeing. They were worried that looters would clear it out before they were able to come back. Obviously, they never came back. Most of the records of this place were lost. Zak's research led us here."

"Very good, Mr. Mesa, very good! What can we expect to find in there?"

"I can't tell you for sure," Zak managed. Lang's expression darkened, and Cecil visibly winced. "M-most of the records were lost," Zak continued. "I'm not sure what's in there, but there *are* alien artifacts in there. It's listed as a contingency storage site, and that's coming from multiple sources."

Lang's frown turned back into a smile. "Ha! Excellent, my boy, excellent! An old dog such as myself could hardly hope for a better historian. Tell me, how soon until we are able to penetrate the sealed chamber?"

The vault was at the end of a ten meter wide, hundred meter long tunnel that had been bored into the base of a barren hill, eroded smooth by eons of unceasing wind. The tunnel had been reinforced with composite braces that were still as strong as the day they had been placed, and had not caved in or crumbled in the time it had sat abandoned. It had been sealed by a deliberate cave-in at the mouth and another deep inside, at the end, to confound the efforts of looters. Air was condensed and pumped in to keep the tunnel pressurized so that the crews could work without getting winded, and to keep oxygen flowing deep underground. Lighting had been strung up all along it. At the very end, the tunnel widened into a large cavern, but the entrance was buried under tons and tons of rock.

"I talked to your foreman," Cecil said, indicating the crew of Lang's men that were using machines and hand tools to remove the crumbling stone. "I very specifically told them not to use explosives. They might damage the artifacts or cause a cave-in."

"A wise decision," Lang agreed. "But how long?"

"He told me several more days. The rock slide goes deeper than we thought."

"I see, I see," Lang replied, rubbing his chin. "I will talk to the foreman myself. I expect they can have that chamber open sooner than you think. Until then, make sure these fools don't do anything stupid. I will not risk the artifacts! My men are replaceable. The artifacts are not."

"We will, Mr. Lang," Cecil agreed nervously.

"And you, Mr. Mesa," Lang said, pointing a crooked finger at Zak. "Find me that vault!"

"I guarantee that he will!" Cecil said, stepping in before Zak could say anything.

Aristotle Lang's demeanor darkened again. "For your sake I hope so. Good day, gentlemen." He turned and left, his hangers-on in tow behind him. Cecil and Zak looked at each other again, and exhaled. Sooner or later their luck was going to run out.

New Austin
Lone Star System
Laredo Territory, Southern Hemisphere

Eleanor Winchester was not happy. She kept herself busy making a nice, home-cooked meal for the family and their expected guests, but she barely spoke a word to anyone. Marcus knew the silent treatment when he didn't hear it. He did his best to give her space.

She had not been pleased when Marcus played back the conversation he'd had with a crewmember of a privateer ship called the *Andromeda*. Even knowing their financial situation full well, she was pregnant and Marcus was talking about *leaving*, for over a year! Nonetheless, Ellie had consented to his talking further to the spacers to see what the specifics were. She said she didn't want to stand in his way, even if she disapproved.

When the captain of the ship and a couple of her crewmen asked if they could come to the house to talk to Marcus, Ellie had even put on a big, fake smile and invited them to dinner. She was now busy in the kitchen, resentfully cooking a meal by hand for guests she really didn't want, instead of just letting the kitchen appliances handle it. When Marcus asked if he could help, she just said she was fine.

Marcus had been with his wife long enough to know that when she said she was fine, things weren't actually fine, and that he was in trouble. He couldn't really blame her, though. He had been gone a great deal when he was in the military, and had promised her—given his word—that after they settled on New

Austin he would be there for his family all the time. He hated that he'd gone back on that promise, hated it, and hoped Ellie would forgive him.

He knew that if, deep down, Ellie was truly, adamantly opposed to him doing this, she'd have said so, asked him not to go, and that would've been the end of it. She'd instead told him to do what he "thought was best" and had spun herself up into a good *mad* over it. But she understood their financial situation better than he did, and she understood what he was trying to do. This job offer could be the blessing the Winchester family badly needed.

That didn't mean she had to like it.

So Marcus gave Ellie a wide berth while she made dinner, and took the time to reread the contract the crew of the *Andromeda* had sent him. It was pretty vague in the details of where they were going and why, but was very blunt about some other things. *Hazardous conditions. Long spaceflight. Austere environment. Safety not guaranteed. Death or dismemberment clause. Lost in space clause. Long-term health effects clause.* Some of that left Marcus wondering, but there was one part of the contract that focused his interest very well: *half up front.*

If they were willing to pay half of the not-insubstantial salary up front, that meant they were serious. It meant that this was a legitimate job, not some shady operation that would just as soon screw a guy over as pay him. That part had made Ellie feel a little better, even if she didn't want to admit it. Marcus freely admitted that it made *him* feel better.

Annie, on the other hand, had surprised Marcus with her reaction. She seemed more excited than anything else, and jealous that he might be going on a *space adventure* without her. He had to remind himself that she had still been little when he got out of the Espatiers and the family emigrated to New Austin. She didn't really remember him being gone all the time. She instead bombarded him with questions about the ship he might be departing on, and he repeatedly had to tell her that he didn't know. Undeterred, she looked up the ship on the colonial network, since it was listed as being docked at Capitol Starport. She had practically memorized every detail about it, and Marcus hoped that the captain wouldn't mind being bombarded with questions about her ship.

Lone Star was sinking toward the eastern horizon when Marcus was alerted to the approaching air car. The house's security system picked it up and sent a notification to his handheld. Dressed a little nicer than usual, in a jacket and slacks, Marcus headed outside to greet his guests.

Annie followed on his heels, acting unusually sociable. Being an only child out in the deserts of Laredo Territory, she didn't interact with other people face-to-face very much. She normally only saw her friends online, and Marcus worried that this was stunting her social development. She was usually shy, reclusive, and even disinterested when people came to visit, but not tonight. Tonight she'd even put on one of the dresses she very rarely wore, a dark blue one that her mother had gotten her last Landing Day. In keeping with her sense of style, though, Marcus noted that his daughter was wearing black leggings and combat boots that almost went to her knees. That was about as dressy as Annabelle Winchester ever got.

The shrill whine of the air car's ducted-fan engines grew louder as it approached. The small aircraft circled gracefully around the house and slowed to a hover. Its engine ducts flared outward, and the vehicle settled onto Marcus' long driveway, kicking up a huge cloud of dust as it did so. The air car's pilot had politely landed about fifty meters away from the house so as not sandblast it. Air cars generally made poor ground vehicles; this one came lumbering up the drive, lift fans retracted, reminding Marcus of nothing so much as a beached sea mammal. It rolled to a stop and cut its engine.

The front doors opened and two men got out. One was muscular, dark-skinned, with a cybernetic implant replacing one of his eyes and a portion of the side of his face—Mr. Broadbent. The other, the one that had been flying the craft, had the pale complexion typical of spacers and blonde hair cropped into a buzzcut. He wore denim blue jeans, but had them tucked into combat boots, and wore a long leather coat and dark glasses. *Definitely not from around here,* Marcus mused.

The oddly dressed spacer came around the vehicle and opened the passenger door. He extended a hand to help a woman climb out of the rear passenger seat. She was tall, and like her compatriot, had a fair complexion. Her dark hair was done up into a tight bun. Her eyes were concealed behind mirrored sunglasses, aviator-type, in the style of ancient Earth. A leather flight jacket with the traditional four bars of a captain on the shoulder boards told Marcus that this woman was the skipper of the *Andromeda*.

She approached confidently, removing her sunglasses. She had strong, angular features and a hard gleam in her eye. The woman offered Marcus a firm, Earth-style handshake. "Marcus Winchester?"

"Guilty as charged," Marcus said with a grin. "You must be Captain Blackwood."

"Catherine," she said. She turned to Annabelle and shook her hand as well. "And who is this lovely young lady?"

Normally Marcus would introduce his daughter, since Annie had a tendency to be very shy during face-to-face encounters with people she didn't know. But with Captain Blackwood, she seemed resolute. She kept her shoulders squared and looked the captain right in the eye. "Annabelle Winchester," she said. "Nice to meet you, ma'am."

"And you," Captain Blackwood said. "Allow me to introduce my associates." She indicated the oddly dressed fellow with the buzzcut. "This is Herr Wolfram von Spandau, my executive officer." Herr von Spandau gave Marcus a single, crisp vertical handshake and a firm nod. "And this," the captain said, pointing at the man with the face implant, "is my security officer."

The security man had a deep voice and a grip like a mechanical vice. "Mazer Broadbent," he said.

"Nice to meet you face to face," Marcus said. "Now, if y'all are hungry my wife is preparing a nice, home-cooked meal."

Captain Blackwood raised an eyebrow. "By hand?"

Marcus nodded. "She never has the appliances make dinner when we have company over."

"It's never as good when the machines do it," Annie added.

"It certainly smells delicious," the captain said. "We'd be honored to be your dinner guests."

Despite her unhappiness with the prospect of Marcus leaving, Ellie was a great cook and a gracious host. She'd grown up on Hayden, and as crowded and crime-ridden as some parts of that colony were, hospitality was a deeply held social value there. Guests at Winchester Ranch were always treated to a fine meal, prepared by hand, drinks if they wanted them, and a pleasant atmosphere. In any case, Ellie liked entertaining, and they didn't get company very often living way out in Laredo Territory, so she was making the most of it. Marcus noted, as the evening wore on, that his wife seemed to be genuinely enjoying herself.

His daughter was too. They hadn't gotten around to discussing business yet, so Annie took the opportunity to ask the captain as many questions as she could. For her part, Captain Blackwood pleasantly and patiently told Annie just about everything she wanted to know. She could probably tell that Annie was completely enamored with her, and Marcus appreciated that she was nice to his daughter. It made him feel better about the whole proposition.

After the meal was cleared away and drinks were poured, Ellie had Annie come "help her in the kitchen" so Marcus could talk business with the crew of the *Andromeda*. Captain Blackwood sipped the stout New Austin whiskey and studied Marcus for a moment before speaking.

"So, Mr. Winchester," she began, suddenly sounding very businesslike, "I take it you've had the opportunity to go over the information I sent?"

"I have, Captain Blackwood."

"Please, it's Catherine. I'm not your captain unless you join the crew. Tell me then, what do you think?"

"You were a little vague on the details."

Catherine took another sip of whiskey. "Mm. We were. Posted on an open network like that, we kept the specific operational details to a minimum, for security reasons and to protect client confidentiality. I don't expect you to sign without knowing some specifics, though, so allow me to explain. I originally hail from Avalon, Mr. Winchester. Have you ever been there?"

"Just Marcus. No, I haven't. I might've guessed from your accent. It's subtle but you have a hint of ancient Scotland in your speech."

Catherine smiled. "Aye. It comes out more when I drink. The Blackwoods are a very prominent family on Avalon. My father holds a seat on the ruling Council there, and serves as the governor of Aberdeen Province. He also owns the Blackwood and Associates Trading Company."

"I see. Is your father the client, then?"

"Technically his company is, but yes. He went to the trouble of tracking me down because of the sensitivity of this matter."

"Wanted to keep it in the family, did he?"

"He did. I've been charged with locating and recovering my brother, Cecil. Not only is he family, he's the rightful heir to my father's name, business, estate, and titles."

Marcus detected a hint of bitterness in her tone, but made no mention of it. "Okay, so he's important. Where is he? Why do you need a team of military-trained mercenaries? I can only assume he's gotten into some sort of trouble."

Captain Blackwood sipped her whiskey again. "Indeed, you could say that. He's on Zanzibar."

"Zanzibar..." Marcus thought out loud. "That's... wait, is that that failed colony world way the hell out on the frontier?"

"It is."

"Catherine, what in the hell is your brother doing out there?"

"That's an excellent question," Catherine replied. "My father was, to be blunt, aggravatingly sparse on the details. Being perfectly honest, the Blackwood name and holdings are in financial trouble. My father believes that Cecil went to Zanzibar on some kind of ill-conceived profit-seeking venture. A treasure hunt, even."

"How did he get there?"

"He hired some assistants and chartered a ship. He invested a great deal of his personal fortune into the endeavor, so whatever it is he thought was there, he believed it would make him a lot of money."

"And your old man just let him traipse off into the unknown like that?"

"So it would seem. There's more, though. The reason we were brought in is not because Cecil has gone missing. He's being held for ransom. Last year a courier ship arrived in the Arthurian System. Part of its bulk information download was a message from the skipper of the ship that Cecil had chartered. He said that a local warlord calling himself Aristotle Lang is keeping Cecil and his associates as hostages. He was, the last we heard, alive, unharmed, and being treated well. If we want him to stay that way, it was suggested that we start negotiating."

"I see. So this guy Lang obviously knows who your brother is."

"I very much doubt my brother was discreet on Zanzibar. Discretion was never his strong suit."

"Ah. Rich off-worlder comes to town, starts throwing money around, gets kidnapped by the local bad guys. This sort of thing happens in the less pleasant parts of some colonies."

"The last update we got from Zanzibar was months out of date. The situation may have changed. We haven't heard anything from Cecil or his captor. After we landed I uploaded a message for this Lang fellow to a courier ship that is headed that way. It'll be some time before they get it." The lag time inherent to interstellar communications had a frustrating way of dragging dramas like this out for months, sometimes years.

Marcus shook his head. "Damn. It's like kidnapping Christopher Columbus and sending the *Santa Maria* back to Spain with a ransom note. So, what are you looking to do? Are you planning on having the team you hire go in, guns blazing, and rescue your brother?"

"Absolutely not," Catherine said firmly. "Not if it can be avoided. I've been entrusted with a large amount of hard currency from my family's estate. I'm prepared to simply pay for Cecil's safe return and leave without incident, if the opportunity presents itself. My mission is to recover my brother, dead or, preferably, alive, not to overthrow a petty brigand on some far-flung rock. If it can be done without bloodshed then that's what I'll do. But you and I both know how these things play out. Once I show up with money in hand, there's a very good chance our Mr. Lang will get greedy and demand more, see how much he can milk us for. I'm not prepared to make multiple trips between Zanzibar and Avalon to settle this matter. One way or another, I will resolve this situation."

Marcus appreciated the captain's candor. He appreciated the fact that she wasn't a trigger-happy nut dead-set on shooting her way in and out of the situation. Marcus had done more than his share of counterinsurgency and irregular warfare work while with Special Operations. Sometimes firepower alone wasn't the answer.

Mazer Broadbent spoke up for the first time since the discussion began. "This is why we'd like to bring you on, Mr. Winchester. I took the liberty of reviewing the parts of your service record that are public information. For the sake of full disclosure, I did twenty standard years in the Defense Force. I served on Mildenhall as well."

"Is that how you..." Marcus trailed off, but pointed at the side of his own head.

Mazer grinned. "This?" he said, pointing at his facial/ocular implant. "Oh yes. I was with the Military Police Corps. We were escorting a Provincial Reconstruction Team and their robots to a work site. Despite the fact that we were hundreds of kilometers inside the Green Zone, we were hit with a complex ambush. Heavy weapons, rockets, everything the insurgents could throw at us. It was, no joke, the last month of my deployment. I got to rotate home a little early, with a little less of my natural skull weighing me down."

Marcus chuckled at the spacer's dark humor. "I was with Twenty-Second SOG over in Regional Command Southwest."

"That was right on the border of the Red Zone, wasn't it?"

"Yeah. We ran ops pretty deep into the Red Zone frequently, right up until the end."

"Saints and prophets," Mazer cursed. "I heard stories from out that way, but it was all just rumor."

Marcus nodded slowly. "Yeah, they kept a pretty tight seal on RC Southwest. The press was kept out completely. They'd even shoot down aerial media bots and unauthorized satellites."

"Right before I left," Mazer said, "they were blockading the system completely. No media was allowed in at all. I hear the whole system is quarantined now."

Marcus' expression darkened. "That's what they should've done in the first place: just evacuated the colonists and pulled out. There was nothing on the planet worth that many lives." A lot of people said they'd been on Mildenhall when they hadn't. The bloody conflict there had almost a romantic mystique in popular culture, made all the worse by the fact that most people had no idea what had gone on there. He could tell that Mazer Broadbent was a real Mildenhall vet; he had the look to him, like a black spot on a man's soul. There's nothing like watching your government sacrifice thousands of lives on a lost cause to dispel any romantic notions of war that you might have had.

"I bring this up," the spacer said, "to assure you that this isn't some fool's errand. The captain is deadly serious about accomplishing our task in a clean, preferably bloodless manner. That said, the people holding Cecil Blackwood, the followers of this Aristotle Lang, are dangerous. Negotiation may not work. The captain recognizes that her small crew doesn't have much experience in ground combat, and especially in dealing with situations such as this. You, on the other hand, do. Your Special Operations background makes you an almost ideal candidate."

"It does, Marcus," Captain Blackwood added, leaning in intently. "Being very blunt, I want you to lead my ground team. We don't have much time to assemble that team, but with your knowledge of New Austin and connections here, the whole process will go more smoothly. I have a substantial operating budget for this. You'll get your pick of personnel and equipment, within reason."

"A year or longer is a long time to be gone from my family," Marcus admitted. "That's the real sticking point for me."

"I don't intend to be on Zanzibar that long if I can help it," the captain assured him. "It doesn't take that long to make the trip from here to there and back. That's just a contingency."

"I assumed as much. I'd be lying if I said I wasn't interested. My wife is pregnant. We just found out not that long ago."

"Congratulations. It must be hard missing the birth of your child," Catherine said.

"It was. I was deployed when Annie was born. I had just left for Mildenhall when she took her first steps. One of the reasons I got out and emigrated all the way out to New Austin was so I could live a quiet life, and be there for my family."

"But you still responded to our query."

"I did. I have another mouth to feed on the way. Emigrating out here wasn't cheap. Getting my dream home out in the country wasn't either. Providing for the education and welfare of my children costs money too. The money you're offering could be a godsend for us."

Catherine spoke softly. "I understand your hesitation. I don't have children, but I know how important family can be. To tell you the truth, I had been, well, estranged from my own family on Avalon for many years. Despite the falling out I had with my father, my brother needs my help now. The past doesn't matter so much in the face of that. I will have a contract sent to you before we leave. If you decide to sign, we'll arrange to bring you to the Starport. I don't mean to rush such a big decision, but sooner the better. The sooner my team is assembled, the more time you will have to train together before we leave. Either way, if you know of anyone else who might be interested, I'd appreciate it if you'd have them contact us."

"I understand. My partner is interested. He'll probably go if I do."

"What's his background?" Mazer asked.

"CDF, same as you. He was in Nuclear/Explosive Ordnance Disposal. Spacewalk and EVA rated and everything, even if it's been a few years. He's solid. His area of expertise might come in handy."

"Very well. Marcus, I'm afraid I need to get back to the Starport now. I'd like to thank you for your gracious hospitality. Please tell your wife her cooking is fantastic."

"Why, thank you," Eleanor said, reappearing from the other room with Annabelle in tow. "It was just a few things I threw together."

Marcus smiled. His wife had spent all day making that meal.

"Thank you for your time," Captain Blackwood said politely, "and for having us in your home. I'll be waiting for your response."

Handshakes were exchanged, and the spacers excused themselves. Ellie made her way back to the kitchen, and Marcus followed.

"What do you think?" he asked.

"I wasn't snooping," Ellie said defensively. Her expression softened. "I may have been monitoring the security camera feed, though."

Marcus smiled. "I figured as much. Look, I know you're not sure about this. If you want me to stay, I'll stay. We'll figure something else out."

"I don't want to stand in your way."

Marcus stepped forward and took his wife's hands into his own. "Baby, we're a team, remember? *I* don't make decisions, *we* make decisions, especially if it affects the family like this."

"I feel like I'm being selfish if I ask you *not* to go. I know you're doing this for our family." She placed Marcus' hand on her belly. "Our growing family."

"I'd get half the money up front. That would be a huge help right now."

"I know you, Marcus Winchester," Eleanor said. "I know you've been restless. I didn't marry you without realizing what kind of man you are. I know you miss the travel and excitement you used to have. You gave that up for us. That was a big deal for you."

"After Mildenhall, I was ready to get out anyway."

"Oh, that's a load of horseshit, Marcus," Ellie said with a tear in her eye. "You were a lifer. I knew that when I married you. And I know you want to take this job. I can hold down the homestead while you're gone. I'll still be here when you get back." The tear trickled down her cheek. "I'm just scared. I used to be scared all the time, scared that I'd get *that* call."

Marcus embraced his wife and held her tightly. "You know how careful I am," he said, trying to sound reassuring.

"You'd damned well better be careful," Ellie said. "Don't you dare make me tell your daughter that her father isn't coming home. Don't you dare."

"Speaking of... where did Annie go?"

"I think that went well," Catherine said. She and her shipmates made their way back to their rented air car.

Wolfram agreed. "I expect that he will sign on."

"I hope so," Mazer said. "He's got the experience we're looking for."

"Do we have any other candidates to meet this evening?"

"Not tonight, *Kapitänin*."

"Good. Let's head back to the Starport then."

Catherine was surprised to hear a girl's voice call to her. "Captain Blackwood?" It was Annabelle, Marcus Winchester's daughter. "Can I talk to you for a second?"

The captain told her shipmates to wait for her in the air car, and went to speak with the young woman. "Hello, Annie," she said with a smile.

"I'm sorry to bother you. I just..."

"It's okay. Go ahead."

"How did you get where you are? How did you come to be the captain of your own ship?"

"Honestly? Fifteen years of hard work. There weren't any shortcuts for me. I'm a graduate of the Avalonian Space Forces Academy, but... well, things didn't work out. I signed on with the *Andromeda* as a junior officer and never looked back."

"I want to do that," Annie said. "I want to be a spacer."

Catherine smiled, and put her hand on the girl's shoulder. "There's no reason why you can't. Concordiat worlds don't have the, ah, biases against female spacers that I had to contend with."

"I'm sorry. I know I'm being dumb. I'm acting like a little kid. But you're where I want to be. I want to go with you. You know, to look out for my dad."

"I rather doubt your mother would approve," Catherine said. "I was just like you at your age," Catherine said. She was being sincere; the Winchester girl very much reminded her of herself as a teenager. "Ready to leave my dull life behind and chase adventure amongst the stars. I have no doubt you can do the same if you set your mind to it. Just remember, a career in space isn't as glamorous as the media likes to portray it. The vast majority of it is routine boredom while you're in transit. You can't have much of a life outside of your ship, either."

"Where do you live? If you don't mind me asking. The information I have says the *Andromeda* is registered out of Heinlein."

"It is. I live there a few months out of the year, and have a few friends there that I never see. I pay people to manage my estate and affairs while I'm away. It's not much of a life."

Annie seemed conflicted. "Then why do you do it?"

Catherine smiled. "Because I *love* it. The sense of freedom you get out there is indescribable. The pride of watching a well-trained crew run your ship so flawlessly that you have almost nothing to do, the wonder at visiting strange new worlds... it's exhilarating. The love of my life. Someday I will settle down, stay planetside for a while, maybe even have a family of my own. Someday, but not today." There was an undeniable twinkle in the captain's eye.

The teenager smiled back at her. "Thank you. I'm... I'm sorry to have held you up."

"Not at all. And listen, I want you to know that if your father decides to come with me, I will do everything in my power to bring him home safely. I take care of my crew. I'm also very, very good at what I do. He'll be in good hands."

"Thank you, Captain."

"And when I do bring him home, you'll get a tour of the ship. Deal?"

"How about before he leaves?"

Catherine raised an eyebrow. "Planning on coming to the city, are you?"

"I am!" Annie said excitedly. She raised her handheld for Catherine to see.

"The New Austin Colonial Chambers of Commerce proudly present the ninety-second annual Aterrizaje Stampede," she said, reading the text on the screen. "What is it?"

"It's a rodeo," Annie said.

Catherine felt slightly embarrassed. "A what?"

"A rodeo! People bring their horses in from all over the terraformed zone for the event. There are barrel races, bull riding, calf roping, mounted shooting, tons of different events. It's a big thing here."

"I see! Your father told me you had an interest in horseback riding. He said you were quite the, um, cowgirl."

"Did you grow up with horses?"

"As a matter of fact I did," Catherine said with a smile. "Avalon has an equestrian culture dating back centuries, to the founding of the colony. Here, look for yourself." The captain tapped the screen of her handheld a few times, pulling up her extensive photo library, and showed a particular picture to Annie.

"Is that you?" she asked, studying the picture. In it, a darkhaired young woman sat proudly atop a silvery Avalonian steed. She was dressed in traditional equestrian garb: red coat, white trousers, knee-high riding boots, and a riding crop tucked neatly under her arm.

"It is, my dear. I was about your age."

"What are you wearing?" Annie asked, incredulously.

Catherine chuckled. "Ah. The riding traditions on Avalon descend from the English back on Earth. Different than your North American style."

"What is that on your head?"

"It's a helmet, child. Don't you wear a helmet when you ride?"

"No, ma'am," Annie said with a toothy grin. She showed the captain a picture of herself, hair done up in braids, with a widebrimmed white hat on her head. "This is how a real cowgirl does it. Hey! You want to see Sparkles?"

"*Kapitänin*," Wolfram grunted. "We should be getting back to the ship."

"There's plenty of time, my friend," she said, patting her exec on the shoulder. "I'll only be a few more minutes. Do you know how long it's been since I've been around horses?" She turned her attention back to Annie. "Lead the way."

New Austin
Lone Star System
Aterrizaje, Capital District
Southern Hemisphere

The Capital District Fairgrounds were a bustle of activity. The Aterrizaje Stampede was a huge annual event, with dozens of high profile corporate sponsors and local media coverage. The rodeo featured numerous events and was a major tourist attraction for off-worlders.

Annie and Sparkles were enrolled in the junior division barrel racing competition. Sparkles wasn't a great jumper, and Annie was never able to rope worth a damn, but the two together were hell on hooves when going around the barrels. Annie hadn't participated in the rodeo in several years, and this was the first time she was old enough for the junior division. As she coaxed Sparkles out of the back of her travel trailer, lead rope in hand, she watched hundreds of other rodeo participants doing the same thing. The huge, temporary stables set up around the fairgrounds were big enough to house hundreds of horses, and the animals called and whinnied to each other. Some of the other entrants were ranchers from the Outback, like Annie. Many were obvious hobbyists, for whom horses were a passing fad, not a passion. She had been practicing all year and was eager to show these strutting city slickers what a real cowgirl could do.

Annie paused when a clunky looking utility robot rolled to a stop in front of her. Sparkles balked a little as it spoke. "Good afternoon, sir or madam. What is your name? I can help you find your ... stall." Dozens such bots were moving about at the fairgrounds, trying to make sure everything got to where it was supposed to go.

"Um, Annabelle Winchester," Annie said, looking the robot up and down. It had a mostly conical body topped with a trapezoidal head on a skinny neck. A pair of thin, articulated arms, terminating in wide, padded claws, hung from its sides. It rolled across the dirt floor of the stables gyroscopically balanced on a single large wheel.

"I'm sorry," the robot said in a tinny, gender-neutral voice. "I cannot find any registration for Umanna Bell Finch-Esther. Are you in the right place?"

"Hellfire, yes, I'm in the right place!" Annie snapped. "My name is Ann-a-belle Win-ches-ter," she said, pronouncing each syllable angrily.

Sparkles stamped uneasily. The robot swiveled its head toward Sparkles. A green light mounted above its binocular lenses blinked. It then raised an arm, causing the horse to balk, and sprayed a puff of vapor at her.

"What the ... what the Sam Hell did you just spray my horse with, you stupid garbage can?" Annie demanded. Sparkles sniffed and shook her head.

"*Equi-Calm*," the robot said. "Equi-Calm is an all-natural combination of pheromones and soothing aromas specially formulated to calm anxious horses."

"Oh my God, I don't care, I just ..."

The robot ignored her interruption. "Equi-Calm is safe and has been shown to be over ninety-six percent effective in clinical trials," it said. "Equi-Calm is generously provided by one of our sponsors ..."

"I don't care!" Annie yelled, throwing her hands up at the robot.

The machine was undeterred, and continued its advertising spiel. "... quitoral Veterinary Pharmaceutical. Free samples of Equi-Calm are available to all Aterrizaje Stampede participants and staff members."

"Say Equi-Calm one more time, you stupid scratching machine!" Annie snarled, pointing a finger at the robot. "Say it! I dare you!"

"Ann-a-belle Win-ches-ter," it said phonetically, "welcome to the Aterrizaje Stampede. Your horse ... Sparkles ... is berthed in stall zero-six-seven." A skeletal, claw-tipped arm extended and pointed to where Annie needed to go. "That way. Thank you, and have a lovely day." The robot indifferently rolled away, no doubt to harangue the next person about Equi-Calm.

Annie shook her head angrily and led her horse off to her assigned stall. "Sparkles, this is how the robot war starts." She found Stall 067 clean, stocked with hay and water, and ready to go. She led Sparkles inside and unhooked her lead rope. "There you go," she said, resting her head against the horse's. "This is pretty nice, hey?" Sparkles grunted and pulled away before lowering her head into the hay trough.

Annie was startled when a trio of girls appeared at her stall door. One of them, taller than the other two, and pretty in that wears-too-much-makeup way, leaned in. "Hey, kid. This your first time at the Stampede?"

Annie wasn't sure why, but she didn't like this girl. She gave off a bad vibe. "It is," she said. "Who the hell are you?"

The two girls to the rear glared at her, but didn't say anything. The taller one, with curly blonde hair hanging from under her hat, chuckled. "Relax, newbie, no need to get bitchy, yeah? You're a barrel racer, aren't you? So am I. I'm Victoria Alexander. Before you ask, yes, I'm one of *those* Alexanders. It's not a big deal, so don't get all sloppy over it."

Annie looked at the girl quizzically. "*What* Alexanders? I don't know any Alexanders."

"Wow," she said, turning to her friends. Victoria's pair of flunkies giggled and shook their heads. "You from off-world or something? The only Alexanders on New Austin that matter. My family owns this stupid fairground."

"That's great," Annie said, turning her attention back to her horse. "Now go away."

Victoria was obviously unaccustomed to being dismissed. "What did you say to me?"

"What, are you deaf *and* bitchy? I said go away. You're bothering Sparkles."

Victoria and her friends erupted into a cackle of forced laughter. "Sparkles? You're definitely not from around here. You're one of those off-worlders that comes to New Austin and lowers our property values, aren't you?"

"Huh?"

"That's what I thought. You're one of those desert rats what lives in a shack in the outback. Don't deny it, I can tell from your shabby clothes. Every year you people come into the city with your skaggy mutant farm animals, thinking you're going to win a pretty blue ribbon to show everyone back home around the watering trough." Victoria cocked her head to one side and leaned in closer. "And every year, I hand you cockies your asses and you go home with nothing."

"No she didn't!" one of other girls said.

"She did! She burned that little bird, didn't she?"

Someone else spoke up, a young man. "And every year, Victoria, you end up sneaking to the free clinic so your papa doesn't find out you got pregnant, a sexual disease, or both. I heard last year it was both." He was tall, handsome, possessed of dark hair and strong Latin features. He was young, about Annie's age, and he looked familiar.

"Fuck you, you jumped-up, rock-hopping dirt farmer!" Victoria sneered. "You think being the white knight is going to get you a piece of that?" she said, pointing at Annie. "You get used to that, because you ain't gonna get any of *this*." She pointed at herself.

"I'm also not going to get any chlamydia, I think," he said. "You should go, or I'll tell my father to tell *your* father about that baby you almost had last year."

Victoria's eyes went wide, but she didn't say anything. She turned on her heel and stomped off in a huff. The young man then turned his attention to Annie. "Hello, Annie," he said. "It's been a long time."

It hit her then. "Carlos? Carlos Martinez?" she asked, and immediately felt her face flush. "Is that you? Holy hell, it's been a long time."

Giving Annie a perfect smile, Carlos stepped forward and leaned on the stall door. "Four years, *chica*. How have you been?"

Annie knew Carlos from their distance learning program, and had met him in person a couple of times. He'd started going to a private school a few years back, after his parents moved to the city. She'd stayed in touch with him online, if only barely. "Yeah!" she said, heart racing. "Um, wow! Look at you! You're, uh, taller." *And gorgeous.* He certainly wasn't the awkward, lanky preteen she remembered. "I didn't know you, you know, did horses. I mean rode horses. I didn't know you rode. Horses."

Carlos nodded. "My papa let me try it once he thought I was old enough. What events are you here for?"

"Barrel racing," Annie said proudly. "I don't mean to brag, but Sparkles and me are gonna mop the deck with that skaggy whore."

"I'm sorry about Victoria. I wish I could tell you she's not always like that, but she is."

"How do you know her? She your ex-girlfriend or something?" *Please say no.*

Carlos laughed. "Good God, no. The Alexanders are old money. They go back to the founding of the colony. They don't like to mingle with people like us."

"I could tell. So how do you know her?"

"I go to school with her."

"Wow, your parents must be doing alright for themselves. You used to live in...where was it?"

"North Sierra Territory," Carlos answered. "Up in the mountains. We do okay, but I got a scholarship to go to her school. I don't think my parents could afford it otherwise. Victoria goes because that's where her parents both went. It's where all the rich kids go. I kind of hate it."

"So what's her deal? It's my first day here, I've never met her before, and she comes up out of the blue acting like the queen of the shrews. What the hell did I ever do to her?"

"She does this. She likes to go around, name-dropping, trying to intimidate her competition. I'm surprised you haven't heard of her family, though. Her older sister hosts that entertainment gossip netcast."

Annie shrugged. "I guess. Is she good?"

"She is. She did come in first place last year, even with chlamydia. Don't let her get to you, and never mind her anyway. How have you been? I don't hear from you much these days. Do you still live in Laredo Territory?"

He remembered? Annie nodded. "Yeah, we do. It's so boring. There's nobody around for kilometers. Our nearest neighbors are seriously ten klicks down the road. My dad says that's why he picked the place, but I think it's because he doesn't want me to have a life. Just getting here was like a thirteen-hour truck ride. What event are you here for?"

"Calf roping!" Carlos said. "It's my second year. Last year I did not do so good, I think. But this year? I've been practicing. In the simulator, on the maintenance bots, and on a real calf!"

"I'm glad somebody I know knows his way around," Annie said, looking across the huge stable building. "I haven't been to the city in like two years, and apparently I've already made an enemy of the local rich-bitch socialite."

"No worries, *chica*," Carlos said, flashing her a smile so perfect she wanted to punch him in his stupid, beautiful face. "Forget her. I'll show you around. She's probably off doing drugs and getting pregnant again."

Annie laughed out loud, awkwardly, before realizing how loud she was being and wanting to die of embarrassment. "Okay," she squeaked.

The western sky was on fire, a tapestry of red, orange, and gold as Lone Star crept above the mountains. It was as glorious a sunrise as Marcus had seen in a long time, fitting for his last morning at home.

It had taken a couple of days to arrange a leave of absence from the Marshals Service, but everything had fallen into place. His contract with Captain Blackwood was electronically signed and notarized, and the half of his pay to be delivered up front was deposited into his account the very next morning. Marcus packed light, out of habit and because of the cramped conditions of space travel. He had only one bag with him as he stood in the dry morning air.

Ellie was still asleep. He'd crept out of bed, gotten dressed, and stepped outside without waking her. He'd already said his goodbyes and made passionate love to his wife. There was nothing left to say, and nothing to be gained from dragging it out. He'd shipped Annie off to Aterrizaje two days prior, renting her passage on an automated truck that could pull his single-horse trailer. In any case he was going to be on New Austin for another twelve days, and he could message his family whenever he wanted. He intended to visit his daughter in the city before he left, and the captain had agreed to let her tour the ship if there was time.

His handheld would no longer be able to connect to New Austin's colonial network once the *Andromeda* lifted off, but with the ship's communications systems, he'd be able to send messages until they translated out of the system. After that, though, he'd have no way of calling home. That bothered Marcus. There was a chance something could happen to the ship, that he could just disappear in the unforgiving darkness of space, and his family never know what happened to him. It was, in a lot of ways, like being a sailor on ancient Earth, before the invention of the radio or telegraph. For centuries, mankind had been spoiled by ubiquitous, instant communication capability. With the right equipment, it was possible to never be out of touch.

After the development of interstellar travel, that changed. A ship in an empty system was truly on its own. Spacers learned the sense of loneliness that terrestrial mariners once knew. Even some fifteen hundred standard years into the era commonly known as the Space Age, this aspect of it was unchanging and inevitable. Marcus never cared much for the feeling; he'd opted for the Espatiers over the Fleet, many years before, for that very reason. At least on a planet, there was ground beneath your feet, (usually) air to breathe, and a sun shining overhead. Even if people were shooting at you, it was preferable to spending your life sealed in a metal can sitting on top of a fusion-powered rocket.

Marcus had not been idle since signing his contract. He'd been in constant contact with his new skipper, and had taken the lead on recruiting, vetting, and interviewing potential candidates for his ground team. As he said he would, Wade had jumped on board. It would be good to have someone he knew and trusted with him, and Wade did have a potentially useful skill set.

Mazer Broadbent's assumption about New Austin had proven correct; there were many qualified candidates to choose from, all with relevant experience. With input from the *Andromeda*'s crew and after a few teleconference interviews, Marcus was able to select five more team members. With Wade and him, that made seven. The candidates chosen, like Wade, had experience and skills that Marcus thought might come in handy, given the mission at hand. More importantly, they were crazy enough to want to go, but not so crazy as to put the operation at risk.

He had interviewed them all, but had not actually met any of them in person yet. There was little time to waste. Using the budget Captain Blackwood had allocated for him, he had arranged for his team to take a tactics and combat shooting course at a private training center outside of Aterrizaje. He'd booked eight straight days of training, with the best instructors on New Austin. It would get his team used to working together, refresh their skills, and let them test the equipment they'd be using.

Of course, he had to go inspect and pick up that equipment first. There was a lot to do, and not much time. Marcus tended to stress when there wasn't enough time to do things correctly, but there was no way around it. The long passage to Zanzibar couldn't be delayed. In any case, he figured, a little stress would do his new team some good.

A shrill whine announced the approach of an aircraft. It was louder than the air car Captain Blackwood had arrived in before. He caught sight of the vehicle as it approached from the north, slowing and descending as it neared his home. The bulbous craft sported two large ducted-fan engines and a V-tail. In place of a cockpit was a cluster of sensors and antennae; this bird was unmanned. The scream of its engines climaxed, then dissipated, as it settled down on his drive and throttled back its engines to idle. Like all vertical take-off aircraft, it kicked up a huge cloud of dust and made enough noise to wake the dead. Shaking his head, Marcus hoisted his bag and approached the vehicle as its engines spun down to idle.

As he drew close, a sliding door on the side of the craft opened. Wade was inside, strapped into a crash seat. *Not entirely unmanned.* "Hey boss!" he said, grinning. "Sorry about the noise." He extended a hand and took Marcus' bag.

Marcus climbed into the cabin, and buckled himself into a seat across from Wade. As the door closed, he noticed Ellie standing in front of his house. A warning alarm sounded as the VTOL prepared to lift off. Marcus waved to his wife as the self-piloting vehicle rose into the air. He watched his house for as long as he could as the VTOL sped away.

"We're really doing this, huh?" Wade asked.

"Yup," Marcus said.

"Are we crazy?" his partner asked.

"Yup. Money's good though."

"What'd you do with your half up front?"

"Paid a bunch of bills, got Ellie some mining equipment. You?"

"Not a damn thing, Boss. I just rented a storage unit and put all my stuff in it. I turned my keys over to my landlord this morning. When we get back, I think I'll make a down payment on a nice house. Nothing too big, you know. It's just me."

"Hellfire, Wade, you almost sound like you're planning to settle down. What's the matter, your sexbot getting tired of apartment living? Did the little missus insist you buy her a house?"

Wade's face flushed. "You know . . ." he trailed off before shaking his head and laughing. "I swear to God, I won it at a raffle at a New Year's party. I don't use it."

"Uh-huh," Marcus said. "Horseshit."

"Why does nobody believe me?"

"For one thing," Marcus said, "who would invite *you* to a party? Now keep your perversions to yourself. I need to call my daughter."

"Already? You've been gone for five minutes."

"No, you damn hooplehead, she's in Aterrizaje. She's at the rodeo there. Shut your yapper a minute." Marcus raised his handheld and placed a call to his daughter.

"Daddy?" Annie asked. Her reddish-brown hair stuck to the side of her face, and her eyes were only half open.

"Rise and shine, pumpkin," Marcus said.

"Holy hell, Daddy, it's early," she complained. "Where are you?"

"I'm on a flight to the city now, with your Uncle Wade." He turned his handheld so Wade could see the screen.

"Hi, Wade," Annie said.

"You look like hell, kiddo," Wade said teasingly.

"It's because it's stupid early in the stupid morning!" Annie insisted.

Marcus turned his handheld back toward himself. "Annabelle, did you stay out late last night?"

"What? No, daddy, I just couldn't sleep."

"Uh-huh. Are you having fun?"

"I am! I met up with Liam and Sandra, since they live in the city." Marcus nodded. He was glad she got to spend time with her friends. Aside from the occasional field trip, she never actually saw her classmates. "Also, Carlos showed me around."

Marcus raised his eyebrows. "Who the hell is Carlos?"

Annie rolled her eyes. "Oh my *God*. You remember Carlos! He was in my class until like four years ago."

Marcus dimly recalled a boy named Carlos on her class roster. "Right. You know the rules, Annie."

"I'm not having anyone stay in my room, Daddy. The hotel autoclerk checks in on me at night and in the morning, just like you told it to. It's like being in prison."

Good, Marcus thought. "Don't be so dramatic. I'm just being careful. Remember what I told you: no boys until you're married."

Annie rolled her eyes again. "Oh my God, Daddy."

"Look, just mind yourself, okay? I don't think your mom was kidding about building a tower. She's preggers and super emotional right now."

"I'll be okay," Annie said. "I can take care of myself."

"I know you can, baby. I'll come see you as soon as I can, okay? I love you."

"I love you too. I'm going back to bed." Annie cut the connection.

Wade was laughing. Marcus shook his head at him. "Someday, you're gonna have a daughter, and this shit won't seem so funny anymore."

Wade folded his arms across his chest. "You make fun of the sexbot, but robots don't have pretty daughters that attract every horny, teenage shit-bird within a hundred klicks of the rodeo."

Marcus sighed. "I can't fault your logic there."

Zanzibar
Danzig-5012 Solar System
Equatorial Region

Cecil Blackwood held his breath as Lang's workers used a power drill to breach the final layer of rock blocking the tunnel. Dust drifted into the stale air of the newly opened chamber as the air pressure equalized. Cecil lifted his respirator and took a long drink from his water bottle. Zanzibar was a miserably dry world to begin with; these tunnels were even worse.

Zak Mesa was right on top of the breach, making sure the workers halted as soon as it was big enough for a man to crawl through. "Okay, okay, that's good. Everyone shut your tools down. We're through."

Cecil joined his dour partner, looking into the impossibly dark cavern they'd just opened. No light had touched the chamber in over a century. "Well," he said, turning on his light. "Shall we?"

Zak may have been unhappy with the circumstances, but even he couldn't completely conceal his excitement. "You men," he said, addressing the dig crew. "Stand by here. Nobody come in unless we call for help, understood?" He was answered by several dull nods. "Good. Mr. Blackwood and I will make sure this is the right chamber, and that it's safe, before anyone else goes in. We don't know what's in there. They buried this place for a reason. Whatever is in there could be toxic, radioactive, or even infected with some kind of alien disease."

Cecil very much doubted any of that was the case, and knew Zak did as well, but that wasn't the point. Lang's men looked at each other wide-eyed, now hesitant to go any further. *Good,* Cecil mused. *Keep the skags out until we can figure out what's in there.* The last thing the two off-worlders wanted was a bunch of ignorant locals rummaging through a treasure trove of alien artifacts like they were searching for parts in a scrapyard. The relics inside were *priceless.*

"That should keep them out for a bit," Zak said. "You ready?"

"You did most of the work, my friend," Cecil said. "Take the first step inside."

Zak actually cracked a smile. He tapped his gaudy smart glasses, setting them to record, adjusted the brightness of his light, and stepped through the breach. Cecil followed immediately behind him.

Inside, the air was stale and dry. Dust danced and swirled in their flashlight beams, disturbed for the first time in over a century by their excavation. The chamber had smooth walls, and had been precisely cut out of solid rock. It was rectangular, five meters high and eight meters wide. They could barely see the back wall through the dust and darkness; Cecil estimated it to be twenty-five meters long.

"Holy shiz..." Zak said, trailing off.

"Indeed," Cecil agreed. Each side of the chamber was stacked with containers and crates. They were covered in a thick layer of dust, but all appeared to have their seals intact. Each was marked with a hard-copy contents manifest, several pages long.

Zak examined the manifest on one of the crates. "Cecil, this...this is big."

"So it would seem, mate."

"No, look at this! The contents, the grid coordinates of where it was found, how old they think it is, all of it! Everything has been extensively cataloged! This will lead us to more dig sites!"

"You mean it'll lead Lang to more dig sites," Cecil said gloomily.

Zak's brief moment of cheer drained out of him. "Damn it. Damn it all. This is an archaeological gold mine. This isn't right, Cecil. It isn't right that that maniac is going to hoard this stuff and sell it to the highest black market bidder! It doesn't belong to him."

"Steady, man. You're right, of course. It doesn't belong to us, either. Or the Concordiat. The beings it does belong to have been gone for millions of years, Zak."

"I get that. But...damn it, Cecil, this stuff needs to be studied! It belongs in museums and laboratories! There's so much we could learn from it."

"We're not going to learn anything if Old Man Lang has us shot. These artifacts have waited for eons. If they have to wait a few more years to have their secrets revealed, it doesn't matter so much."

Zak exhaled in obvious frustration. "You're right. Let's just get this over with and get off this stupid rock." He swung his flashlight back toward the door. "I suppose there's no sense stalling. Lang is going to—*augh!*"

Startled, Cecil spun around. "What...?" He then saw what Zak's light had settled on. "My God."

"You okay in dere?" one of the workers called, approaching the breach with a light.

"Ah, yes, we're fine," Cecil replied. "Stay outside, please. We, uh, need to make sure it's safe before anyone comes in."

In a dark corner, off to the side of the breach, partially concealed behind a stack of crates was what looked like a campsite. On a crumbling bedroll were two mummified corpses, holding each other in a silent embrace. In the impossibly dry, virtually sterile tomb they had been sealed in, the two people had been remarkably well preserved.

The two adventurers approached the bodies quietly, as if they were afraid of disturbing them. Their eyes were gone, their skin dried out into a grayish-brown, leathery texture, and their teeth had yellowed, but they were unmistakably human. One man had died sitting up, with his back against the cold chamber wall. The other was lying so that his head was in the sitting man's lap. Both of their mouths gaped open; their empty, dry eye sockets stared into oblivion.

"They must have been trapped when the tunnel was sealed," Zak observed.

"But look," Cecil pointed out, "they have a stockpile of supplies. This wasn't an accident. This was done intentionally."

"Why bother bringing supplies?" Zak wondered. "This had to have been a suicide mission."

"Perhaps not. Perhaps...I don't know. This tunnel was sealed right before the Maggot assault on Zanzibar, correct?"

"That's what the records say. The artifacts were hidden as the Maggots approached the planet."

"I wonder...suppose this was meant to be temporary? Suppose they wanted to stay with the artifacts, hoping to be rescued when the fighting was over?"

"This place is probably a better survival bunker than any other place you'll find on Zanzibar. There weren't many survivors from the Maggots' orbital bombardment, only a few thousand out of some fifty thousand colonists."

"A tragic fate," Cecil said quietly. "Surviving the bombardment only to die in here, buried alive."

"They didn't use all of their supplies."

"They may have run out of air. There's a CO_2 scrubber over there," Cecil pointed, "but it could have failed on them."

"Maybe they gave up and just killed themselves," Zak wondered, darkly.

Cecil managed a morbid grin and patted his partner on the shoulder. "As always, you are the ray of sunlight that warms my life, Mr. Mesa. If we get out of this alive, I'm going to triple what I promised you in our contract."

"Yeah, well, worry about the *staying alive* part before you worry about the money part." He glanced down at the two mummified corpses again. "Hmm," he muttered. The historian bent down and picked up a dust-covered tablet computer off of the floor. "I wonder if I can get this working. There might be useful information on it."

"It's worth a try," Cecil said. "I'm curious about what brought these two down here. It'll also give us something to do while Lang's people sort and carry off the artifacts." He watched Zak's demeanor darken as he swept his light across the rows of sealed containers. The historian said nothing, but shook his head sadly.

Aristotle Lang's workers were impressively gentle with the ancient alien artifacts. The old man had given explicit instructions that they be delivered intact, and no one wanted to provoke his wrath by damaging something. Before the containers were removed from their now-unsealed tomb, Zak scanned their manifests and uploaded them to his handheld. The information on those documents would be useful not only to Zak and Cecil, but to future generations of archaeologists and historians.

Assuming, of course, they were able to get that information off Zanzibar.

Rather than let Zak indulge in his moping about their unfortunate situation, Cecil encouraged him to examine the dead men's tablet and see if its data storage was intact. It had been sitting on the floor of that chamber for over a hundred standard years, but it wasn't as if such personal devices had changed much since then. On the contrary, the technology had plateaued long before that. The software changed over the years, but the hardware remained essentially the same.

The tablet's battery had long since died. Cecil had to dig through a bag of adapters, but he was able to find one that would allow Zak to connect his handheld to the found device. The climate in the tomb was dry enough that the tablet's systems were intact. Cecil went off to run interference with Lang for a while, and let Zak focus on his discovery in peace.

A few hours later, the Avalonian aristocrat rejoined his partner at his ad hoc work station in the tunnel. Lang's men were nearly finished clearing out the artifacts, and paid the two off-worlders no mind. "Any progress?"

"Quite a bit," Zak said absentmindedly. "It's slow-going. The operating systems aren't compatible, so my handheld has to translate everything."

"Is it working?"

"Yes. It is now. I actually planned for this, you know."

"You planned on finding mummified corpses with an intact computer?"

"Not exactly, but I expected to find a few prewar devices during this treasure hunt. I downloaded a program designed to let my handheld talk to old or unknown systems. It seems like it's working pretty well. I'm getting just about everything."

"Show me."

Zak nodded toward his screen. "Cecil, look at this. They weren't just two random guys. They worked for the colonial government. They were xenoarchaeologists assigned to the excavation of the alien artifacts!"

"Lang will be happy, I suppose," Cecil said.

"No!" Zak looked around conspiratorially. The two adventurers were out of earshot of Lang's men. "We can't give this information to him, Cecil! We can't! We have to get this off-world!"

"What good will that do us?"

"It probably won't do us any good. But it'll spread the word. People will know."

"All it means is that treasure hunters will come to this planet by the score."

"Maybe. But it also means the Concordiat will send in research teams. They'll send security to protect them. With a find like this, they may even get off their asses and annex Zanzibar. It could civilize this place, put an end to the warlords and the chaos and the fighting."

"Cecil, everyone already knows that Zanzibar was once inhabited. Hardly anyone cares."

"It's because they don't know how much of that civilization remains! Look at this, Cecil! The xenoarchaeologists deliberately scrubbed the records. They were hiding the information!"

"But why?"

"Here," Zak said, turning his handheld so Cecil could see the screen better. "The owner of the tablet was this guy, Dr. Meriadoc Loren. The other guy was Dr. Lee Potts. I think they were a couple."

Cecil raised an eyebrow, and his lip curled slightly, but he didn't comment. "I see. So what happened, then?"

"Dr. Loren was a dedicated diarist. He kept a running video journal of his work on Zanzibar. I haven't had time to go through all of them, there are hundreds of entries. But this file was flagged; they wanted someone to find it. Watch."

The long-dead Dr. Loren appeared on the screen. His skin was pale and his hair was a silvery color. He removed his eyepiece before he spoke. "My name is Dr. Meriadoc Loren. I am a senior researcher at the Archaeological Administration for the Colonial Government of Zanzibar. If you're watching this, it most likely means that I'm dead. I can only hope that this is being watched by human eyes, and that humanity survives somehow.

"Four million standard years ago, Zanzibar was a living world with a thriving ecosystem. It was home to countless native species, including an intelligent, sentient, monument-building indigenous race we call *Sapio zanzibarensis*, or commonly, the *Zanzibari*. We don't know by what name they called themselves, if indeed they had names in the way we understand them."

The image of Dr. Loren faded into the background, and was

replaced with that of a short, bipedal being with grayish brown skin and a cluster of three dark eyes. It was holding a spear in its three-fingered hand, and wore what appeared to be polished metal armor. Curled up against its torso was an additional pair of arms, these smaller, each equipped with three long, delicate-looking fingers. "As you can see," the archaeologist continued, "they didn't much resemble humans, but were capable of making tools. We believe they were at a level of technological development roughly analogous to the Bronze Age on Ancient Earth. They built great cities, catacombs, bridges, and pyramids. They fought wars, they raised crops, they employed beasts of burden, and they utilized a primitive, hieroglyph-based written language.

"There is no question that they were sentient, but there's more to it than that. Some of the artifacts we've uncovered are anomalous. They don't fit with the technology level of the Zanzibari. Some of these artifacts are made of advanced materials, through means the primitive natives couldn't have managed on their own. I'm not supposed to talk about this, but I've heard that other teams of researchers are looking into it. What I am and am not supposed to talk about doesn't really matter anymore."

The scientist could be heard taking a deep breath before continuing. "The mystery only deepens from there. Four million years ago, something happened to this planet; we have not yet ascertained what. What we do know is that whatever it was, it *killed* Zanzibar. Today, the surface has been all but swept clean. It no longer supports native life of any sort, not even at the microscopic level. The planet's seismic and volcanic activity ceased, its magnetosphere vanished, the oceans boiled away, and everything was just...wiped out. There's still some debate over the nature of this cataclysm, but I personally do not think it was natural. And...it seems that we humans on Zanzibar are about to share the natives' fate."

Dr. Loren's face reappeared on the screen. He looked resigned. "As I record this, the extraterrestrials have broken through our defenses. The Zanzibaran Astro Guard and the ships from the Concordiat Fleet have all been destroyed. The aliens are approaching now, and if their actions on the frontier are any indication, the orbital bombardment should begin soon.

"The transit points are blocked. There is no escaping now. We are completely cut off. There is something larger at stake here than our own lives, however. Whatever happens here today, humanity will likely, hopefully survive elsewhere. Zanzibar is just a small colony. We have thousands of them across known space. But for these people, the indigenous beings, this world was all they had. Nothing survived the last cataclysm on Zanzibar. Someone has to speak for them." The camera panned, showing the two scientists' campsite inside the freshly sealed chamber where their bodies now resided. "My husband, Lee, and I volunteered to stay here. We've been sealed in. Our odds of surviving the attack are probably better here than anywhere else on the planet. I'm not holding out much hope, but it's possible someone will be left behind to dig us out.

"If not...if not, then at least the artifacts are protected. Sealed in these crates is part of what little remains of a once-mighty civilization. If the worst happens, they will be preserved. They will be protected from the assault, but also from looters and grave robbers." Zak and Cecil looked at each other uneasily. "We've scrubbed everything about our work off the network. We've seen what happens on other colonies after the aliens attack: as soon as they leave, the vultures descend to loot, steal, and take whatever they can, so we've hidden everything."

Dr. Loren's eyes, despite being on a small screen, seemed to bore right into Cecil and Zak, judging them, damning them, pleading with them. "If you're watching this, and you understand what I'm saying, I implore you: these artifacts are priceless. Please treat them with respect. Humanity itself may one day share the same fate. Perhaps one day soon."

The archaeologist trailed off, then addressed the camera one last time. "My name is Ozymandias, king of kings: Look upon my works, ye Mighty, and despair!" The video ended then, leaving Cecil with a knot in his stomach.

New Austin
Lone Star System
30 km north of Aterrizaje, Capital District
Southern Hemisphere

"Contact right!" Marcus shouted, directing his team's attention to the quartet of hostiles at their three o'clock position. "Thirty meters!" He ducked behind a crumbling wall as the enemy's weapons opened up. Leaning from behind cover, he selected the underslung 30mm grenade launcher bolted to his carbine, found a target, and fired. "Grenade out!" An instant later, the smart grenade air-burst inside the window that two of the hostiles were firing from. Their silhouettes disappeared in a cloud of smoke and dust. "Covering fire!"

"Engaging!" shouted Hondo, who was equipped with a heavy automatic rifle. He poured bursts of fire onto the position of the two remaining enemy, keeping their heads down as Devree, the team sniper, lined up a shot with her powerful rifle. She fired in rapid succession, taking three shots to punch through a wall and tag one of the hostiles. Hondo's machine gun chewed through the wall the other was hiding behind, and the rest of the team poured the fire on.

"Halifax! Tanaka! Wade! On me!" Marcus took three of his shooters and assaulted forward, pushing through the ambush to counterattack. They rounded a burnt-out building and were able to flank their remaining enemies, cutting them down in a matter of seconds. The team formed up once more, entered, and cleared the building they had taken fire from. Marcus was impressed with how smoothly the whole thing went this time.

"Clear!" Marcus shouted. His team responded similarly, letting him know the entire building was secure. "Good job. Check for injuries, form back up, and let's keep moving."

An alarm buzzed loudly. "Cease fire, cease fire, cease fire," came over the team's headsets. "End-ex. Put 'em on safe and let 'em hang." Marcus and his team exited the building, dusting themselves off, weapons lowered. The seven hired guns were covered in dirt and sweat. Their body armor chafed, despite the latest and best active comfort enhancements.

"Damn it," Marcus swore. He had managed to tear open the crotch of his trousers when diving to cover.

Devree approached, removing the magazine from her large sniper rifle as she did so. She whistled when she saw the hole in her team leader's pants.

"Hey, my eyes are up here," Marcus said with a grin. "This happens every time. I guess my massive cock can't be contained by ordinary pants."

Wade patted his long-time partner on the shoulder as he walked up. "That's not what Ellie told me."

Devree said "oooooh!" theatrically as Marcus laughed. The former marshal turned to Wade. "Yeah well, you don't have to worry about impressing your lovebot, do you?"

The sniper's cold blue eyes lit up as she grinned evilly at Wade. "You have a lovebot?"

Wade's face turned red. "No!"

"It's more of a sexbot," Marcus said. "I don't think there's anything loving about what he does to that thing."

"Lies! Lies and slander!" Wade protested.

Marcus chuckled as the dark-haired sniper made his partner blush like a schoolboy. He was pleased with how well his team was getting along, even though they'd only been training together for a matter of days. He'd made it a point to get to know each of them individually, and encouraged them to go out together, as a team, after the day's training was finished. Getting drunk together often improved team integrity as well as training together.

Captain Blackwood's recruiting effort had produced a pretty decent team, Marcus thought. Devree Starlighter was a former law enforcement sharpshooter from the Concordiat Inner Colony world of Mandalay. Even with her extensive cybernetic prosthetics, she was beautiful. During the interview with Marcus and Mazer

Broadbent, she described in grim detail how she'd ended up so far away on New Austin, escaping the hitmen of a powerful crime syndicate that murdered her partner and nearly killed her as well.

Jeremiah Hondo had been a grunt in the Espatier Corps, and had seen a little combat on a couple of short contingency deployments. He'd been out of the military for over a decade, but had impressed Marcus with how motivated he was and how fit he'd kept himself. He was a lean, muscular man of Earth-African descent. His dark skin was covered in ornate tattoos that traced his family and tribal heritage back more than fifteen hundred years, prior to the dawn of the Space Age on Earth. He'd spent his time on New Austin raising six children, managing a herd of cattle, and brewing his own beer.

Randall Markgraf had been a noncommissioned officer in the Concordiat Defense Force. He was a military intelligence interrogator by trade, and Marcus thought his particular skill set would be very useful once they got on the ground on Zanzibar. He was a veteran of the counterinsurgency effort on the troubled colony world of New Caledonia. He was still forbidden to discuss the details of his work in that conflict, but his résumé and service record all checked out. Like Marcus, he'd emigrated to New Austin on his discharge bonus, and had been making a living as a private investigator in Aterrizaje. Captain Blackwood's offer was considerably more than he made in an average year, however, so he jumped at the opportunity.

Ken Tanaka hailed from Nippon, the Concordiat colony known for being home to the largest number of ethnic and cultural Japanese in known space. He had been on a prestigious law enforcement tactical team that was a first tier asset for the colonial government. He resigned after an incident resulted in an innocent being killed during a shootout with an infamous, blood-thirsty crime syndicate. After studying the reports and listening to Ken's description of events, Marcus concluded that the former policeman had been a scapegoat for politicized administrators, and was the victim of people who hadn't been there second-guessing a split-second, life-or-death decision. In the Espatier Corps, Ken wouldn't have been punished for what happened. But Nippon was Nippon, and they did things their own way there. In any case, the quiet Nipponese expatriate was more than competent and stereotypically stoic. Marcus hired him without hesitation.

The last addition to the team was Benjamin Halifax. He was a short, broad man with a muscular body and a hard gleam in his eye. His pale, freckled head was shaved, except for a strip of red hair down the middle, and a scraggly red beard hung from his chin. He didn't have a record of military service like most of his teammates. Instead, he'd spent several years as a mercenary, serving in several small, bloody conflicts on independent worlds. More importantly, he was the only man qualified for the job who had actually been to Zanzibar recently. Given that much of the information available to Marcus was patchy at best and possibly years out of date, having a guy who actually knew his way around their destination could be immensely helpful. That made it worth bringing him on board, despite his sketchy background.

A few moments later, a pair of instructors approached the team of mercenaries with Captain Blackwood in tow. They wore high-visibility red armor vests and ball caps, and carried holstered sidearms. The two men were employees of the Aterrizaje Tactical Institute, the most prestigious (and only) advanced weapons training facility on New Austin. They had been observing the live-fire exercise remotely, controlling the enemy combatant bots and monitoring the students for safety.

"Very nicely done," the lead instructor said, greeting the team. "You've only been training with us for eight days, and you're working together like professionals. A couple of you got hit in the close ambush, but the sim says that none of you would've died from your wounds."

"I caught one in the ass," Halifax said. "I'll be sitting on a cushion for a few days." The target bots carried lifelike representations of enemy personnel, and could fire at students with what was colloquially known as "stinger" rounds: low velocity, non-lethal projectiles that didn't cause any serious harm, but hurt like being stabbed with a hot blade.

"We saw that," the instructor said with a chuckle. "Mr. Tanaka got his arm clipped, too. Nonetheless, you assaulted through, outflanked your opponents, cleared that structure, and prevailed. We'll go over some learning points on the replay, but all in all you did very well."

"I found the whole thing to be most impressive," the captain mused. "Marcus, I think you chose your team well."

Marcus was pleased that the captain seemed satisfied. Taking seven people through the advanced combat tactics course at ATI, after purchasing the necessary weapons, equipment, and ammunition, was not inexpensive. He wanted to make sure the captain knew she was getting her money's worth. He didn't know what they would encounter on Zanzibar, but he found himself increasingly confident that his hastily formed team could handle anything thrown at them.

The instructors were pleased as well. "Excellent work today. You passed your final exercise with flying colors. Tomorrow we'll go over the lessons learned as a group and sign off on your certifications."

Marcus grinned. This was better training than the Marshals Service ever paid for, and damned if it wasn't fun. His team seemed to be enjoying themselves, too. It'd be less enjoyable once real bullets started flying, but until then, he wasn't going to be a wet blanket. It was bad for morale. "It's early still," he told his assembled team. "Let's meet up in a couple hours for dinner and drinks. You all did a damned fine job today, and we ought to celebrate."

In his career in the Concordiat Espatier Corps, Marcus had been hauled across space in many different ships, most of them military troop transports. He'd never served on a small patrol ship like the *Andromeda,* as they typically didn't perform the sort of missions that required a complement of Espatiers.

She was a Polaris Class patrol ship from Winchell-Chung Astronautical Industries, and she was big for her class. Standing seventy meters tall on her landing jacks, she outmassed most ships designed for her mission by quite a bit. She also was capable of longer duration patrols than most ships of her type.

Her hull was thick and cylindrical, coming to a blunt nose at the tip. Around the base of the hull were four conformal engine nacelles which housed her primary rocket motors. Four stubby airfoils protruded from the hull, in between the engine nacelles. As Captain Blackwood had explained, the bottom half of the ship was almost all propellant tankage, surrounding the thermonuclear motor which powered her. Near the nose was a cockpit, much like you'd see on a conventional aircraft. When the ship was planeted, the pilot's back was to the ground, but when she was in flight he was facing forward. Many of the smaller, transatmospheric ships featured this archaic arrangement. It wasn't necessary—the pilot didn't fly the ship by eye, and in fact the *Andromeda* could be controlled from several different stations—but it was tradition going back to the dawn of spaceflight.

Docked on a launchpad at the Capitol Starport, the *Andromeda* had been serviced, refueled, and rearmed for the long haul to Zanzibar. Patrol ships of this class weren't generally designed to be away from their home station for more than a couple of months. The planned round trip to Zanzibar and back would take much longer. Even with the *Andromeda*'s long legs, they were going to need to tank up on propellant more than once during the journey.

Marcus, Wade, and their team made their way up the large mechanical gangway which connected the landing tower to the ship's open cargo bay. The cargo hold itself was the largest single compartment on the ship, aside from the propellant tanks. It took up the entire diameter of the ship, and was more than twice as tall as most decks.

Inside, the ship's cargomaster, a man named Kimball, greeted Marcus and his associates. "Good afternoon, gentlefolk," he said with a smile. Kimball was short by normal human standards, standing only 1.3 meters tall, and had curly hair and a trimmed goatee. He hailed from the world of Darwin, a Concordiat Inner Colony that was first colonized in the Mid-Diaspora period. The huge, dense planet had almost half again as much gravity as the Earth. The early colonists engaged in genetic modification treatments to help their descendants adapt to the high gravity. Centuries later, most Darwinites were extremely short, but possessed dense muscles and strong bones. "How went the controlled violence today?"

"It went well," Wade replied. "We completed our final exercise today. How are things going here?"

"All is in order," Kimball said. "We've stocked the necessary provisions for the journey. We're on schedule to lift off in four local days."

"Very good," Marcus said with a nod. "We're headed back to our racks to get cleaned up, change, and then we're going out for the evening." It was not only polite, but long standing tradition, to let the ship's crew know of your comings and goings.

"Most excellent," Kimball beamed. He wasn't really looking at Marcus, so much as he was focused on his eyepiece, but he was paying attention. "I'll let the watch officer know of your plans, for the log. We're still connected to the Starport's water supply, so there are no time limits on showers. Water is included in our berthing fee."

Marcus nodded and headed toward the crew quarters. Water was a precious, limited resource in deep space. Once underway, showers were allowed only with the bare minimum amount of (recycled) water necessary to do the job. Even still, he didn't want his team to hog the *Andromeda*'s limited shower space. The ship's crew only got to enjoy that kind of luxury every so often.

The crew quarters were located just below the cargo bay. It, too, was a taller-than-normal deck, as it accommodated two levels of individual bunks. Each bunk was a small compartment, 2.5 by 1.25 by 1.5 meters in size, containing acceleration-adaptive bedding, a power source, and an onboard computer. They were, mercifully, soundproofed to give the occupants about the only privacy they'd get while underway. During their orientation, it had been explained to the mercenaries that each berth could also function as an emergency survival pod. If the crew compartment were to depressurize, the compartments would seal air-tight. Onboard CO_2 scrubbers would allow a crewmember to survive for a lot longer than he would in just a spacesuit. Ships in the *Andromeda*'s mass class rarely came equipped with escape pods, so this was about as good as it was going to get. Marcus didn't mind; it was better protection than he'd had on some of the big troop transports he'd ridden.

Two levels of berths ringed the crew compartment, fifteen in each layer. They were separated by sections of life-support equipment, compartments for storage of personal effects, and structural supports. The top level was offset slightly from the bottom one, and could be accessed by a narrow catwalk when the ship was under gravity. In the center of the crew compartment was a commons area and recreational center, complete with screens, games, a zero-g-capable kitchenette, and seating. The commons was deserted presently, as most of the crewmembers who weren't on watch were off ship, enjoying their last few days of planetside leave.

A latrine and shower room was adjacent to the crew deck. While each berth had its own relief tube, the regular zero-g-capable toilets were much less awkward to use. The showers, likewise, were designed to work in freefall, though they functioned just fine when the ship was planeted. Marcus' brief, hot shower was nonetheless glorious after a day of running around in full battle rattle under the blazing light and heat of Lone Star.

New Austin
Lone Star System
Aterrizaje, Capital District
Southern Hemisphere

The Aterrizaje Stampede was a big event, spanning six days and dozens of events. It was as close as New Austin came to having its own Olympic Games, and this year was its biggest showing yet. The whole thing had been a whirlwind, and Annie found herself in awe of the spectacle. At its peak, there were fifty thousand people in attendance at the fairgrounds, and countless more watching the media coverage. It was positively overwhelming for a simple country girl from the outback, but Annie was holding her own. She was enjoying the freedom of being away from her parents, but at the same time found herself wishing they could be there too. Her mom was busy opening a new mining claim, trying to get it up and running while she could still travel comfortably. Her dad was off playing soldier somewhere in the city. Both of them called her every night.

In any case Annie wasn't lacking for company. Carlos had made good on his offer to show her around the city, and she'd visited her friends from school as well. Aterrizaje was a small but rapidly growing city of a quarter million people. It could be tough to navigate sometimes, but between the mass transit system and the autotaxis, getting where you needed to go wasn't too difficult. There was a lot to see and do, even outside of the rodeo. Annie's event wasn't until the final day, so until then she was free to explore. There was one place in the city she really wanted to see, though.

"Here we are," Carlos said, stopping his father's automobile in an otherwise empty parking lot. "The northwest viewing area of the spaceport. Why did you want to come here?"

Annie didn't answer. She hopped out of the vehicle, closing the door behind her, and looked longingly to the south through a high, chain-link fence. As the sun sank toward the horizon, a dozen ships of various shapes and sizes were silhouetted against the fiery red sky and golden clouds. "There," she said, pointing at one of them. "That one off to the left? That's the *Andromeda*."

"Did you read that from your eyepiece?" Carlos asked, standing next to her.

"Yeah, but I already knew which one it was. I know her captain. Nice lady named Blackwood. She had dinner at my house. It was no big deal."

"Really? That's crazy."

Annie's expression sank. "My dad is leaving on that ship. He'll probably be gone for over a year."

Carlos' expression softened. He very lightly patted Annie on the shoulder, but quickly yanked his hand away, as if he thought she would bite. "I'm sorry. Why is he leaving?"

"Work. It's a long story."

"You want him to stay, don't you? It's okay. I'm close with my papa, too."

"No, that's not it."

"You don't want him to stay?"

"No, *I* want to *go* with him!" Annie insisted, looking up at her friend. "I want to be on that ship! I want to go to space! It's not fair. Dad doesn't even really want to go, we just need the money. It's my dream and I can't go."

"Do you really want to leave? Things aren't so bad here."

Annie looked up into Carlos' big brown eyes and felt her face flush again. "No... no they're not," she said, managing a smile. He moved closer to her then, gently taking her by the hand. Her mind racing, her heart pounding, not knowing what to do, she closed her eyes and let it happen. Their lips touched, butterflies fluttered around in her stomach, and she wanted to melt. Then the ground started to shake. *Wait,* she thought. *The ground is shaking.*

Pulling away from Carlos' embrace, Annie ran forward to the fence and watched, in awe, as one of the ships lifted off from its launchpad. Her eyepiece identified it as the *Amerigo Vespucci*, a merchant vessel registered on Earth itself. She was tall and sleek, a new design from the heart of the Concordiat. The ground shook and a huge plume of dust and smoke spewed forth as she lifted off like a volcanic eruption. The fires of her fusion rockets were nearly blinding as she throttled up and began to accelerate. She watched the ship roar into the darkening sky, leaving a trail of smoke behind it, for what seemed like a long time. The rumble of her engines faded as she disappeared over the horizon.

"Wow," she whispered. Carlos coughed awkwardly. Annie spun around to face him, hands behind her back. She could tell she was blushing. "Sorry about that."

"No, I am sorry," Carlos said sheepishly. "I was an ass. I didn't mean to... you know. I'm sorry."

"What? No! No, no!" Annie said, stepping forward and looking up into his eyes. "That was... that was amazing. I just... I'm sorry I'm such a schiz. I get distracted easy. My mom says I get that from my dad."

"So," Carlos said, looking around. "What do you want to do now?"

Annie raised an eyebrow and folded her hands across her chest. "I don't know what you think you're going to get, cowboy, but let me tell you something..."

"No no no!" the young man pleaded, the color draining from his face. "That's not what I meant, I swear!"

Annie softened her expression, smiled, and shook her head. Before Carlos could protest anymore, she shushed him. "I'm just teasing you, stupid. I'm sure you don't want to sit out here and watch ships lift off with me all night."

"I will if that's what you want to do," he said. "But I'm hungry."

"Me too. You want to get something to eat in town?"

"I know some places that are good. Do you like tacos?"

"Everybody on New Austin likes tacos," Annie said.

"There's also a party tonight, if you want to go."

"I heard about it. People say it gets crazy."

"It's not bad. Everyone is easygoing. No drama."

Annie looked longingly at the spaceport one last time. "You know what? Let's go. I haven't been to the city in years. I never get to have a life. Tonight, I'm going to have a life. I'm going to have fun and not worry about tomorrow."

"Don't you ride tomorrow?"

Annie frowned. "Okay, I'll worry about one thing that happens tomorrow. I ride in the afternoon. When is your event?"

"A little earlier than yours, but still after lunch."

"Good. I want to sleep in in the morning."

Carlos' jaw fell open. "What?"

Annie punched him in the arm and laughed at him. "You're so easy to mess with. It's adorable."

After the sun had gone down, as New Austin's twin moons rose into the night sky, Wade found himself driving the rented van on the way to the evening's entertainment. Their destination was a popular bar called Denim & Diamonds. It was a stereotypically New Austin establishment, complete with twangy Western-style music and line dancing (which New Austin classified as a Heritage Art Form), but the drinks were cheap, the beer was good, and they had plenty of pool tables. Wade didn't like to drink much, so he volunteered to drive the van so everyone else could have a good time. They could've simply hired an autotaxi, of course, but why spend the money when Captain Blackwood had already paid for rental vehicles?

Denim & Diamonds was jumping, but Wade had screened ahead and reserved a table for the team. He sipped water for the next few hours while the team caroused, drank, laughed, and enjoyed greasy bar food. Marcus didn't drink that much, but he got goofy when he'd had a few, and was laughing at Randy Markgraf's dumb jokes. Randy didn't stay too long; he lived in Aterrizaje and went home most nights, preferring to sleep in his own bed. Marcus said he'd be going to bed before it got too late; Annie was in town for the big rodeo and he wanted to watch her ride the next day. Hondo took an autotaxi back to the ship so he could screen his wife and children, as he did nearly every night. Ben Halifax was last seen leaving the bar with two pretty young women, and had them both laughing and giggling as they went out the door. The brash, loud, abrasive mercenary certainly had a way with the ladies. It was baffling.

Ken Tanaka, despite his reserved, quiet demeanor, lightened up after a few shots of sake and whiskey. He was off at the billiards tables with Marcus, who was teaching him to play pool. Marcus was so good at pool that Wade had accused him of being some kind of wizard. He'd spent half the night whupping all comers and winning a few credits in the process.

Wade found himself alone at their table, sipping a fizzy soft drink and feeling a little bored. He didn't abstain from drinking on any religious grounds. He just didn't like the feeling of being drunk. He didn't like the loss of control or cognition. It was a personal quirk, but he'd seen enough of his compatriots in the fleet get in trouble from alcohol-related incidents that he thought of it as an advantage. He'd never had to go stand in front of the CO and explain some ridiculous behavior from the night before. No, being sober allowed Wade to execute shenanigans without getting caught, and usually without being suspected. He smiled at the thought.

"What's so funny?" It was Devree Starlighter. Wade hadn't noticed her come back to the table. "Where is everybody?" she asked.

"Marcus and Ken are shooting pool. Everybody else left, and I think those two are going to want to go after they finish their game. Where have you been?"

"Dancing!" she said with a grin. She'd had a few drinks and was a lot bubblier than usual. "I've lived on New Austin for almost three years now and have *never* been line dancing. I can't believe how fun it is!"

Wade couldn't help but size the lovely sniper up as she sat down next to him. She had dressed the part for a night of line dancing at Denim & Diamonds: short denim skirt, cowboy boots, sleeveless blouse, and a cowboy hat. All of the stuff was brand new, but she wore it like it had been made for her. Despite being a little tipsy, she gracefully crossed her legs after sitting down.

And what nice legs they are, Wade thought, trying not to stare. He could see the line where flesh gave way to prosthetic, but it was barely noticeable at a glance. There was another such fine seam on her arm.

"See something you like there, buddy?" Devree said, with a twinkle in her cold blue eyes.

Wade felt his face immediately flush. He'd been caught staring. *Smooth,* he thought to himself. "Uh, sorry," he managed. "I was just...you know, your prosthetic." *Yeah, that sounds reasonable.*

"They're pretty realistic, aren't they?" Devree said. She hiked up her skirt a little and slid a finger along the fine line where biology met machinery. "I've seen a lot of people with ugly gray replacements, where they look like robots. That's the fashion in a lot of places. I paid the extra for the insurance coverage to get the top quality replacement parts, and I'm glad I did." She took a sip from a bottle of beer.

"You can barely even tell they're not real," Wade said.

He fell silent when Devree grabbed his hand and placed it on her thigh. "Right?" she asked. "It's okay, touch it. My legs use the heat produced from their normal operation to make the synthetic skin warm to the touch. It feels almost like real skin, doesn't it?"

"It...uh...it sure does," Wade managed.

Devree's expression softened. She sat up a little straighter, pulled her hemline back down, and looked apologetic. "Oh my God, I'm sorry," she said. "I'm embarrassing you."

"No!" Wade protested. "It's okay."

"Oh, I'm sure you enjoyed that," she said slyly. "But this is unprofessional. I just haven't dressed up and gone out in a long time. I sure as hell shouldn't have had that shot of tequila. Nothing good comes of it when I drink tequila. That's how I ended up married."

"You're married?" Wade asked, mortified.

"No! I mean, I *was*. Not anymore. Back home. I went to the academy with him, we were young, we were stupid, we got married on a crazy impulse, and it was a terrible idea. We lasted six months before we split. Luckily, getting divorced on Mandalay is pretty easy." She chuckled.

"Well, I'm sorry it didn't work out," Wade said.

She shook her head. "It's better this way. His name is Heath, and we're still friends. Marrying another cop is a bad idea anyway. Too many work problems get brought home." She took a sip of water from a glass on the table. "What about you? Are you married?"

"Me? Nah. I, uh, wouldn't have been touching you like that if I was married."

"Oh really?" Devree laughed and shook her head. "You've been on New Austin for a while though, haven't you?"

"I immigrated here...it'll be four years ago, four local years I mean, next month."

"What in the world brought you all the way out here?"

"I lived on Hayden, like Marcus. We were stationed at the same place. There's this giant CDF base outside of the city of Langley, I mean, a *huge* base. Probably fifty thousand personnel there. I lived on base, in bachelor quarters. I'm glad I did, actually. Langley is a shithole."

"I've heard that," Devree said. "I've never been on Hayden, but you don't hear a lot of good things about it."

"They got the hell blasted out of them by the Maggots during the War. Hayden isn't that big, and it's like eighty-five percent covered by ocean to begin with. The Maggots leveled most of the terraformed landmass, and I mean they *obliterated* it. If you go up north there are crater fields stretching as far as you can see in every direction. They say it took years for the dust to settle. There are the ruins of cities and towns, parts of ships that survived reentry, all kinds of stuff, but almost no one goes up there. The colonial government tries its best to keep people out. A lot of the ruins are still radioactive from the Maggots' particle beams, they say, and the place is a graveyard. They don't want grave robbers looting what little remains."

"That's . . . depressing," Devree said. "Mandalay is beautiful. It didn't get hit in the war. The terraformed zone is huge, and outside of that it has its own ecosystem. Plants, animals, everything. There are jungles of these . . . well, they're not really trees, but they kind of do the same thing. Some of them are eighty meters tall. When they bloom, it's the prettiest thing. They turn dozens of shades of bright colors. If you see it from a distance, the whole forest looks like a bowl of candies."

"Wow. I don't really know much about Mandalay. What's it like in those forests?"

"Oh, you don't go into the forest, not if you don't need to. There are all kinds of things that will kill you there: plants that will wrap you in vines and suck the juices out of you, animals that will swallow you whole, even a kind of fungus-type stuff that'll dissolve you in acid. The local wildlife doesn't care that it can't digest our alien protein. Everything on Mandalay wants to kill you. The terraformed zone is surrounded by a fifty-meter-high wall to keep the native species out as much as possible. But you didn't answer my question. What brought you out to New Austin?"

"Huh? Oh. Well, like I said, Langley isn't a great place to live. The remaining inhabited landmass is crowded. They had this big population boom after the war, with refugees from other colonies moving in and people deciding to have a lot of kids. I guess a brush with extinction triggered the 'go forth and multiply' instinct. Most people around Langley live in these massive arcologies. Each one is a self-contained little city, hundreds of stories high, with thousands or tens of thousands of residents, shops, services, you name it. The place is so crowded there aren't enough jobs for everybody. With that kind of unemployment, crime is high. The government starting cracking down more and more on the crime, and it just got to be ridiculous. There were police checkpoints all over the place, the government monitors electronic transmissions, there were cameras everywhere, and where there weren't cameras there were robots following you around, recording everything you do. They used to joke that you couldn't swing a dead cat without breaking ten different laws, but one time I watched this crazy homeless guy *literally* swing a dead cat around, by the tail, outside the northwest gate of the base. Right in the middle of an intersection! Turns out, that *is* illegal. This cop tried to talk him down and he hit him, you know, with the dead cat. Right in the face. Three other cops shot the guy and dragged him off while the first cop tried to wipe, I don't know, whatever juices come out of a dead cat, off his face."

Devree snorted loudly, trying not to choke on her water as she laughed. "I shouldn't laugh. They shot an obviously disturbed man. It's screwed up. Still funny, though."

Wade continued, "I know, right? I swear to God, that actually happened. That's when I told myself that I needed to get off that fucking rock. The worst part is, even with all the heavy-handed policing, the cameras, the searches, the checkpoints, it's *still* not safe to go into some places in the city. The gangs there are well armed, and they fight with each other and the cops all the time."

"Holy shit. I can see why you left."

"Yeah. I knew I wanted to get out of the Defense Force, but I sure as hell didn't want to live anywhere on Hayden. There are places that aren't as bad as Langley and places that are really nice, but there are no jobs in the not-bad places and I'm not rich enough to live in the *really* nice places. I found these advertisements for emigration to New Austin, and it looked amazing—wide open spaces, clear skies, fresh air, plenty of room, low crime, and a government that minds its own business. I said, sign me up!"

Devree took a long sip of water and ate some of the tortilla chips that were left in the basket on the table. "That's what they told me when they offered me a list of places I could go. No crime syndicates on New Austin, they said. No native ecosystem trying to kill you, either. Just mild weather and friendly people. At least that's what they said."

"If you don't mind my asking, what happened to you? Mandalay is an Inner Colony world, right? What brought you out to the frontier?"

Devree stirred the ice in her water for a moment, thoughtfully, as if trying to decide what to say. "I was a sniper on one of the Colonial Enforcement Bureau's tactical intervention teams."

Wade raised an eyebrow.

"Yes, we called them *TITs*," Devree said with a grin. "It's actually a really prestigious unit, and it's hard to get into. The regular Police Academy was tough, but the selection course for the TITs has something like an eighty percent washout rate. Not a lot of women make it through, but I did."

"Your prosthetics are...extensive. How did you get them?"

Devree held up her artificial right arm, and examined it quietly for a moment. "That's kind of how I ended up out here. I was flesh and blood when I went through the academy. I mean, afterwards, they gave me the usual boosters to keep me in top shape, but I got through selection on my own. These," she said, indicating her prosthetic legs, "these are the result of an attempt to kill me."

"Jesus," Wade said quietly. "How bad was it?"

"Both of my legs were traumatically amputated above the knee. My right arm was mangled so badly that it couldn't be saved. My left arm was in better shape, but I lost fingers on the hand. I had extensive internal injuries, my eardrums were burst, I was temporarily blinded by the explosion, and I had extensive second and third degree burns."

"Explosion?"

Devree nodded. "We'd been cracking down on a crime syndicate called the Black Hand for over a year. When we started, they ran a good portion of the capital city of New Dawn. When all was said and done, they were on the run, but they didn't go out without a fight. There was a standoff. We had one of their big-time players, son of one of the Black Hand's bosses, surrounded in a warehouse. We busted him in human trafficking and smuggling. He took one of the kids hostage."

"Kids?"

"Yeah, kids. They were his cargo. There's still a market for that kind of shit in some places, I guess. He took a hostage, this terrified teenage boy. My spotter, Samseer, was with me. I took the shot. I blew that son-of-a-bitch's head clean off, through a skylight, from this really tall communications tower nearby."

"So what happened?"

"The syndicate boss went insane. He had his few remaining loyal soldiers just start wreaking havoc in New Dawn. They killed police officers, judges, lawyers, city and government officials, whoever they could take a shot at. It got so bad that the governor declared a state of emergency and sent in the Colonial Guard. But the Black Hand had eyes and ears everywhere, even in the Enforcement Bureau. Somebody talked. They found out I was the one who made the shot."

"Oh no," Wade said.

"Samseer and I were in an unmarked ground car, headed out to lunch one day. All I remember is a car pulling in front of us, and this woman standing in an open sunroof with a missile launcher in her hands. I was on the passenger's side. The missile hit the driver's side. Samseer was killed instantly. I don't know how I survived. I woke up in a city hospital a few days later. I couldn't see, I could barely hear, and I was missing my limbs. Machines were keeping me alive."

"I'm so sorry," Wade managed. "That's horrible."

Devree shrugged. "Is what it is. They fixed me, as you can see. My arms and legs are better than real ones. They feel pretty real to me. It's still a little different, but it feels mostly natural when someone touches me. My new organs are better than the ones I was born with, I can run faster, and I don't have to worry about spraining an ankle anymore. It could've been a lot worse. Like Samseer."

"You seem pretty positive about it."

"I have to be. My partner was killed, I was blown to pieces, and I had to drop my entire life and come out here just to be safe. I can't dwell on all that. I'm lucky to be alive and I need to focus on that."

"It sounds like you've had this argument with yourself before."

"I drank heavily when I first got here. I was out every night almost. I'd go home with just about anybody, I'd start fights, I even spent a couple nights in the Aterrizaje city jail. That's when I realized how stupidly I was acting. I quit drinking for over a year, got a job, and put my life back together. I figured I owed it to my partner to not waste the rest of my life."

"So what brought you on this mission?"

"Same thing that brought you, Wade," Devree said with a smile. "The money. Also, I'm bored. I'm not the workaday kind of person, never was."

"Well, if you're interested, when we get back Marcus and I might be able to get you on the Marshal's Service. They're pretty shorthanded. The pay's not great, and it's usually dull, but it's not a bad job."

"Well...one thing at a time. When we get back I just might take you up on that. And I'm sorry I told you my entire life story. I get chatty when I drink. Thank you for being a good listener. Most guys only listen to me when they're trying to get in bed with me."

"Wouldn't dream of it," Wade said with a wry grin. Devree laughed.

Near the Aterrizaje fairgrounds was a large caravan park. People came in from all over the terraformed zone to attend the Stampede, and the caravan park was full. So full, in fact, of mobile homes, trucks, trailers, and other vehicles that they had spilled over into the dusty open areas beyond the park. Annie had heard about the parties that could happen out in the caravan park. Tonight was a big one. Multiple bonfires had been lit. Dozens of horsemen, cow punchers, riders, party girls, and roughnecks drank, caroused, blasted music, and had a good time. The Aterrizaje city police didn't bother them unless someone reported destruction of property, and the fairgrounds' robots generally stayed away as well. They were tasked with monitoring the livestock and weren't concerned with drunken human antics.

At sixteen standard years, Annie was below the legal drinking age on New Austin, but tonight nobody seemed to care. Young people, teenagers to twenty-somethings, gathered around a large bonfire as music played. People danced, drank, played games, and made out. Nobody asked her to verify her age before handing her a bottle of beer.

"See? It's not so bad," Carlos said, sipping his own drink. Nobody was getting out of control or anything.

"I guess," Annie said, sipping the beer in her hand. "My dad would be so mad if he knew I was here, though." She took another sip and frowned. "Drinking, no less. What is this stuff, horse piss? Is someone playing a joke on me?"

Carlos looked at her bottle. "It might as well be horse piss. Try this."

Annie took the bottle from Carlos and took a long swig.

"Easy there. I don't think you drink much."

"I don't drink at all," she said, handing the bottle back. "That's better, but...ugh."

"What's wrong?"

"Nothing, I just think I'm done with this," she said, pouring the remainder of her beer into the dirt. She tossed the bottle into a waste receptacle and looked up at Carlos. "So is this what people do in the city?"

"What do you mean?"

"I live in Laredo Territory. The nearest actual town is Red River."

"That's not much of a town."

"It's not. It has maybe four thousand people, and it's an hour away by road. I almost never see people my own age, you know? Or people at all, except for my parents. I guess I thought it'd be more exciting than this. I don't know." She looked around at the revelers. It was getting late and things had calmed down somewhat. "Everyone is just sitting around, or drinking, or making out. Nobody is talking to anybody."

"Parties are more fun when all your friends are there," Carlos said.

"I don't have a lot of friends. Not face to face friends anyway."

"You had fun in the city though, didn't you?"

Annie smiled. "I did. You've been the sweetest tour guide. Thank you for showing me a good time." Nearby, a woman, probably in her early twenties, kneed a drunk, oafish young cowboy in the balls and knocked him to the ground. A group of people cheered and laughed at his pain as the woman grabbed her hat and stormed off. Annie shook her head. "And thank you for being a gentleman, Carlos. Hey, you want to get out of here?"

"Where do you want to go? My dad's car has autodrive."

"I want to go check on Sparkles."

Carlos nodded. "The robots will let us in if we display our passes. Do you have yours?"

Annie nodded, pulling her ID pass out of her pocket and hanging it around her neck. "Let's go."

The huge stable was darkened, except for navigation and safety lighting, to calm the animals. As expected, a robot checked their passes when they entered, but ignored Annie and Carlos after that. They made their way along a row of stalls to number 067, but stopped when they saw a group of what looked like teenagers gathered around Sparkles' stall.

"What the fuck?" Annie snarled, and took off at a run, leaving Carlos to try to keep up with her. Swearing aloud, she pushed her way through the gaggle of inebriated teens to find Victoria Alexander in Sparkles' stall. The horse was taking something from the palm of her hand.

"What the fuck are you doing to my horse?" she said. With a push of her arms she cleared the stall door and landed next to Victoria. "What did you give her?" she snapped, shoving Victoria with both hands.

The rich girl slammed against the stall wall, but only started laughing. She wasn't looking so good; her hair was a mess, her clothes were disheveled, and she stank of alcohol. Her eyes were bloodshot and red. "Hey there, desert rat," she said. "Just seeing if your horse likes to party. Want some?"

Annie's heart was racing, her hands shaking. She grabbed Victoria by the shirt and pulled her in close. "What did you do to my *horse*, you fucking bitch?"

Her head lolling around, Victoria showed Annie a small, empty vial. "Red Eye, baby. You want some? It makes you fly, fly, fly!"

The group of teens were watching uneasily, and no one said anything. Annie could feel the rage boiling up from deep inside her. She didn't know if she wanted to scream or cry. Shoving Victoria aside, she turned to the group. "You let her do this? You let her? Somebody call the vet! She poisoned my horse!"

"I'll do it," Carlos said, touching his handheld. "What the hell is wrong with you people?"

An older guy, probably in his twenties, smacked the device out of Carlos' hand. "Who you calling there, dirt farmer? You trying to bring the law down on us?" Red Eye was a dangerous synthetic drug, one of a few such substances that was banned for personal consumption on New Austin. It caused erratic and sometimes dangerous behavior in its users, and simple possession was a criminal offense. Carlos shoved the older guy back and bent to pick up his handheld. "I don't give a damn about your stupid Red Eye, asshole! Her horse will die if we don't—" Before Carlos could say anything else, the other man punched him in the face, and the fight was on.

The group of teens formed a semicircle to watch Carlos fight Victoria's friend. The older man was bigger than Carlos, but he was inebriated and clumsy. The young gaucho grabbed him by his shirt and flung him into the boards of the stall, following up with a flurry of punches. Some of the teens fled, but others stayed and cheered. The bigger man shoved Carlos back and came at him once more.

Victoria was laughing uncontrollably the whole time, leaning on the stall door. Annie was on her handheld with emergency services, explaining that her horse had been poisoned. The call finished, she was about to throw Victoria out of the stall when Sparkles convulsed.

The horse, her breathing labored and slow, fell to her knees, then collapsed to the dirt floor of her stall. Annie watched helplessly as she convulsed, cried, and kicked, foam coming from her mouth and nostrils. Annie felt sick as Sparkles suffered, vomiting up a bloody mess before lying still.

"No . . ." she said, dropping down next to the animal. "Sparkles?" The fight going on right outside of her stall, Victoria, the drugged-up teens, all of it faded away as she placed her hands on her horse's still form.

Sparkles' ragged breathing slowed and then stopped. She died.

Tears streamed down Annie's cheeks. She buried her face in her hands and wept. She was snapped back to reality when Carlos slammed the other man into the stall door again. Startled, she stood up to see what was going on.

The other teens scattered as a trio of utility robots rolled up to the scene of the disturbance, politely insisting that the two men stop fighting. The lead robot was knocked to the ground as Carlos threw his opponent into it, sending man and machine tumbling to the stable floor in a heap. The robot's wheel spun helplessly, kicking up dirt, as it tried to right itself, but the weight of the unconscious man on top of it was too much.

Carlos, with a swollen face and blood leaking from his nose, stepped over to the stall door. "Are you okay?" he asked Annie, breathing heavily. "What . . ." his voice trailed off when he noticed Sparkles' body on the floor of the stall. "Oh no. Victoria, how could you do this? What is wrong with you?"

Victoria seemingly ignored him as she tried to climb over the stall door. Before she could make it over on her own, Annie grabbed her legs and shoved her over the top. The rich girl fell face-first to the dirt floor and struggled to get up.

Annie wasn't about to give the bitch the chance. In a flash, she leapt over the door and came down on top of Victoria. She dragged the inebriated girl to her feet and threw her back to the ground as hard as she could. Before the robots could do anything, before Carlos could say anything, she came down on Victoria like an orbital strike. "How could you?" she said, so enraged that she was crying. "How could you?" She didn't give Victoria the chance to answer; she sat on top of her and punched her in the face, then again, then again. "You fucking bitch!" she shrieked, hitting her over and over.

A mechanical claw clamped down onto Annie's arm, snapping her out of her rage. The robot ground its wheel into the dirt, pulling her off of Victoria. "Get off of me!" she said, shaking free of the robot's grasp.

Carlos was at her side then, and helped her to her feet. "Annie, you need to stop," he said quietly.

Annie didn't say anything. She looked down at Victoria, bloodied and bruised, and felt sick. Victoria's eyes were swollen shut, blood leaked from her nose and mouth, and her breathing was ragged. Annie's knuckles were bloody. Shaking her head, not knowing what to do, she turned to Carlos, buried her face into his shoulder, and cried.

Annie opened her eyes, squinting in the dazzling lighting of the holding cell. Despite how uncomfortable the bed was, she'd managed to sleep for a while. She'd been taken into custody by the Aterrizaje Police, but they were mostly nice. They bandaged her hands and didn't restrain her when they drove her to the station. Once they got her there, though, they did a blood test and found a little bit of alcohol in her system. They promptly wrote her a ticket for underage drinking.

Still, they let her tell her side of the story, and said they would look at the logs from the security cameras and the robots. They said that the veterinarian had taken a blood sample from Sparkles and would be able to determine if there were any illegal substances in the horse's system. Annie's handheld had been broken in the scuffle, but the police said they'd notify her parents for her. This mortified Annie, but there was no way to hide this from her parents. She wasn't under arrest, technically, but they wouldn't release her without a legal guardian. They put her in a holding cell so they could monitor her until someone came to get her. It had been hours and hours. It had to be mid-morning already. She had no idea how long she'd been in there, or when anyone would arrive.

Annie sat up quickly when she heard the door unlock. It slid open and her father stepped into the room. Jumping off the bed, she ran to him and hugged him tightly, trying not to start crying again. "Daddy, Sparkles is dead! She killed her!" she sobbed.

Her father held her tightly for a long moment. "Come on now, baby girl," he said. "Let's sit down a moment."

"We're not leaving?" Annie asked, unable to hide the fear in her voice. Was he just going to leave her here?

"I need to talk to you about what's going to happen," he said. "Then we'll go." He seemed tired.

"Okay," she sniffled, sitting back down on the bed. After her father sat next to her, she asked him what was going on.

He shook his head sadly. "I'm going to be straight with you, honey: this isn't good. That girl you beat down, Victoria? She's in the hospital with a fractured skull and a broken nose. You did a number on her."

Despite the pit forming in her stomach, Annie was defiant. "She killed Sparkles! She poisoned her with Red Eye! Red Eye, Daddy!"

"I know, I know," her father said reassuringly. "The city police have the video recordings from the cameras and the robots. Your friend Carlos corroborated your story, though the police told me both of you had alcohol in your system."

"I just tried beer," Annie pleaded. "I didn't even finish it. I didn't like it."

"Ok, honey. Neither one of you was intoxicated. It certainly seems like Victoria was, but they're not going to tell me the results of her blood test. They *did* find vials of Red Eye on her and that clown that Carlos whupped the shit out of, though."

"*She* should be the one in jail!"

"You're not in jail, Annie. Calm down. If she wasn't in the hospital getting her face put back together she probably would be. Things being as they are, though, it's not so cut and dry. Her father is an influential man with a lot of money. That son of a whore actually had the gall to call me, a peace officer, and offer me a shady deal."

"What?" Annie asked. "What kind of deal?"

"He said he'd pay me a lot of money if I didn't press charges for his daughter poisoning your horse. He said that if we didn't press charges, then he wouldn't either, and this would all go away."

"But she *had* Red Eye!"

Her father shrugged. "He has enough clout to make sure she just gets sent to rehabilitation."

Annie was scared now. "Why didn't you take the deal?"

"Because it's not right, Annabelle. Guys like that need to learn that sometimes, having money to throw around doesn't mean you can do whatever the hell you want. If this thing just gets quashed, that girl won't learn anything from this. Nothing will change, and she'll grow up to be a horrible human being because she never had to live with the consequences of her actions."

"She's already a horrible human being."

"I agree, honey, but she's seventeen years old. *Nobody's* life is over at seventeen. There's always time to turn it around."

"But she killed Sparkles!" Annie said angrily. "Why are you taking her side? Now I'm going to go to jail!"

"Annabelle Winchester, I am *not* taking her side, and you're not going to jail. Calm down and let me finish. That girl's daddy threatened me up and down. Threatened to sue, threatened to ruin our lives, threatened to get the book thrown at you, and threatened to have you tried as an adult. He made those threats and I have witnesses that saw him do it, like your Uncle Wade. I didn't, uh, exactly tell him other people were listening, but it's not a recording and their testimony will hold up in court if he tries anything."

Annie looked down at her lap. "What's going to happen now?"

"Right now? I'm going to take you back to your room so you can get cleaned up and get some rest. We'll get something to eat on the way there if you're hungry. Worst case scenario, you might be looking at a year in juvenile detention for assault."

Annie looked up, eyes wide, feeling sick. "A year?" She couldn't hold back the tears anymore. "It's not fair. You said to always finish a fight. You said."

"Hey now, baby girl," her father said, putting his arm around her. "I didn't mean you just beat the shit out of someone who wrongs you, even if they have it coming. This is the real world, honey. There are consequences for your actions, even if you thought they were justified. Juvy ain't the end of the world. It won't keep you out of most schools."

"I don't care about schools. I want to go to space."

"I know. Don't worry, some time in the pokey won't keep you out of the Spaceflight Academy or the Defense Forces, either. You're going to be okay."

"But I don't want to go to juvy," Annie cried. "It's not fair!" *How is he letting this happen?*

Her father gently brushed the hair out of Annie's eyes. "Come on, honey, no more tears for right now. I'm going to talk to the judge and see if there is another arrangement we can work out. You're a minor, you're under a lot of stress because your mom is pregnant and your father is leaving, it was your first time alone in the city, and a drugged-up hooplehead poisoned your horse. Those are some pretty extenuating circumstances. I called my lawyer and she's pretty confident we'll be able to make a deal."

"But..." Annie protested.

"No 'buts' now," her father said. "There's nothing for it. Come on, let's get you out of here. Captain Blackwood gave me a pass for two days, so I'm here for you."

Annie sniffled as she stood up. She felt sick. It was all too much. "I wish I could just go with you, Daddy," she said. "I just want to leave this stupid planet."

Annie's father stood up and looked thoughtful for a moment. "Yes, well, one thing at a time. Let's get you signed out."

It had taken some legwork, and he'd had to call in some favors, but Marcus was able to get his daughter a court hearing the very next day. This was fortunate, because he was scheduled to lift off from New Austin shortly after that, and didn't want to have to ask Captain Blackwood to delay for his sake.

Marcus had been afraid that Ellie would go ballistic when he told her what happened. Annie had tried beer and beaten a girl so badly that she'd been hospitalized. She was mad at Annie but she was furious at Victoria Alexander and her sleazy father. She considered him and his entire family a bunch of degenerates who were a blight on New Austin. Marcus happened to agree, but they were a blight with a lot of money and good lawyers. He had to take that into consideration.

Marcus' lawyer, an old friend of his named Serendipity Kim, represented Annie during the hearing. The Alexander family lawyer, a well-known, high-priced celebrity attorney, made an appearance and demanded the hearing be dismissed. He insisted an adult criminal trial be scheduled, but the judge wasn't having any of it. Especially, Marcus noted with a smile, when both Wade and Captain Blackwood herself testified to the judge that they'd overheard the conversation wherein Mr. Alexander threatened Marcus and his family. The judge had dismissed him from the courtroom, and made it clear that the Alexander family was to leave the Winchesters alone.

Upon the advice of Ms. Kim and her father, Annie pled guilty, as a minor, to an assault charge. It could have been a lot worse, but given the circumstances the judge didn't want to throw the book at her. By old law going back to the founding of the colony, stealing or harming another colonist's livestock was a serious offense on New Austin. Given that, Ms. Kim was able to convince the judge that Annie didn't deserve to go through an adult criminal trial.

The question remained of what was to be done with her? Marcus knew there was no way the judge was going to let her be released into the custody of her mother, especially since Victoria wasn't going to get off so easily either. In trying to calm Annie down, Marcus had downplayed juvenile detention somewhat. It wasn't horrible, but he didn't want his daughter out doing manual labor projects with a bunch of underage criminals, separated from both of her parents and far from home. She was distraught enough with everything going on, especially with her horse having been poisoned, and he feared juvy would make a bad situation for Annie a lot worse.

Not having many options, Marcus approached Captain Black-wood with a proposal: Annie would be released to her custody and would serve as a crewmember-in-training for the duration of the mission. Space was dangerous, yes, but at least he didn't have to worry about her being all alone, or getting attacked by some crazy delinquent.

Captain Blackwood surprised Marcus by readily agreeing to the proposal. She had the bunk space, she explained, and such arrangements were quite common on her adopted homeworld of Heinlein. A shipboard environment offered discipline and structure that would straighten out a rowdy teenager. She'd be in a secure environment, and the mission to Zanzibar wasn't as risky to the ship itself as, say, pirate hunting.

Annie, predictably, was thrilled at the proposition. Ellie, on the other hand, was adamantly against it. She wasn't going to allow her daughter to leave her for up to two years, with no real way to communicate with home. "I'm losing my husband," she'd said, "I'll be damned if I'm losing my daughter too!" She especially wasn't happy with some of the hazard clauses in the proposed contract, similar to the one Marcus had signed.

Captain Blackwood must have taken a shine to Annie, Marcus thought, because she was being very helpful through the entire ordeal. She'd sat down with Ellie for an hour, over coffee and tea, explaining exactly what shipboard life was like, the risks, the realities, and what Annie would be in for. Marcus didn't know what she said to her, exactly, but after they were done talking Ellie agreed. She broke down and cried, hugging Annie tightly, but she agreed to let her go.

And why not, Marcus thought to himself. He was only a couple years older than Annie was now when he'd enlisted in the Espatier Corps, and he'd been a hell of a lot less mature than his daughter was. At least this way he could keep an eye on her, and she'd be a very long way from Carlos and other teenage boys. Not that Carlos was a bad kid. He'd gone to the hearing to testify on Annie's behalf. He'd stood up for her and beaten the shit out of a drugged-up adult. If Annie insisted on growing up and having a boyfriend, Carlos seemed like an alright kid.

Marcus was relieved, and Annie ecstatic, when the judge agreed to the proposal. She was to be released into the custody of Captain Catherine Blackwood for a period of not less than one local year. He reminded Annie that if, upon her return, the captain reported that she was not satisfied with her service, that she could be sent straight to juvenile detention. Annie said that she understood, the judge banged his gavel, and that was that.

So it was that shortly before he was supposed to leave New Austin, Marcus found himself outside of a courthouse in Aterrizaje with his wife, his daughter, his new captain, her XO, Wade, and his lawyer. It was enough to make a man's head spin, but he was happy that it had all more or less worked out. Annie had loved Sparkles dearly, and losing the horse was devastating for her. Shipboard life, with the discipline and work that it entailed, would keep her from dwelling on the loss.

Annie approached her parents in tears nonetheless. "Thank you, Daddy," she said, hugging each of her parents tightly. "Thank you, Mom."

Ellie was crying too as she held her daughter. "You be careful, do you hear me?" She looked over at Marcus. "You bring my little girl home safely, Marcus. You bring her home to meet her sibling."

"We'll be home before you know it, baby," Marcus said, even though they all knew that wasn't true. "I'll look after her."

"Please don't make me regret this," Ellie said. "Please, Marcus. Look after our little girl."

Captain Blackwood approached. "I hate to interrupt, but we do need to be going. Crewman Apprentice Winchester has a lot to learn and will be doing a lot of on the job training. I'll keep her busy." She looked Marcus' wife in the eyes. "And I'll keep her safe."

Ellie nodded, wiping the tears from her cheeks. Annie stood up a little straighter and thanked the captain for her help.

"Don't thank me yet, crewman," Captain Blackwood said. "I promise you this will be the hardest thing you've ever done."

The resolute expression on Annie's face made Marcus proud. "I won't let you down...Captain," she said.

Captain Blackwood nodded at Annie, then looked over at her executive officer. "Wolfram? She's all yours."

Nodding, the stern, Germanic spacer turned to face Annie. "Crewman, come with me. We're heading directly back to the ship. We don't have time for a proper orientation before liftoff. You'll need to pay attention and learn fast."

"Okay," Annie said.

Wolfram leaned down so that he was eye to eye with Annie. "Crewman, when addressing an officer, you *will* address him by his title and call him sir. Am I making myself clear?"

Annie's eyes were wide. "Y...yes sir!"

"Good," Wolfram said. "This is not like the netcast shows, Crewman. The *Andromeda* is not staffed by a band of plucky misfits. Space is a harsh mistress, an alien environment unfit for human life. We survive there only through good order, discipline, and hard work. Failure to do your duty, and do it correctly, will get you and others killed. *Do you understand*?"

"Yes, sir!" Annie replied, standing up so straight she looked like she was going to break. Marcus remembered his first day in boot camp and tried not to laugh at his poor daughter.

"Good," Wolfram said. "Now come with me." He looked up at Captain Blackwood. "*Kapitänin*," he said with a nod, and led Annie off to the rental van.

Captain Blackwood looked apologetically at Eleanor Winchester. "Wolfram can be tough, but he's fair. He runs a tight ship. Annie's in good hands. We'll make a spacer out of her."

Ellie looked thoughtful. "You know what? Maybe this is good. She's out here drinking beer, getting into fights, and who knows what else. She thinks she's all grown up now? Let her live by grown-up rules. She'll appreciate how good she had it."

Captain Blackwood nodded. "I need to be going myself. Mr. Winchester," she said, looking at Marcus, "you can take the rest of the day off to spend with your wife. We're in final preparations for our departure, but I don't need you on the ship for that. Just make sure your people are all accounted for and in place well before our scheduled launch."

"Yes ma'am," Marcus said. As the captain left, and his lawyer excused herself, he turned to Wade. "Hell of a day, huh?"

Wade agreed. "It worked out. Too bad about the horse, though."

"If I ever get my hands on the little bitch that did that to my daughter, I'm going to choke the life out of her. I'm glad Annie broke her face."

"I'm gonna take off, Boss," Wade said. "I'll screen the others and let them know we're on liberty until liftoff. Go spend some time with your wife."

"You should go visit your sexbot," Ellie said, a twinkle in her teary eye. "She probably misses you, all alone in that storage unit. You keep neglecting her and she'll start cheating on you with the other appliances."

Wade shook his head. "You know..."

Marcus laughed out loud. Ellie was sad, but she was tough. She'd get through this.

The Privateer Ship *Andromeda*
Capitol Starport, Aterrizaje
New Austin

Captain Catherine Blackwood steepled her fingers patiently as she reclined in her command chair. The entire crew was strapped in, either at their duty stations or in their racks. New Austin had made for a pleasant visit, but Catherine had business to attend to, and it was time she got underway. Her command screens showed her that everything was in order and that all systems were functioning as they should be. The ship rumbled quietly as the engines idled hot.

A window popped up on her screen. At the same time, a calm voice came over her headset. "*Andromeda*, this is traffic control. You are cleared for launch on your planned trajectory."

"Roger that, control. Thank you," Colin, who was up on the flight deck, replied. "*Andromeda* out."

A klaxon sounded and red lights flashed. All boards were still green. Satisfied, Catherine tapped her headset. "Colin, take us up."

"Roger that, Captain."

The low rumble of the idling engines grew into a throaty roar. The vibration increased to a rattle as the ship was buffeted by the thrust reflecting off the landing pad. All at once, the roar reached its crescendo, and Catherine was pressed back into her seat as the *Andromeda* left the surface of New Austin. She kept a watchful eye on her screens, even though she had complete confidence in her pilot and wasn't expecting trouble. Launch and landing were the two most dangerous parts of a ship's flight. An accident or failure that would, in space, be an annoyance, could be catastrophic during atmospheric flight.

On another of her displays, Catherine watched the dusty surface of New Austin recede into the distance as the *Andromeda* rocketed toward the heavens on a plume of smoke and fire. *My God, I do love it so,* she thought to herself with a smile.

Spaceport control contacted the *Andromeda* one last time. *"Andromeda, spaceport control. You have left our airspace. You are go for throttle-up. Safe travels."*

Colin replied crisply, "Roger that, spaceport control, we are go for throttle-up. Thank you. *Andromeda* out." He then announced over the intercom, "Stand by for throttle up. Three . . . two . . . one . . . mark."

On Colin's mark, he opened up the ship's engines a little more. Most spaceports had altitude and thrust restrictions on inbound and outbound ships. An engine sufficient for interplanetary travel could be extremely destructive to ground infrastructure if not managed safely. Catherine was pressed deeper into her acceleration seat as the ship rocketed away from the surface at four gravities. She was unable to suppress the wide grin that appeared on her face. She loved this part, the launch, screaming into the heavens on a tin can spitting hellfire. It was a sensation the very first astronauts on Ancient Earth had experienced, and it bound spacers of every era together.

Stuck in her chair until the ship reached escape velocity, Catherine had little to do unless disaster struck. Her crew was competent and her ship was in good order, just as it should be. She thought it would be unprofessional of her to gush to her crew about how proud she was of them, and how much she loved watching them work, but she made her feelings known in subtler ways. Still, just to keep herself from daydreaming too much, Catherine pulled up their planned trajectory on one of her displays.

In ninety-six hours, they would rendezvous with an automated fueling station in high solar orbit. Getting from the surface into space consumed a lot of propellant, so much so that larger, capital-class ships were typically not capable of atmospheric flight. This limited their versatility and left them reliant on orbital infrastructure for support and maintenance, but it allowed for hull designs much larger than even the biggest of atmospheric ships.

Her reaction mass tankage topped off, the *Andromeda* would then boost along a trajectory that would take them to the Lone Star System's third, and least used, transit point. It was there that her long journey would *really* begin.

I hope you're still alive, Cecil.

I hate this part, Marcus thought to himself. He'd spent plenty of time aboard ships while in the Espatiers, but he'd never been fond of getting shot into space on a thermonuclear blowtorch. Travel from civilized spaceports generally had an impressive safety record, but Marcus could never shake the feeling that the ship was going to rattle itself apart, leaving him to plummet to his death.

Annie, on the other hand, seemed to be enjoying herself. "This is amazing!" she said over the intercom. The strain of the acceleration did nothing to dampen her enthusiasm. The eight newcomers to the *Andromeda* were each secured in their individual berths, which doubled as acceleration couches, but had an open channel with one another so they could chat. Wade remarked that it had been a long time since he'd done this, but seemed fine. Ken Tanaka had fallen asleep somehow. Devree Starlighter cried out with excitement as the *Andromeda* hit four gees; she found the whole thing as thrilling as Annie did. Benjamin Halifax grunted tersely and muttered the occasional obscenity. Jeremiah Hondo seemed perfectly at home under acceleration, and chatted with Wade. Randall Markgraf joined the conversation briefly, complaining of light-headedness, before blacking out.

The team had nothing else to do while the *Andromeda* was accelerating at more than one gee, and Annie was too much of a novice to be allowed to roam the ship while it was under high acceleration. At two gravities, Marcus recalled, you could get up and walk around. It was like carrying another man on your back. You just had to be careful about falling down. Many spacers wore shoes with arch supports, and swore by them.

At four gravities, though, it wasn't safe to move about unaided. A fall that would result in only a bruised butt and ego under normal circumstances could break bones and burst blood vessels at four times the gravity that the human body was designed for. Falling any kind of a distance could kill a man as if he'd flung himself off of a building. Driving the point home, a small red light above the hatch to his berth informed Marcus that it was sealed. He couldn't get out if he wanted to.

It's a good thing I'm not claustrophobic. The kind of berth he found himself in was often derisively referred to as a *coffin,* but it was actually comparatively spacious. Marcus had enough room to stretch, move about some, and climb in and out without bumping his head. That in and of itself was a luxury he would have paid good money for on more than one long haul in a Concordiat Fleet troopship. "Hey kiddo," he said, straining under his own weight. "How you holding up?"

"I'm okay!" Annie insisted, though she sounded a little less enthusiastic now.

It's also a good thing there's a relief tube in here, because I have to piss. Being compressed under four times one's normal weight tended to dramatically exacerbate a full bladder. "Good. I'll be right back," Marcus grunted to the group. "I gotta piss."

"Good luck," Wade said with a strained grin. "Don't hurt yourself."

"That'd be a hell of a thing," Marcus mused. "All this planning and preparation, and I get incapacitated trying to take a leak." Chuckling to himself, Marcus signed off of the group chat and strained to get the relief apparatus into place.

This is the first day, he thought to himself, straining to urinate under his present apparent weight of 332 kilograms. *What have you gotten yourself into?*

Zanzibar
Danzig-5012 Solar System
City of Freeport, Equatorial Region

Freeport wasn't much of a city, but it was the only real city left on Zanzibar and the closest thing the desolate rock had to a capital. At its center was the lonely planet's only functioning spaceport, and a town had sprung up around it in the aftermath of the war. Every few local weeks or so, Zak was permitted to take his assistant, Anna Kay, into town to gather supplies and do research.

At first, Aristotle Lang had sent one of his goons to act as an escort. Zak made it a point to appear too afraid to try to escape, and eventually the old warlord stopped worrying so much about him. These days, Zak was permitted to take Anna and roam Freeport at will. Lang still had spies everywhere, and he was forced to wear a tracking device that recorded everything he said and everywhere he went.

It didn't work that well, though. Zanzibar's satellite network was patchy and unreliable at best. There were times when the entire planetary network would go down, and it could be days before someone would get it running again. The device itself was old and had not been properly maintained. In any case, Zak had more initiative than Lang imagined he did, and he was good with electronics. He had long since been able to hack his electronic babysitter, and there were plenty of dead zones in the city where it would lose contact with its home station. Even Cecil didn't know about this—it wasn't that Zak didn't trust him, it was just that Cecil sometimes had a hard time keeping his stupid mouth

136

shut, especially when he was in bed with the woman that Lang had given him.

It's better this way, Zak thought to himself. *If I get caught, they probably won't kill Cecil, since he didn't know anything about it.*

Freeport was a crowded, noisy, dirty, and dangerous city. It was a cluttered mess of poverty, crime, and advanced off-world technology. Those who survived the Maggots' assault on the planet and its desolate aftermath were a hardy folk. "Native" Zanzibarans tended to be clannish, suspicious of off-worlders, fiercely loyal to their own, and tough. Their ways often seemed strange or even cruel to outsiders, but they were the descendants of the survivors of this world's second apocalypse. As backward and sometimes barbaric as they seemed, Zak had a lot of respect for them. If you could survive on Zanzibar, you could probably survive anywhere.

The "natives" weren't the only people on Zanzibar, however, especially in the notional city of Freeport. When he'd first arrived, Zak had been surprised by the amount of commerce and interstellar traffic coming and going through the system. With no planetary government and no official ties to the rest of inhabited space, Zanzibar had become a hub for illicit trade of every kind. A few pirates made the planet their home port. Traders and corporations used the system for illegal or unethical deals that needed to be kept off the books. Criminals, fugitives, refugees, and exiles also often made it their home. Zanzibar was hard to get to, but it seemed to Zak that for a lot of people, that was the planet's best quality.

Freeport's streets were narrow, crowded, and cluttered. Structures had been haphazardly thrown up wherever the builders fancied over the years, and there was little rhyme or reason to it. The nicest buildings tended to be the oldest—prewar relics that had survived the alien bombardment. The newer stuff was either imported prefabs or structures cobbled together with locally acquired supplies. Most of them were dirty and many looked unsafe.

The streets were often too narrow and too crowded with pedestrian traffic for ground cars. As Zak and Anna wove through the crowds, they had to dodge bicycles, electric scooters, and even the occasional rickshaw to avoid being run over. Vendors peddled goods from carts or small trucks, shouting at passersby for business or loudly haggling with customers. Small shops lined the streets, selling every imaginable product, including weapons, drugs, prostitutes, and even livestock. The air stank of trash, an inadequate waste management system, and animals.

I hate this place, Zak thought to himself, not for the first time. Zanzibar's quaint, third-world charm wore off quickly, especially when the food gave you diarrhea and you witnessed a group of local teenagers beat a man and steal everything he had, including his shoes. In many ways, Zanzibar's tough conditions had brought out the worst in the people who lived here. Most seemed to carry a kill-or-be-killed, take-whatever-you-can attitude. Not unsurprising in people for whom day-to-day survival is an uncertain struggle, but still depressing.

As if Zak needed something else to be depressed about. *Focus.* The little program he'd written was about to start spoofing his tracking device, but it could only operate for so long before running the risk of the deception being detected. He had a limited window to get his real business in Freeport done. Anna would take care of the stuff he'd ostensibly set out to do, and hopefully that'd be enough to fool Lang's spies.

Zak took a quick look around, then leaned over to his assistant. "It's time, Anna. I'm going to split off here. Just do your shopping. Please be careful."

"You're the one who needs to be careful," Anna retorted. "I can take care of myself. If Lang finds out what you are doing, he'll have you flayed alive."

Zak worried about his assistant. She was a dark-haired woman of Greek ancestry, hailing from the Concordiat colony of New Constantinople. She was a veritable encyclopedia of historical knowledge, and actually held doctorates from that colony's prestigious University Byzantium. She didn't talk about her family much, but he knew she came from a background of wealth and privilege... and she'd walked away from it all to go with him.

So Zak worried. They were unarmed, except for a few knives between them, and Freeport could be dangerous. A woman all alone in this trash heap could be subjected to worse things than just petty robberies and beatings. But Anna was Anna, with enough stubborn courage to dismiss Zak's concerns as more pointless worrying (which, he had to admit, he was prone to).

"You're not wrong," he said glumly. "But you're the only person on this damned planet I care about, so please be careful."

"I appreciate your sentimentality," she said, trying not to

sound aloof (she always sounded aloof despite her best efforts), "but we cannot lose sight of our objective."

She was right, of course. Zak nodded. "If I don't make it to our meetup point, you know what to do. I need to get going. If I'm late they'll get suspicious."

"Go, then," she said. "Mind yourself!"

"You know me." Zak gave her a lopsided grin. "I'm always careful."

Anna rolled her eyes, pulled her hood up over her head, and disappeared into the crowd.

Zak's contact was waiting for him as expected. The man was dressed in typically shabby Zanzibaran garb. He looked as if he just walked out of the shantytown on the outskirts of Freeport. His face was concealed by a common respirator and dust goggles. Had the man not given Zak the expected signal, he never would've picked him out of the crowd.

The mysterious individual told Zak to follow him, but after that said nothing. He led Zak on a winding path to the outskirts of Freeport, through alleys, markets, slums, and crowded streets. The off-world historian didn't blend in nearly as well as his guide, and Zak began to get nervous. It wasn't good for foreigners to be in this part of Freeport. The shantytown was dangerous. There were people here that would kill a man for his shoes, and to their eyes the historian probably looked like a prime target: a rich off-worlder, out of his element.

As if sensing his concern, the guide paused and turned to Zak. "Do not worry," he said, his voice sounding strangely mechanical. "You are safe with me. I am called Strelok."

"Where are we going?" Zak asked nervously. "I was told not to come to this side of town."

"That is because your *benefactor's* men are not welcome here. They are rivals to the gang that controls the shantytown. They are less likely to have spies here. Anyone caught working with them is usually killed."

That didn't make Zak feel any better. He took a deep breath through his respirator. "I've been planted with a tracking device. I created a program to fool it, but I need to be careful."

Strelok looked at a handheld device. "I see. It's crude, nothing I can't block. Will your program provide false location data, or will this leave a blank spot on your record? Will it draw attention? Can you take it off?"

"It falsifies my location data," Zak said. "Shows me moving back and forth across the bazaar and market areas. It's a compilation of previous visits to town, randomized and stitched together. If you can jam the signal it won't show up as a lack of location information." Zak rolled up his pant leg, showing a metal bracelet locket around his ankle. "I can't get it off, though."

Strelok said, "very well," and double-checked the screen of his handheld. He seemed satisfied that the device was being neutralized. "Follow me."

Zak nodded, and followed as his guide continued on. The shantytown was constructed of whatever materials could be found to build with. There were a few intact prewar buildings, and a few ruins of old buildings, but mostly it was row after row of cobbled-together shacks and hovels, where Zanzibar's poor scraped a living off of an inhospitable planet. Improvised moisture condensers collected what little water there was from the air. Crude solar panels provided a modicum of electricity, which was necessary for survival. There was no wood to burn on Zanzibar, and the winters were terribly cold.

Beneath the crumbling ruin of a highway overpass stood a sturdy-looking prewar building. It had once been two stories, but the top floor had been blasted away, leaving only part of a wall. The windows had heavy metal plates bolted over them, and the door appeared to be reinforced as well. Behind the building was the crude wall that surrounded Freeport and kept out those deemed not fit to live in the ramshackle city.

"What is this place?" Zak asked. Strelok didn't answer. He rapped on the metal door three times and waited. A camera on the outside of the building was trained on him, and Zak had the uneasy feeling that someone was hiding nearby, pointing a weapon at his head. After a few agonizingly long moments, the door clunked metallically as it unlocked and swung open. The guide motioned for Zak to follow and disappeared into the darkness inside. Zak was hesitant to enter, but he could feel eyes on him. If he turned back now, he doubted he'd make it out of the shantytown in one piece. With nothing else to do, he steeled himself and followed his guide.

The building was dimly lit and dusty. There were multiple

cots stacked against the walls, and what looked like stockpiled rations and provisions. It was some kind of safe house or hideout.

"Were you followed?"

Zak jumped a little at the voice from the darkness. Out of the shadows stepped a silver-haired woman with deep lines in her face. She had a boxy flechette gun leveled at Zak's chest. He quickly raised his hands and tried to think of what to say. He had no idea if he'd been followed! He was a historian, not a spy!

Before the woman painted the walls with the contents of Zak's torso, Strelok stepped in and addressed her. They both spoke Commerce English with the same odd accent, but did so almost in whispers. Zak couldn't quite make out what they were saying. Some of the words he did overhear didn't make sense, as if they were mixing languages. The woman had a dull gray synthetic plate on the side of her head, at her temple, but whatever had once been attached there was now gone.

After a few tense moments of heated but quiet discussion, the woman lowered her weapon and addressed Zak. "My comrade insists that you can be trusted, young man. He tells me this even though you are in the employ of Aristotle Lang. Tell me, then, how can we trust you?"

"I don't work for Lang willingly," Zak said defensively. "I'm a hostage."

"Hostages don't get to wander around Freeport unescorted."

"I spent a lot of time convincing him I'm not a flight risk. Besides, Lang cares about my employer, whose family is very wealthy. He's the real hostage. I just got swept up in the whole affair."

"You do not belong on Zanzibar, young man. What is it you do here? Who is this employer?"

Zak removed his respirator and took a deep breath. The building was pressurized and had a functioning filter. "My name is Zak Mesa. I'm a historian. I spent years researching the pre- and postwar history of Zanzibar. Much was lost in the war, as I'm sure you know, especially regarding the native species that lived here millions of years ago. I published a dissertation covering several theories as to what happened, and my work slowly circulated through inhabited space. I was living on Columbia at the time. Out of nowhere, I'm contacted by a man named Cecil Blackwood. He tells me he's basically a big deal on his homeworld of Avalon, he tells me that he wants to go on an expedition to Zanzibar, and he's willing to pay me a lot of money to do it. I jumped on his offer. It sounded like an adventure, and it sure sounded better than the dead-end job I was doing there."

"Why did this Cecil Blackwood want to come to Zanzibar?" the woman asked.

"Alien artifacts," Zak said quietly. "Items from just about any alien species are worth a lot of money. But stuff from the ancient, native Zanzibari? It's exceedingly rare in a market full of exceedingly rare things. They're priceless."

"So you came here, seeking treasure, to rob the tombs of the dead?"

Zak's eyes sunk to the floor. "It sounds bad when you put it like that. But that's why I'm here. I've heard that you folks can help me."

"What is it you want from us? We do not traffic in alien relics."

Strelok spoke up then. "He wishes to send a message off-world."

"You could do that from the communications facility in Freeport," the woman said suspiciously.

"Uh, no I *can't*," Zak replied. "If I tried, one of Aristotle Lang's spies would see me, and he'd have me skinned or something. He may not have power in the shantytown, but he has spies and contacts all over the city proper."

"Indeed, he does," the woman agreed. Her skin was very pale, but her eyes were sharp and piercing. "So you came to us? Why?"

"I've been doing nothing but researching the history of Zanzibar since I made planetfall last year. Cecil was able to throw enough money around to get people to talk to an off-worlder about the history of this place. I learned a lot, stuff that's not generally known to the rest of inhabited space."

"Yes. Zanzibar has very little contact with anywhere else. That is one of the reasons we chose it."

"Money talks. It was through talking to the locals that I first heard rumors of your group. Zanzibarans are so clannish and paranoid that they avoid off-worlders as much as possible. They didn't know much, and it was hard separating rumors from the truth. But I determined that a group of political refugees from the Orlov Combine had formed a colony on Zanzibar, and were maintaining a low profile while they smuggled more of their fellows away from Orlov's Star."

The silver-haired woman looked thoughtful for a moment, unconsciously touching the plate attached to the side of her head. One corner of her mouth curled up in a lopsided grin. "Well done, Mr. Mesa. You came looking for us, and now you have found us. The question is, why should we help you? Even bringing you here entails quite a bit of risk."

"Look, I've spent more time with Aristotle Lang than I like. I'm sure he's heard of you, but I don't think he's worried about you."

"It is not Lang that we fear," the woman said sternly. "If the Orlov Combine were to become aware of our efforts here, what do you think would happen?"

"The Combine has no power here," Zak managed. "I mean, do they? They're pretty isolationist."

The woman's eyes narrowed. "I know full well the nature of their policies, Mr. Mesa. They are indeed isolationist. They are also xenophobic and paranoid. If there is one thing that would cause them to send a punitive military expedition, it's the knowledge that there is a colony of defectors living on an undefended world, who have been smuggling out refugees and dissidents for decades. If the Combine sends a fleet out and simply blasts Freeport to dust, who will stop them? Who will even care? No one cares about Zanzibar. You risk not only our operation, Mr. Mesa, but everyone on this miserable world. So I ask you again: why should we help you?"

Zak's mind raced. The woman's eyes were boring holes in him. Strelok was immutable, impossible to read. Zak feared that he was once again in over his head, and that the wrong answer would bring him to a swift and unpleasant end. *This was a bad idea. One more bad idea at the end of a chain of bad ideas.*

"Listen to me," Zak began carefully. "Please. Lang isn't interested in the ancient artifacts out of some historical curiosity. He means to sell them to the highest bidder. He intends to use the money to buy weapons from off-world, heavy weapons that you can't find on Zanzibar, like power armor, missiles, and combat robots."

"It is no surprise that a petty warlord enjoys such toys, Mr. Mesa."

"He doesn't want them so he can *enjoy* them! I believe he means to take control of Freeport! Think about *that* for a moment, will you? He may be a petty warlord now, but what happens when he gets his hands on military-grade hardware, takes control of this stupid planet's only functioning spaceport, and has a vast supply of impossibly valuable artifacts to sell on the black market?"

The woman's eyes widened slightly.

"What happens to your colony then?" Zak asked more quietly. "Do you think for a moment that Lang won't buy weapons from the Combine? They'll probably be his biggest trading partner. Orlov's Star is the closest major inhabited system, after all."

Strelok removed his cowl. Like the woman, he had a plate embedded at the temple, an attachment point for some device that was no longer there. "This is why I brought him to you, Maggie," he said quietly. "If there is even a chance any of this coming to pass . . ." he trailed off.

The woman, Maggie, nodded slowly. "You were right to do so." She looked thoughtful for a moment, then addressed Zak once more. "Mr. Mesa, you have made a compelling argument. But I cannot make this decision alone. I will need to consult with the others."

Zak felt a pit forming in his stomach. He couldn't risk multiple meetings with these people while whatever committee they had deliberated and discussed the matter. Sooner or later his luck would run out. "It is extremely risky for me to get away like this," he said, "and I do not want to risk sending you a message remotely, even if it's encrypted. If Lang even suspects that I'm talking to someone on the outside . . . well, let's just say that I've seen him crucify people."

Maggie raised an eyebrow. "Crucify?"

"Yeah, crucify. Like from the Christian Bible? Ancient Rome? He takes people, nails them to a big cross, and leaves them up there to die slowly. And that's what he'll do to all of you, in a heartbeat, if he thinks it'll get him weapons from the Combine. So whatever meeting you need to have, I suggest you have it soon."

"I am afraid I am not familiar with the myths of Ancient Earth, but you have made your point. You need not be concerned. While you were talking, I contacted those I need to discuss this matter with, and have relayed to them our conversation in full." There was a pause, as if she were listening to a voice Zak could not hear. She probably was. "We will help you send your message. First we will need to know what it is you wish to say, and to whom you wish to send it. You can record it here, if you are ready, but we cannot send it right away. We will have to wait until a ship comes to Zanzibar that can carry your message. Couriers do not come here often, but they do come here. It will take some time, but your message will be sent out."

A euphoric wave of relief washed over Zak, so much so that he wanted to sit down. "My God...thank you. Thank you so much. I'll do whatever it is you need, whatever I can do. Thank you."

"What I do not understand," Maggie said, "is what you think will become of you. Are you calling for a rescue?"

"No. This is bigger than me. There's more at stake than saving my own skin. It's not right that a madman like Lang can rob the graves of the dead to buy weapons to further terrorize the people here. Zanzibar has suffered enough."

"We can keep you safe, Mr. Mesa. You needn't go back. You can stay with us, and Aristotle Lang will never find you."

"I appreciate the offer, but no I can't. My partner, Anna, is shopping for supplies in Freeport. That's the pretense we used to come here. If I don't come back, Lang will kill her, or worse."

"It is risky, but we may be able to get her to safety before she leaves the city."

"It's...it's not just her. It's Cecil."

"The Avalonian?"

"The same. He's not a bad man. He just made some very bad decisions, and I made most of them with him. I can't leave him like that. Lang probably won't kill him if I disappear, but he'll do terrible things to him all the same. Me searching for that vault keeps Lang happy, and that keeps Cecil safe. I can't just save my own skin and leave him to his fate. It's not right. He stuck his neck out to save me from Lang more than once."

"Your loyalty is admirable, Mr. Mesa. It gives us more confidence in your intentions. Are you ready to record your message?"

"I think so, yes."

"Very well. Where would you like this message to go? I hope you don't expect to send it to the Concordiat Security Council on Earth."

"What? No. No, I have a better idea. I'll address my message to the Historical, Archaeological, and Anthropological Society of Columbia. HAASCA has ties to the most prestigious universities on Columbia, the colonial government, and its counterparts on other worlds. They know me there. I've presented dissertations and published papers with them. They'll listen. They'll bring it to the right people. It's the best hope I have."

"Very well, Mr. Mesa," Maggie said. "The camera is ready. Stand over there when you're ready to record your message."

"I also want to upload some data from my handheld."

"If you insist," Strelok said. "Give it to me. I will copy the data and we will send it with your message."

A few moments later, after smoothing his clothes and going over what he wanted to say, Zak stepped into the indicated corner. A camera mounted to the ceiling was aimed at him; Maggie and Strelok fell silent and indicated that he should begin. He cleared his throat and said, "my name is Zachary Dionysus Mesa, formerly of the University of Columbia on the colony of the same name. This message is intended for my peers and fellow scholars of the Historical, Archaeological, and Anthropological Society."

Zak fetched from a pocket one of the ancient alien rune stones, so well preserved after millions of years. "I am presently stranded on the frontier world of Zanzibar, in the Danzig-5012 system. I am being held captive by a brutal warlord named Aristotle Lang. This artifact is a relic from the ancient Zanzibari species, who vanished four million standard years ago. Against my will, I am being forced by Lang to hunt for and turn over these artifacts. He intends to sell them on the black market and use the money to buy weapons.

"I send this message not as a plea for rescue. It is likely my fate will have already been decided by the time anyone receives this. This is a plea for intervention. The people of Zanzibar live in poverty and fear. Warlords and bandits control everything outside of the city of Freeport, and the planet is a refuge for pirates, criminals, and smugglers. These artifacts are the last remnants of an extinct species. We know so little about the Zanzibari, and we still don't know what happened to them or what killed their homeworld. Colonial researchers were working on this same problem over a century ago, when the Maggots attacked. They hid everything to save it from destruction, and to prevent looters from stealing it later on.

"Don't let the efforts and sacrifices of these people be in vain. Don't let a madman like Lang rob the graves of extinct beings so he can spread more misery and suffering on an already miserable world. The records left behind by my predecessors indicate that they were hiding something big, some major discovery. I have not yet ascertained what; the xenoarchaeological program was secretive and compartmentalized. It could be something dangerous. In any case these artifacts cannot be allowed to flood the black market unchecked. Once they get off-world, they'll never be recovered, and so much knowledge will be lost forever. Something must be done."

Zak took a deep breath, and looked up. "This is Zak Mesa, from Zanzibar. Uh, signing off."

Maggie seemed satisfied. "Well said, Mr. Mesa. Our people will edit your message and incorporate the data you indicated. As soon as a ship arrives that can carry your message, we will get it sent off."

"My God, thank you," Zak said, relieved. "Thank you so much. I do need to be going, though. Lang's spies will grow suspicious."

"Very well," Maggie said. "Strelok will escort you back to the market. Try to stay alive, Mr. Mesa."

Zak managed a weak smile. "No promises, but I'll do my best."

The Privateer Ship *Andromeda*
Deep Space
JAC-83-45891 System

With a silent flash, a ripple in the quantum foam, and a pulse of x-ray radiation, the *Andromeda* winked into existence one hundred and forty million kilometers from a red dwarf star known only as JAC-83-45891. It would take her a hundred and ninety-nine hours on the planned trajectory to swing across the system to the next transit point. Such was the unglamorous reality of interstellar travel—countless hours with little do while the ship coasted through one empty system after another. This system had no planets or asteroids, or anything of note. It was simply one stop of many on the *Andromeda*'s long journey.

Down in the crew compartment, Marcus Winchester's head was spinning. He fumbled for his space sickness bag, feeling severely nauseated, but couldn't muster the necessary fine motor function to grasp it. It mocked him, tumbling lazily in the air a few centimeters out of his reach. Every time he reached for it, it simply glided out of the way, spinning and dancing merrily in freefall.

"Fuck you, bag!" Marcus growled. At least, that's what he intended to say. What actually came out of his mouth sounded more like "F-f-f-fuuuuu—yoooo..." accompanied by a spray of spittle. The droplets of Marcus' saliva joined the vomit bag in its zero-gravity dance, orbiting it and shimmering in the light like so many tiny stars. The lights in Marcus' berth flickered unevenly, and his display screens remained dark as the system struggled to reboot.

What Marcus was experiencing was formally known as the Vestal-Black Effect, named for the two physicists who first postulated it. In over a millennium of effort, no truly effective counter to the effect, known colloquially as "transit shock," had ever been devised. It affected the human mind and electronic devices alike, and was thought to be the byproduct of these complex systems being shunted from one star to another, effectively leaving the physical universe for an infinitesimally short amount of time. That kind of space-time displacement had side effects, and the side effects were unpleasant.

It had been years since Marcus had experienced transit, and he was all the worse for wear because of it. With a grunt and a lunge, he managed to snag the wayward vomit bag just as his acceleration restraints locked. With both hands he brought the bag to his mouth and threw up. Acrid fluids burned his nose and mouth, and made his eyes water. He desperately held it to his mouth, dry heaving several times, before sealing it and releasing the bag of puke to float around his berth.

I forgot how much I hate this. His head was mushy, his eyes were still half focused, and his thought processes were slow. It was like waking up after going on the worst bender ever. His motor skills were coming back, though; he successfully retrieved his water bottle on the second try. His berth stunk of sweat and vomit, and was growing uncomfortably warm. The environmental systems hadn't turned over yet. *And she wants to be a spacer, she says.* His daughter had been in cold sleep when they made the long journey from Hayden to New Austin. She'd never experienced the misery of transit shock.

Until now. Through the throbbing of his head, Marcus remembered that his daughter was on the ship with him. *Why is she here? What's her name again?* He clenched his eyes shut, trying to concentrate through the pounding in his skull, as he struggled to remember his daughter's name. *Starts with an "a"... Anna. Ann. Annie.* "Fuck," he said aloud, before having another drink of water.

TAP TAP TAP.

Marcus froze. It sounded like someone had just tapped on the hatch of his berth. *Did I imagine that?* He strained to listen, but heard nothing but the air circulation system and other ambient ship noises as the *Andromeda*'s systems slowly came back online.

TAP TAP TAP. He definitely heard it that time. Somebody was rapping on the hatch. Marcus strained to sit up enough to see past his feet to where the hatch was. He was still restrained in his acceleration couch (which was also his bed), and didn't know if he had the dexterity to get the restraints unfastened. He tapped the panel on the wall that was supposed to open the shutter, revealing the small window in the hatch. After four tries, the system finally responded and the shutters opened.

Black eyes studied Marcus from behind blood-matted hair. A stained, tattered purple scarf hung from the girl's neck, her face was shrouded in shadow and confusion, but Marcus immediately knew who she was. He covered his face with his hands and tried not to scream. His heart raced, his head spun, and a pit of cold fear formed in his chest. *TAP TAP TAP. TAP TAP TAP.*

"Go away!" Marcus shouted, his eyes still clenched shut. He opened them in horror when he realized the hatch was being unsealed. Blinding white light poured in as the door slid open. "Leave me alone!" he cried.

A reassuring woman's voice answered. "You're okay! Hey! Look at me!"

Marcus' eyes slowly came into focus, and so did the haggard-looking young woman drifting just outside of his berth. Her hair was tied in a tight bun, and what looked like vomit stained part of her sage green flight suit. She had a medical bag in her hands.

"My name is Felicity," she said. "I'm a medic. You're experiencing severe transit shock."

"No shit," Marcus managed.

"What did you see? I think you were hallucinating."

Marcus was quiet for a moment. "Nothing," he lied. "It was nothing." The dead girl from Mildenhall would never let him go.

"All of you groundhogs are having bad reactions," Felicity continued. "Here," she said, producing an auto-injector. "This will level you off."

"I don't need—gah!" Marcus wasn't able to finish his sentence before Felicity jabbed the needle into this thigh.

"The hell you don't," she mused. "I don't want to get puked on again, if it's all the same to you."

Marcus' heart rate slowed as the chemical concoction made its way through his veins. The overwhelming sense of anxiety faded away, and his head stopped spinning. "Is my daughter okay?"

"The kid?" Felicity asked. "Don't worry, I checked on her first. She's doing okay, better than the rest of you. Is this your first time translating or something? Did we just pop your quantum cherry?"

"Believe it or not, no," Marcus said. "It's just been a long time. Ugh." He shook his head. "So, which one of us puked on you? Rest assured, I won't let him live it down."

Fastened into her seat on the command deck, Catherine idly sipped nutrient- and electrolyte-infused water while she waited for the dizziness to reside. Even experienced spacers were not immune to transit shock. Neither, for that matter, were the *Andromeda*'s systems. Catherine's own displays were mostly offline, leaving her to look through a few blank transparent screens. One screen was solid blue, with a standard fatal system error message in white text.

The more complex the system, the more susceptible it was to the ravages of transit shock. Usually systems would come back online after a few minutes, but not always. As a safety measure, most ships, especially those operating alone, had as many redundancies and manual backups installed into their systems as possible. Fully automated ships were rarely trusted for anything more than in-system duty, or routine transits between star systems (and unmanned ships were generally prohibited from transporting human cargo).

There was only so much one could do with manual or analog backups, however, especially regarding something as complex as an interstellar-capable ship. Catherine waited patiently, relaxing in her chair and trying to get her bearings, as three separate computers ran test problems over and over again. When all three agreed on the answer, systems would automatically be brought back online, and the *Andromeda* would be underway again.

"Status report," Catherine ordered.

Luis Azevedo rubbed his eyes, then looked groggily away from his myriad of displays. "Captain, life-support is one hundred percent. Engineering reports the reactor is in the green. The transit motivator will be fully cycled in approximately four hours. Medical reports no injuries, though our guests downstairs are still having a hard time with transit shock. Med Tech Lowlander got vomited on, and one of the mercenaries admitted that she saw a ghost."

Spacers' tales, going back more than a thousand years, often mentioned sightings of ghosts or apparitions on board a ship after completing a transit. The superstitious liked to say that when a ship translates between systems, it leaves the universe completely. When it returns, the tales went, it carries with it the souls of the restless dead who follow the ship to its next port.

Catherine didn't put much stock in any of the old stories. Transit shock was hard on the human mind. People hallucinated, especially if they were not used to it, and that's all there was to it. At least, that's what Catherine told herself, even though she'd seen some strange and unsettling things in her career. Shaking off her wandering thoughts, she focused on the task at hand. "Sensors?"

Nattaya Tantirangsi turned from her screens full of error messages and looked at her Captain apologetically. "Still not up and running, Skipper," she said. "Radar, infrared, and passive sensors are all being difficult. Optical tracking is online now, so we can eyeball it if we have to. We may have to pull some components on the main sensor suite though."

"I see. How long?"

"It'll take me about an hour, Skipper. I apologize. We should've done it after our last transit."

"It's quite alright, Nuchy," Catherine said, addressing the junior officer by her nickname. "These things are unpredictable. Get started on that. We'll navigate by the stars if we have to." She tapped a control that gave her voice communication with the ship's pilot. "Flight Deck, how are we doing?"

Colin sounded tired, but coherent, when he responded. "Five by five, Skipper. Aside from my scopes being down, all controls are responding. The autopilot crashed when I tried to reboot it, so I left it off for now. I've already laid in the course sent up from Astrogation. We can begin our boost anytime you like, ma'am."

Catherine smiled. "Flying by the seat of our pants, under manual control, while navigating by the stars. This is *real* spaceflight, ladies and gentlemen. Run final checks and prepare for acceleration. Let our guests know that they'll have gravity for a while. I'm sure they'll appreciate it."

Half an hour after transiting from the Lone Star system, Annabelle Winchester was hurriedly getting ready to report to the cargo deck for more OJT. She'd spent the entire flight from New Austin to the transit point getting a crash course on the day-to-day operations of the *Andromeda,* and the First Officer von Spandau had been right: it was *hard*. The ship's schedule was confusing at first, and she'd been working twelve hour shifts every day. There were texts she had to study, emergency procedures she had to memorize, and much she had to learn.

Cargomaster Kimball, her immediate supervisor, had explained to her that on a small ship like the *Andromeda*, every crewman must be able to do multiple jobs. Everyone had an assigned job, of course, but cross-training was highly encouraged, and the more skills and certifications a crewman had, the more useful he could potentially be. Kimball, for example, was the cargomaster. He was also the ship's extravehicular activity procedures expert, held a certification for a basic emergency medical technician, and had extensive training in damage control, emergency repair, and spaceflight firefighting.

Even being a cargomaster was more involved than Annie had assumed. Kimball was required to account for every gram of mass the ship was carrying. Not just the cargo, but consumables and reaction mass alike. It all had to be stowed and secured correctly, and the ship's cargo mass had to be symmetrically balanced around the axis of thrust. As supplies were consumed or cargo offloaded, everything had to be reshuffled to maintain that mass balance. Yet for all that, they had assigned Annie to Kimball because his area of responsibility was one of the *less* technical ones on the ship. Annie didn't know anything about engineering, software writing, electrical systems, plumbing, astrogation, or thermonuclear propulsion above what she'd learned in her primary school education. She was told she didn't need a lot of specialized training to move containers around and help clean the ship.

As she was leaving her berth, a klaxon sounded and the pilot announced that the ship would be getting underway. With a dull roar, the *Andromeda*'s engines ignited. Annie felt a sense of weight returning to her body as the ship hit one gravity of acceleration and held there. The pilot announced that the burn would last for ninety minutes, and Annie was grateful for it. She wasn't used to freefall and had been on a strict liquid diet as her body adjusted. Being dropsick was a miserable experience that had left Annie wondering what she'd gotten herself into.

A few minutes later she was greeted by Systems Tech Daye, one of the crewmen who seemed to have many jobs. Annie had worked with Daye a lot since leaving New Austin and thought he was nice. He was a pale, skinny young man with long, dark hair that he kept tied up in a bun while on duty. "How are you doing, groundhog?" he asked, politely letting her go down the ladder first.

"Transit shock wasn't as bad as I thought it would be," Annie said, climbing down to the cargo deck. "I guess my dad and his team all got sick."

"I saw that," Daye said. "Did you not get sick as well?"

"I did," Annie admitted as she reached the deck below, "but at least I didn't throw up on the medic like that guy Markgraf did."

"I may have laughed at her when that happened," Daye said. "Felicity didn't think it was as funny as I did. I'm glad you're holding up, though, kid," he said, joining her on the cargo deck. "That was our first translation. We're in orbit around JAC-83-45891."

"I know that one," Annie said.

"Did you study the flight plan?"

"All four thousand hours of it! But I knew that star from before. It's a class-M red dwarf, five-point-three light years from Lone Star. You can see it from where I live on New Austin for most of the winter."

"Okay, but like I said, that's our first translation. We have a lot more of those ahead of us before we get to Zanzibar."

Annie's stomach churned at the thought. "Does it get better?"

"Indeed it does, Crewman-Apprentice," Cargomaster Kimball said, approaching his two subordinates. "With time and frequency, the effects of transit shock aren't as bad. You get used to it, as they say."

"Good morning, sir," Annie said respectfully, though she towered over Kimball.

"Good morning to you, young miss," Kimball replied. "You as well, Tech Daye. Shall we begin another day of bringing the Crewman-Apprentice up to speed?"

Daye patted Annie on the shoulder. "She's a fast learner, Mr. Kimball."

"I agree," Kimball said, looking up to study Annie. "She took to freefall maneuvering rather quickly, didn't she?"

"Today was her first translation, and she's holding up a lot better than those big tough mercenaries upstairs."

"Ah," Kimball said, smiling up at Annie. "A quantum deflowering, as the crude joke goes. Well done, young miss. I can think of no better way to celebrate than by introducing you to the basics of shipboard firefighting. Have you ever been in a spacesuit before?"

"No, sir," Annie said.

"I thought as much. Both of you, this way," he said, heading toward a row of storage lockers. "We'll get one adjusted for you so you can begin your training. The firefighting suits differ from regular suits only in their improved resistance to heat and flame. A shipboard fire is one of the most dangerous situations a spacer can face. Fire in freefall moves and flows like a vapor. If contained it will quickly consume the oxygen in a compartment and extinguish itself. If not contained, it can rapidly spread, especially in an oxygen-rich environment, or if there is, say, a hydrogen leak. Many of the materials used in standard ship construction, such as titanium, magnesium, and aluminum, are extremely flammable and burn very hot. There are oxidizers on board as well. Shipboard fires have killed plenty of spacers over the centuries, and must not be taken lightly."

"Aren't there automatic fire-suppression systems?" Annie asked.

"There are, young miss, but those systems will not help a shipmate who has succumbed to smoke inhalation or has lost consciousness from lack of oxygen. If the ship is damaged in combat or in an accident, those systems may not be working correctly. Catastrophic shipboard fires are very rare, but we always train for the worst-case scenario as if we expect it at any time. To do otherwise is to court complacency, and complacency is the enemy of the spacer. Complacency kills."

"I understand, sir," Annie said.

"Good girl," Kimball said with a smile. "Let's get you suited up."

Zanzibar
Danzig-5012 Solar System
Trench Town, Northern Hemisphere

Six thousand kilometers north of Lang's Burg was an isolated settlement built in an eighty-meter deep gash in the surface of Zanzibar. The windblown ceramicrete highway, built more than a century before, was raised just high enough above ground level to keep it from getting buried in dust. The long, lonely road had withstood the forces of erosion well, Zak thought. He'd had plenty of time to think about the road; the caravan from Lang's Burg had spent over a local week making the treacherous journey. Dozens of vehicles traveled in a tight convoy, laden with supplies, fuel, weapons, and Lang's soldiers. Trench Town wouldn't know what hit it. Zak quietly hoped and prayed that they wouldn't resist, that nobody would be killed.

The settlement had, before the Maggot bombardment, been little more than a mining outpost. It was so remote that even the Maggots ignored it, not hitting it with their particle beam weapons. After the fall of Zanzibar, the survivors at what later became known as Trench Town had several advantages. Their location protected them from the incessant, howling winds that plagued this region of the planet. The mines gave them access to valuable commodities like iron and salt, as well as ice—deep below the settlement was a vast, frozen underground lake. The citizens of Trench Town had been able to grow crops in greenhouses, raise livestock, and take in survivors from other parts of the ravaged world (the few that made it that far north, in any case).

Trench Town was far enough away from Lang's Burg and Freeport that the society there posed no threat to Lang and his machinations, but that didn't matter to the warlord. He wanted every settlement on Zanzibar under his thumb and paying tribute so that he could better equip his army. More importantly, Zak's research had revealed that miners that had, long ago, before the war, discovered buried artifacts, a hidden treasure trove from the lost native Zanzibari civilization. Upon learning this, Lang immediately began planning to capture the town at all costs. Zak, Anna, and Cecil were dragged along to exploit the find after the town was secured.

It took Lang's militia about two days to pacify Trench Town. The citizens put up a valiant defense, but they had few weapons and fewer people who knew how to use them. Lang's forces were not well trained, but they were battle hardened veterans of countless such conquests of independent settlements all over Zanzibar. During the battle, Zak and his companions were held back in the encampment Lang's men had built in the rocky highlands surrounding Trench Town. There they waited with Lang, his guards, and his camp followers, as his militia assaulted the town with gun trucks and heavy weapons. Zak watched helplessly as the defenders were cut down.

When the fighting was over, Lang rode triumphantly into Trench Town with the rest of his caravan. During a big, theatrical show trial, he acted as a judge while the citizens who fought back (and survived) were given a choice: they could pledge fealty to Aristotle Lang, or be executed. Those that chose death were hanged, strung up from rocky outcroppings of the trench in which the settlement was built, and were left to swing in the wind as a warning to the others. Zak had thrown up after watching this.

Lang was brutal in his pacification efforts, but he was also smart. While his men forcibly confiscated all the weapons they could find from the citizens of Trench Town (only Lang's men were allowed to have guns), they also distributed food and medicine. The isolated northern settlement had been hanging on for all these years, but they were desperately short on some supplies, and Lang provided them. He even gave a big, pompous speech about how he was going to reunite all of Zanzibar, bringing civilization back to the ravaged world at any cost. It almost made Zak sick again.

This is how the wayward historian, along with his compatriots and surrounded by Lang's guards, found himself being led deep into one of Trench Town's mines. Only a few of the settlement's prewar computers worked, but Zak was able to get enough information off of them to understand where he was being led. It was during this operation that the miners had discovered a natural cave system which had been sealed for millions of years. Deep in this cave system, several kilometers underground, the miners discovered what they had called "the tomb." Leading them underground was a guide from Trench Town, a gray-haired man named Linus.

"Do you think we'll find an actual skeleton of a native Zanzibari in there?" Cecil asked, his voice muffled by his respirator.

"I don't think so," Anna answered. "Unless they fossilize, bones turn to dust in a matter of decades."

"In any case we're not the first ones here," Zak added. "The prewar scientists went through this place and collected everything they could find. According to the records, they used the site to store artifacts when the Maggot assault was imminent."

Linus spoke up sullenly, leery of the armed guards all around him. "My grandfather was a small boy when the war started," he said. "He told us stories of the splendor of the old colony, of how comfortable life was despite the harshness of our world. His father worked in the mines, and he told us stories of how they found the relics of the Zanzibari. You won't find any skeletons in there. Everything they found was boxed up and sealed for long-term storage."

"I suppose that will make Lang happy," Cecil said glumly. "It'll be easier to transport them south."

Zak shook his head slowly at the thought, but tried to stay focused on the task at hand. It was all he could do.

The Privateer Ship *Andromeda*
Deep Space
Baker-3E871 System

Baker-3E871 was a pale white dwarf star, slowly dying an eons-long death. Its dim, harsh light was filtered through beautiful rings of debris, a stellar disk that surrounded the star and made for an awe-inspiring image on the *Andromeda*'s screens.

Or at least it would have, if the damned screens would work, Catherine thought. In terms of transit shock, not all translations were created equal. Being shunted into the Baker-3E871 system had been particularly hard on the ship's systems. The captain monitored the process of getting underway, noting happily when systems came back online, as a pair of systems technicians were replacing electronic components on the command deck.

The transit point was presently outside of the dying star's debris disk, if only barely, but was still uncomfortably close to the star itself. Momentum is not retained when translating into a new star system, and the *Andromeda* had to consume a lot of reaction mass to get up to orbital velocity so as not to fall into the white dwarf. The acceleration gave her technicians the sensation of gravity as they worked to replace burned-out optical computer boards behind Nuchy's console. Now, once again in freefall, they were finishing up their task.

"Captain!" It was Luis Azevedo. "You need to see this!"

"Send it to my...damn it!" Catherine snarled. Her screens were still locked up. She unfastened her safety restraint, pushed herself out of her chair, and gracefully drifted across the command deck toward her junior officer. "What is it, Luis?" she asked, bracing herself on a nearby handhold.

"We didn't notice at first because sensors were offline. But the optical auto-tracking picked it up as soon as the system cycled. Look."

Catherine moved in closer to get a better look at the young officer's display. Against the starry background of space, a shimmering blob reflected the light of Baker-3E871. It was surrounded by other such blobs, chunks of rock and ice in the star's debris disk, but it stood out nonetheless. The image slowly zoomed in, magnified hundreds of times, until she could make out the silhouette of a large ship. The spindly vessel appeared to be slowly rotating, end over end.

"It looks like she's adrift, Ma'am," Luis said.

"Range?"

"Point-nine million kilometers. She's skimming the edge of the debris disk."

"Any radio traffic coming from her?"

"None that we've picked up so far."

"Very well." Catherine pushed herself away from her junior officer's console, flipping over as she did so, landing right in her chair. She tapped the intercom. "Colin, are you tracking that unknown contact?"

"Roger that, skipper. Sensors are still giving me error messages, but I've got her on optical."

"Good. Lay in an intercept course, shortest time. Start broadcasting a standard emergency response message. If there's anyone alive on board, maybe they can hear us." Catherine rapidly tapped the controls on her command console. She was pleased to see that systems were starting to come back.

Kel Morrow looked a little ragged when he appeared on her screen. Of her officers, he was the most sensitive to transit shock, and it was often a miserable experience for him. "Astrogation," he said tersely.

"Kel, we've got an unidentified contact nine hundred thousand klicks ahead of us. I'm not ready to trust the sensors yet, but optical telemetry leads me to believe she's adrift. Once you can access the database, do a historical records search and see if there are any reports of a derelict in this system."

Astrogator Morrow raised an eyebrow. "Thinking of taking a detour, Captain?"

"I wouldn't, but it's not far off of our planned trajectory. It'll give the crew something to keep busy with." Catherine didn't need to mention the potential monetary gain from recovering a derelict ship. If the core systems of its transit drive, which required extremely rare elements and were difficult to manufacture, were intact enough to salvage, it would pay for the reaction mass needed for the intercept hundreds of times over.

If the ship wasn't a derelict, and was in fact in distress, then all the better. Ancient Laws of Outer Space demanded that any available ship come to the aid of another in need. In an empty system far from civilization, there was no one to enforce such laws, but that didn't matter to Catherine Blackwood. The skipper of the *Andromeda* wasn't the sort to ignore a call for help or leave a ship in obvious distress to its fate.

Klaxons sounded and Colin's voice was broadcast throughout the ship. "Stand by for acceleration, two gravities. T-minus ninety seconds and counting. All personnel stay in your acceleration couches. Personnel not on watch, return to your berths. Stand by for acceleration, T-minus eighty seconds and counting."

Catherine calmly fastened the restraints on her command chair, and reclined it back into the acceleration position. Her eyes lit up as she studied the blurry, magnified image of the unknown ship on her screen. Even if it proved to be nothing, at least it broke up the monotony.

Long hours ticked by as the *Andromeda* boosted along an intercept course intended to match the trajectory of the unknown ship. With her sensor suite fully operational once again, the *Andromeda* was able to thoroughly scan the adrift vessel in the visible spectrum, in the infrared, and with radar. What telemetry revealed was startling: the unknown contact was not a ship in distress. It undoubtedly had been at some point in the past, but presently it could only be classified as a derelict. She was cold, with no active emissions signature at all. Only the pale light of Baker-3E871 slightly warming one side of her hull caused her to stand out from the cold background of space.

The intense ultraviolet radiation of the dying star had bleached her hull almost white, but the computer was able to identify the ship. Her name was *Agamemnon,* and she was huge. From nose to tail she was seven hundred and forty meters long, and she outmassed the *Andromeda* by an order of magnitude. Her primary hull was long and cylindrical. Four cylindrical habitat modules were folded against this section; under acceleration, their decks were perpendicular to the ship's axis of thrust, so that passengers could enjoy a sense of gravity. While the ship coasted, the arms were intended to rotate ninety degrees outward. They would then be spun around the ship's axis, using centrifugal force to simulate gravity for the crew during the long haul between transit points. A lengthy but narrow spine connected the primary hull to the propulsion unit, a bulbous cluster of massive rockets, propellant tanks, and radiators.

She rotated lazily, end over end. Her hull was peppered and pockmarked with micrometeorite damage, but she was remarkably intact for being adrift in the rings of Baker-3E871.

"It was an exploration ship," Kel Morrow reported, "constructed in Earth orbit. It departed on what was intended to be a long-duration survey mission, mapping out new transit routes along the frontier, studying worlds that had been identified as potentials for colonization, and cataloging scientific discoveries along the way. The records from this time period are incomplete, patched together by historians, but it seems it was one of a dozen in its class commissioned by the Survey Fleet."

Catherine's eyes widened. "*Survey Fleet*? Does that mean what I think it means?"

Kel nodded at his captain through her screen. "The program was called Cosmic Odyssey VI. It was the last such venture ever commissioned by the Second Federation."

"My God, Kel," Catherine said, unable to hide her excitement. "That ship has been waiting to be found for, what, eight hundred years?"

"Something like that, Captain," Kel agreed. "Cosmic Odyssey VI was initiated just as the First Interstellar War was getting into full swing."

"How is it she hasn't been found, in all this time?"

Kel shrugged. "Transit points move over time. In a high solar orbit like this, in a system this far from most of inhabited space, the odds of a ship translating into the system when the *Agamemnon*'s orbit and the transit point were close to each other are very, very small. Not much trade traffic comes this way, and we're off the normal trade routes anyway. This isolation, juxtaposed with the fact that the derelict would be hard to pick out of the star's rings if you were much farther away than we are, and it makes sense. It's a remarkable find, but not a shocking one."

Catherine shook her head slowly. Humanity had been a space-faring race for something close to fifteen hundred standard years, depending on whose calendar you went by. The Second Federation represented to its era what the Interstellar Concordiat did to the present: the interstellar polity that presumed to unite most of humankind. Its era was known as the "Diaspora": centuries of rapid outward expansion, colonization, and exploration. It was during this period that most of the now-long-established colony worlds, including Avalon, were first settled. It was seen by some as a golden age, an era of unprecedented discovery and achievement. Even in the present day, it was considered to have been the peak of human civilization. Technological wonders were devised that had not been eclipsed in the subsequent eight hundred years.

The Diaspora came to an end with the outbreak of the First Interstellar War. What started as a localized conflict between the Federation and the Post-Humanist Movement spread, like wildfire, into a conflagration that engulfed the heart of known space. Warfare in an age of unchecked scientific advancement proved to be more destructive than anyone could have imagined. Orbital bombardment, nuclear weapons, biological weapons, and even nanotech weapons were all used with reckless abandon as both sides attempted to annihilate one another. Both were ultimately successful; the Post-Humanists were destroyed, and the Second Federation collapsed shortly thereafter.

Billions died in the war. A massive amount of critical space infrastructure was destroyed. Entire colonies were wiped out, and others lost contact with one another as interstellar traffic tapered off to a trickle. Earth itself was subjected to orbital bombardment. The end of a war heralded the beginning of a new dark age, the Long Night, formally known as the "Interregnum." For four hundred years, technology stagnated or even regressed, an unknown amount of knowledge was lost, and human society backslid into an earlier era. Even in the present day, hundreds of years later, there were technologies from the era of the Diaspora that could not be replicated.

What all of this meant for the crew of the *Andromeda* was that the *Agamemnon* was potentially a very valuable find. Too valuable to pass up, in fact, despite the urgency of the present mission.

Catherine's officers agreed with her assessment: the amount of time they would lose was acceptable, given the potential payoff. There was no way the *Andromeda* could salvage the massive relic on her own, but the find was valuable all the same. If nothing else, the location of the ship could be sold to a salvage operation for a hefty payout. The *Agamemnon* was so big, and was in such a remote location, that nothing but a professional salvage effort could successfully bring her back to port. That didn't mean vultures hadn't picked her clean over the centuries, but judging from the sensor feed she appeared remarkably pristine.

The intercept of the derelict went smoothly, and the *Andromeda* precisely matched the trajectory of the *Agamemnon*. As they closed in on their target, Catherine made her way up to the flight deck.

Colin Abernathy was startled when she appeared behind him. "Skipper! What can I do for you?" Lean, dark-skinned, and possessed of a head of short, curly, black hair, Colin was the only member of the crew who hailed from Earth. He had spent several years as an apprentice pilot with a small, family-owned trade company before being recruited for the *Andromeda*. He had spent most of his life in space, and was extremely skilled for one so young.

Catherine smiled at her junior pilot. "Don't let me disturb you. I don't get up here as much as I like these days, and I want to see her with my own eyes." She climbed into the acceleration chair to the right of Colin's, and reclined. There were windows on the flight deck, part of an aerodynamic protrusion from her hull. If you stood on the deck, they were above you, but reclined in the pilot's chairs they were ahead of you, as if you were flying an airplane. This cockpit wasn't necessary; there were several stations from which one could take complete control of the ship. It was more tradition than anything else, a throwback to the early days of space travel on Ancient Earth, when the lines between spacecraft and aircraft were more blurred. Catherine loved it.

"You want to take the controls on the approach, Skipper?" Colin asked. "The *Andromeda*'s your baby. I won't be offended."

Catherine was *sorely* tempted by her pilot's offer, but only smiled and shook her head. "You're doing a fine job, Colin. Carry on." She didn't mention it, but was pleased to see her young pilot with his hands on the controls, tapping the retro-rockets and making tiny course corrections manually. Too many spacers were far too reliant on the computer, in Catherine's opinion.

"Yes ma'am," Colin said. "You can see her in the distance now."

The *Agamemnon* appeared as little more than a particularly bright star, shining against the tapestry of the rings of the white dwarf star. As the minutes ticked by and the two ships closed, Catherine was able to make out the shape of the derelict more clearly. "That is a *big* ship," she said absentmindedly. Vessels of that mass displacement were rarely seen in the modern era. The power requirements for pushing such a monster through a translation were astronomical. Few places were able to produce transit drives with that kind of mass capability, and few organizations could afford to field a ship so large. Even a veteran spacer like Catherine Blackwood found the technological prowess of the long-defunct Second Federation to be awe-inspiring.

"Are you piping this throughout the ship?"

"Yes ma'am. The feed is available on every screen on board. How close do you want me to get? She's got a debris field around her, but we can avoid the big chunks, and at our current relative velocity the little chunks pose no threat. The same goes for the asteroids—nothing presently poses a threat to us."

"Well, then . . . shall we make this challenging?"

"What did you have in mind, Skipper?"

"Find a docking port."

It took Colin a brief moment to process what his Captain was telling him. A toothy smile appeared on his face. "Yes ma'am! The way she's tumbling like that, though . . ."

Catherine smiled back. "I said it was going to be a challenge."

Colin tapped his control panel. "Attention all personnel, return to your acceleration stations. I say again, return to your acceleration stations. Stand by for docking operation. This might get a little bumpy."

The *Agamemnon* had a docking module just aft of the primary hull. It was located by design at the huge ship's center of gravity. Through a combination of skill, experience, and computer assistance, Colin was able to bring the *Andromeda* in close on an approach vector while avoiding the debris field that drifted through the darkness along with the derelict. With a coordinated burst of the maneuvering thrusters, the pilot spun the *Andromeda* clockwise, matching rotational speed with the larger ship.

With their rotation matched, the *Andromeda* cautiously closed with the docking hub. The privateer ship's docking port was located at her nose, and had a variable coupler that could work with ports of various types and sizes. The stars wheeled around the two ships as the distance between them decreased. Colin turned on a pair of bright floodlights, illuminating the derelict's hull during the approach. It was obvious that she'd been drifting out there for a long time—her hull was scarred, dented, had been perforated by micrometeorites time and time again. She had long since depressurized.

A burst of the retrothrusters slowed the ships' relative velocity to a crawl. The *Andromeda*'s nosecone opened, her docking umbilical extending like a proboscis from her hull. From under her belly a heavy-duty mechanical arm unfolded, extending forward with the umbilical. As the *Andromeda* came to a halt, relative to the *Agamemnon*, her arm silently clamped down onto the exposed support beams that surrounded the docking module. Stabilized, the docking umbilical extended further, and latched onto the long-sealed port on in the larger ship's hull.

In the *Andromeda*'s nose, Wade Bishop and a small boarding team made final preparations for the upcoming extravehicular activity. Wade's Fleet EVA certifications had long since expired, but he had conducted such an operation much more recently than any other of the hired mercenaries. The spacesuit he was using was actually nicer than the one he'd had in the fleet, and old habits came back to him quickly. He'd be clumsier in freefall than he was before, and he had to take a pill to settle his stomach, but he was excited to go. After all, how often did one get to explore a genuine ghost ship, a relic from another era?

Besides, Wade rationalized, there could be explosive hazards on that ship. Emergency demolition charges, propellant, even military ordnance. As the only one on board qualified to render safe such hazards, he was able to convince Captain Blackwood that he should go. She hadn't been particularly disagreeable about it; the skipper was paying her hired guns a lot of money, so it made sense that she'd want to get as much use out of them as possible.

Accompanying Wade were three technicians, each experienced in boarding operations. Captain Blackwood didn't want to send over a large team, risking more lives than necessary. Something had obviously gone wrong on the *Agamemnon*'s journey, and there could be danger hidden in her long-silent passageways. Moreover, the task at hand was merely to complete an initial survey of the ship. The *Andromeda* had a more important mission at hand, and wasn't equipped for a salvage operation of this magnitude in any case.

Officially leading the expedition was Kimball, the *Andromeda*'s diminutive cargomaster. On a ship with a crew of only twenty-one, personnel often performed duties outside of their normal roles. There wasn't much for the cargomaster to do in transit, so Kimball pulled double-duty as one of the ship's chief EVA experts. Being small of stature and physically strong were advantages in zero-gravity operations. In addition to being more maneuverable than most, Kimball required less oxygen than a larger individual, and could operate for longer periods of time on a limited air supply. Wade was impressed with how gracefully he handled himself in the docking bay, checking and rechecking his team's spacesuits and equipment.

The other two were members of the ship's crew that Wade had seen before, but didn't actually know. One was a pretty woman with ebony skin and a bald head, the assistant engineer, Wade thought. The other, a thin, unassuming man with pale skin, blonde hair, and a dour demeanor, was a communication technician. None of the boarding party, including Wade, were vital to shipboard operations. Should the worst happen and the entire party be lost, the *Andromeda* could complete her mission mostly unimpeded.

Suited up, sealed, and with oxygen flowing, the four-person boarding party pulled themselves upward to where the internal hatch was. The room fell silent as it was slowly depressurized, and the internal bay doors opened. Wade found himself looking down a long, flexible, illuminated tube that connected the two ships. His sense of equilibrium was off, and maneuvering was difficult, as the two ships were still slowly rotating together. The centrifugal force was slight, but it was enough to throw off maneuvers if you didn't account for it. Kimball had no apparent difficultly, but the rest of the party moved awkwardly through the umbilical, pulling themselves along the guide lines that ran along the wall of the tube.

The docking port doors to the *Agamemnon* were closed, and had been powered down for centuries. With extensive improvised wiring, it might be possible to apply power and get them open, but the team instead opted to do it the (relatively) easy way: with high-energy laser cutters. The lasers were connected, via a long, retractable cable, to a power outlet in the *Andromeda*'s docking bay. Many times more powerful than any handheld laser weapon, and designed for short-range cutting applications, the laser cutters were the fastest way to get into the derelict short of blasting a hole in her hull.

The process was still slow, taking the better part of an hour. The cutters were ultimately successful, and Wade helped Kimball push in the two-meter-across circular section they'd cut out. It disappeared into the dead ship's interior, leaving the boarding party to stare into utter darkness.

"Off we go, gentlefolk," Kimball said somberly. "Please be respectful. This ship is a tomb. We don't want the restless dead coming on board the *Andromeda* with us."

If any member of the boarding party thought such ancient spacers' superstitions were silly, they didn't say so. The docking bay was a spherical room a dozen meters in diameter. As their helmet lights shone on the interior of the *Agamemnon*, the first light to illuminate her corridors in centuries, Wade felt a sense of cold unease crawling up his spine. Pieces of metal and debris drifted around them as the team moved into the compartment. Bits of ice sparkled in their helmet lights as they scanned back and forth, looking like nothing so much as very light snow.

"Control, this is the entry team," Kimball said, transmitting on his radio. "We've entered the docking bay. The ship is depressurized, but other than natural damage from extreme age, seems to be intact. We're going to split up. Myself and Gentlewoman Delacroix will head aft, to the propulsion section. Mercenary Bishop and Technician Love will head up to the crew module, to see if they can download the ship's logs from the command deck. We may lose comms once inside. She's a very big ship. The cables on the laser cutters won't reach into the interior. We may not get very far."

"Copy all," Captain Blackwood said crisply. "Use extreme caution. Your air should last for about four hours. That's all the time you're going to get. Salvage whatever you can. Try to find out what happened to this ship. If you find the bodies of the crew..."

"We will pay them our respects, Captain. They haven't had a proper burial. Entry team out."

Stabilizing himself in the cavernous, yet surprisingly empty docking bay, Wade looked up at Kimball. "Are you sure splitting up is a good idea?"

"No, Mr. Bishop, I am not, but we are on a tight schedule. If you feel unsafe at any time, come back to the *Andromeda* as quickly as you are able. This ship has seen enough death. Let's not add to it."

"Holy shit, this is creepy," Wade muttered, forgetting his radio was on.

Kimball grinned through his helmet's face plate. "What's the matter, Mr. Bishop? You're not afraid of a few ghosts, are you?"

"I don't believe in ghosts," Wade said, sounding dreadfully unsure of himself. In the darkness of a long-dead ship, it was easy to let one's imagination run wild.

Kimball grinned again. "Good, good. I am sure the dead here will take that under advisement. Move along now, time is of the essence. Be careful."

"Yeah," Wade said, pushing off into the darkness with the technician named Love. "Careful."

The central docking hub was located at the bottom of the ship's primary hull. It was connected to a massive cargo bay. Whatever supplies the *Agamemnon* had been carrying were still in place, secured and tied down inside the huge compartment. Wade and Love drifted through the quiet darkness, their helmet lights shining the way ahead, as they explored the hold. Random debris and ice particles drifted in the vacuum; the occasional pinprick of light from Baker-3E871 shone through small holes in the hull.

"Well, this is pleasant," Love said anxiously. "This isn't anything like a typical horror story. No, wait, I'm mistaken. It's *exactly* like *every* horror story."

Wade patted the vacuum-rated pulse laser pistol attached to the front of his suit. "That's why I brought this."

"Well, you have more sense than most horror story characters," Love said, pushing aside a free-floating crate that had crossed trajectories with him.

"I don't think we're going to find aliens or anything up there. This ship has been dead for eight hundred years. Nothing could've survived that long."

"We assume," Love added.

"Look," Wade said, shining his light on a set of stairs. They led upward into the primary hull. "The doors aren't sealed. Everything is open. The whole ship is probably depressurized."

"If they were in trouble, why didn't they lock down?" Love wondered. A standard emergency function of nearly every spacecraft was to seal pressure hatches in the event of a hull breach.

"Maybe they didn't know," Wade mused, grabbing onto the staircase railing. His body flipped around and he nearly lost his grip. "Argh," he growled. "Damn it."

"You okay?" Love asked, steadying himself on the railing with much more grace than Wade had.

"I'm fine. Just going a little too fast. Anyway, maybe they didn't know there was a problem until it was too late? There's no sign of an explosion, major hull breach, or anything."

"That's what's so weird," Love said, leading the way into the crew module. "It's like the crew were all incapacitated."

"I've heard stories," Wade said, following Love through the hatch, "about ships that arrive through a transit point, and the entire crew has vanished."

"I've heard those stories too. Another version has the crew all dead, of asphyxiation, like they ran out of air. Some kind of time distortion. There's no verified report of such a finding, though."

"Maybe not," Wade agreed. "Or maybe it never gets reported because no one is alive to report it. Maybe records of that were lost during the Interregnum. Who knows? I mean, let's be honest, the transit drive itself is basically magic."

Love chuckled. "It's not magic. It's math. Really, really complicated math."

"Same thing. Okay...where the hell do we go now?" The habitat module of the *Agamemnon* was a cylinder over two hundred meters long. The four rotating "arms" were folded into semicircular recesses in the hull. The primary hull was topped with a huge shuttle bay. The compartment the spacers found themselves in was an impressively large open space, almost like the lobby of a building. Long dead plants, preserved in the icy vacuum, decorated the room, as did several large displays. The screens weren't attached to the wall so much as they were part of it. "This ship is huge. The crew must have been in the hundreds."

"The actual crew was only a couple hundred," Love said.

"And it was only that big for damage control purposes. This is a Second Federation vessel. She was very likely controlled by an artificial intelligence."

"How did that work?" Wade asked. "What did they do about transit shock? My handheld was wiped after our last translation."

"The AI would've been rather more sophisticated than your handheld. Aside from that I don't know. They did have problems with AIs, which was probably the only reason ships of that era were manned at all. We can't make such systems today."

"I don't know why anyone would want to," Wade said. "The last time we tried to play God it caused the bloodiest war in human history and the collapse of interstellar civilization. Why screw with that again?"

"Have you read much on the Post-Humanist Movement?" Love asked.

"Not since school," Wade admitted. "They were led by an AI, though, I know that."

"Not just led by it. On the inner colony world of Hera, they built themselves a machine god, an entity they called Euclid. They gave it more and more power, more and more control, let it make decisions affecting the entire colony. They let it reprogram itself, helped it expand its own processing power. The machine was mad, and they didn't know it. They practically worshiped it as a deity, but in their hubris they denied this. They believed Euclid's decisions were based in science, and therefore everything it did was logical. Those with spiritual beliefs were mocked, then persecuted, and eventually were considered to be mentally ill, even as the rest knelt before their machine god."

"Wow," Wade said.

"I apologize," Love said. "I didn't mean to give you a sermon. My faith, the Universal Stellar Union, originated on Hera as well. My ancestors were persecuted terribly by the Post-Humanists, who declared their atheism while bowing their heads and groveling to a computer. You are correct, though: Euclid started a war that destroyed much of human civilization. Anyway, back on task. From what I read about the ship design, the command deck is in the upper levels of the habitat module, just below the shuttle bay."

"It's a long way up there. The interior doors might be sealed."

"We can follow the elevator shaft," Love said. "There's no reason to assume it doesn't go up to the very top, is there?"

Using a mechanical entry tool Love had strapped to his back, the two spacers managed to force open the elevator doors. They floated into the tube, the only illumination coming from their helmet lights. Low-light enhancement assured them that the lift itself wasn't stuck above them, blocking their way. They could make it out hundreds of meters below them, probably down in the engineering module.

"I feel like a gnat crawling down the barrel of a rifle," Wade mused as they drifted upward. The inside of the elevator shaft had a ladder, so that it could be traversed in zero gravity or under acceleration.

"A what?" Love asked.

Wade didn't bother explaining what a gnat was. He instead studied the labels on the walls as they drifted past each deck. Each set of access doors had a sign next to it, in standard Commerce English and two other languages that Wade couldn't read, listing the deck number and the purpose of the level. As was expected, the interior habitat spaces of the main hull were used primarily for storage, including a gigantic cargo bay. Wade had been on some massive Concordiat warships, but he had never seen a ship design so opulent, so expansive, with so much open space. It was decadent, almost wasteful. "I don't understand why they built a ship like this," Wade said. "So much internal space. The shaft that connects the hab module to the engineering module, why is it so long? It's like they were less concerned with mass ratios than they were with how big they could make the ship. Can you imagine the reactor output of this thing?"

"I can imagine the payout from the salvage rights if it's still intact," Love said. "A Second Federation vessel? Gods, we could all retire."

Wade snorted in his helmet. "Ha! As if a career spacer like you is ever going to retire. You'll be underway until they have to launch you out of the casualty chute. In any case, I wouldn't count your currency just yet. There's no way we can recover this monster ourselves. It's going take a fleet of transports to break it down into pieces small enough for them to translate with and get it somewhere else."

"It's kind of callous, if you think about it," Love thought aloud. "This ship is a historical artifact. Perhaps Kimball was right. It seems disrespectful to the dead."

"Maybe so," Wade agreed. "But someone else will find it eventually. How it sat out here for eight centuries without being discovered, I have no idea. But sooner or later, someone will find it. We can either benefit from the find, or someone else can."

"True enough, mate, true enough. Ah," he said, grabbing onto the ladder to stop himself. "This is the stop for the command deck. Stand by. Kimball, this is Love, do you read me, over?"

Kimball's voice came back over the radio, heavy with static. "Copy that. Have you broken but readable. We have no comms with the *Andromeda*." That was no surprise. A ship as massive as the *Agamemnon* would be equipped with heavy shielding to protect the crew from cosmic radiation and the hull from micro-meteorite impacts. Their suit radios didn't have enough power to transmit through all that. "Engineering is sealed. We're trying to get in now. How goes it for you, over?"

"We're in the lift shaft, about to enter the command deck. No sign of the crew yet, over."

The cargomaster could barely be heard over the white noise of static. "Roger. Use caution. Kimball out."

"Ready?" Wade asked.

Love nodded inside his helmet, and prepared the mechanical breacher again. "Let's get this door open and see what we can see." The device took a few moments to place. Once secured to the doorframe, powerful jaws dug into the doors and forced them apart, bending and twisting them as it did so. There was no sound in the depressurized ship, but the two spacers could feel the vibration in their hands as they gripped the ladder. "That's it. We're through."

"I'll go first," Wade said, pushing off of the ladder. He moved across the lift shaft, grabbing onto the pried-apart doors, and pulled himself through.

"What do you see?" Love asked, moving closer. "Wade? Any sign of the crew?"

"No... there's just a helmet floating around in here, and some other junk. Let me take a look... AUGH!"

On the *Andromeda*'s command deck, Captain Blackwood kept herself busy running system checks and going over the planned route to Zanzibar for the hundredth time. There was precious little she could do at the moment, and it frustrated her. She had very badly wanted to go on board the derelict herself. She abhorred the idea of sending her crew into the unknown while she sat safely on the ship, and she was just as curious as anyone to explore an ancient relic from an earlier era. But that wasn't the captain's place. If something happened to the boarding party, the mission had to go on. A good skipper knows when to take charge, but more importantly, she knows when to trust her crew to do their jobs. Sometimes, being a good skipper was no fun.

It was disconcerting for her, all the same. The ship's sensors couldn't get a good lock on the boarding party's suit transponders, and the away team had no direct communication with the ship. It had been long enough that Catherine was getting concerned, and was about to order the rescue team to report to the docking bay.

Before she could give the order to proceed, Luis Azevedo looked up excitedly at his control station. "Captain! The boarding party just entered the docking umbilical. They're ... they're moving fast. Something's wrong."

"I'm going up there, Luis." Catherine hit the emergency release on her seat harness and made for the hatch. "The ship is yours."

Up in the docking bay, Catherine waited impatiently behind a heavy pressure hatch as the airlock was sealed, and the nose of the docking bay repressurized. The four members of the boarding party had all returned and, judging from what she could see on the camera feed, they all seemed to be okay. They had certainly returned to the *Andromeda* in a hurry, coming through the umbilical so fast they crashed into personnel waiting for them.

Once the pressure was equalized, the door opened, and Catherine pushed herself into the docking bay.

Annabelle Winchester was the first to notice her. "Captain on deck!" she announced.

"As you were," Catherine said, grabbing onto a handhold. The ship's flight surgeon, Harlan Emerson, Med Tech Lowlander were checking the boarding party's vitals.

Cargomaster Kimball and Assistant Engineer Delacroix seemed fine, if a little confused. Wade Bishop and Tech Love, on the other hand, looked as if they'd seen a ghost. All color had drained out of their faces, and sweat droplets floated off of their heads as their helmets were pulled away. Love was on the verge of hyperventilating, and the med tech placed an oxygen mask over his face to keep him from fainting.

"Mr. Bishop," Catherine said, drifting closer to her hired mercenary as the Winchester girl was helping him out of his suit. "What happened in there? Are you alright?"

Bishop nodded his head. "I'm okay, Captain, I just...I just..."

"Kimball said you and Love had just entered the command deck. Did you find some sign of the crew?"

"That we did, ma'am. All over the walls."

"What?"

"As soon as we opened the door to the command deck, we found a corpse. Frozen, largely preserved. He'd been decapitated. I mean, I found the head first. I thought it was just a helmet, until I saw, you know, the eyes. Frozen eyes. But, accidents happen in space, right? Sooner or later we were going to find bodies. So we pushed in, tried to find a way to access the ship's computer, get at the logs, see if any of it is intact."

"I see. Did you have any success?"

"What? Oh, no ma'am. Nothing we had with us is compatible with their systems. Love said it was all quantum positronic whatever. Way more advanced than anything we have. Second Federation stuff. This ship doesn't have a computer, she has an honest-to-God *AI*."

There were few places, even in Concordiat space, with the technology to create a powerful, self-aware artificial intelligence. Much of that knowledge had been lost in the Interregnum, and attempting to create such things in the modern era was something of a taboo.

"I see. What happened then?"

"We recorded everything. It's all on the video. We just...we explored the command deck a little. Huge, multiple rooms. We found the entrance to the actual bridge and popped the door open."

"And you found the remains of the crew in there?"

"If you want to call it that," Wade managed. "Captain, the ship itself is intact. There is no apparent damage to the interior that isn't consistent with being adrift for hundreds of years. But the crew...there were a dozen bodies on the bridge. All frozen. Some of them were naked. Some of them looked like they'd been torn apart by animals or something. There was frozen...blood, guts, whatever, stuck to the bulkheads. I think we found the ship's skipper, too. He was sitting in a big chair in the center of the bridge, still strapped in. He was even wearing his spacesuit, but the helmet visor was up. He'd been stripped down to the bone. There was a fucking skull grinning at us from inside his helmet, Captain."

"Dear God," Catherine said quietly. She noted that the color had flushed from Annie Winchester's face.

Bishop continued, "I've seen a lot of shit in my career. I've rendered safe unexploded missiles from ships that had been mangled in combat, where there was blood and body parts floating around me as I worked, but I've never seen anything like *that*. I don't know what the hell happened on that ship, but there's something *wrong* in there."

"I see," Catherine said reassuringly. "Just try to relax, Mr. Bishop, I won't be sending you back over there." She looked over at her cargomaster. "Mr. Kimball, did you find anything as gruesome?"

"Nothing, Captain," Kimball replied. "The aft section was completely deserted, no sign of the crew whatsoever. We were beginning to think they'd all abandoned ship. We weren't able to get into main engineering, though. The pressure doors were sealed, and it's going to take heavy laser cutters to get through. May I speak freely?"

"Of course, Mr. Kimball. Give me your honest assessment."

"Mercenary Bishop is correct. I don't know what happened on this ship, eight hundred years ago, but there's a wrongness about her. At first I thought it was just the mind playing tricks, in the silence and blackness of such an old relic, but after what was found on the bridge? Who knows what we might find behind those pressure doors, or in the crew habitat arms. Better to just mark the location of the find and sell it to someone else for exploitation. We don't have the capability to get much out of her in any case. She's just too big, and we have places to be."

"I hate to leave such a find for someone else to take," Catherine said. "Aside from everything else, if that AI is intact, the Concordiat authorities will pay a hefty salvage fee for it."

"Indeed, Captain," Kimball agreed. "If we don't sell the AI core to them they'll try to take it by force. They're quite serious about AI control."

Catherine nodded. "We'll leave a claim beacon on the ship, one that responds to a coded signal, so whoever we sell it to can find the *Agamemnon* again. If someone else finds her in the interim, there's no guarantee that anyone will respect our claim out here, but it's better than nothing." She observed Tech Love, breathing rapidly into an oxygen mask. "As you said, Mr. Kimball. She's been waiting out there for eight hundred years. She's not going anywhere. You all did an excellent job in there. Mr. Kimball, see to securing the docking umbilical. As soon as the ship is buttoned up we'll be getting underway."

Kimball nodded. "I'll take care of it, Captain."

"Excellent," Catherine said, pushing herself back toward the hatch. "Carry on."

Zanzibar
Danzig-5012 Solar System
Lang's Burg, Equatorial Region

Cecil Blackwood popped the cap of his flask and poured a shot of stiff local booze into his coffee before turning back to his compatriots. Zak Mesa and Anna Kay had an improvised lab set up on the ground floor of the building they had been allotted, and were both lost in their work. Cecil was the idea man, he liked to think, and the money guy. He didn't really do much of the research stuff. He had *people* to do that.

People who were now hostages, just like him. People whose lives he'd put in danger. Cecil took a deep breath, then sipped his alcohol-laced coffee. He didn't really need to be here. He wasn't contributing much to the effort, as Zak and Anna burned the proverbial midnight oil, but he had never been the sort to go off and relax while his team was on the job. Good leaders lead from the front, his father used to say, whether he's a commander of a warship or a foreman on a job site.

Zak and Anna were an odd pair, Cecil thought, watching them. Zak was reading something on one screen while analyzing high-resolution pictures of various artifacts on another. Anna had one of the ancient Zanzibari artifacts that had been recovered from Trench Town, a sword with an oddly curved blade, in a laser mass spectrometer. She studied the results and took copious notes. The two of them spoke only occasionally, and a person who didn't know them might think they didn't like each other.

Cecil didn't think they were screwing each other, but suspected

178

they both secretly wanted to. Stressful situations like being a prisoner tended to bring people together, forming strong bonds through shared misery. Cecil could read it in the way Anna interacted with Zak. Back home, he was considered something of a womanizing scoundrel, but he liked to think of it in more romantic terms. However one chose to look at it, he knew how to read women, and it was obvious to him that Anna had fallen for Zak.

The historian, for his part, was either a master at keeping his private life private, or was utterly oblivious to his partner's affections. Cecil strongly suspected the latter. Zak was a dour man who wore his emotions right on his sleeve. He was one of those quiet, bookish types who were usually too introverted to have much success with women. Anna was just like him, which is probably why they hadn't jumped in bed with each other yet: both were too shy to make a move.

Cecil found the whole thing grimly adorable, but at the same time annoying. All men, especially men of note, were expected to know how to properly court a lady on Avalon. He had wined, dined, danced with, courted, and bedded plenty of women on Avalon, commoners and aristocracy alike. He was confident that he could have married any of a dozen women if he had wanted to settle down (he didn't). The confidence and the charm came naturally to him, but he knew it didn't for most men. It frustrated him to see Zak missing an opportunity like this; Anna was quite comely, remarkably intelligent, well-traveled, and came from a prestigious family. She'd be a prime candidate for marriage for any young man on Avalon, but Zak ... poor Zak just didn't see it. Like a couple of awkward adolescents, Zak and Anna rotated around each other, but neither could muster the courage to voice their desires.

Finishing his coffee, Cecil resolved to pull Zak aside one of these days and have a man-to-man talk with him. He very much doubted the shy historian would find himself a better woman than Anna. In any case, life was short, too short to waste on being shy ... especially when you're being held for ransom by a petty, sociopathic warlord, Cecil thought bitterly. He set his mug down and took a long swig from his flask. "So," he said, putting the flask back in his vest. "How goes things?" He was glad that they'd found some ancient novelty to keep themselves busy with. Lang's brutal conquest of Trench Town had deeply disturbed the two intellectuals.

Anna glanced up at him briefly. "Well enough, Mr. Black-wood. Spectrograph readings aren't really telling me anything about this particular item that wasn't included in the manifest, but I scanned it just in case. It's fascinating."

"It's some kind of dagger, isn't it?" Cecil asked.

"More like a short sword," Anna said. "See how the blade is curved? It's meant for slashing, not stabbing. The Zanzibari were smaller than humans. This would be about perfect size for them to use as a one-handed weapon. The metalwork is beyond that of any culture of a similar technology level back on earth. The blade isn't steel. It's an alloy, with some synthetic materials that my spectrometer can't identify."

"That's...unusual, isn't it? The Zanzibari were at a rough equivalent to the Bronze Age, weren't they?"

"Indeed they were. This is puzzling, and it seemed to vex the prewar archaeologists that were studying their civilization as well. They were not primitives. They had a sophisticated, technological society that would have rivaled Ancient Rome at its zenith. Even still, the materials science needed to make a blade like this had to have been beyond their capabilities."

"I see. How is it so well preserved? Even high quality steel rusts away with enough time." The short sword's blade was darkened and worn, and whatever material the handle had been made of had long since disintegrated, but the weapon was otherwise intact.

"It has gotten brittle with extreme age," Anna said, "but otherwise is in excellent condition. The soil of Zanzibar is dry. There's been no rainfall here for millions of years. Being buried kept it from being eroded by the wind, and there are no plate tectonics or volcanism on this world. Zanzibar being a dead rock contributed to the blade's preservation. According to the manifest we..." she paused, uncomfortable with how the blade had come into her possession, "That we *recovered*, it was originally found sealed in a deep chamber in the cave system beneath Trench Town. It had been found in a polished stone container that was also intact. The Zanzibari made things to last. Whatever material the blade is made of withstood the test of time."

"So it would seem," Cecil agreed. "I don't suppose you've been able to divine what happened to the Zanzibari, then, from studying that blade?"

"I wish," Zak said, without looking up.

"That would get our names in the history books," Anna agreed. "That's another thing our predecessors here were struggling with. They had archaeologists, geologists, climatologists, volcanologists, chemists, and physicists all working on that question, and they didn't seem to be any closer to answering it than we are."

"Some of the media I recovered shows their scientists actually *arguing* about it," Zak said. "Not as in having a vigorous discussion. They were *shouting* at each other. Seemed like a passionate bunch, if nothing else."

"They were frustrated," Anna added. "According to the journals we've recovered, they'd been working very hard on this question, and were constantly pressured by their corporate and government sponsors. Zanzibar likes to keep its secrets, though."

"I don't think it was natural, what happened," Zak added, "and neither did Dr. Loren. He wrote about it extensively in his journals. Their end was too abrupt. This planet changed too quickly."

"Four million years is a long time," Cecil pointed out.

"Not in planetary terms. The dinosaurs, giant reptiles from Earth, went extinct sixty-five million years ago. The Earth had a different climate and geography back then, but was still habitable. Even the extinction event that killed the dinosaurs didn't wipe out all life on earth."

"Even more perplexing," Anna injected, "there's no evidence on Zanzibar of a massive impact from space. There have been impacts, of course, but nothing big enough to wipe out an entire planet, and nothing that corresponds with the time frame. Even a massive asteroid impact, one sufficient to *sterilize* the surface, wouldn't cause the oceans to permanently vanish, end plate tectonics, and curtail volcanic activity. It doesn't make any sense. Planets don't just suddenly *die*."

"Apparently they do," Cecil mused. "How big were these oceans?"

"Nothing like Earth," Anna said. "They covered, at most, a fifth of the surface, and were shallow. But they just disappeared."

"The poles have ice. There is also a lot of ice below the surface." Mining subterranean ice is how most of Zanzibar's scattered settlements survived. Water was a precious commodity on the barren, windswept world.

"That's true. Zanzibar is cold enough that there is now ice where once there may have been a water table, and both poles are largely frozen over. Even still, that's not nearly enough to account for all of the water that would've been in this world's seas."

"That's . . . rather chilling, if you think about it," Cecil said. "A world is suddenly wiped clean, and an entire team of scientists couldn't determine why. It leaves a lot to the imagination, and what the imagination comes up with is frightening."

"It's the stuff horror stories are made of," Zak said. "I doubt Anna and I are going to solve this quandary by ourselves, but to even have access to this data is unbelievable. If we get off of this planet alive, I'm going to send this to every research institute in known space. This is huge. And . . ." he looked at the sword again. "And people died for it."

"Let's not get ahead of ourselves, Zak. By all means, save all the data you can. But for now, let's just keep Lang happy so we don't end up strung up like those poor bastards up north."

Aristotle Lang himself entered the room unexpectedly. "Now, now, Mr. Blackwood, you don't give me enough credit! Have I been anything but hospitable during your visit?"

Zak nearly opened his big mouth, but Cecil piped up before the historian could spout off. "Of course, Mr. Lang, of course. I was just using a figure of speech. We, ah, didn't hear you come in."

The stocky warlord was dressed in a long, furry coat that hung nearly to his ankles. What sort of beast the fur came from was anyone's guess. He had a very large pistol hanging from his belt in a crossdraw holster. Two of his omnipresent bodyguards quietly entered the room, and posted themselves by the door. "I just wanted to pay my valued researchers a visit, see how you were doing."

"Well, ah, we've been analyzing this blade, as you can see. It's very well preserved, given how old it is."

"Fascinating. Millions of years have passed, and it looks only a few hundred years old. How much do you suppose one could fetch for that, on the market?"

"There really aren't any pieces like it on the open market, not that we can tell. You know how the Concordiat is about the trade in alien artifacts."

"Ha!" Lang snorted. "To hell with the Concordiat, I say. They imagine themselves masters of humanity, but they are not the masters of me. What price could we fetch for it on the *private* market?"

Cecil put a hand on Zak's shoulder to stop him from saying anything. "Several million, easily, given the condition that it's in."

Lang's dark eyes lit up a little. "Good, good. As well, I have good news for you. A courier ship arrived in-system this week. On the bulk download was a message for me." He held out a small tablet computer, and tapped the screen. "It seems your ordeal will be at an end soon, my friends."

Cecil and his compatriots looked at each other in disbelief. It had been months, many months, since the original message to his father had been sent out. He had all but given up hope of ever hearing a reply. His excitement turned to shock when the video began to play, however. He absolutely had not expected to see *her*.

"Greetings, Mr. Lang. I am Captain Catherine Blackwood, commander of the merchant vessel *Andromeda*. As I record this message, my ship is on New Austin. We are stopping here to resupply before setting out for Zanzibar. My father has contracted me to negotiate for the release of Cecil Blackwood and his entire staff. I come prepared to negotiate in good faith, and want nothing more than to resolve this matter as quickly and painlessly as possible. The specifics of our flight plan are included in this message, so that you know when to expect us. It is not a short journey, so I must ask for patience on your part." Catherine's demeanor softened ever-so-slightly. "Stay safe, little brother. I'm coming to take you home." The message ended abruptly.

Cecil and his compatriots were left speechless. He hadn't seen his sister in years, and now she was coming to pay his ransom? Without a word, he retrieved his flask and downed the rest of it in one gulp.

Lang beamed. "You see? I know you doubted me, but you are not in any danger. You are not any use to me strung up, as you say. I have plenty of malcontents to hang, if I wish, like those fools in Trench Town who did not accept my generous offer to join the revolution. I only have one rich man's son to bargain with."

"Yes...well..." Cecil stammered, still in shock.

"One last thing before I take my leave," Lang said. "How much closer are we to that vault?"

Zak looked up, staring the old warlord right in the eye, before Cecil could stop him. "We're *working* on it," he said coldly. "All of your blustering, all of your veiled threats, and all of your pressure doesn't make the work go by any faster. We're trying to solve a mystery here, and honest-to-God treasure hunt. Most of the records were deliberately scrubbed, and most of those that *weren't* were destroyed in the war. It's going to take *time*. Research can't be *rushed,* Lang. All these interruptions do is disrupt our workflow!"

Cecil's mouth fell open. Anna coughed uncomfortably, and kept her eyes fixed on her lap.

Lang's eyes narrowed. His two bodyguards looked at each other with disbelief. Nobody spoke to Aristotle Lang that way. The old warlord stepped across the room, until he was standing over Zak. The historian stood up, eye to eye with Lang, and glared at him.

This is it, Cecil thought, cringing. *The damned fool just got himself killed.*

"Ha!" Lang barked. He slapped Zak on the shoulder, laughing heartily. "I *like* this historian of yours, Mr. Blackwood! He's quiet, like a mouse, but he has the heart of a lion! I'm surrounded by fools who are afraid to tell me the truth, but this man, this man has *balls!* Ha ha! Very well, Mr. Mesa. I will leave you to your studies. It will be some time before the ship arrives to collect you all, so perhaps we will find it by then?"

"P . . . perhaps," Cecil squeaked.

"I have faith in you, Mr. Blackwood," Lang said. "Do this thing for me, and I will let your sweet Bianca leave with you. I think you both would like that, yes?"

"Yes. Yes, of course. That's very generous of you."

Lang smiled evilly. "I am *very* generous to those who do well for me. Very generous." He turned on his heel and strode out of the room, pausing only to berate his two bewildered bodyguards. "Come, you fools, leave these scholars to their work. Can't you see you're disturbing them?" A door slammed as the warlord and his entourage left the building, leaving the three captives alone again.

Cecil, wide eyed, heart racing, slowly sat down. A bead of cold sweat trickled down his right temple. He looked over at his partner and shook his head slowly. Zak seemed like the quiet type, but Lang was right: the man had *balls.*

Anna was staring at Zak in disbelief. It would seem that she'd never seen this side of him before either, and it was apparent to Cecil that she liked what she saw. Her face flushed, just a little.

"Say Zak," Cecil said conversationally. "I need you to help me with something upstairs."

"What? We're pretty busy here, Cecil," Zak said, as oblivious as ever.

"I'm aware of that, but I really need to discuss something with you. Please, it'll only be a moment."

"Fine," Zak muttered, standing up. "I'll be right back, Anna."

She seemed surprised by the statement. "Hmm? Oh! Okay," she said, her face turning red. She looked back down at her console.

"This had better be important," Zak groused as he followed Cecil out of the room.

"Oh, it is," Cecil insisted, "it is."

The Privateer Ship *Andromeda*
Deep Space

While the ship was under acceleration, Marcus thought the journey was much more enjoyable. A steady 0.85 gravities of thrust wasn't exactly real gravity, but it was enough to settle the stomach and allow the team of mercenaries to enjoy a solid meal. After forty-five minutes of physical fitness training and a quick shower, the hired guns gathered around a circular table in the ship's common area. An impromptu game of poker had broken out while they ate a meal together.

Marcus chewed his food idly while reading from his tablet. He was terrible at poker and wasn't playing. Devree Starlighter, on the other hand, had a poker face worthy of a professional card sharp, and seemed to be cleaning up nicely. She didn't even crack a smile as Randal Markgraf folded in frustration, but Wade laughed at him.

Marcus chuckled and returned to his reading. On his screen was an encyclopedia, and he passed the time reading everything he could find on not only Zanzibar, but also Avalon and the Blackwood Family itself. The captain hadn't been exaggerating when she explained that she'd come from a powerful family. Clan Blackwood was an ancient family line on Avalon, going back centuries to the colony's founding in the Late Diaspora. They were one of a number of original stakeholders, colonial founding fathers who set themselves up as a sort of aristocracy.

Avalon's government was not democratic by any means. The heads of the Stakeholder Families served on a high council, a legislative body that held most of the political power. They would choose a High Councilor who served as the colony's head of state, but his powers were specific and limited. The stakeholders' power and prestige seemed to come from the size, wealth, population, and economic productivity of their respective provinces. Clan Blackwood, lords of Aberdeen Province, had been one of the most powerful and influential for centuries.

The Blackwood & Associates Trading Company was one of the largest and most widely traveled merchant fleets from an independent world, and they had a virtual monopoly on interstellar trade to and from the Arthurian System. Their earnings had been slowly declining for years, however, as Avalon's trade regulations made it difficult for them to break into new markets, and in the face of increasing competition from independent free traders.

"So what's our next stop, Marcus?" Devree asked, scooping an armful of poker chips toward her.

Benjamin Halifax stopped frowning at his cards for a moment. "It's probably Opal, lassie. Not many places to resupply this far out. Really, not enough traffic out this way for many traders to establish themselves, especially since to get to Zanzibar from here you have to go through Combine space. Most choose to take the long way 'round."

Randall Markgraf spoke up. "Why didn't we take that way? Why in the hell are we going through Combine space if there's another way?"

"It's a *lot* longer," Wade answered, looking up from the game he was playing on his handheld. "There aren't a lot of places to resupply that way, either, and they're spread further out."

"A ship of the *Andromeda*'s class would be pushing its luck to take that route," Marcus said. "She's still a patrol ship, even if she's a big one. She wasn't designed for one-way missions this long. The captain didn't want to risk running low on remass or stores."

"Let us not forget," Ken Tanaka said, "that this is a rescue mission. Time is of the essence."

Wade nodded. "And the long route would add . . . hell, maybe months to the trip, depending."

"I've never heard of Opal," Devree said.

Halifax folded his cards. "I'm not surprised. The colony there is all of one small city, maybe ten thousand people. They're independent, not affiliated with anyone. Not enough there for anyone to bother with, I suppose. The planet has a fully developed eco-system, but it's completely incompatible with terrestrial biology. The atmosphere is breathable, but only barely. Humans can't even digest any of the native plant matter. Just growing food there is a challenge, needs to be done in greenhouses. There are hardly any metals close enough to the surface to bother mining. It's not a good candidate for colonization."

"Why in the hell does anyone live there? How are we supposed to get supplies from this place?"

"Just enough traffic to Zanzibar, and to the Orlov Combine, comes though this way that traders have set up shop. At least, they were there last time I came through this way."

"When was that?" Marcus asked.

"Seven years," Halifax replied. "New Austin years, I mean."

"How does a colony that small even sustain itself?" Devree asked.

"Their primary economic resource is the export of locally grown plant matter and alien artifacts," Wade said, reading from his handheld. "I just looked it up."

"Alien artifacts?"

Halifax grinned. "Aye. Opal is inhabited."

Devree's eyes grew wide. "I've never seen an alien before."

"You may or may not see one while we're there," Halifax said. "They're reclusive."

"It says that they're at a stage roughly equivalent to the Stone Age," Wade said, reading further. "Their population is small, estimated to be only a few million on the whole planet. They trade trinkets and crafted goods to the human colonists, who sell them on the open market."

"The big money is in relics from *extinct* alien species," Mark-graf said. "That's probably why the colony on Opal isn't booming. There are a few known planets with indigenous civilizations at that level. Their artifacts are expensive novelties for collectors, and that's about it."

"What do these beings look like?" Hondo asked, setting down his cards.

Wade raised his handheld so everyone at the table to could see the screen. "Check it out."

"I can't tell if it's cute or horrifying," Devree said. The crea-ture on the screen was short, little more than a meter tall, with smooth, leathery skin that varied from blue to brown. Its short arms and legs both ended in hands with opposable digits, tipped with claws. It had a mouth full of pointy, needle like teeth, and two large, round red eyes.

"They're unsettling when you first see them," Halifax said. "Opal's ecosystem is similar to Earth's, and these beasties fill the role that our ancestors once did. But when you get close, you realize just how alien they are. They don't have noses, for example, like mammals on Earth do. They breathe through their mouths, make this sickly wheezing sound. They don't talk to humans—they *can't*. Their mouths are too different, they can't pronounce human languages. They're not dumb, though. They learned a crude form of sign language, which they use to communicate with the colonists."

"They reproduce asexually," Wade said, reading from his screen again. "They don't really have sexes. Or sex, I guess."

Devree raised an eyebrow. "How dull."

"They'll bash your head in and eat your guts if you walk in on one of their gatherings at the wrong time," Halifax continued, "but they're mostly harmless. Humans are a curiosity to them, nothing more. It's the colonists you need to be wary of." When the group looked at question at him, he leaned in closer and explained. "They've been isolated on that world for a long time, since first contact with the Maggots. They were like a doomsday cult, hoping that if they settled there they'd be overlooked by the Maggots while the rest of humanity was slaughtered."

"It worked," Wade said. "It says here that even when the war came through this sector, the Maggots never even approached Opal."

"Aye, and that's where it gets strange," Halifax said. "The Maggots did come through this system. I read up on all the reports the last time I was through here. It wasn't a big force, but they were tracked by Concordiat ships. They could've easily blasted the colony from orbit. They never left any other human colonies unscathed. But instead, they just left the system and never returned."

"After the war," Wade read, "the Concordiat government sent an envoy to Opal to try to learn why the colony wasn't attacked. Rumors were flying that the colonists had made some kind of deal with the Maggots, but that doesn't make sense, because we never were able to communicate with them at all."

"What did they determine?" Hondo asked.

"Pretty much nothing," Wade said. "It says here that the inquiry was inconclusive, and they left. That was over a hundred years ago. They were mostly forgotten about after that."

"As I said, they're strange folk," Halifax said. "If the captain lets us off the ship while we're planetside, you'll do well to stay out of their settlement. The traders had a nice little trading post established while I was there. You won't likely see too many of the locals. Rumor has it they tried to forget that they're the aliens on that world, never told the children about humanity's real origin. I don't know if there's anything to that, but they do act as if they worship their planet. They fancy themselves its guardians and servants. They're especially protective of the natives."

"How do you know all this?" Marcus asked. "How long were you there?"

Halifax crinkled his brow as he tried to remember. "Maybe a couple of local weeks? The ship I was on needed engine repairs while she was there. We stayed for longer than planned. Anyway I was plowing this local girl, if you follow me. Buxom young thing, inexperienced but eager. She told me all this." Devree frowned, and Halifax grinned sheepishly. "Begging your pardon, lassie. I said too much."

"I thought you said the locals are reclusive," she said.

"Aye. But they're still human, and there are thousands of them. It's frowned upon, but some of them fraternize with off-worlders, especially the young people. Colony Fever is universal, you know."

"So, you said it'd be a good idea to stay out of their settlement?"

"It really depends. We may get a cool reception, but there are things to see there. It's best to abide by all of their rules, no matter how strange. They punish infractions harshly, so they say, but I don't really know. All of that is kept quiet, and even the lovely lassie with the enormous knockers wouldn't tell me the details."

Markgraf looked thoughtful for a moment. "If I didn't know better," the veteran intelligence officer said, "I'd say you were using that girl as a way to get information. Classic honeypot."

Halifax grinned. "Believe it or no, I'm not just a handsome face who's handy with a gun."

"You're not handsome, for one thing," Marcus said. "It's a good thing you're handy with a gun."

"I think you're all gross," a familiar voice said. The mercenaries looked up to see Annabelle Winchester enter the common area.

"Good to see you too, baby," Marcus said. His daughter hugged him, then sat down at the table with the group. She was dressed in the same green flight suit the rest of the crew wore, with her hair done up in a tight braid to keep it out of the way in freefall. Marcus didn't want to embarrass her by saying so, but he was so proud of her he felt as if he might burst. "How you been holding up?"

"They keep me busy," Annie said, peeling the top off of a heated flight meal. "Twelve-hour shifts every day." She took a bite of her meal and frowned.

Marcus smiled. "You said you wanted to be a spacer, kiddo."

"It's not bad," she said. "I'm not whining, I was just saying."

"I think it's a fine thing you're doing, little lassie," Halifax said. "You may be surprised to learn that when I was your age, I got into a bit of trouble with the law myself."

"Yeah, no one is surprised by that," Devree said.

Halifax laughed and shook his head. "All this defamation of my character, it's unfair. But it's true. At fifteen standard years I was in a street gang on Olympus."

"You're from Olympus?" Markgraf asked. "You don't sound like you're from Olympus. You don't have the accent. Olympians talk like they've got a mouth full of rocks."

"Aye, but, I wasn't born there. My mum took me there when I was just a babe, got passage on a free trader somehow. Grew up in the slums there, though, and it was the law of the jungle." He looked up at Marcus. "Being on a ship is good for the girl. She's safe, she's busy, keeps the youthful piss and vinegar under control. When I was her age I'd have killed to get off that miserable rock."

"I like the *Andromeda*," Annie said. "Everyone is nice, except for First Officer von Spandau." She looked around to make sure no one else was listening. "I don't know what that guy's problem is," she said more quietly. "He never smiles or anything."

Wade shrugged. "I heard he's from the Concordiat Fleet. I was in for twelve years, and I saw more than a few officers like that. He's not a bad guy, he's just serious about running a tight ship. Believe me, kiddo, I saw a few free traders and independent spacers in my time, and none of them were as disciplined as the crew of this ship. None of their ships were in as good a shape, either. This ship is in top condition. That's good. Space is unforgiving."

192 *Mike Kupari*

"That's what he told me," Annie said. She badly mimicked his accent. "Space is zee harsh und un-forgivink mistress! Now report to your station, *schnell!*"

The table of mercenaries erupted in laughter. Marcus shook his head. "Where did my daughter learn to be so sarcastic?" he wondered aloud.

"Uh, I *wonder*, Dad," Annie said, rolling her eyes.

"Oh. Right," Marcus admitted. "Probably my fault."

Annie looked at her chrono. "I need to get going." She stood up and cleared her tray from the table.

"Where you off to, kiddo?"

"Gotta help Daye do some systems maintenance down in engineering."

"Yikes, how is that?" Devree asked. "The engineer seems like a real hardass."

Annie shrugged. "I haven't really worked for her yet."

"Just do your best, honey," Marcus advised, "and be respectful. Let Daye do the talking if you're not sure what to say."

"I'll be okay, Daddy," Annie said. "I gotta go, though. I'll see you guys later." She dumped her waste in a receptacle and disappeared up the ladder.

Devree smiled at Marcus. "She's such a sweetie," she said. "I can't believe that girl got in trouble with the law."

"Believe it. You oughta see what she did to that other kid. Fractured her skull and broke her jaw. It was either this or she was going to juvenile detention for a year."

"Aye," Halifax said, "but this other lass poisoned your girl's horse, didn't she? At her age, I'd have killed anyone what took from me what that little sodding wretch took from your daughter."

"It was Red Eye," Marcus said. "The other girl, Victoria, she was hopped up on Red Eye. Makes you do crazy things."

Devree shook her head. "Red Eye made the rounds on Mandalay when I was a patrol cop there. One time a bad batch went around the slums. It was making people go insane, like violently insane, attacking others and trying to bite their faces off. By beating the shit out of that girl, your daughter probably saved her life, Marcus. She'll get the help she needs now, before that poison kills her."

"I think it worked out pretty well, all things considered. I'm just worried about her mom. She's at home, alone, pregnant, and her little girl is light-years away and can't communicate. I know it's hard on her." Marcus sounded guiltier than he would've liked.

"Ellie's tough," Wade said. "You know she'll be fine. When you get home, you're going to have a son to meet."

"You're expecting a son?" Devree asked.

"Not exactly," Marcus admitted. "It was too early to tell when we left. I'm just... well, you know, a father hopes."

"I don't know what you're hoping for," Wade said. "Annie's just like you. She's a little female clone of you. If anything, your boy's as likely as not to take after his mom."

Marcus sipped his coffee thoughtfully. "You know, that wouldn't be bad. This trip notwithstanding, mining is the family business now. It'd be nice if we had someone to take it over down the road."

"See?" Wade asked. "Everything's going to be fine. Quit worrying."

Devree had been right about one thing, Annie thought to herself: Chief Engineer Indira Nair was a hardass. The job that Annie and Tech Daye were tasked to do was fairly straightforward; the life-support system on the engineering deck had been acting up ever since the last translation, leaving it unpleasantly warm down there. A systems check had revealed that one of the computer subsystems was "fried" (as Daye had described it) and needed to be replaced.

"It shouldn't take too long," Daye explained to Annie as they arrived on in engineering. "The ship's internal systems are all modular, and components can be swapped out on the fly."

"Do you have to replace them often?" Annie asked.

"It depends, really," Daye said. "Some translations are harder on the systems than others. Transit shock is impossible to predict. Usually the hardware is unaffected, but sometimes the software gets so buggered up that the whole thing locks up. Sometimes we can run diagnostics and unbugger it, but other times it's easier to swap it out with a spare from our supply, and work on getting the problem component running again later. Once in a while transit shock is bad enough that critical components like cooling fans or voltage regulators stop working, and it causes actual physical damage to the component. That's what I think happened here."

Annie thought for a moment. "What happens when the spares in our supply get messed up, too?"

Daye shook his head. "Then you're in for a fun day. It doesn't happen often. Usually components that are powered down are less likely to be affected, but not always. I've swapped out components before, only to find the replacement is just as nonfunctional as the original. It's a headache."

"How is it we've been traveling in space for fifteen hundred years and we still haven't figured this out?"

Daye shrugged. "Chaos theory. It's impossible to predict because there are too many variables, and some of the variables happen in the quantum space-time shunt and can't be measured, because the shunt takes an immeasurably small amount of time. That's one theory, anyway. There's a lot about translating between systems that isn't well understood, even though we do it on a routine basis. In ancient times, it was thought that such modes of travel would be impossible. It conflicted with their understanding of the universe. But even today, there are contradictory theories about what goes on during a translation. It's all above my level. I tried reading some of the texts about it in school and it gave me a nosebleed. There is a lot they can't explain yet."

"Like what?"

"Like if one ship translates right after another, the one that went second might arrive first. Or, there might be a long delay between when the first and second ship arrives, even if they departed within minutes of each other. Sometimes, very rarely I mean, but it does happen, ships just disappear. The theory is it's some kind of extreme time distortion, but that's just a theory."

Annie blinked hard. "You're right, it does give you a headache."

Someone else spoke up then. "Hello. We ran every diagnostic subroutine available and the system is still nonresponsive." It was Assistant Engineer Delacroix. Annie remembered her from the boarding of the *Agamemnon*. The assistant engineer looked at her and smiled. "Hello, Annie. It's good to see you again."

Annie smiled back. She loved the woman's Classical French accent. It made her sound so sophisticated and cultured. "We'll get it running again in no time, ma'am," she said, doing her best to sound confident. She looked at Daye. "Uh, won't we?"

Daye nodded as he began to remove an access panel from the bulkhead. "I think so. The sooner the better. It's damned hot in here."

"It's insufferable!" It was Chief Engineer Indira Nair. Delacroix quietly stepped away as the chief engineer stood over Annie and Day, hand on her hips. She was sweating through her flight suit and was in a foul mood. "We can't work like this."

Daye, crouched down on the deck, removing the panel, looked up at the engineer. "Understood, ma'am. We'll have it up and running shortly."

Engineer Nair glanced at her transparent eyepiece, and didn't look at Daye when she spoke to him. "Keep me updated." Without another word, she walked away, climbing into her acceleration seat and workstation.

The engineering deck was not large, so Annie had to talk quietly to ensure the engineer wouldn't overheard. "What the hell is her problem?"

Daye glanced over at Nair, then back at Annie. "She just likes things nice and ordered. Every really good engineer has a case of obsessive-compulsive disorder, they say."

"She's so antisocial and bitchy!" Annie whispered, helping Daye remove the troublesome computer subsystem from the wall.

"She's an engineer," Daye said simply.

"I'm serious," Annie said. "Even the XO isn't that tight-assed. I've seen her around the ship. She barely talks to anybody, even in her down time. When the captain took me down here during my orientation, she didn't say a word to me."

"I'm serious, too," Daye insisted. "She's an engineer, and a good one. That's just how they act. I know it looks like everything pretty much runs itself down here, but this is the heart of the ship. A small problem here can turn into a big disaster for everyone if it's not caught and corrected right away. Mechanically, the ship's fusion motor is a fairly simple system. There are very few moving parts and very little to go wrong. It doesn't require complex programming or sophisticated computers to keep it operational, so it's not as likely to be affected by transit shock. If something does go wrong, though, it can be catastrophic. If containment fails, the fusion reaction can't be controlled, and that's the end of us. If there's a radiation leak, the engineering deck will get the worst of it. Basically, any serious problem down here will probably see Ms. Delacroix being promoted to chief engineer shortly thereafter. Most shipboard engineers tend to be neurotic about keeping things in top condition. Everybody's life depends on it."

As she helped Daye replace install the new components, Annie glanced over at the chief engineer, sitting in her workstation, monitoring the reactor and the propulsion system. She listened to the rumble of the engines as they accelerated the *Andromeda* through the void and thought about the incredible forces that had to be not only contained, but controlled to make that possible. It left her in awe.

"Hey!" Daye said, interrupting her daydreaming. "Focus, kid. Hand me that fastener."

"Oh, right," Annie said, embarrassed. "Where to next?"

Daye looked at his eyepiece and frowned. "Upper level latrine is backed up. Ugh."

"Shit," Annie said. Daye laughed.

Using a bit of aerobraking to slow to descent speed, the *Andromeda* circled the little blue planet of Opal one last time before retracting her primary radiators and plunging, tail-first, into the atmosphere. While there was no shortage of terrestrial planets in explored space, worlds with fully developed ecosystems were rare. This sometimes caused them to be ruled out as candidates for colonization, due to the difficulties in getting Earth life to adapt. Opal was an exception to this rule, though its colony of determined settlers was small and isolated.

Scans from the *Andromeda*'s sensors showed a world teeming with life. The poles were buried under massive ice caps, and three-quarters of the surface was covered in shallow oceans and warm seas. Opal seemed to lack the frighteningly deep oceans of Earth and Avalon, but nonetheless supported an abundance of marine life. The dense atmosphere easily slowed the ship to a safe landing speed high over the trading post's tiny spaceport. In a spectacular cloud of smoke and flame, the *Andromeda* lowered herself onto one of the spaceport's two launch pads, and settled onto her landing jacks with a deep, metallic groan.

The nameless human colony on Opal was some twenty kilometers away from the traders' spaceport, a tiny outcropping of civilization in a clearing of the extremely dense flora. It was surrounded on all sides by a tangled jungle of plant life that resembled terrestrial trees, save for their bluish tint and odd bioluminescence. Puffy white clouds filled an intensely blue sky, as the world basked in the yellow-orange light of the system's star.

The only paved road on the entire planet connected the lonely colony to the trading post, and no traffic could be seen on it.

The colony itself was a crowded, sprawling cluster of boxy, prefabricated buildings that had been added on to over the years, repainted, or rebuilt completely. The largest structures by far were the domed greenhouses in which the colonists raised their staple crops of soy, wheat, barley, rice, and beans. Its common areas appeared neat and clean on telemetry, with residents going to and fro on their daily business. Every building's door seemed to function as a sort of airlock, keeping climate-controlled, filtered air inside so humans could live more comfortably.

Outside the small city, partially covered in vines and plants, was the towering, skeletal hulk of the ship which had brought the colonists to Opal more than a century before. It had been stripped for building materials and supplies over the years, but its primary spaceframe remained. Standing some eighty meters tall, it towered ominously over the settlement, and was now home to native flora and fauna of many types. The thick, humid atmosphere of Opal had long since rusted the exposed metals that were vulnerable to corrosion, but the primary spherical structure of the ship remained largely intact. Her main hull was a great metal ball, fifty meters in diameter, sitting on top of a large cluster of engines, fins, landing jacks, and support structures. A large flock of flying creatures were frightened out of the stripped vessel as the *Andromeda* set down at the spaceport.

The arriving privateer ship wasn't the only vessel presently at the spaceport. Five hundred meters away, on the other landing pad, stood a mid-sized free trader with a pointed nose and a bulbous hull. Her transponder listed her as the Armed Merchant Cutter *Ascalon*, registered out of the Llewellyn Freehold. Catherine sent the *Ascalon*'s skipper a courtesy message. She kept the details of her mission to herself, but discreetly inquired as to whether the merchant cutter had been to Zanzibar.

A few moments after sending her greeting, as her ship was being spun down, she received a brief text message from the *Ascalon*. It was an invitation to her captain's cabin for dinner. It was customary for ship's officers to have dinners with one another, but this usually included the first officers at least. This invitation, on the other hand, was for the captain alone, and was to be a private affair with the *Ascalon*'s skipper. Before sending a reply, Catherine consulted her first officer via text message, not wanting the junior officers on the command deck to overhear.

Wolfram von Spandau replied quickly, in his usual terse style: *I do not like this. If you meet with him, I wish to go with you.*

Catherine replied: *That's not what he's asking. He wants to have a private dinner with me.*

Perhaps he imagines himself irresistible to women? Wolfram typed. *He will be disappointed, if that is the case.*

Catherine chuckled to herself. *I don't actually know if their captain is a man. It could be a woman. I could meet the love of my life over there.*

The executive officer was less optimistic. *Or you could be held for ransom. Such things are not unheard of out here on the frontier. This so-called merchantman could easily be a pirate.*

Catherine grinned widely as she typed, her command crew oblivious to the nature of her conversation. *My goodness, captured and ravaged by a pirate queen! I believe I've seen that video before. Do you suppose I'll be tied up as well? I think I might fancy that.* She could almost feel Wolfram blushing through the text interface. Sparing her XO the effort of coming up with an awkward response, she continued: *In all seriousness, how about this: I will go over there and meet with him. Instead of wearing my frilliest space damsel dress, I'll wear my regular flight suit. I'll take a sidearm, as that's customary anyway. Perhaps their captain isn't a presumptuous lecher—perhaps he just wants to share some information, and doesn't want his crew to hear too much. Not all spacers are as reliable as mine.*

Wolfram von Spandau took a few moments to type his response. *Very well. Please be cautious. I will see to the replenishment of our remass tanks and set up a maintenance rotation while we're dirtside, as we discussed. Three local days will be more than enough time for the maintenance. The crew can get off the ship for a time and waste their money at the trading post.*

There is one last thing, Catherine typed. *While I see to this, I want you to run an emergency drill on the crew. Hostile natives threatening the ship in port. We've been underway for a long time. They're tired and won't be expecting it.*

I agree, Wolfram typed. *It will give Mr. Winchester a chance to organize his people on the fly as well.*

Very good, Catherine typed. *Start the drill in one hour. I want the crew ready to defend the ship until it can be brought back up for launch. Notify traffic control, Mr. Broadbent, and Mr. Winchester of the drill, but no one else. The ship is yours.*

Logging off and shutting down her command console, Catherine stood up and stretched. "Mr. Azevedo," she said, "I have business to attend to. *Herr* von Spandau has the ship. The command deck is yours."

Showered and refreshed, Catherine made her way down to the *Andromeda's* cargo deck. She wore a fresh flight suit and her genuine leather flight jacket, with a gun-belt around her narrow waist. The large ventral cargo bay doors were opened, connected and sealed to the spaceport's landing tower. Down the ramp was an elevator that led to the base of the landing tower. From there, a series of underground tunnels connected the various areas of the spaceport and trading post, so that travelers could move from one area to the next without having to brave the sweltering climate outside. The dense atmosphere made it difficult for those unaccustomed to it to work, and the humidity level was always murderously high.

The spaceport's underground tunnels were well lit, but practically deserted. A small, three-wheeled electric scooter was available for rent for a small fee. As Catherine rolled along the tunnel connecting the *Andromeda's* landing pad to the *Ascalon's*, she didn't see another soul. The only activity was a couple of service robots going about their appointed tasks. Soothing mood music played over speakers and resonated off of the bare block walls.

The landing tower that led to the cargo bay of the *Ascalon* was identical to the one Catherine had come down when leaving her own ship. As she made her way up the ramp, she saw quite a bit of activity in the merchant ship's cavernous cargo bay. An alarm chirped as she approached, and the crew members inside took notice of her.

"Good evening," she said crisply. "I am Captain Catherine Blackwood of the privateer ship *Andromeda*. Your skipper was gracious enough to invite me to your ship. Permission to come aboard?"

A waifishly thin crewmember in a red coverall spoke up. "I am Cargomaster Mearl," he (or perhaps *she*; Catherine couldn't really tell) said. "We have been expecting you. Permission granted, Captain. Welcome aboard the armed merchant cutter *Ascalon*." The androgynous cargomaster had very pale skin, a shaved head, and never set down the tablet he/she was holding. Behind him/ her, the cargo bay was stacked with shipping containers of goods, all secured and balanced so as not to throw off the ship's center of gravity. From the looks of things, the *Ascalon* would be leaving Opal soon.

"Your ship is impressive," Catherine said. "I can see you run a most efficient cargo deck. I've visited a lot of merchant ships, and have seen few in such impeccable shape. I assume you're departing soon?"

Mearl perked up and actually smiled at Catherine's offhand flattery. "Thank you, Captain. Indeed. Our launch window is in a matter of hours." He/she turned and waved toward another crewman. "This is Cargo Tech Samuel. He will take you to see the captain."

The hulking crewman stood in stark contrast to his supervisor. He towered over Catherine, his dark skin rippling with muscles. "Please follow me," he said tersely, his deep voice booming. "Our captain is waiting."

The *Ascalon* was large enough that it had a small lift running up its centerline. The *Andromeda*, in comparison, had no such luxuries; the crew had to use ladders to traverse between decks. The merchant vessel was rather larger than the *Andromeda*, but unless it had a surprisingly potent engine cluster, Catherine suspected it wasn't nearly as capable. The *Andromeda* could pull ten gravities of acceleration under full afterburner; a ship like the *Ascalon* probably couldn't do half that. The two ships were designed for very different roles—much of the *Andromeda*'s internal volume was used for redundant systems, armament, and armor. As a merchant cutter, though, the *Ascalon* was impressive.

A tinny robotic voice announced that the lift had stopped at the officers' quarters deck. Samuel led Catherine through a narrow, circular corridor, lined with doors to small cabins for the ship's officers. Each appeared to be as big as Catherine's personal quarters, and a four such cabins ringed this deck of the ship.

One of the cabins had an ornate door, and seemed to be larger than the other three. Samuel banged on the hatch three times, then stood up straight, hands folded behind his back. With a clank and a hiss, the door slid open, and he spoke up. "Cargo Tech Samuel reporting, sir. I am escorting Captain Catherine Blackwood of the *Andromeda*. I believe you are expecting her."

A cheery male voice spoke up from inside the cabin. "Send her in, please!" Samuel stood aside, nodding as Catherine stepped past him and entered the cabin. "Welcome aboard the *Ascalon*, Captain," the ship's skipper said. "I'm so pleased that you accepted my offer." He was an average-looking man with an average build, red hair, a red goatee, and freckles. He stood at the far side of a small table. Like his crewmembers, he was dressed in a dark red coverall, though over it he wore a more formal tunic with four gold bands around the cuffs of each sleeve. "I am Captain Matthew Atkins of the Llewellyn Freehold."

"Pleased to meet you," Catherine said, stepping across the cabin to shake his hand. Captain Atkins seemed to have his own private dining area, another decadent luxury the *Andromeda* had no room for. "Your ship is most impressive."

Captain Atkins brimmed with pride. "Isn't she? So many free traders are little more than tramp cruisers in poor condition, crewed by shady individuals. Then they wonder why they can't get contracts with the big corporations and colonial governments! My predecessor ran a tight ship. Matt, he would always say, a ship's got to be in shipshape! It's hokey but it's true." He paused, before motioning to Catherine to sit. "Please, Captain, have a seat. You'll get me talking if you ask me about my ship!"

Catherine smiled at him. She didn't think she was in any danger of getting abducted (nor in any danger of getting ravaged by a lusty pirate queen), and Captain Atkins seemed unusually personable for a Freeholder. "If I may ask, why all the secrecy?"

"Ah," he said. "Wine? Water?" He poured Catherine a glass as he continued. "Many of my crew are new hires from the Freehold. They can be a rather mercenary bunch. You asked me about Zanzibar, so I thought we'd have a private conversation, face-to-face, captain to captain. Discretion is part of my professional code."

"I certainly understand," Catherine said, sipping her wine.

"Dinner should be ready shortly. I hope you like roast chicken?"

"I do."

"Then you'll really like this. It's an actual chicken my men acquired."

"From the colony?"

"No, from the trading post. The locals don't raise livestock. But it's not dehydrated, frozen, or otherwise preserved."

Catherine thought for a moment. "The locals don't raise livestock?"

"You don't know? I suppose the information available about this place is pretty sparse. The colonists are all strict vegans, by law. All they eat are the plants and nuts they grow in their greenhouses. The consumption of meat, fish, or animal products is forbidden. Rumor has it they put people to death for it."

"That's insane," Catherine said.

Captain Atkins could only nod. "It's just a rumor. I'm sure they'd be unhappy if they found out we were eating meat in here, though there's nothing they can do about it. These people have been isolated on this rock for over a century. Until this trading post opened up, maybe forty local years ago, they were completely cut off from the rest of inhabited space."

"How in the world did they sustain themselves on such an inhospitable planet?"

"Their original colonization mission was intended to be long term. Their ship, the one rusting away to the north of the settlement? They completely stripped it for parts and equipment. The ship's fusion reactor was moved, and now powers the colony. Compared to fusion rockets, the colony doesn't need very much power, so they leave it more or less in standby mode. With a minimum of maintenance, it can run for a very long time like that."

"One of my crew spent some time here a few years ago. He told me the colonists on Opal were strange."

"Oh, they're an odd bunch all right. Their colony is a commune. Everyone pitches in to the best of his ability, and is in turn given what he needs to survive. There's no money, no private property, and no taxes."

"I see. And who decides who needs and gets what?"

Captain Atkins chuckled. "That is the rub, isn't it? They call them the Elders. They run the show here. Really reclusive bunch. Supposedly they're the living survivors of the original colonial mission. They'd have to be really, really old for that to be the case, but I suppose it's possible. They make the laws, and they have so-called Peacekeepers to enforce them. But mostly people abide by the laws without the threat of force. They're indoctrinated from the time they're children, taken from their parents, raised in communal crèches. This whole colony is basically a cult, except they're not religious."

"The trading post...they're Freeholders as well?"

"Yes. Not affiliated with my business, and believe me I don't get any kind of a discount for being from the same home port. There's just enough traffic coming through this system these days to make it worthwhile."

"Trade from the Orlov Combine, I assume?"

Captain Atkins took a long sip of his wine. "I don't like dealing with the Combine. I know what they are, you know. But their raw materials are good, and they're cheap. The profit margins are too big to pass up."

"If I may ask, what are you doing on Opal?"

"Same as you, I suspect. Stocking up on remass and supplies. I do trade with the colonists here. I have a contact and, before you ask, I'm not inclined to share."

Catherine smiled. "Wouldn't dream of it. Not my sort of contract, really. But what do you trade? The information I have is vague."

"The trinkets the natives make fetch a pretty credit from collectors. But the real money here is in the wood."

"Wood?"

"It's not technically wood, I suppose. The flora that fills the role of trees on Opal aren't really trees, in strict biological terms. But their hides, the bark, wood, whatever you want to call it, is beautiful." He reached behind him and produced a small box. Inside was a sample of the plant matter. It had rich, deep, purple coloration, and swirled with intricate patterns and grains. It dimly glowed indigo.

"It *is* beautiful," Catherine said, touching it lightly. It felt like finely polished wood. "Did you finish this?"

"That's the real beauty of it, Captain," Captain Atkins said. "This is just a sample cut from a pseudo-tree. The texture and color varies widely from breed to breed, but a lot of them are just as lovely. The bioluminescence lasts for years, even after the sample has been cut from the tree, so long as it's exposed to UV light daily."

"I can see how selling this would be profitable. I've never seen anything like it."

"I've got a deal worked out with the colonists. I bring them supplies they need, mostly from Orlov's Star, and they let me take wood and trinkets. It's all kept on the down-low, of course. The trading post gets a cut of the profits. Apart from my ship, there are only one or two others that have such a deal worked out, and it's good money. It's the secret that makes this place profitable."

A rap on the hatch announced that dinner was served. Catherine hadn't smelled fresh roast anything since leaving New Austin. The scent of the chicken was almost intoxicating as two crewmen set the table. After they excused themselves, she dug in greedily, savoring every bite of her meal. The vegetables were fresh as well. It was glorious.

"My God, this is good," she said, washing down a bite with a sip of wine.

"I saved the best for myself. Being captain has its privileges. But don't think I haven't taken care of my crew; I purchased some pigs from the trading post and had them butchered. We'll be having quite the feast before we lift off. It's a long way back to the Freehold, and we've been gone from home for a long time. I want to treat my people."

"I guess my question is, why are you divulging all of these secrets to me? Aren't you afraid I'll try to move in on your territory?"

Captain Atkins only smiled. "Not at all, Captain. For one, you're a privateer, not a free trader. You might make a few extra credits running cargo, but your ship isn't suited for it. Secondly, your reputation precedes you."

"My reputation?"

"Absolutely. I've heard of you, Catherine Blackwood, and the *Andromeda* as well."

Catherine couldn't stop a devilish grin from appearing on her face. She folded her hands under her chin and leaned in. "Oh really? And what is it you've heard?"

Captain Atkins may not have been Catherine's *type*, and maybe it was the wine talking, but he was quite the charmer. "I'm sure you recall an incident a few years back, where the *Andromeda* was brought in to protect merchant vessels transiting into the Coleman-2203 system?"

"I could hardly forget it," Catherine mused. "I had just officially taken command of the *Andromeda*. My predecessor, Captain Roberts, was serving as my exec on his final job before he retired. Raiders were preying on merchant ships coming through the transit point, hitting them before they had time to recover from transit shock."

"It put a real damper on trade with that system, which was a pity, because the asteroid belt there is overflowing with iridium, uranium, and cobalt."

"There's no colony in that system, just a cluster of hollowed-out asteroids and space stations in the asteroid belt." Asteroid miners, sometimes called Belters, were often portrayed in popular culture as rugged, independent, nomadic people, who answered to no one and made a living wherever they could. It had been Catherine's experience that there was more than a little truth to that stereotype. The Belters in the Coleman-2203 system tried, but didn't have the means to protect themselves from the raiders that had set up in their system.

"The raiders were choking them off," Captain Atkins said. "I was part of a five-ship convoy, full of relief supplies, contracted by the Belters themselves and some outside parties. We hoped that there'd be strength in numbers, but that transit point is a cast-iron bitch."

Catherine's eyes widened slightly. "I thought your ship looked familiar. We'd been chasing the raiders all over the system, but just couldn't get close to them. As soon as your fleet came through, though, they took the bait. We splashed both of their ships. My first mission as skipper and we got two pirate kills!" Catherine took a long sip of wine. "I don't mind telling you, Captain, that that was the greatest day of my life."

"Please, call me Matt. It was a pretty good day for me as well. We were struggling to get our weapons online when you intercepted the raiders. Had you not been there, it would have ended badly for us. I invited you to dinner, Captain..."

"Please," Catherine said, interrupting. "Just Catherine."

Captain Atkins smiled. "I invited you to dinner, Catherine, because I never got to thank you. I owe you my life and my ship. Sharing a bit of chicken and some information is the least I can do."

"I'll be glad for any information you have on Zanzibar or Orlov's Star," Catherine said. "It's hard getting current, accurate intelligence about those places. I'm afraid I can't get into specifics of my mission, however. Client confidentiality and all."

"No worries, Catherine, I completely understand. You are in luck, though. I was on Zanzibar a few months ago, and went through Combine space on the way here."

"Really? So tell me, what is the secret to getting through Orlov's Star unmolested?"

"The short answer? Be prepared to pay a couple of big bribes, and hope for good luck."

Exhausted, Annabelle Winchester climbed down the ladder into the crew deck. She'd just come off of a twelve-hour shift and wanted nothing more than to crawl into her berth for some badly needed rack time. There was a lot for the crew to do after the ship set down at the trading post on Opal. Being on duty, Annie had been running around like a crazy person, helping everyone who needed help only to be sent off to the next person. Kimball had kept her busy on the cargo deck, rearranging containers to make room for the supplies they would be taking on. As soon as that was done, he'd told her to report to the ship's purser, Mordecai Chang.

Annie was surprised to learn that Mr. Chang seemed to live in his tiny compartment above the crew deck, adjacent to the supply locker. He didn't come out even when Annie banged on his hatch. He just addressed her through a screen and gave her a list of items that needed to be checked out of storage on the cargo deck and stocked in the supply locker, so the crew could access them as needed. It was a task fit for a robot, but there were no robots on the *Andromeda,* so it fell to Annie. It had taken her three trips to get everything to where it needed to be.

The crew deck was unusually crowded. With the ship planeted and postflight checklists completed, there wasn't much for the crew to do if they weren't on watch or maintenance duty. Most of the *Andromeda*'s sixteen-person crew seemed to be crowded into the habitat area. Annie's dad and his mercenaries were there too, sitting around one of the tables in the common area having an animated conversation. Everyone seemed to be in a good mood, excited at the thought of getting off the ship for a while.

Everyone except her father. He wasn't bantering with his team the way Wade was. He just quietly studied a tablet in his hands, occasionally looking around the room.

"What's wrong, Dad?" Annie asked.

He looked up from his tablet, surprised to see her. "Huh? Oh, hey, sweetie. Nothing's wrong. How are you?"

"Tired."

"Ship life wearing you down yet?"

Annie felt defiant. "No! I just had a long shift, is all. I feel at home on the *Andromeda,* Dad."

Her father smiled. "I'm glad. Your mother and I used to worry, with you growing up without any other kids around. We thought it might stunt your social development."

What is he talking about? "Dad, I have a lot of friends," she said.

"I know, baby, but you almost never get to see them. That's not how it's supposed to be. You're supposed to, you know, spend time with them, do stuff, be a kid."

"Hey now," Wade said, noticing Annie's conversation with her dad. "I was in the same situation as her when I was growing up. I turned out fine."

Annie's father held his hand out, offering his partner as an example. "See? I was worried you'd turn out like Wade."

"Hey!" Wade protested.

Annie rolled her eyes. "Obviously, I'm not going to turn out like Uncle Wade, Dad."

"Hey!" Wade said again.

"Sorry, Uncle Wade," Annie said, flashing him her sweetest smile. "No offense, you're kind of lame."

Wade just shook his head. He looked over at Devree, who was sitting next to him. "I'm being verbally abused by that girl, and her father is encouraging her."

"Aww," Devree said, making a pouty face. "Did she hurt your widdle feewings?"

Wade folded his arms across his chest. "You know..."

Laughing, Annie looked at her father again. "Anyway, I like it here. It's just hard sometimes. I miss Mom."

Marcus put a hand on his daughter's arm. "I miss her too, honey. I'm sorry there haven't been any courier ships lately. I know you want to send a message home. I do too."

"Do you think she's okay? With the baby and everything, I mean."

"Everything will be fine, baby," Marcus said reassuringly. "Your mom is tough, and stubborn. You don't need to worry about her."

Annie didn't like to admit it sometimes, but the way her father projected confidence always comforted her when she was worried. It was like no matter what life threw at them, her dad knew just what to do, and things always worked out. Annie figured having been a chief warrant officer in special operations had a lot to do with her dad's demeanor. He was used to making quick decisions under stress.

Her father looked her in the eye. "I want you to know I'm very proud of you, Annie."

Annie felt her face flush a little. "Dad . . . come on."

Marcus smiled. "Just remember: no matter what happens, stay calm, keep your wits, and do what you've been trained to do."

Huh? "Dad, what are you—"

A piercing warning klaxon sounded throughout the ship, interrupting all conversations. It was followed by the voice of Wolfram von Spandau. "Attention all personnel. Go to general quarters, I say again, go to general quarters! Essential ops personnel report to your duty stations and get the ship prepped for emergency liftoff. All other personnel, report to security. I say again, report to security, draw weapons, and stand by to repel boarders." The klaxon sounded again as the message ended.

The crew deck exploded with activity as everyone scrambled to get to where they needed to go. Her heart racing, Annie looked to her father. "Dad, what's going on?"

He smiled at her again. "Everything will be okay, honey. Just follow your shipmates and do as you're told. Get going now."

"For real? The ship is being attacked?"

"Get going!" her father ordered. He then turned his attention to his teammates. "Come on people, you heard the man, assholes and elbows! Move it! I want everyone armed up, kitted up, and on the cargo deck in five. Not you, Halifax. You go straight to the cargo deck. It's time we unwrapped that present we've been saving."

The red haired mercenary's eyes lit up, and a vicious grin split his face. "Aye."

"What are you still doing here?" Marcus barked, startling Annie. "Quit screwing around and go!"

Annie didn't take the time to answer her father. She turned on her heel and ran for the ladder.

Marcus was pleased with how fast his team had gotten their gear together. Most of their weapons were stored on the cargo deck, so after suiting up in body armor and battle rattle, they had made their way there. While the crew of the *Andromeda* hurried to issue out weapons from the ship's arms locker, the mercenaries were already locking and loading.

"Mercenary Winchester!" It was Kimball. He was carrying a compact laser weapon and, from the look of him, hadn't been informed of the drill. "It's good to see you."

"Kimball, we need to get the big package unwrapped so we can do an emergency startup on it."

Kimball checked his eyepiece. "I see. I'll need help."

"Halifax will help you. The rest of us will secure the landing tower until it's ready to go."

"I'm here!" It was Annie. She slid down the ladder like a veteran spacer and jogged over. "Sorry." Marcus noted the laser carbine slung across her back and smiled.

"What took so long?" Kimball asked. "Come on, your father wants a piece of equipment pulled from storage and ready to go."

"I'm sorry!" Annie said. "Mr. Broadbent didn't want to issue me a weapon!"

"Wait a second," Marcus said. "Why not?"

"He said I hadn't qualified with one or something, like I don't know how to shoot."

Marcus chuckled. "You ever use a laser before?"

"No, but it's basically the same thing. Power cell in, charge the weapon, safety selector, look through the scope, squeeze the trigger. Easy-peasy."

"Come now!" Kimball said. "There'll be time for chit-chat later!"

Marcus stepped back and felt himself swelling with pride as he watched his daughter work. Dressed in her green flight suit, laser carbine slung, she pulled the securing bands from a large container and used a heavy-lift cargo dolly to move it to the center of the cargo deck. A moment later and the crate was open, revealing the hulking powered armor suit inside.

Halifax looked up at the war machine and smiled. He tapped controls on his handheld, causing the suit to boot up and come to life. The armor stood nearly three meters tall. Calling it a "suit" was something of a misnomer, as the operator didn't wear it so much as he rode inside its armored shell. Its main body split open, revealing the cockpit and access for the operator. Halifax climbed in and began rapid startup procedures.

Meanwhile, Wade led the rest of the team out the cargo bay doors and down the ramp that connected the landing tower to the ship. This was fully enclosed, not allowing it to be used as an elevated firing position, but that could be quickly corrected if necessary. When a ship was planeted it was extremely vulnerable, even more so if it was locked into the landing tower, because it couldn't leave. Most atmospheric ships carried small crews and were lightly armed, if at all. A ship of the *Andromeda*'s class wasn't vulnerable to small arms fire, but it could easily be damaged by explosives or anti-armor weapons. Heavy weapons weren't the biggest threat to a ship in port, however. An intact ship was extremely valuable; boarding and capturing it intact was often easier than destroying it outright, and was much more lucrative for the aggressors.

There were only two ways to board the *Andromeda*: through the cargo deck via the docking tower, and through the crew hatch down by the landing jacks. The crew hatch was easy to secure by retracting the ladder and sealing the hatch. The landing tower was the more likely assault route. It provided no cover for attackers or defenders, but with the small crews ships carried it was possible for a mob of hostiles to overwhelm the defenders.

Marcus told his team to halt on the gangway and wait for the heavy. As several more armed crewmembers appeared on the cargo deck, Kimball and Annie kept them clear of the hulking powered armor unit as its hydrogen engine roared to life. Doing his final function checks, Halifax drove the armored juggernaut forward. Its clanked and clunked on the deck as it strode out of its container. Once clear he unlocked its arms and began arming its weapons. Marcus waved the powered armor forward, toward the cargo elevator, after reminding Halifax not to use its plasma gun in an enclosed space with friendlies nearby.

The mercenaries fell in behind the lumbering armored giant as it smoothly clanked and clunked down the gangway, using it as cover. Anyone attempting to board the ship would be in for a nasty surprise. Marcus was pleased to note it had taken barely six minutes from the time Kimball asked him what was going on to the time Halifax was piloting the powered armor toward the cargo elevator.

A warning klaxon sounded throughout the ship. "Attention all personnel, this is the executive officer. End-ex, I say again, end-ex. This has been a drill."

"What?" Devree said, sounding frustrated. "This is bullshit." Hondo shook his head, and Tanaka remained silent.

Halifax's voice sounded over the armor's PA system. "What

a cock tease. It's a cruel thing, getting a man all spun up and then telling him it was a joke."

"Stow the bitching, people," Marcus said. "It wasn't a joke. It was a drill. We've been sitting on our asses for weeks. The captain wanted to make sure the ship's crew wasn't getting complacent, and I wanted to make sure you guys could get your shit together in an emergency."

"I think we did well," Tanaka said.

"You did," Marcus agreed. "We got the heavy out of storage and ready to go in less than six minutes. Any angry mob this planet could muster would be hard-pressed to overcome that kind of firepower."

"What would have been our plan of attack in this scenario, Marcus?" Tanaka asked. "I assume you meant to engage the attackers in the service tunnels?"

"You know it," Marcus said. "It's tough planning an impromptu defense like this, but I believe our best bet would've been to move down the elevator and engage the hostiles in the tunnels. A firefight down there would be a lot less likely to damage the ship, and we wouldn't have a bunch of spacers with laser weapons running around playing soldier, getting in our way. I would've had them stay up here and secure the gangway while we took the fight to the enemy. Thoughts?"

"That sounds like a good strategy," Hondo said, resting the buttstock of his heavy automatic rifle on the deck. "We would have to make sure we didn't get stuck in the tunnels, though. There could be more attackers approaching on the surface. They could access the landing tower while we were underground, take the elevator up, and go around us completely."

"Good!" Marcus said. "Good thinking! That's a possibility in a situation like this. There are ways to access the surface from the tunnels. The ship can monitor the area around it and let us know if hostiles are trying to swing around our defenses."

"Can't we just disable the elevator?" Devree asked.

"That's a tougher problem. In most cases, short of coming out here and physically breaking something, no. Spaceport authorities rarely, if ever, give up any control to the ship. Once we're locked in, we're locked in until they decide to release us. Getting the landing tower to release us if they don't want to is not a quick or easy process."

"Lots of cutting," Wade said. "Or tapping into the landing tower and seeing if we can override it. The ship's system techs might be able to."

"That is a possibility, if you have time. As a last resort, you might have to go to spaceport control and convince them to release the ship, by force." It was the price ships paid for landing at a functioning spaceport. The amenities were valuable, and spaceport controllers liked to make sure they were paid before letting ships go. "Anyway, good job, everybody. Head back in. Once your gear is stowed and the heavy is secured, you're on liberty until we lift off. Check with the flight schedule *before* you go anywhere, please."

"What's there to do in this place?" Wade asked.

Halifax chuckled over the armor's PA system as the machine lumbered back up the gangway. "More than there is to do on the ship. They locals will probably let people take a tour of their town as well."

"Enjoy it," Marcus said. "This is the last time we land until we get to Zanzibar. Get out and stretch your legs. Just be careful."

Standing in the shadow of the looming trading post, Devree Starlighter took in her surroundings as she waited to board a small bus. The spaceport, though small, still covered a vast area cut out of the dense alien jungle. The trading post itself was a prefabricated building that reminded Devree of a bunker, ugly and square, decorated with huge, gaudy advertising screens.

Opal was a bluish-green world, colors that oddly clashed with the orange light of the star she orbited. Still, the rich biosphere of a truly living world reminded Devree her homeworld. The life on Opal was completely different, but it *felt* similar enough.

With Devree was a small tour group from both the *Andromeda* and the *Ascalon,* which wasn't due to lift off for another thirty hours. This was probably the last chance she was going to get to walk on an actual world before reaching Zanzibar, and she didn't want to miss the opportunity. It was also the only chance she was going to get, on this trip, to see an actual alien.

With her was Wade Bishop, the only other member of Captain Blackwood's hired guns that wanted to go, Annie Winchester, and a couple of other crewmembers from the *Andromeda* that she hadn't really gotten to know. Marcus had told the team not to go anywhere alone (especially where his daughter was concerned). Being there to look after Annie was the excuse Wade had used to come along, but Devree was beginning to suspect the demolitions technician had a bit of a crush on her. She was still embarrassed about her drunken, flirty behavior with him back on New Austin, and hoped he hadn't gotten the wrong idea about her. Still, he *was* kind of cute, in a weird, awkward way.

Annie, on the other hand, was adorable. She wore sunglasses and a respirator to help her cope with Opal's harsh atmosphere, but she was just bursting with excitement. She hadn't stopped talking about how amazing it was to be on another planet and maybe seeing an alien since they'd left the *Andromeda*'s cargo bay.

The only other person from the *Andromeda* she really recognized was Kimball, the cargomaster. He was easy to pick out of a crowd, given his short stature. It was kind of sad that she'd been cooped up on a ship with these people for weeks and still couldn't pick most of them out of a lineup, but she was really bad with names. She'd meet someone, shake his hand, then immediately forget his name. The doctors told her that short-term memory problems were one of the things she'd have to learn to live with, after her brush with death. She'd accepted that, but it was still frustrating. It made people think she was a ditz.

"The bus is finally here," Wade said, his voice wavering in the sweltering heat. Rolling up the only highway on Opal was a small bus, its electric engine whining shrilly in the morning air. As it pulled to a stop, Devree was surprised to see it had a human driver, one of the colonists.

"Good morning travelers!" the man said eagerly. He, too, wore sunglasses, and was dressed in a bland, beige outfit that seemed to wick away moisture. This part of Opal was hot and insufferably humid, and Devree was sweating heavily just from standing outside. The bus was mercifully cool as the spacers-turned-tourist boarded one by one. "Sit anywhere you like," the driver said. "I am Slevin, your guide. Welcome, welcome to Opal!"

So much for the frosty reception Halifax warned us about, Devree thought. This Slevin character seemed personable enough, but then again, he was moonlighting as a tour guide, so he pretty much had to be. Devree found a window seat and sat down as Slevin read a very long list or rules about visiting the colony on Opal. Annie plopped down next to her, and she realized how small the seats were. Wade sat just across the narrow aisle. *I hope Wade can't smell me from over there.*

The bus pulled slowly away from the spaceport, heading back down the long road to the nameless colony. "As you can see," Slevin said, speaking over a PA system, "Opal is utterly teeming with life. It has a rich, fully evolved ecosystem of a type rarely found in explored space. Native life abounds here, on land, in the seas, and even in the sky. I must insist, however, that should we encounter any native life-forms, that you be respectful and keep your distance. Please remember that this is their world, and that we are the aliens here. If you start to feel faint or sick, let me know, and I will provide you with supplemental oxygen. The atmosphere here is not toxic, but it takes some getting used to."

The tour wasn't especially interesting at first. The human colony on Opal amounted to little more than a small city. The buildings were the same boxy prefabs you'd find on a hundred colonized worlds, though they had been added onto over the years in a haphazard fashion. Some looked downright ramshackle, but others had native pseudo-trees growing out of them and were very beautiful. Aside from Slevin, none of the locals acknowledged the tourists, not even so much as a nod. Devree still took dozens of still pictures with her handheld. *How often do you get to visit another planet?*

Compared to what Halifax had told her, Slevin was pretty sparse on the details of the history of the colony. He mentioned that they had been here since the time of the Second Interstellar War, and seemed proud that the tiny colony was completely independent. (He claimed it was completely self-sufficient, too, but Devree wasn't buying that.) He showed them the massive, domed greenhouses where they raised their crops, and boasted that everything they ate was completely "natural." What that meant, exactly, escaped Devree, considering that food crops intended for planetary colonies had been genetically modified for centuries, but she didn't feel like nitpicking the poor man. He was just trying to show them around, after all.

After an hour or so of leading the tourists around the colony on foot, in the sweltering heat of the day, Slevin brought them into what he called a fair-trade bazaar, where they could purchase or barter for locally made goods. "We have no use for your money on Opal, of course," he said proudly, "but we pool it into a common fund and use it to trade with off-worlders from time to time. We ask that you either pay in hard currency or barter with material goods. Electronic banking is unavailable here. All goods in the bazaar are handmade by local artisans, who simply want to share the fruits of their labor with travelers such as yourselves."

Once the doors had cycled, Devree took a deep breath and sighed with relief. The cool air inside was refreshing. "Wow," she said, looking around the bazaar. More than a dozen colonists had set up stands or displays, with goods for sale or trade. "My mom would love this place. I should get something for her."

"Your mom emigrated to New Austin with you?" Wade asked, wiping his brow.

"She's my only living relative, and she was in danger too, so they sent her with me. Oh, look at those pots! I'm gonna go look."

"I want to see!" Annie said, following on her heel. As she and Marcus' daughter browsed the merchant's wares, Devree caught Wade rolling his eyes and smiled to herself.. He wasn't the least bit interested in shopping, but was letting her drag him around to be nice. It was kind of sweet, in a sad, pushover kind of way. He stood nearby, idly looking around with his hands in his pockets as she haggled with a local over a beautifully painted clay pot. Annie browsed a table full of handmade bead necklaces and charm bracelets.

Wade tapped on Devree's shoulder as she exchanged a handful of hard currency with the woman selling pots. "Devree?"

"Just a second," she said, not looking up.

He tapped harder. "Devree, *look*."

She stood up, pot in hand. "Holy hell, Wade, what—oh my God."

Wade grinned and put his hands back into his pockets. "Thought you'd want to go see." At the far side of the room, surrounded by the bulk of the visiting tourists, were two of the short, leathery creatures that called Opal their home. One had skin that shaded from brown to blue. The other, slightly taller, was green with reddish patches. Their round eyes were shiny and red, and their pointy teeth gave them an unsettling look. With them was a human woman, dressed in baggy, moisture-wicking garments. She was skinny and sickly looking like most of the other colonists. She communicated with the aliens in sign language and translated for the visitors.

"Hold this," Devree said, shoving her newly acquired pot into Wade's hands. "I'm gonna go get a picture! Come, on, Annie!"

One of the creatures signed rapidly to the translator with its clawed fingers. She replied to them, then turned to the cluster of off-worlders surrounding her. "He says greetings, strangers, and welcome. He and his partner have been chosen by their tribe to meet and trade with strangers. They have brought some trade goods for this purpose. Please be advised, though, that they won't accept currency. They may accept items of yours for trade, however."

A crewwoman from the *Ascalon* raised her handheld. "Is it okay if I take a picture?" she asked.

Before the translator could reply, the two aliens noticed the device in her hands. They stood close to each other, putting their arms over each other's shoulders in a remarkably human manner, and very obviously mugged for the camera. Their mouths hung open in a ghastly approximation of a smile. "Yes," she said, smiling herself. "They enjoy being photographed. Just make sure you show them the pictures after. Sometimes, we trade hard copies of photographs with them."

Annie stood next to Devree, seemingly mesmerized. She didn't even take pictures at first. "Devree," she said quietly, "this is so incredible!" The girl then raised her handheld and began to snap a barrage of still pictures.

"You'll have to send me those when we get back to the ship," Wade said. He'd caught up to her, still holding her pot in his hands.

Stepping through the crowd, Kimball slowly approached the small beings. Intrigued, Devree raised her handheld and set it to record video. The aliens seemed utterly fascinated with Kimball. Unlike most humans, the *Andromeda*'s cargomaster didn't tower over them. One of the creatures raised a clawed hand to the top of its head, comparing height. It then signed rapidly to the translator.

"He wants to know what you are," she said apologetically. "Please take no offense. They've never seen one such as you before."

"Offense?" Kimball asked. "Gentlewoman, rest assured that I am as fascinated with them as they are with me. I am from a world with high gravity, and it tends to leave us shorter in stature. Would you be so kind as to relay this to them for me?" The translator did so, pausing as she thought about how to translate gravity. The two aliens spoke to each other after she had finished. Their language was a series of huffs, puffs, clicks, and grunts to human ears, but it worked well enough for them.

The being closest to Kimball had a crude belt around its midsection, attached to which was a sheathed knife. Taking the hilt into a clawed hand, the alien drew his weapon, which had a blade of black stone, and presented it to Kimball.

The translator seemed as surprised by this as Kimball was. She signed to the other alien briefly, then turned to the cargo-master again. "He wishes to offer his knife, if you have anything you're willing to trade for it. This...this is fascinating. They're normally so shy around humans. We've warned them about how cruel and exploitative humans can be."

"Perhaps, Gentlewoman, that that is the reason they are so shy," Kimball said. "I don't have much on me, I fear. However..." He pulled a folding knife from where it had been clipped to the pocket of his coverall. Very slowly, so as not to startle the aliens, he opened the blade, and presented it, handle-first.

"What...what is that?" the translator asked, her eyes wide.

"It's a knife of course," Kimball said. The alien took the blade eagerly, and showed it to his companion. In turn, he let Kimball take the obsidian knife. "A blade for a blade," the cargomaster said, examining his new acquisition. "He seems happy enough with the trade. That knife is well used, but it's made of the finest alloys and holds its edge. My new friend will get many years of service out of it."

The translator looked aghast. "You brought a weapon here?" She stepped back timidly, as if she expected Kimball to leap up and slash her with alien stone knife.

"Gentlewoman," he said levelly. "There is no need for any alarm." He indicated his blade, which the aliens were opening and closing repeatedly, having figured out the locking mecha-nism. "It's a tool for these fellows to use. They offered me one of theirs, so I offered one in kind. It only seems fair. I mean no one any harm."

"But you were told!" she stammered, stepping back further. "They said you wouldn't have any weapons! Why are you carrying weapons?" She looked around at the rest of the tourists, eyes wide.

Devree stepped forward, but kept recording with her handheld.

Things were going sideways in a hurry and it was best to document it. "Hey, look at me. It's okay. This is just a misunderstanding. Please calm down. We'll leave, we'll go back to the spaceport."

"I . . . I have to report this," the translator said. Before anyone else could say anything to her, she hurried off. She took the driver of their bus in tow and disappeared into a small room off to the side of the bazaar. The two aliens, no longer able to communicate with the humans, seemed just as confused as the spacers.

Kimball nodded to the creatures, then turned to the group. "Gentlefolk, I fear I have caused a drama. I apologize for this. If any of you are carrying pocket knives, I suggest you keep them hidden until you get back to spaceport. It seems these people take their no weapons rule well into the realm of the absurd. Mercenary Bishop," he said, handing his alien knife to Wade. "Please hold onto this for me. Having a simple blade is apparently cause for alarm in this strange place. It makes one wonder how these people slice their vegetables without succumbing to panic attacks."

The other colonists at the bazaar were hurriedly packing up their things and heading for the airlock. Before the spacers could decide what to do, the translator returned, leading a trio of security men. Instead of the plain garb worn by most of the colonists, they wore blue uniforms with armor and helmets. Their faces were concealed behind respirators and goggles. The first two appeared to be carrying stun batons, but the third had a flechette gun in his hands.

"That's the one!" said the translator, pointing at Kimball. "He had a weapon in the presence of the protected ones!" The two aliens' faces couldn't be read by humans, but for all that they looked bewildered as the translator hurried them away and the security men moved in on the group of tourists.

"You are coming with us," one of them said, pointing at Kimball. His voice was disguised with a modulator, making him sound robotic.

"Gentlemen," Kimball said, hands raised in the air. "There is no need for this. This has all been a misunderstanding. I meant no one any harm. If you'll just let me return to my ship, I'll leave your world and there won't be any issues."

The security man stepped forward and shoved Kimball down to the ground. "Place your hands behind your head. Comply!"

The other drew his stun baton, crackling the electric shock

device in warning to the group of spacers. "Do not interfere. Interfering with Peacekeepers in the discharge of their duties is a crime." The spacers from the *Andromeda* stepped forward anyway. Devree put a hand on Wade's arm; he looked like he was going for a gun.

"Stand down, all of you," Kimball grunted as he was roughly restrained. "Do not make this worse than it is. Mercenary Star-lighter, you recorded this, correct? Please send the video to the captain and return to the ship. This will get sorted out."

"But," Devree began.

"No buts!" Kimball interrupted. The security men were already leading him away. "Notify the captain!"

Annie looked up at Devree, fear in her eyes. "We have to do something! We can't just let them take him!"

"I'm sending the video to the captain now," she said quietly. "This is bullshit."

"Captain Blackwood will do something," Wade said. "She doesn't fuck around. This won't stand. Send it to Marcus too, just in case."

"My dad won't let this stand," Annie said defiantly.

Devree put a hand on the girl's shoulder. "No, sweetie, I don't expect he will."

Captain Catherine Blackwood sat up straight in her chair on the command deck of the *Andromeda*. She smoothed the wrinkles out of her coverall and made sure her hair was all in place. Appearances counted for a lot in these sorts of dealings, and she wanted to be the very picture of the master-after-God of her ship. Standing behind and to the left of her chair was her executive officer, Wolfram von Spandau, with his hands held neatly behind his back. Marcus Winchester stood off to the side, arms folded across his chest, so that he couldn't be seen on screen. The normal watch-standers had been dismissed from the command deck for the call. Taking a deep breath, Catherine tapped the controls on one of her several screens and waited for the call to connect.

After a moment, a young man in the drab gray outfit with a stand-up collar appeared on her screen. Like most of the colonists on Opal, he was almost sickly thin. "Greetings, Captain," he said, speaking Commerce English with the unfamiliar accent the colonists all seemed to share. "My name is Desh. I am an appointed speaker for the Council of Elders. My word comes directly from them, and anything you tell me is the same as telling them. What is it you'd like to discuss?"

You know damned well what I want to discuss, Catherine thought. She didn't say that, though. *Losing your cool doesn't help your negotiations any.* "Greetings, Mr. Desh. I am Captain Catherine Blackwood, commanding officer of the privateer ship *Andromeda*. I'd like to discuss the status of my cargomaster, one Jason Kimball. There was a misunderstanding at the trade bazaar this afternoon, and he was taken into custody by your security forces."

Desh cocked his head to the side slightly. "Misunderstanding? Captain, there was no misunderstanding. I've seen video of the incident, and that video was corroborated by the testimony of multiple witnesses. Mr. Kimball was, in fact, carrying a weapon, specifically, a knife with a metal blade. It was made very clear by the guide that weapons are completely prohibited in our colony. This is doubly true in the presence of the indigenous beings. We are, after all, guests on *their* world."

The indigenous being seemed bloody well delighted to receive that knife, you ass. Catherine rested her elbows on the arm-rests of her chair, folded her hands together, and glared at the Speaker. "I also have seen video of the incident, sir. Indeed it *was* a misunderstanding. The so-called weapon the woman was hyperventilating about was a simple folding pocket knife. It's a tool for opening packages and cutting things as needed. Every member of my crew has one. It's very easy to become tangled up during an emergency in zero gravity, and a knife can be a lifesaving tool in that situation. It probably never occurred to my crewman that anyone would consider it a *weapon*."

Desh narrowed his eyes and spoke in an almost scolding tone. "Captain, I mean no disrespect, but if there was a misun-derstanding then it surely lies in the reading comprehension of your crew member. The terms and conditions listed as part of boarding the tour bus explicitly state, among other things, that metal-bladed weapons are as prohibited as firearms and energy weapons. Your man came into our home and violated our rules, Captain. Ignorance is no excuse for violating the law here."

Her face was a mask, but Catherine's blood was boiling.

Either these people really were that unreasonable, or they were fishing for a bribe. "I see," she said diplomatically. "Having traveled all over inhabited space, I'm well-versed in the importance of respecting local laws and customs. In the contract that each of my crew members signs is a clause stating that they are personally responsible if they should commit a crime while off of the ship. That said, I am on a mission of some urgency, and my cargomaster is currently incarcerated. I am unfamiliar with the specifics of your judicial system. Would it be possible for me to pay his bond and have him released? Rest assured I'll take it out of his pay. We do need to be on our way soon."

"I'm afraid that is not possible, Captain," Desh said coolly. "Under our code, your crewman must remain in our custody until the next scheduled meeting of a Judiciary Tribunal. At such time, he can argue his case before the Council of Elders, and his fate will be decided then. If you wish, you can send a representative to speak for your crewman at his trial."

They really are *that unreasonable,* Catherine thought grimly. "I see. When, may I ask, is the next meeting of this tribunal?"

"Tribunals are held regularly, on the first day of the month, assuming there are cases to be adjudicated. The next one is scheduled in twenty-nine days."

Opal's day was thirty-four and a half hours long. Catherine barely managed to maintain her calm demeanor. "I see. And you're sure that there's nothing I can do to expedite this process?"

Desh raised his head, looking down his long nose at Catherine. "Captain, I don't know what you're insinuating, but I've explained our laws as plainly as I am able. We will not violate the sanctity of our laws merely because some off-worlder imagines herself to be important and is in a hurry. Mr. Kimball's trial will be in twenty-nine days. You can wait until then, or come back at that time and speak for him if you wish. Good day, Captain." Desh's image disappeared, and the screen flashed CONNECTION LOST.

"Goddamn it!" Catherine snarled, slamming a fist onto an armrest.

"They are being unreasonable, *Kapitänin,*" Wolfram said, stating the obvious. "I feared this would be the case."

"This is my fault," Catherine said, rubbing her temples. "My gut told me not to let my crew venture into that bizarre little colony, and I just didn't listen."

"These things happen," Wolfram said. "They are unfortunate, but they happen. It was a necessary risk. We have a long flight ahead of us. Letting the crew out on leave while we're planeted is good for morale."

Marcus spoke up. "I hate to be the one to say it, but maybe Kimball should've been more careful about what he had on him. Though, being honest, I'm willing to bet my two people both had 'concealed weapons' on them as well."

"Rest assured," the captain said, "when this matter is resolved I'll be docking Mr. Kimball's pay for the trouble. That said, I am not amused with the colonial authority's nonsense, and I am not about to leave a man behind at the behest of some petty bureaucrat on this backwater swamp." She looked to Marcus. "Mr. Winchester, do you feel your team is up for an extraction mission?"

Marcus rubbed his chin for a moment. "It's very doable, Captain. From the video my daughter and Ms. Starlighter recorded, and other media we've been able to obtain, including telemetry from the ship's sensors, their security is crude. These so-called Peacekeepers, the local constabulary, are few in number, and I have no reason to believe they're particularly well-trained, not on an isolated colony like this. The colonists are pretty tight-lipped, but between our observations and what Mr. Halifax has told me of his previous visit, I have enough information to devise and effectuate a rescue plan. I think this would be a good real-world training opportunity for my team."

Catherine looked thoughtful. "But?"

"Captain?" Marcus asked.

"But," Catherine repeated. "I sense a 'but' in your assessment."

"Captain, the question is, how many casualties are you willing to accept? I'm confident my team can accomplish this with a bare minimum of bloodshed. Even though we've lost the signal from his locator beacon, we believe Mr. Kimball is being held in a structure called the Office of the Peacekeepers. It's basically a police station. While these Peacekeepers might be poorly trained, I don't expect they'll let us take Kimball without a fight. It could get ugly in a hurry. I believe we can retrieve your crewman, but there might be broader consequences to this course of action."

Catherine's eyes narrowed. "Are you suggesting I leave my crewman to his fate?"

"Ma'am," Marcus said calmly, "I'm not suggesting anything. You're paying me a lot of money for my expertise, and I'm giving you an honest assessment of the situation. I can get your man back. The consequences of that course of action are yours to deal with, not mine. We're outside of Concordiat space, and by extension the jurisdiction of my government."

Wolfram von Spandau spoke up then. "He is correct, *Kapitänin*. This colony does not have any extradition, law enforcement, or recognition treaties with any other colony or government. Their laws are not recognized by the Concordiat or anyone else. Regardless, we must proceed cautiously. Our crewman broke one of their asinine laws. Retrieving him by overt force and killing their citizens could be considered an act of piracy. If these people successfully lodge a complaint against us with Concordiat authorities, we could be blacklisted. We'd never be able to safely operate in Concordiat space again."

Catherine knew all this, and her executive officer shouldn't have had to remind her. But he was doing what a good exec does: keeping his Captain out of trouble. She took a deep breath and forced herself to calm down. "You are right, of course, both of you. I'm just frustrated, forgive me. I have no patience for tyrants of any sort, and I find the petty ones to be the most insufferable. I could *destroy* their colony if I was willing," she said darkly. "I wouldn't even need to waste our ammunition—landing the ship in the middle of town would turn most of it to glass. But ... obviously I won't do anything like that. The question is, gentlemen, what *can* we do?"

"We need more information, Captain," Marcus suggested. "I doubt any of us would be able to blend in with the locals in town, but we have other tools at our disposal. We need to determine what kind of security measures are in place and whether or not the people keeping him can be bribed or threatened."

Wolfram nodded thoughtfully. "What if they will not be bribed or threatened?"

"It's risky, but ... we have less-lethal options at our disposal. The people holding him won't grant us any such consideration, of course. It's like bringing a pillow to a knife fight, but with good intel, a good plan, and a particularly firm pillow, we may be able to pull it off."

"They may still complain to the Concordiat authorities," the executive officer said.

Marcus nodded in agreement. "They may. But we're a long way from the nearest Fleet patrol. It would be weeks before anyone even hears their complaint, and probably months before an investigation is launched, *if* an investigation is launched, which is not likely. I seriously doubt the Fleet would send an envoy all the way out here because some privateers sprung one of their guys from the clink. If we go in guns blazing and shoot up the colony, well, that's different. But if we do it quietly and cleanly... I can't make you any promises, Captain, but I think I can get your man back without causing an interstellar incident. All the rumors that they execute people for minor infractions work in our favor. They refuse to confirm or deny it. Extreme measures seem more reasonable if you're trying to save your man from the gallows."

Catherine's brow furled in concentration as she thought for a few moments. Nodding to herself, she looked to Marcus again. "Very well, Mr. Winchester. Enlist the aid of the crew as necessary. Find out everything you can, and come up with a plan as quickly as possible. We're still on a schedule here."

"Consider it done, Captain," Marcus said, heading for the hatch. "I'll brief you as soon as I know more. I need to go talk to my team."

The darkened sky of Opal shimmered with the light of a thousand stars and two small moons as Marcus and his team made their way through the dense alien forest. The foliage glowed blue, green, violet, and indigo through natural bioluminescence. Countless tiny creatures, some flying, come crawling, went about their business in the darkness, themselves glowing faintly like fireflies. The pseudo-trees swayed and shifted in the darkness, and shuddered slightly when bumped, as if startled by human touch. It was beautiful, ethereal...like a vivid dream.

Marcus noted thankfully that the native life didn't seem interested in the human mercenaries. The weird forests of Opal weren't anything like the vicious jungles of Mandalay, where every single lifeform seemed to be out for blood. He felt peaceful, despite the tension of the situation. The flying creatures emitted a melodious hum as they passed by, and the pseudo-trees would answer with a deep, rhythmic pulse of their own. It was still warm and murderously humid, but of the many alien ecosystems

Marcus had found himself in over the years, this was one of the more pleasant ones.

Devree Starlighter's calm soprano voice piped into Marcus' headset. "Cowboy-6, Overwatch. In position. Eyes on the BOI. Almost no activity in the street. Multiple security cameras around the structure. Over."

"Cowboy-6 copies," Marcus replied. He grinned at the first official use of their unofficial team name. Devree, with Randy Markgraf serving as a spotter, had crept into town under the cloak of darkness and active thermoptic camouflage. Devree had found a good sniper's hide for herself, high above the town, on a maintenance access platform of a communications tower. The remaining five mercenaries approached the town from a different direction. They didn't have enough thermoptic camouflage garments for the entire team, so Marcus thought it best to give them to the sniper team.

"*Andromeda* copies as well," said another voice. "There's very little activity across the entire colony. Early to bed, early to rise, it seems. Over." Kilometers away, on the command deck of the ship, Captain Blackwood and her crew were monitoring the entire mission. They had a small, stealthy, nearly silent drone circling above the colony, providing real-time information to both the ship and the ground team.

Marcus was pleased that Captain Blackwood didn't seem interested in micromanaging her people. She was observing and acknowledging, but didn't try to tell Marcus how to run his team. He greatly appreciated the professional trust in him she displayed. "Roger. We've reached Waypoint Charlie," he said, indicating that his team was on the edge of town. The foliage abruptly ended in a vast clearing, in which the colony was situated. The Office of the Peacekeepers, a bland, windowless structure, stood less than a kilometer away from the edge of the forest. The colony's streets were narrow and cluttered, which would aid the team in approaching undetected.

"Cowboy-6," a crewman on board the *Andromeda* said, observing through the multispectral cameras of the drone, "I've mapped a route for you, sending now. This will get you to the building of interest."

Devree spoke into her radio once again. "I've got the cameras identified and targeted. Standing by."

"Copy all," Marcus said. His eyepiece blinked. "Received. Moving."

Captain Blackwood herself spoke into the communications link. "Good luck and Godspeed."

The team didn't have a direct line of sight to the Office of the Peacekeepers as they wove their way through the cluttered town. This was good, as that building had security cameras on it, mounted on the corners of the roof, whereas most of the other structures didn't. Hugging walls and crawling through ditches, the team approached their target in silence. All of their gear had been secured so as not to make noise. Smart glasses enhanced their vision in the low light, and active headsets enhanced their hearing. From what he'd observed, Marcus didn't think these Peacekeepers had any such modern equipment at their disposal.

Still, he wasn't about to let his team get complacent, not on their first real operation. They communicated through hand and arm signals as they moved swiftly through the darkened colony. Half the team would move up while the other half held position and provided cover. In this way, they approached very close to the Office of the Peacekeepers before Marcus indicated that they should hold up and take cover. "Overwatch, Cowboy-6. Holding at Waypoint Delta."

Devree acknowledged. "Roger. Stand by." An instant later, a pivoting security camera in a transparent protective bubble shattered, followed by a sonic crack, as a high-powered rifle bullet punched through it. From her elevated vantage point, Devree angled her scoped, sound-suppressed rifle and rapidly snapped off several more shots, destroying every security camera in her line of sight.

At the same time, Marcus pointed to Ken Tanaka, who was positioned across a narrow street from him. He and Tanaka each lobbed two screening smoke grenades forward, filling the narrow streets with dense white smoke. The thick, humid air and lack of wind enabled the smoke to hang over the street like a bad memory, limiting unenhanced vision to a couple of meters and interfering with even multispectrum cameras.

As planned, the team quietly rushed forward through the smoke. The front door to the Office of the Peacekeepers was reinforced, not something you could just kick in, but Wade was prepared. As the others provided cover, the explosives technician vaulted up the short steps to the building's front door. He unrolled a linear shaped charge along the hinge-side of the door, pressing it into place as he did so. That done, he jumped down from the front steps and crouched by the wall. He looked to Ken, who was scanning the doorway with a handheld scanner. The Nipponese mercenary shot Wade the thumbs up when the scanner told him the other side of the doorway was clear. Wade nodded back and readied his initiator. "Fire in the hole!"

BOOM! With a loud, metallic bang and another cloud of smoke, the door was blasted off its hinges and clattered to the steps. Marcus and the team were moving in an instant, weapons up and ready. In a tight stack, they maneuvered up the stairs and into the now-open airlock as alarms blared and fire-suppression systems sprayed purple retardant. The interior door of the entryway was locked, but the team was prepared for that as well. Halifax and Hondo stepped forward, aiming their big-bore flechette guns at the door's hinges. *BA-BLAM!* Powdered tungsten breaching rounds disintegrated the hinges. Marcus raised his foot and kicked the door in, sending it flying to the floor. Without breaking his stride, he led the team through the door and into the Office of the Peacekeepers, amongst the scream of klaxons and the shouts of men.

"Contact front!" Marcus shouted, firing off a rapid shot at a Peacekeeper who was stumbling out of a room, having barely finished putting his mask on. His flechette gun bucked against his shoulder, launching a less-lethal round into the unsuspecting constable. The slug hit its target with enough blunt force to cause him to double over in pain, and latched onto him. Then it shocked him senseless, disrupting his central nervous system and causing him to black out. The shock rounds were about seventy-five percent effective against nonaugmented humans, and were the most reliable way to put a man down short of killing him outright.

"Contact rear!" Ken Tanaka said, his voice elevated but still calm. Several frantic gunshots rang out in the building's main corridor before a shock round put the pistol-wielding Peacekeeper on the floor. "He's down!"

"Bishop, Halifax, on me!" Marcus ordered. "Tanaka, Hondo, secure the entry point. *Andromeda*, Cowboy-6, we've breached the BOI and are conducting our search. Overwatch, move in."

To a chorus of acknowledgment, Marcus, Wade, and Ben Halifax moved down the corridor, searching for the way down to the detention facility. The doors were labeled, but the signs were in Esperanto and were hard to read. "I think this is it!" he said, indicating another reinforced door which was labeled "malliberigon facilecon."

"I'm picking up his locator beacon again," Halifax said.

"The door is secured," Marcus said, trying the handle. The whole building went into lockdown the moment the door was breached.

"On it!" Wade said, stepping forward with another, smaller breaching charge. He attached it to the door as Marcus and Halifax took cover behind a corner. He ducked behind cover himself, shouted, "fire in the hole!" and mashed the initiator.

BOOM! The concussion in the corridor was head-splitting, and had it not been for the mercenaries' active hearing protection they'd all be deaf. Wade moved forward first, checking his shot. The door, mangled and twisted, barely hung on by one bent hinge. Wade booted it once, then twice, then a third time, which broke it free and sent it clattering down the stairs below. "We're through!" he announced.

Without missing a beat, Marcus and Halifax rounded the corner, guns up, and headed down the narrow stairwell. Lights flickered in the aftermath of the blast, and the corridor was filled with smoke. Even with vision enhancement, it was hard to see.

Tanaka's voice crackled in Marcus' ear as he made his way carefully down the stairs. "This is strange. We're encountering almost no resistance. The two men we've dropped are still incapacitated, and there's been almost no sign of anyone else."

"The building went into an automatic lockdown when we breached," Halifax said, breathing heavily in his mask. "And it's the night shift. Probably only had a couple Peacekeepers on desk duty. More will come, lads, so keep your wits about you. The whole town knows we're here now."

"This is Overwatch," Devree said breathlessly. "The whole town lit up when you guys breached. People are mostly staying indoors, but the feed from the ship shows multiple personnel on foot, headed our way."

"We're in the detention center," Marcus said, static fuzzing over his transmission.

"Roger," Devree acknowledged. "Extraction Team, now would be a good time!"

Mazer Broadbent responded. "Understood. Extraction team moving." Kilometers away, at the outskirts of the spaceport, the *Andromeda*'s security officer and another volunteer from the crew sped toward town in a ground van they had rented from the traders. At the same time, Captain Blackwood was running her crew through the final checks for a short-notice emergency launch. The powerful fusion reactor of the *Andromeda* was running hot, ready to lift the ship into the safety of space at a moment's notice.

Down in the subterranean detention center, Marcus and his team found themselves shrouded in darkness and smoke. They hit their vision enhancement as they came around a dogleg in the corridor. He gasped aloud as a dumpy Peacekeeper, mostly clad in ill-fitting riot armor, crashed into him coming the other way. The startled colonist dropped the helmet he hadn't yet put on as he tried to bring his carbine to bear, but Marcus grabbed the barrel, shoved it aside, and cracked the constable upside the head with his flechette gun. Before the Peacekeeper could recover, Marcus shoved him back a bit and hit him with a full-on butt-stroke from his weapon. The Peacekeeper's weapon clattered to the floor as he collapsed against a wall, coughing and wheezing.

Wade slung his flechette gun full of less-lethal rounds. He faced the injured colonist, kicked his carbine away, and leveled his big 12mm revolver at the man's face. "Stay down!" That gun was loaded with *especially* lethal rounds, and the dazed jailer gaped at it wide-eyed. He raised his hands slowly and didn't move.

Across the detention center, Marcus and Halifax had located a bewildered Cargomaster Kimball. They handed the spacer a respirator mask through the bars of his cell as they struggled with the door controls, trying to figure out how to let him out. He might have to run, and Opal's thick atmosphere made aerobic activity difficult if you weren't used to it. Wade marched the injured jailer over at gunpoint and sat him down in his work station. It took a couple of prods with his big sidearm, but the Peacekeeper relented and shakily tapped the controls.

With a loud buzz barely audible over the constantly blaring klaxons, every single detention cell opened at once. The other prisoners, wide-eyed and confused, mostly stayed in their cells, afraid to do anything, but two of them bolted, running up the stairs and out the door. Where they thought they were going to hide on an inhospitable planet with only ten thousand permanent residents was anyone's guess.

The mercenaries led Kimball out of his cell and handed him the Peacekeeper's very old-looking carbine. "Don't shoot unless you have to," Wade said. "We're trying not to kill anybody."

Marcus keyed his microphone. "*Andromeda*, this is Cowboy-6. Package in tow, headed back to the barn." As his team checked Kimball for injuries and got him ready to move, Marcus took a quick look around. Two of the rooms in the detention center had large chairs in the middle, fastened to the floor, complete with restraints for the arms, legs, waist, and head. The floors were bare, complete with a drain. "Does that look like a torture chamber to you, Wade?" he asked.

"It sure as hell does, Boss."

Kimball spoke up after tightening the straps on his mask. "They were constantly accusing me of trying to threaten the aliens, their so-called protected ones. They pointed guns at me and accused me of being a weapon-loving fanatic. I pointed out the inherent irony in that situation," he said, pointing to a large bruise on his brow, "and they responded with a demonstration of their nonviolence."

"He has a few bruises and swelling, but he's good to travel, Marcus," Tanaka said, switching off the flashlight he'd been checking Kimball with.

"Good. Alright, boys, let's get the hell out of here. We just kicked a hornets' nest."

Mazer Broadbent rolled the van through the narrow streets of the colony as fast as he could manage without crashing. He hadn't driven a ground vehicle in quite some time and was a little rusty. This became perfectly clear when he bucked the wheels over a curb and scared the hell out of the young Tech Daye, who had volunteered to come rescue Kimball. The colony had woken up. Nearly every light was on, people were peering through their windows, and a few were running through the streets.

Fishtailing around a corner, Mazer stomped on the accelerator and raced the boxy vehicle down a slightly wider street leading to the Office of the Peacekeepers. With vision-enhancing goggles, he could see the mercenary team holding a tight perimeter by the building's entrance, awaiting his arrival. Coming to the end of the street, he hit the brake, cut the wheel to the right, and spun the van around, lifting it briefly up on two tires, so the rear doors were facing the waiting mercenaries.

The van's cargo door was yanked open, and the mercenary team shoved poor Kimball in with such force that Mazer thought that they *threw* him. The seven mercs piled in after their quarry, faces concealed behind masks and tac helmets. Two of them were very difficult to see in the gloom of the night until they deactivated their thermoptic camo. Those two, Starlighter and Markgraf, climbed in last and pulled the door shut.

"We're in!" Marcus Winchester announced. "Drive!"

"Hold on!" Mazer replied, hitting the accelerator again. The mercs were tossed around in the cargo space of the van, not having seats nor anything to hold on to, as the security officer roared the vehicle back through the city the same way he'd come in.

As he made a hard left turn onto the main road which led to the spaceport, he saw a group of men hurriedly trying to pull barricades into the street.

"Roadblock!" Daye announced.

"Brace!" Mazer said, pushing the accelerator to the floor and bringing the van to its top speed. Terrified Peacekeepers dove out of the way as the clunky vehicle smashed through their plastic barricades, sending them clattering down the street. Mazer had no idea why they thought those would stop a speeding vehicle, but they were certainly unhappy about it. In the van's wake, orange muzzle flashes appeared in the night as a couple of the constables opened fire.

"They're shooting at us!" one of the mercs shouted, as small-caliber bullets punched through the back door, narrowly missing the occupants. But in a flash, the van was too far away from the Peacekeepers for their sidearms to be of any use, and rounding a bend, put the colony out of sight.

"I think we're in the clear," Mazer said, and immediately regretted it.

"Mr. Broadbent!" Daye said, tapping the security officer on the shoulder roughly. "Mr. Broadbent!"

"What is it, man?"

Before Daye could answer, Marcus, in the back of the van, peered out of the rear hatch. "Hellfire," he spat. "Mazer! We've got company! Inbound hovercycles, coming in fast!" Mazer hadn't known the colonists actually had any vehicles, much less hover-cycles. But there they were, skimming low over the pseudo-trees, twin lift-fans screaming in the dark. They would've been hard to see except for the bright spotlights they shone on the van as it sped up the highway.

Daye ducked down in his seat as bullets *pinged* and *dinged* against the van's body. "They're shooting at us!" Each hovercycle carried two Peacekeepers; the one in front drove while the one behind him aimed a pistol as best he could. Their accuracy was terrible, but one lucky hit and the van would crash.

In the rearview mirror, Mazer noticed Halifax changing magazines in his weapon. Wind filled the cab of the van as the mercenary slid open the top hatch and stood up. "Marcus, I have a shot!"

Mazer swore to himself. "Marcus, shoot them down!"

The mercenary team leader nodded and gave Halifax a thumbs-up. The stout merc laughed aloud and opened fire. Between the hovercycles zipping back and forth, being blinded by spotlights, being shot at, and the van weaving all over the road, Halifax could barely hit anything. But the cycles weren't armored to save weight, so one lucky shot... "Yes!" he exclaimed victoriously. One cluster of flechettes had struck something critical on the closest hovercycle. It rolled over and crunched into the pseudo-trees, disappearing from sight. The other one slowed down and backed way off.

Halifax ducked back into the van. "I got one! The other bas-tard's runnin' home to mama."

"We're almost there!" Mazer said, as the van sped through the gates of the spaceport at well over a hundred kilometers per hour. Hardly slowing down, he maneuvered the van down into the subterranean service tunnels. The vehicle entrance ended at an airlock. The Security Officer hit the brake and cut the wheel. The van's wheels screeched as it slid to a stop, barely two meters from the wall. Mazer took a moment to exhale heavily as the mercenaries kicked open the back door and piled out. "I don't think we'll be getting the deposit back on this," he said, examin-ing the holes in the vehicle.

Leaving the van where it was, the spacers cycled through the airlock as quickly as possible. Once inside, they discarded their respirator masks and ran down hundreds of meters of tunnels, dodging oblivious service robots and knocking over a garbage can. Rounding a corner, the group ran down another, shorter corridor and came to a massive cargo elevator. The doors opened, and all nine people piled in, breathing heavily. The elevator moved slowly upward, taking almost a full minute to reach the cargo deck of the *Andromeda*. The three spacers and seven mercenaries, sweating and panting, said nothing as tinny, electronic music played softly.

The music gave way to a chime as the elevator came to a stop. The doors opened, and the group ran up the long, ramping tunnel, the arm of the spaceport's service tower, and into the open cargo bay doors of the ship. Crewmen were waiting for them inside. They had barely cleared the entrance when the cargo doors began to close and the service tower began to retract. Med Tech Lowlander, checking them for injuries as she led them through the ship, hurried them to the crew deck and got them strapped in for liftoff.

Up on the command deck, Captain Blackwood received word that the ship had been secured, all personnel were accounted for, and all stations were secured for liftoff. At the same time, one of her screens flashed a warning and displayed more incoming hovercycles. There were six of them in total. Hovering at low altitude, they circled the *Andromeda* like vultures as the service tower slowly retracted.

One of Peacekeepers transmitted a threat to the *Andromeda* in a thick Esperanto accent. "Stand down at once! Stand down! You are all under arrest! Comply!"

Catherine had had *enough* of these people. She tapped the transmit button on her display. "Officer, this is Captain Catherine Blackwood of the *Andromeda*. Be advised, we have been cleared by the spaceport for launch. We are lifting off in T-minus ninety seconds. If you value your lives, you will be clear of our exhaust plume by then. *Andromeda* clear."

Catherine listened to their frantic transmissions as the Peacekeepers, completely unsure of what to do, called back to the colony for instructions. Their leader radioed Spaceport Control, demanding that the *Andromeda* be detained. The traffic controller, a quintessential Freeholder, calmly explained to the Peacekeepers that as a sovereign and free individual, not only did he not recognize their authority but he had no authority of his own to detain a ship. As a matter of fact, he said, detaining them would be tantamount to *piracy*. The *Andromeda,* he said, hadn't broken any spaceport rules and had filed its flight plan twenty hours in advance, as requested. He repeated Catherine's suggestion that the hovercycles clear the launch area before the ship lifted off, and reminded them that the spaceport would not be liable for any injury or death that might occur if they chose to stay.

Catherine actually laughed out loud as the Peacekeepers broke and fled. As the countdown reached T-minus twenty seconds, she reclined her command chair back into the launch position. The deal she'd worked out with the Freeholders who ran the spaceport hadn't been inexpensive, but it had proven worthwhile. Freeholders, by nature, disliked the weird, authoritarian rules of the tiny colony, and only accommodated them to the extent necessary to do business. She'd gotten her crewman back, and these backworld crazies could go pound sand.

"This is the captain," she said, broadcasting over the ship's intercom moments before launch. "Well done, all of you. Stand by for liftoff."

Zanzibar
Danzig-5012 Solar System
Lang's Burg, Equatorial Region

Pale light from Danzig-5012 peeked in through the shutters as Zak opened his eyes. He stretched lazily, like a cat on a summer morning (a cat with creaky, cracking joints, anyway). While normally a night person, since coming to Zanzibar Zak had been a habitual early riser. He suspected it had something to do with the planet's lack of a magnetosphere screwing with his sleep patterns, but that was only a guess. It would be a while before Anna got up, and even longer before Cecil crawled out of bed. He retrieved his handheld from the nightstand and took it out of standby.

Zanzibar didn't have a functioning planetary network. There were a few satellites in orbit, but they were strictly pay-for-use, and Zak didn't have access to them. Lang's Burg had its own crude local network, but it was monitored and had nothing of interest on it. Little, if any, news from the rest of inhabited space ever made it as far as Zanzibar, and what news did arrive was months out of date. Fortunately, Zak had thousands of texts saved on his handheld: history books, novels, poetry, anthologies, fiction and nonfiction alike. He was a voracious reader in his free time, and found solace in the quiet solitude of a good book.

His current fascination was an ancient epic poem titled *The Fall of Mankind and the Coming of the Long Night*, written some eight hundred years before. It was a romantic, tragic, and sadly beautiful retelling of the First Interstellar War, the horrific atrocities committed as both sides struggled to exterminate each other, and the ultimate collapse of interstellar civilization. It was a woeful lament of humanity falling from its zenith, destroyed by its own hubris, returning to pre-Space Age barbarism and continual struggle.

The long-dead author of the poem had seen his civilization destroyed. He wrote the poem not knowing if or when the Long Night would ever end, and the sense of loss he felt was palpable with each verse. It made Zak think of the ancient Zanzibari; did they know their end was coming? Did they write epic works lamenting their impending doom, or did it happen suddenly? How many times, on how many worlds, had such a cycle of achievement and destruction been repeated, over billions of years? What great civilizations had lived, flourished, and died in the countless eons before humankind had taken its first step? The Milky Way Galaxy was but a grain of sand on a vast beach, stretching across the cosmos and through time. What difference did any of it make? What did it matter?

The author of *The Coming of the Long Night* pondered these possibilities as well, and felt insignificant because of it. Perhaps it was just the melancholy that comes with witnessing an apocalyptic war unfold, but Zak could feel the bleak hopelessness, the futility of man's insignificant struggles, in the words. It was depressing, more depressing than merely waking up on a dead rock like Zanzibar.

After an hour or so of reading, Zak heard Anna quietly moving around downstairs. She, too, was an early riser, and typically started her days with yoga, then breakfast and tea. He pulled up a picture of her on his small screen. It had been taken right after their arrival on Zanzibar, before their ordeal of captivity began. She was actually smiling. Such a beautiful smile. She undoubtedly had her pick of suitors on her homeworld.

Yet, apparently, she had set her sights on Zak. Cecil had pulled him aside and told him, bluntly, that Anna was in love with him, but he didn't believe it. At first he thought the Avalonian aristocrat was playing a joke on him. After all, Anna had always seemed all business to Zak. She never made any flirty gestures, seemed to dislike physical contact, and was almost standoffish at times.

Cecil had laughed at Zak when he said that. "You just described yourself there, my friend," he'd said. "Did it ever occur to you that she's just like you?"

As a matter of fact, that *hadn't* occurred to Zak. But why hadn't she said anything about how she felt? Anna was a strong woman from a powerful family, and never had any trouble speaking her mind.

Cecil had laughed at that, too. "It wouldn't be proper," he explained, "for a woman of her position to go chasing after a man. That's not how they do things on New Constantinople. Supposedly sophisticated societies sneer at how backward it all is, but in some places a man is still expected to court a lady, to earn her favor. Women don't necessarily give their affections away. You have to work for it. She's not going to risk humiliation by expressing her interest in you. That's your job, as the suitor, to read the signs and make the connection."

The cultural differences between Zak's home of Columbia and the colony of New Constantinople seemed greater than just the fluid accent Anna spoke Commerce English with. He'd made it a point to read everything he could find about the history and society of Anna's home. Cecil had told him that he wasn't going to find a better woman than Anna, and as condescending as it may have sounded it was probably true. The clichéd advice usually given to people in his situation was to "just be yourself"; Zak had been himself for his entire life, and had never won the affections of a woman like Anna before. He had to do it right if he hoped to . . . *to what? What is it you think is going to happen? Focus, man. Get her off this rock alive, then worry about romance.*

Driving the sentiment home, a message box popped up on the screen of his handheld. *What?* Zak hadn't received a message since he'd been on Zanzibar. Without access to a network, his handheld was as isolated as he was, and there wasn't anyone to send him a personal message anyway.

He tapped the screen to bring up the text message. His handheld didn't recognize the sending address. *Mr. Mesa,* it said simply, *your message has been sent.* That was it. A ship willing to carry his message must have left Zanzibar, bound for Concordiat space. A feeling of relief washed over Zak; no matter what happened to him now, he'd done all he could do. He didn't know if the plight of the Zanzibaran people, or the theft and sale of alien relics being used to fund a warlord's army, would be enough to move anyone to act, but at least he had tried.

Zak felt good, for the first time in a long time. He had to

tell Anna the news! Jumping out of bed, Zak ran downstairs and entered the kitchen, where his partner was making herself a modest breakfast out of the food supplies provided by their captors. She looked up at him quizzically when he entered the kitchen, waving his handheld around like a madman. "Well, ah, good morning," she said, raising an eyebrow.

Zak held his screen for Anna to read. "It's done. We did it."

Anna looked thoughtful for a moment, then smiled. "Good. Very good. It doesn't change our situation, but at least we did *something*. We may just get through this yet, Zachary. Our ride home is on its way, and Lang has been happy enough with our work of late."

Zak's expression darkened. "I hate that man," he said quietly. "I hate what he's doing. I hate being so powerless. Anna I..." he trailed off, taking a deep breath. "Anna, I'm sorry I dragged you into this. I'm sorry...for everything."

Anna smiled. "Stop apologizing. You and I, and Mr. Blackwood as well, we are all of us victims of circumstance. I don't blame you for what's happened to us, and neither should you. I knew the risks when I signed the contract. Do you know what my life was like before we became partners?"

Zak simply shook his head. He'd met Anna at a historical symposium on Columbia, where he presented his paper on the history of Zanzibar.

"New Constantinople has been a center of trade, commerce, and culture for a thousand years. My world was burned in the fires of the First Interstellar War, but instead of backsliding into chaos and barbarism, my ancestors held fast and rebuilt our civilization. My family can trace its lineage back to the colony's founding during the Diaspora. I...there's something I have to tell you."

Zak's heart quickened. "Yeah, sure, go ahead. You know you can always talk to me."

Anna looked down. "I'm afraid I've not been entirely forthcoming with you about things...about myself. My name isn't Anna Kay."

Wait, what? "Okay," Zak said. "What *is* your name?"

"My name is Anna Komnene. When I said my family can trace its lineage back to the founding of the colony..." She trailed off.

Zak's mind raced. "Holy hell. You weren't joking. You're a

member of the royal family? Anna...why didn't you tell me? Why are you even here? Why...?"

Anna hushed her partner so she could speak. "I'm not an *important* member of the royal family. I'm not going to be empress or anything, if that's what you're wondering." New Constantinople was a constitutional monarchy. The royal family rarely involved itself in day-to-day governance in the modern era, though their leadership had been key in pulling the colony through the Interregnum. "I didn't tell you because I wanted you to treat me like a partner, not nobility. Before I met you, I lived a life of leisure and luxury. I was free to pursue whatever interest or activity I desired, or not. Anything I wanted, I could have. If I wanted to marry, there was no shortage of men, men I'd never met mind you, willing to propose. Growing up, I was always treated differently, deferred to even, out of respect for my family."

"That...I mean, I'm not trying to be mean, but that doesn't sound that bad to me."

Anna laughed. "I know. Rich girl problems, right? But that's just it: it wasn't hard. I've never known struggle, or want, or danger, or adventure in my entire life. They were abstract concepts that I read about, not things that happened to me. I was free to do whatever I wanted, but nothing I did mattered. Most people who knew me didn't actually know *me*, they knew Anna Komnene, of the Komnene Family, descendants of Alistair Komnene, one of the founding fathers of New Constantinople. People assumed I was vapid, spoiled, and out of touch with the world. You know what? I *was*. The superficial charity work I did, the ceremonies I attended, it was all a chore for me, just doing what was expected of me. None of it mattered."

Zak shook his head. "What were you doing on Columbia then?"

"I ran away," Anna said, smiling. "Not that it was any great sacrifice. I had quite a bit of money put away, after all. After I was awarded my doctorate in archaeology, I told my family I was moving off-world, gathered my things, and left. Columbia was the closest major colony. I wanted to see how the rest of the galaxy lived, and your world was as good a place to start as any."

"Why tell me this now, Anna? Do you want me to try send a message home for you? Will your world send a rescue mission?"

"My world doesn't have much of a military, Zak. No punitive expeditions are going to be sent on my behalf. My title, my position, they were mostly ceremonial, and I walked away from them of my own accord. I didn't tell you before because I thought...well, I thought you'd be mad that I've been dishonest with you. I was worried that if Lang found out who I was, he'd hold me for ransom the way he's been holding poor Cecil. But I want you to know the truth now, because I want you to stop blaming yourself for my situation. You and I are both in over our heads, but we're in it together. I have you to thank for a great deal. You treated me like a regular person. You gave me the dignity of a meaningful task. You let me do things on my own, instead of treating me like a precious artifact. I want you to know that no matter how this ends, even if...even if we both die here, I'm grateful. I truly am."

A tear trickled down Anna's cheek. Zak had never once seen her cry before, and his first impulse was to try to comfort her. He wasn't the hugging type, but she looked like she needed a hug.

Anna stepped back slightly. "Hold on now."

"I'm sorry!" Zak sputtered. "I just thought..."

Wiping the tear away, Anna raised an eyebrow, flashed him a smile, and looked him up and down. "I know we're laying it all on the table, as it were, but perhaps you should get dressed? I'm a lady, Zachary, and that is no way to present yourself to a lady."

Zak's eyes went wide as he realized that for the entire conversation with his partner, he'd been standing in the kitchen in his underwear. In his haste to tell her the news, he had forgotten to dress. His face turned a deep shade of red, and he slowly backed around the corner. "Probably not a good day to wear my lucky rocketship underpants," he said meekly.

"I disagree," Anna said with a devilish smile. "I find them adorable. Run along now, get dressed. We'll talk when you're wearing pants."

Smooth, Zak. Cecil is never going to let you live this one down.

The Privateer Ship *Andromeda*
Combine Space, Orlov's Star System

When transiting between stars, an object's velocity and momentum are not preserved. Ships that come through are left disoriented and vulnerable due to transit shock. The greatest difficulty in defending transit points is the constant expenditure of thrust required. The transit points themselves don't orbit the stars they spawn from; their relative positions are dependent on the position of the stars in relation to one another and the strength of the quantum link between the two. They change their relative positions over time and are difficult to track.

As soon as the *Andromeda* appeared through the transit point, she was locked onto by a cluster of automated defense platforms. These weapons used a combination of huge solar sails and low-impulse ion thrusters to stay with the transit point and not be pulled into Orlov's Star. They were small and low mass, but were bristling with missiles and directed energy weapons. When the ship's communications systems came back online, the crew realized they were being hailed by the defense platforms.

A recorded message followed. The video was of a beautiful, pleasant-sounding woman. She had a flower in her hair, but wore a bland, gray jacket with a stand-up collar. Grafted to her temple was a small electronic device. She spoke Commerce English with an almost mechanical tone. "Welcome, travelers, to the People's Combined Collective of Orlov's Star. Whether our homeworld is your final destination or you're just passing through, you will be pleased with our legendary hospitality. Your first stop will be the

241

customs station, the coordinates of which are being sent with this message. We understand that space is a dangerous place. However, our system is safe and secure. As such, we require all visitors to keep their weapons powered down and offline for the duration of their stay in our system. All weapons and cargoes must be declared to the officials at the customs station and prepared for inspection. Please be advised," the woman said, playfully wagging a finger at the camera, "that attempting to access our system network without authorization is strictly prohibited. Thank you, and have a lovely visit."

Catherine grimaced at the recording through the pounding of her head from transit shock. "Well, they certainly seem pleasant."

Wolfram von Spandau did not share her humor. (He almost never shared her humor.) "We must exercise the utmost caution, *Kapitänin*," he said, turning his seat to face her. It was rare for both the captain and the XO to be on the command deck at the same time, but Catherine wanted her most experienced personnel on duty for this one. "I am sending their instructions to Astrogation and the Flight Deck, so that we may lay in a course and be underway. These customs officials may ask for exorbitant bribes. If we refuse to pay, they may confiscate the ship."

Catherine's eyes narrowed. "Like *hell* they will. You are correct, though, Wolfram." She tapped one of her screens. A moment later, Mordecai Chang, the ship's purser, appeared on her display. The screen split, and Cargomaster Kimball appeared as well.

"Cap'n," Chang said politely. It was obvious he wasn't feeling well either.

"Captain," Kimball acknowledged.

Catherine sipped some water from her drinking tube and addressed her men. "Gentlemen, this is it. We've been given our marching orders from these defense platforms, and we'll be underway shortly. We need to tread very carefully here. They'll want our cargo manifests as well as a weapons inventory. Give them the ones we've prepared for this circumstance. If they send an inspector over, Mr. Kimball, deal with them as best you can. You are authorized to pay out additional bribes if need be. Mordecai, make sure our books are inspection-ready, please."

"Yes ma'am," Mordecai said. He wasn't going to show them the *real* books, of course. He had special sets of books and documentation for inspection purposes.

"When we get through customs, they'll send us to one of their commercial space stations. We need to resupply there. Remass is the number one priority, followed by rations. I want everything we bring on board scanned and inspected for surveillance devices. No matter how long we're docked with the station, the crew is not to leave the ship under any circumstances."

"Understood, Captain," both men said. Catherine signed off, and addressed the others on the *Andromeda*'s command deck. "This is it, people, the last hurdle before we reach Zanzibar. Let's make this as smooth as possible and get the hell out of this system. Wolfram, is our course laid in?"

"Yes, *Kapitänin*."

"Very well. Extend radiators, send our flight plan to the customs station, and initiate the burn."

It was not a short journey from the transit point to the customs station. For twenty-five hours the *Andromeda* pressed on through the night, matching trajectory with the customs station in high solar orbit. Her sensors were tracking over a hundred ships in the system. Orlov had a large population for a colony, over a billion, and had an incredible amount of space infrastructure. The system's most sunward gas giant, Artyom, had a dozen moons and an exceptionally dense asteroid ring, all rich in minerals and heavy metals. Orlov's Star was, by far, the most populous system in its sector of space.

Orlov itself was an inhospitable world, but one incredibly rich in mineral resources, including the very rare elements needed to make transit drives. The planet supported no native life beyond the equivalents of lichens, mosses, plankton, and bacteria, but had an oxygen-nitrogen atmosphere suitable for breathing. Orlov was extremely volcanically and seismically active. Massive volcanoes, deep rifts, and powerful quakes scarred its rocky surface. Most of the population lived near the poles, where slowly melting ice caps provided a source of water and fed large, freshwater seas.

Orlov had never been intended for permanent colonization. During the Middle Diaspora, it was a booming hub of mining and trade, but was home to relatively few permanent residents. Being so remote, the system was completely cut off from the rest of inhabited space during the Interregnum, and it was popularly believed that the stranded residents went mad during their centuries-long struggle for survival. The modern-day Orlov Combine was a tyrannical surveillance state unlike anything else in known space.

As the *Andromeda* approached, long-ranged telemetry gave the crew a good picture of the customs station. It was as bare and utilitarian as anything else the Combine built: A large drum, one hundred meters in diameter, slowly rotating to simulate gravity. Around this was a massive, spindly docking structure, with docking ports for a dozen ships, clusters of radiators, solar panels, and communications arrays. The habitat module spun in the external structure like a wheel in the fork of a bicycle.

Following directives broadcast from the station, the *Andromeda* opened the docking port on her nose and coupled with an open berth on the space station's huge superstructure. The ship's manipulator arm slid forward and clamped onto a load-bearing point, better stabilizing her as she equalized pressure with the station and prepared for inspection. Her crew moved to and fro in freefall, making final preparations for boarding by customs officials. The large stockpile of ground weapons that had been purchased for the ground team were hidden away, buried in several of the sealed containers in the cargo bay. The ship's course logs were altered, showing her coming from Heinlein instead of New Austin, and stopping at the Llewellyn Freehold on her way to Zanzibar. None of these preparations meant the captain wouldn't have to pay some hefty bribes to get through Combine space unmolested, but it would, hopefully, make the process easier.

The shipping manifests, flight plan, and cargo declarations were all checked electronically. Catherine remained strapped into her command chair, watching the various documents scroll across the screen as the customs computer scanned them line-by-line. No red flags had popped up yet, and so far the transit, docking, and customs taxes hadn't been too expensive. She was beginning to hope that she'd actually make it through Combine space without being searched or having to shell out a huge bribe. They usually paid less attention to ships merely crossing their space than those who actually had business in the Orlov's Star System.

Then an alarm chirped and the screen flashed red. *Damn it to bloody hell,* Catherine thought. *That's what I get for wishful thinking.* The *Andromeda*'s falsified flight plan was flagged, though nothing in particular about it was. A baritone computerized voice told her, in Commerce English, that her ship had been randomly selected for inspection, and to stand by for boarding. The message then repeated in Classical French, Esperanto, Mandarin, and other languages before Catherine hit the mute button. *Random my pale Avalonian ass.*

"This is the captain speaking," she said, piping her message across the ship. "We are about to be boarded by Combine customs officers. You all know what to do. Remain calm, be cooperative, and if there are any issues at all, do *not* become confrontational. Let your officers know, and they'll inform me. I'll handle any discrepancies myself. That is all."

A short while later Catherine, Wolfram, and Mazer Broadbent were all clinging to handholds in the uppermost docking bay, waiting to receive the Combine customs officers. Catherine could see the tension on her men's faces. The worst-case scenario, in this particular case, was pretty bad. There were plenty of horror stories about the Combine security apparatus, and no one wanted to learn if they were true.

As it would turn out, the two bored-looking customs officers that drifted downward through the hatch were almost underwhelming. One had very pale skin and white hair, and his eyes darted around nervously. He clutched his tablet computer as if he were afraid one of the spacers would steal it. The other customs officer, despite the electronic monitor bolted to his skull, seemed more like a normal person. He greeted the crew pleasantly, introducing himself as Corbin-17741, and asked to be shown to the cargo hold.

Customs Officer Corbin clung to one of the handholds in the *Andromeda*'s cargo bay and let his flunky do all the work. The pale, nervous-looking man seemed comfortable enough in zero gravity. He launched himself from cargo pallet to cargo pallet, noting the manifest and tapping entries into his tablet. He asked for two random cargo containers to be opened for inspection, which Kimball's team did without hesitation. There was nothing in them but the rations and supplies that were listed on the manifests, after all.

Pulling himself next to Catherine, Corbin thumbed his handheld with one hand while gripping a handle with the other. "Captain, you declared that your ship is armed?"

"I did," Catherine said nonchalantly. "The frontier is dangerous. Pirates and the so-called fleets of petty, third-rate colonies, who may as well be pirates, prey on merchant ships frequently.

We are often tasked to provide security for merchant ships traveling through this sector, and our presence alone has quieted things down."

"I imagine so," Corbin said, sounding unimpressed, and not looking up. "Your weapons systems are..."

"Two rotary missile launchers," Catherine provided, "two heavy laser turrets, and one sixty-millimeter gauss weapon."

"You're not carrying any prohibited weapons, such as nuclear warheads, or other weapons of mass destruction?"

"Absolutely not," Catherine insisted, and it was true. Outside of major fleet battles and orbital bombardment, nuclear warheads were more trouble than they were worth. "All of our warheads are conventional high-explosive/armor piercing, or high-explosive fragmentation."

"Very well," Corbin said, tapping the screen of his device and lowering it. "Everything seems to be in order here, assuming my subordinate doesn't find anything improper."

"I assure you he won't," Catherine said, doing her best to feign sincerity. *Is it really going to be this easy?* It was possible. More and more merchants and traders were braving Combine space every year in search of cheap materials to resell. Maybe the Combine authorities were more interested in business than graft?

"I'm sure," Corbin agreed. "Now, there is one last thing we need to go over, and I have some forms you need to sign. Is there a someplace where we can discuss this in private?"

Bloody hell, Catherine fumed. *Here it is. The part where he demands his bribe. Maybe he'll be decent enough to pretend that it's taxes or fees he's collecting.* "Ah, yes," she said, maintaining her composure. "My cargomaster's office, right over there, is secure. Mr. Kimball?"

"Yes, Captain?" Kimball replied, clutching a handhold and looking daggers at the pale customs officer touching everything in his cargo bay.

"I'll leave you to oversee this for a moment. Mr. Corbin and I are going to your office to sign some documents."

Kimball looked over at the captain knowingly. "Yes, ma'am."

"Right this way, please," Catherine said, pushing off the wall and sailing toward Kimball's small office.

Once inside, Corbin tapped the electronic device on the side of his head, then did something on his handheld. The tiny light on his skull-mount device went out. "I apologize for this, Captain. For the moment, we have our privacy."

Can he do that? Catherine wondered. It was possible, she surmised, that if you were high up enough in the Combine hierarchy that you could get away with turning off the camera for just a bit. She folded her arms across her chest, floating at an odd angle from the customs officer, and glared at him. All pretenses of politeness were gone. "Let's not mince words, then," she said. "What do I have to do to ensure my ship crosses Combine space without incident? We have no business here. We just want to cross your space and be on our way."

Corbin smiled. "I see you know the way of the world. Truth be told, many in my position would demand money from you. We're not exactly paid, you see, and foreign hard currency is accepted on the black market. Other, sleazier individuals may demand something more *intimate* from you."

Every muscle in Catherine's body tensed, and she found her hand moving toward the compact pulse laser concealed beneath her flight jacket. She was of a mind to just shoot this son of a bitch, and damn the consequences.

Corbin raised a hand apologetically. "Such things are strictly prohibited, of course, and are punishable by death. They aren't as common as many would believe, but occur often enough to sully the reputation of the glorious People's Combined Collective. I want to assure you that I'm not here to demand a bribe or sexual favors from you, Captain." He looked out the office's small window, as if to ensure that his subordinate wasn't snooping. "Between you and me," he said conspiratorially, "I'm not actually a customs officer. I'm with Internal Security."

Catherine's heart dropped into her stomach. Internal Security was notorious across civilized space. They were the ones who rooted out all threats to the Combine, real or imagined, and killed or imprisoned anyone they deemed traitorous with impunity. She couldn't have found a worse person to be having this conversation with. "I see," she said, eyes narrowing. "As I said, I'm merely passing through. I'm not interested in the domestic politics of the Combine in the least. I just want to be on my way."

"That's what they all say," Corbin said coolly. "However, I'm not interested in any contraband you may be attempting to get through the far transit point. I'm interested in your destination."

"Zanzibar? What of it?"

"There are rumors about Zanzibar. Internal Security flatly denies any such thing is possible, but sometimes people just... vanish. Sometimes they go to Zanzibar and never return. There are whispers amongst disloyal malcontents that there is sanctuary there. Those with traitorous hearts, guilty of thought-crimes, they say, can escape there and be beyond the reach of Internal Security."

Catherine genuinely had no idea what the man was on about. "I've never been to Zanzibar before, Mr. Corbin, nor have I been through Combine space. I don't know anything about any of this."

"Of course you don't. Few do. The idea that there is any place beyond the reach of Internal Security is almost a thought-crime in itself. Doctrine dictates that the greater good of the collective will always prevail, and those who selfishly wish to pursue their own ends without regard for the needs of the collective will always fail."

"It must be an awful burden," Catherine spat, "trying to keep your thoughts in order so as not to commit one of these thought-crimes."

Corbin smiled. His eyes were dark and cold. "That's the beauty of it, Captain. We are all guilty of thought-crimes. The Proles perhaps not so much; they are a dull lot, by design. But those of us with all of our faculties have all committed crimes of thought at one time or another. It's unavoidable, human nature."

Bewildered, Catherine took off her cap and ran her fingers through her hair. "This is a fascinating discussion, Mr. Corbin, but I wish you would come to your point."

Still smiling, Corbin continued, "When human nature is a crime, all men are criminals. When all men are criminals, the State has power over them as would a warden over his inmates. That is the true doctrine of the Combine, whether they would admit it or not."

Catherine said nothing for a moment. This could easily be a trap, and attempt to snare her into saying something that would give him an excuse to confiscate her ship and put her on trial. "Again, Mr. Corbin, this is fascinating, but it has nothing to do with me."

"But it does," Corbin insisted. He tapped his handheld a couple of times, and presented the screen to Catherine. It was a standard customs inspection form. "I will allow you to proceed. On the far end of the system, closer to Transit Point Beta, is a commercial space platform. There you can purchase reaction mass and supplies as needed, before proceeding through the transit point and out of our space."

"Well, thank you," Catherine said, confused. She outstretched one arm to tap the screen, which would sign the document, but Corbin pulled the handheld away.

"There is one other thing you must pick up from that station," he said. The image on the screen disappeared, replaced by that of a plain young woman in a blue coverall. "This woman is a traitor, guilty of numerous crimes of thought, possession of banned literature, and trafficking in disruptive lies. If you wish to leave this system, you will do exactly as I tell you."

"I'm not going to kill this woman for you, Corbin," Catherine said coldly. "You bastards can bloody well do your own damned dirty work. I'm a businesswoman, not an assassin."

"You are not in a position to negotiate, Captain Blackwood, but you assume too much. You will take this woman on board your ship and you will bring her to Zanzibar."

"Why in God's name would I do that?" Catherine barked. "So you can accuse me of smuggling defectors and confiscate my ship? So I can be part of some elaborate sting operation? To hell with that, and to hell with you, Corbin. I've had enough of this."

Before Catherine could leave, Corbin softened his tone, almost to a plea. "Please, Captain, you misunderstand. This woman? Her name is Lana. She's my daughter."

Catherine took a deep breath, and found herself once again pinching the bridge of her nose between her finger and thumb. *It can never just be simple, can it?*

The Orlov System, though populous, wasn't especially big by most standards. It only contained five planets: Orlov itself, two gas giants, an uninhabitable rock with marginal atmosphere, and a tiny ball of ice furthest out. The locations of transit points, however, had nothing to do with the size of a solar system. Even a comparatively "small" system could take a long time to cross. It took the *Andromeda* over a hundred hours of flight time to match trajectories and rendezvous with the commercial platform. It gave Catherine plenty of time to ponder her next move.

Corbin-17741 was blackmailing the *Andromeda* into absconding with his daughter, a young woman named Lana-90890. She had been a low-ranking officer in the Combine's government-owned merchant fleet, and had helped smuggle refugees to Zanzibar in past. Her role in the matter was small, but simply not reporting the crime was considered an equally grave offense. This didn't bother her father too much. He claimed that he, too, was involved in the smuggling operation. Catherine didn't know if she believed that. He may have just been telling her that to make himself more sympathetic, and there was still the chance this whole thing was some kind of needlessly elaborate ruse.

That didn't make any sense, though. An officer of Internal Security doesn't need flimsy pretexts to confiscate property and incarcerate persons. According to everything Catherine had read, there was very little they couldn't do in the name of state security, and they answered only to their own hierarchy. That left the possibility that Corbin was being sincere, and really just wanted to get his daughter out of the reach of the Combine before she ended up in a concentration camp.

"She doesn't know that I'm aware of her activities," Corbin had warned Catherine. "She and I are not on good terms. I never talk about what I do, but she figured it out, and she hates me for it. She's hated me for years, ever since they took her mother away. There was nothing I could do." He left a recorded message for his daughter, and told Catherine to tie her up and *drag* her onto the *Andromeda* if necessary. He had already gotten her reassigned to manning a commercial platform, trying to keep her out of trouble, but she just wasn't very good at covering her tracks. Internal Security would track her down eventually, Corbin insisted, and he'd been waiting for a ship en route to Zanzibar.

There were other places he could have sent her, he said, but Zanzibar was the only place where he knew she'd survive. A lifetime subjected to the Combine does not prepare you to live with the rest of humanity. He could send her to the Concordiat, but feared that they'd interrogate her and lock her away. He could send her to an independent system like the Llewellyn Freehold, but what was she going to do there, with no money, no job, no family, no support whatsoever?

So for months, Corbin had been working on a scheme to get his daughter to Zanzibar. He'd been deliberately hindering

Internal Security's investigation of the supposed Combine refugee sanctuary there, which was easy enough because the central authorities, in their hubris, didn't want to believe such a refuge was possible. Meanwhile, he pulled some strings to make sure his daughter was reassigned to one of the commercial platforms. It was considered a dead-end job. The platforms were manned only because of bureaucratic inertia. They didn't actually require a human operator, and people assigned there were usually forgotten about, only rotated home for a few months out of Orlov's long year, and left to wither away. She had been alone on that platform for many weeks by that point. Several ships had passed through, going to Zanzibar, but none had arrived at such a fortuitous time as the *Andromeda*.

One would think that Lana would be more than willing to run off on any ship that would take her. Corbin had warned that this might not be the case. Her first impulse, he said, would be to think it was some kind of sting operation conducted by Internal Security, just as Catherine had. Even after she saw her father's video, she might think it to be an elaborate loyalty test. Internal Security had such a cruel reputation that few put such mind games past them. Once Catherine had Lana secured, Corbin insisted that he would see to it that the *Andromeda* would make it through the transit point, regardless whatever else happened.

Catherine didn't like that "regardless whatever else happened" part. She very much didn't like the idea of having to fight her way through God-knows-how-many Combine ships and defense platforms. Orlov's Star was the most militarized solar system in all of inhabited space, by all accounts, and one ship couldn't tangle with that and prevail. Despite her misgivings, however, Catherine didn't have much choice. If she refused Corbin's request, he could, with a single call, have her ship tracked down and destroyed before it ever made the transit point. So despite her misgivings, despite her quiet anger at being blackmailed, she went ahead with the plan to get this Lana on board her ship by any means necessary. She didn't tell the crew about the situation, save for her officers and Marcus Winchester. There was no sense stressing the rest of the crew out over it. There was nothing they could do, and they were already on edge just from having to travel through Combine Space.

The commercial platform was a large, branching structure, capable of docking and servicing up to four ships at once. Among its list of purported services were hull maintenance, reaction mass refueling, supplies of helium-3, deuterium, boron, and lithium (depending on the needs of your ship's reactor), bulk rations for purchase, "luxurious" zero-g showers, and a gift shop/snack bar. At the station's core was a cluster of huge hydrogen tanks, each a sphere fifty meters in diameter. In the middle of the tanks, amongst a mess of solar panels, radiators, and communications equipment, was a group of small cylinders that made up the habitat module for the station's sole occupant. There were no rotating sections on the commercial platform; the unfortunate attendant got to spend her entire time on duty in freefall. The habitat module was larger than just a tiny living quarters. The platform advertised having a "state of the art" medical bay, wherein for a nominal (exorbitant) fee, a sick or injured spacer could be treated by an autodoc. (For the kind of money they were asking, Catherine thought, they could at least offer a human doctor.)

Taking advantage of the platform's services was the pretext Catherine would use to go aboard. Once there, she would attempt to talk Lana into going with her. If that didn't work, Mazer Broadbent would hit her with a stunner and drag her back to the *Andromeda*. Timing was critical in this operation; it would take hours to get the ship loaded up and ready to depart, and they weren't going to make the final leg of the journey without those supplies. Grabbing Lana would have to be the last thing they did before departing, and even then, they'd have to be very fast. Everything in Combine space was monitored. Catherine didn't know how on the ball their security forces actually were when it came to something like responding to an abduction, and Corbin had promised to run interference somehow, but she didn't want to take any more chances than necessary. There were no other ships docked at the platform, but there was at least one military patrol ship close enough to pursue the *Andromeda* as she dashed for the transit point. One unknown ship was en route to the space platform and would arrive soon. Catherine's window was rapidly closing.

Once the ship was coupled to the space station, Catherine made her way up to the docking bay, Corbin's message on her handheld and a compact pulse laser concealed beneath her flight jacket. Marcus Winchester and Mazer Broadbent were with her, both discreetly armed, just in case. The trio floated up through the docking umbilical, pausing at the far end to let the station's airlock cycle. The main compartment of the station was the gift shop and snack bar. Vending machines of every sort were fastened to every surface, signs flashing and screens promising good deals. A hologram of the same pretty Combine woman who had welcomed them to the system was projected in the center, prattling on about the glory and achievements of the People's Combined Collective. Signs in six languages pointed visitors to latrines, showers, and the medical bay. One door was marked "authorized personnel only." That, Catherine surmised, had to be where Lana was.

Getting through the sealed hatch would be a problem. Wade Bishop had volunteered to rig up another shaped charge for the purpose, but Corbin had provided for that. Uploaded to Catherine's handheld was a set of Internal Security access codes that he said would get her through any door, grant her access to any system, everything. The trick was, the handheld would have to be plugged into the stations' computer directly. The codes were designed to not work if broadcast via radio.

Marcus and Mazer pretended to avail themselves to the gift shop while they searched for an access panel. Everything for sale was secured in a vending machine, and they browsed through the menu screens. T-shirts, trinkets, hard copy books, toys, and a variety of electronics were all available. Marcus purchased a t-shirt with the People's Combined Collective governmental seal, an authoritarian logo consisting of a stylized gear, olive branches, a rocket, and stars printed on it. "Annie will love this," he said to Mazer, holding it up for the security officer to examine.

On another screen, Mazer pulled up an image of a ceramic dragon figure, twenty centimeters long. The dragon was perched on a rocky outcropping, holding a crystal orb in its claw. "Who comes all the way across inhabited space and buys a ceramic dragon from a Combine refueling station?" He asked. Meanwhile, on the *Andromeda*'s command deck, Luis Azevedo stood by, waiting for the word from his captain. When he received it, he would initiate the ship's powerful electronic warfare suite. The jammers would prevent the platform for calling for help before they could shut down its communications, but turning them on would cause the *Andromeda* to light up like a nova on sensors.

"Captain," Mazer said. "Come look at this. I think it's just what you've been looking for."

Catherine pushed herself off of a handhold and drifted across the compartment to her security officer. She grabbed another handhold to stop herself, and rotated forward to see what Mazer was talking about. It was a holocube, portraying a ship sitting on a launch pad on a wintry day. If you shook it, holographic snow gently fell on the ship and accumulated on the ground below it. It was an interesting trinket, but the holocube wasn't really what Mazer was indicating. Next to the vending machine, on the wall, was a panel with the markings of computer maintenance access. "I see," Catherine said, nodding. "It is lovely. Shall I get it?"

Mazer and Marcus both nodded. This was it.

"ECM active, Skipper," Azevedo said into her earpiece.

Moving quickly, Catherine drew her utility knife and snapped the blade out. She pried the panel open and found the small computer access port inside, underneath a screen displaying information on the station's computer systems. She connected a data cable to her handheld and plugged it into the port. The screen lit up momentarily as the computer tried to identify the new device attached, but before it could finish Catherine tapped her own screen and ran Corbin's program.

"Got it," she said. After a second, a menu appeared on her handheld, listing the measures available to an officer of Internal Security. The first thing she did was lock down the platform's communications systems, preventing it from broadcasting or receiving. The system would only send out a looped message stating that the station was being commandeered by Internal Security. That would keep the curious away. "Luis, their comms are down," she said into her earpiece. "Shut down ECM."

"Roger, Skipper."

She then disabled the omnipresent monitoring and recording systems. Even Internal Security didn't have the option of deleting the recordings. Next, she unsealed all of the internal hatches and sealed the other docking ports. The other ship inbound wouldn't be able to couple with the station if it didn't have the sense to change course.

"Done!" she said to her men, pocketing her handheld. "Let's go."

The trio moved through the "authorized personnel only" hatch, into the station's cramped living quarters. "Lana-Nine-Zero-Eight-Nine-Zero!" Marcus called. "Lana! We're here to get you out! Where are you?" Bracing himself on a handhold, he cautiously peeked around a corner where two cylindrical sections were joined. He immediately recoiled, cursing, as the loud, crackling snap of a laser weapon discharge rang out. A streak of air just past his head shimmered, and the far bulkhead flashed and smoked where the beam struck. The air stunk of ozone as Marcus pulled his 10mm pistol.

"Let me talk to her," Catherine said, pulling herself forward. "Lana?" she called around the corner. "Lana, can you hear me?"

"Who are you people?" Lana replied, obviously afraid. "You're not InSec. What do you want?"

"We just want to talk to you," Catherine said.

"You can talk to the patrol when they get here!" Lana cried. "I sent out a distress call. You'd better leave now!"

"No, you didn't, Lana. We have control of your communications. Nothing went out, and no one is coming for you. It's just you and us. I just want to talk to you. My name is Catherine."

"How do you know my name?" Lana sounded terrified. "Who... who are you? Who sent you?"

"Your father sent us, Lana."

"My father...? Are you Internal Security? I told you people I don't know anything! I'm not a traitor! Please!" she cried. "Please..."

Instead of trying to talk her down, or rounding the corner and risking getting blasted, Catherine set her handheld to project. She pointed the lens at the far bulkhead, where Lana's laser had struck, and tapped the screen.

The image of Corbin was distorted on the curved bulkhead, but it was clear enough to see. "Lana," he began, looking far less detached than he had in person. "It's me, your father. I need you to listen to me very carefully. Internal Security suspects you're part of a human trafficking ring, smuggling defectors out of the system. I've been keeping them off your trail as best I could. I tried to keep you safe. That's why I had you assigned here, but I can't protect you anymore. I've done all I can do, and sooner or later they're going to come for you. They're coming for you and they're going to make you disappear, just like they did with your mother.

"I know you hate me for what happened to her. Lana, your mother was the only woman I ever loved. If I had known that she was suspected, if there was anything I could've done, I would've stopped it. When they kicked in the door to our flat, I knew immediately what was happening, and it was already too late. That's why I didn't try to stop them: not because I didn't love your mother, but because of what would happen if I had. That's also the reason I had to publicly denounce her after the arrest. If I didn't, they'd have come for me, and also for you. I've worked for InSec for years. I know how they operate.

"I'm sorry, angel. I'm sorry it took me so many years to make it up to you. I'm sorry I didn't have the courage to say this to you before. I just couldn't bear to face you, and I still can't. You look just like your mother. Every time I see you, I see her.

"I want you to go with this woman, Captain Blackwood. She's going to take you to a safe place. You've never trusted me in your entire life, but I'm begging you to trust me this once. I have been planning for this day for a long time. Arrangements have been made, and debts have to be paid. I wish I could tell you this in person, because you very likely won't hear from me again.

"Go with the captain, Lana. Please, go with her. There isn't much time. I love you."

The message ended, and suddenly it was very quiet in the weightless compartment. Catherine could hear quiet sobbing coming from around the corner. Risking a look, she peeked around the bulkhead. Lana was huddled up at the end of the short corridor, floating in a fetal position, face buried in her hands. Droplets of tears, sparkling in the artificial light, drifted away from her face as she wept. The laser pistol rotated lazily away from her.

Motioning for her men to stay out of sight, Catherine pulled herself around the corner and down the corridor, stopping a few meters from Lana. "Hey there," she said softly. "My name is Catherine."

Lana looked up, tears drifting off of her red eyes. She was so young, barely into her adult years. "What's going to happen to me now?"

"Please come with us, Lana. Your father has arranged for us to get through the transit point without being stopped, but we don't have a lot of time. He asked me to take you away, to someplace where you'll be safe."

"Where?"

"Sanctuary," Catherine said, hoping to God that it was actually a real place. "On Zanzibar."

✧   ✧   ✧

Back on the *Andromeda*'s command deck, Catherine moved quickly to strap into her command chair as she scanned all of her displays. The docking umbilical was being retracted, the manipulator arm was being stowed, and the ship was preparing to back away from the station.

"Skipper!" Azevedo said excitedly. "That unknown contact just fired its engine up. It's headed straight for us, must be pulling four Gs! Two thousand klicks and closing!"

"Weapons online, *Kapitänin*," Wolfram said. "I've got a lock."

"Hold your fire! Azevedo, sound general quarters!" the lighting of the command deck dimmed and changed to red, making it easier to see the multitude of displays. "Colin, get us the hell away from this station, full afterburn!"

"Yes ma'am!"

"Astrogation," Catherine grunted, straining to speak under the g-forces as Colin flipped the ship away from the space platform, "send the flight deck a minimum time, maximum thrust trajectory for the transit point!"

"Sending now," Kel Morrow replied. "ETA, eighty-nine minutes."

"Engineering, spin up the transit motivator and keep it hot. I want us through the transit point as soon as we get close enough. Run the reactor hot, full power to all systems and weapons, all the way to the transit point!"

"Roger that, Captain," Indira Nair said. "That is more than our radiators can handle. We will have to dip into the heat sinks for as long as we can."

"Very good, Indira," Catherine said.

Colin's voice echoed throughout the ship, "Attention all personnel! Stand by for emergency thrust!" Seconds later, the crew of the *Andromeda* was crushed into their acceleration couches under the weight of eight gravities. The ship rattled and vibrated on top of an exhaust plume that lit up the night like a newborn star.

After a few minutes, the pilot backed the thrust off to six gravities, and Catherine was able to think clearly again. Her displays lit up as multiple Combine patrol ships fired up their engines and began thrusting in her direction. Targeting sensors swept the *Andromeda*'s hull, but the hostile ships were still too far out to engage; too far out, and too confused. They still weren't sure what was happening.

Driving the point home, a looped transmission was being broadcast from the unknown contact on virtually every standard frequency. "We are the Vox Populi," it said, the speech an electronic amalgamation of dozens of voices. "We are the true voice of the enslaved, the oppressed, the sovereign citizens of Orlov's Star. The Combine believes they are watching us, but we have been watching them. Join us, fellow citizens! Tear down the cameras, smash the recorders, break your chains! Live, love, struggle, and die on your own terms, as human beings, not as cogs in the great, soulless machine! For years we have struggled in darkness, but now we are revealed! Rise up! The revolution begins today!"

Azevedo's voice was strained as the weight of six gravities pressed upon his lungs. "Skipper, that contact is headed straight for the station! There's no way it's going to be able to...holy shit! Impact!" One of Catherine's displays showed a silent flash of light, far behind the *Andromeda*, as the ship smashed into the massive space station at a relative velocity of thousands of kilometers per hour. The ship, the station, the reaction mass tanks, all of it, blazed momentarily before fading to dust and bits of hot metal.

It hit Catherine then: Corbin-17741 had arranged this, somehow. This was their cover to get out of the system. Suddenly, every non-military ship in the Orlov's Star system was suspect. Communications chatter went wild as the massive, unwieldy Combine security apparatus tried to figure out what happened and stop more attacks from being carried out. Ships that were underway were ordered to power down their thrusters and stand by, but those orders hadn't come from their respective chains of command. Many of the messages seemed dumbfounded, waiting for orders from central authority, asking what had happened, or insisting that one set of orders superseded another. Instead of focusing on the *Andromeda*, fleeing from the destroyed station, military ships were being diverted to protect critical infrastructure. According to long-range sensors, some were actually firing at other ships too slow to comply with their demands. It was chaos, beautifully orchestrated chaos.

There was still the matter of getting out of the system alive. The transit point was guarded by a constellation of defense platforms, and as the alert went out across the system, their sensors lit up and began scanning all nearby ships. "We are being targeted," Wolfram said calmly. He paused for a moment, grunting under the strain of acceleration. "Fifteen individual defense platforms have locked onto us. At this acceleration we won't be able to maneuver. We have the momentum advantage, and the platforms cannot maneuver at all. If we fire now, we can destroy some of them before they can effectively engage us, but... the odds are not in our favor."

Azevedo chimed in. "Skipper, that Combine patrol ship is pursuing us now. I just received a message ordering us to find a stable orbit, cut our engine, and stand by to be boarded. At the rate they're accelerating we'll be through before they can engage us. Barely."

This is going to be close. "Hold fire," Catherine repeated. "Luis, broadcast the message that Corbin left us."

"Roger, Skipper. Stand by... broadcasting." He was breathing heavily. "Now what?"

"*Kapitänin,*" Wolfram said. "The platforms have broken their lock. They're... they're ignoring us!"

The message the *Andromeda* was broadcasting was a high-level Internal Security emergency code. It stated in no uncertain terms that the transmitting vessel was on urgent InSec business and was not to be interfered with in any way, punishable by death. The robotic defense platforms responded automatically, but the lone patrol ship seemed undeterred. "Our bandit is speeding up, Skipper," Azevedo observed. "Must be red-lining their reactor. They're pulling eight Gs now. Sensors make that a *Pagan-Hotel* class," he said, referring to the ship by its Concordiat Defense Force codename. "Max acceleration is supposedly seven gravities. He'll be able to engage us before we reach the transit point."

"Can he follow us through?"

"Negative, Skipper. Not transit-capable." The *Pagan*-class was little more than a cylindrical can with an engine cluster on one end and massive radiators coming out of the sides. It was not atmospheric, nor was it particularly elegant, but the Combine military supposedly had hundreds of them in reserve.

Minutes ticked by, agonizingly slowly, as Catherine ran the numbers on her console. The command deck grew noticeably hot, and streams of sweat ran down her head under the high gravity. Running at this acceleration for half an hour was burning through the reaction mass she'd just paid a king's ransom for, and was straining the ship's cooling systems. The radiators could only radiate heat away so quickly, and the internal heat sinks could only absorb so much. Once their capacities were exceeded, emergency cutoffs would engage. If those safeguards were overridden, the ship would overheat and systems would start to fail. The interior could become too hot for the crew to function in. The trajectory Kel Morrow had given her was the fastest route to the transit point, and if that *Pagan-H* kept up its relentless pursuit, she'd have no choice but to engage. Right on schedule, the *Andromeda*'s engines cut, plunging the crew back into the relief freefall. The pursuing Combine ship followed suit a moment later.

The transit point grew nearer and nearer. Despite the Internal Security broadcast, the *Pagan-H* continued on its intercept trajectory, constantly issuing demands that the *Andromeda* stand by to be boarded. On Catherine's display, two circles represented the ships' respective targeting envelopes, drawing inexorably closer like a nascent Venn diagram. As they drew near one another, she ordered Azevedo to engage the ship's electronic countermeasures. The ECM couldn't do anything to hide the *Andromeda*'s massive thermal signature, but it could play hell with incoming missiles' terminal guidance. The crew was already at battle stations; Catherine and her officers on the command deck were still in their flight suits, but those crewmembers who had time to do so had already been ordered don their spacesuits in the event of a hull breach. All crew not on duty were secured in their individual berths, which all had emergency life-support systems of their own.

After thirty minutes of coasting and cooling, the engines fired again, accelerating for the final dash to the transit point. The pursuing *Pagan-H* responded in kind. A long moment passed, then warning tones sounded as she fired off a volley of missiles.

"Skipper!" Azevedo said excitedly. This was his first time in combat. "Incoming volley designated Salvo-Alpha, time to impact, six minutes!"

Catherine nodded. "Wolfram, target the incoming missiles, fire at will. Luis, deploy countermeasures. Try using the radar to fry their guidance systems."

"Targeting missiles," Wolfram confirmed. "I have a lock on the *Pagan* itself."

"Hold your fire," the captain ordered. "This is bad enough without us starting a war with the Combine. Defensive fire only. We'll engage the ship as a last resort. Luis, what's the capability of their laser weapons?"

"Database says they're pretty light on lasers and have no railguns. They're missile carriers, Skipper."

"Excellent. Colin, keep us on course for the transit point. Engineering?"

"Standing by, Captain," Indira Nair replied, sweat dripping down her face. "Transit motivator is spun up, stable, and running hot."

"Very good. It's going to be close. As soon as your boards are green for translation, engage the motivator. Do not wait for my order."

"Yes ma'am!"

"Incoming missiles locked!" Wolfram said. "Firing!"

"Splash one!" Luis announced, as a powerful beam of coherent light caused one of the incoming missiles to detonate. "Splash two!" he said as another, damaged, veered off course. Another was spoofed by the countermeasures.

"Last one destroyed, *Kapitänin*!" Wolfram announced proudly. It had been a long time since he'd manned the weapons station, and Catherine could see her exec was in his element.

An alarm sounded again. "Bandit is firing a second volley, Skipper! Salvo-Bravo, count... eight incoming missiles!"

Catherine's lip curled into a humorless grin. "Not very sporting of them, eh?"

"Skipper! Third volley! Salvo-Charlie! Another four missiles!" Far away, across the void of space, the four rotary missile racks of the *Pagan* spat out missile after missile, ripple-firing the warheads not directly at the *Andromeda*, but toward where the *Andromeda* would be when they intercepted her. "They must be dumping their magazines!"

"Engaging!" Wolfram said. Invisible beams lanced out into the night. Brilliant countermeasures spat out of dispensers across the *Andromeda*'s hull, trying to confuse and beguile the incoming warheads. Numerous missiles were damaged, knocked off course, or destroyed outright by the defensive laser fire, but they were still coming. The *Pagan*, seemingly possessed of an inexhaustible supply of the weapons, vomited out another volley. The crew was floored with G-forces as Colin skewed the ship, consuming some of the incoming missiles in the inferno of the *Andromeda*'s exhaust plume.

Damn it all, Catherine cursed, wishing she would have just shot Corbin with her laser. "Wolfram," she said, resolved to do what had to be done. "Arm missiles. Send our friend a volley, three rounds rapid, on my mark. Maintain lasers for defensive—"

Before she could finish her command, the *Andromeda* plunged into the quantum foam and vanished from the physical universe. The final missiles, no longer having a target, continued harmlessly into oblivion.

Zanzibar
Danzig-5012 Solar System
Equatorial Region, 300 km north of Freeport

Cecil Blackwood lifted his respirator and took a long drink from his flask. The tunnel he found himself in was well-lit with high-intensity work lights. The voices of Aristotle Lang's workers were barely audible over the roar of the earthmoving machinery, even with Cecil's electronic hearing protection.

Nearby, Zak Mesa and Anna Kay watched in silence. Their faces were obscured by respirators and goggles, but Cecil noted that they were holding hands. *Good*, he thought to himself. Happiness was hard to come by on Zanzibar; you had to take it where you found it.

This tunnel wasn't like other hastily dug subterranean storage sites. It was wide enough to have a two-lane road, paved with ceramicrete running its length. The originally installed light-ing and ventilation no longer worked, but the tunnel itself was structurally sound. The only blockages were deliberate cave-ins, intended to keep intruders out.

Intruders like Cecil Blackwood and Aristotle Lang. Cecil took another swig of booze. It had taken weeks of research, false starts, and dead ends, but Zak and Anna had finally located Lang's precious vault. Given how remote and how deeply dug the site was, Cecil was sure there was something of immense value in there. What, exactly, he couldn't say—all records of what had been placed in that vault had been deliberately scrubbed before the Maggot invasion.

Lang seemed confident that it had all been worth it, though. The pompous warlord stood off to the side, not bothering with a respirator, his mouth in a wide grin as machines worked at the heavy blast doors. The tunnel had been deliberately collapsed at three separate points along its long, straight path beneath a barren mountain north of Freeport. Getting through the cave-ins had been slow going, damaging several pieces of equipment and killing four of Lang's workers. The effort had continued though, and now they were at the end: the blast doors to the vault.

Cecil found himself secretly hoping that there was nothing in there. Lang would likely kill Zak out of frustration, but the look on his face would be priceless. Still, he was as curious as anyone else as to what this vault contained. Every storage site they had uncovered so far had contained at least a few items of value: artifacts from the vanished Zanzibari civilization, mostly, but also precious metals, useful machinery, even records of the human colony on Zanzibar before its destruction. It was a historical treasure trove, enough to make even Zak Mesa crack a smile.

Lang's greed was insatiable, though, and he was focused like a laser on finding the vault. Now he waited, believing this to be his moment of triumph. Perhaps it was, and perhaps Cecil's ordeal was almost over. His sister, Catherine, was on her way, and should be arriving on Zanzibar soon. She was coming to take him home. Cecil dared to hope that he would be able to leave this rock behind and never return. He didn't speculate about what he'd do after this, but whatever it was, it'd be somewhere with plenty of sunshine, fresh, breathable air, and every luxury he could afford.

For Zak and Anna, it was also a moment of triumph, if a bittersweet one. The secrets they'd uncovered would go down in the history books. They had learned more about Zanzibar than any researchers had since before the war, and their hard work had paid off. Even Cecil considered it a tragedy that such dedication to research and learning should serve to benefit a maniac like Aristotle Lang, but nonetheless, Zak and Anna had much to be proud of. He doubted they really believed him, but Cecil had promised them both that he'd ensure they were taken care of, once their ordeal was over. They had earned it, after all.

It had taken days of constant drilling to breach the armored, reinforced ceramicrete blast doors, but Lang had kept the pressure on his foremen, and his dig crews had been relentless. Now, as the warlord watched eagerly, a drilling machine was about to punch through the last layer of the meter-and-a-half thick blast doors. The technicians monitoring the drilling robot were intensely studying the displays, sweat trickling down their faces. The machines and lighting had caused it to grow uncomfortably warm in the tunnel, and everyone was nervous as well. One of them, a dark-haired man whose face was covered with a breathing apparatus, cocked his head suddenly. He tapped the controls and the machine ground to a halt. As the heavy, tracked drilling machine backed out, a loud, beeping alarm marking its time, the clouds of dust drifted through the hole it had just dug. A slight breeze wafted through the entire tunnel as the air pressure equalized. When the machine was far enough away, its operators shut it down, and it was suddenly eerily quiet.

Everyone looked to Aristotle Lang. The warlord, for his part, was focused only on the entrance to the tunnel. He approached slowly, cautiously even, as if he were afraid it was all a dream. His mouth agape, he shook his head slowly before looking over at his trio of captives. "Mr. Mesa, come here, my boy."

Zak and Cecil looked at one another anxiously, but the historian approached Lang quietly, saying nothing. Cecil and Anna followed tepidly.

"You've done it," Lang said softly, almost choked up. "You have done this thing for me. I never doubted you."

"Well, yes, but I can't confirm that there's anything of value—"

"Nonsense, boy. No one would go through this much trouble without good reason. Listen to me now. Take your compatriots and go in with me. Together, we will see what you have worked so hard to find. You've all earned it."

It took the trio of off-worlders only a few moments to get ready. Protective hard hats, flashlights, and recorders were all readied. As they prepared to enter, Lang's men clustered around the breach in the blast door in a large semicircle, but kept their distance. They had been afraid that some alien horror was buried in there. Cecil didn't think so, but he certainly couldn't rule it out. He was a little nervous himself, if he cared to admit it.

Lang went in first, his flashlight leading the way as he ducked through the hole in the blast door. Zak followed, then Anna. Cecil was last. Taking a deep breath of filtered, condensed air, the Avalonian aristocrat ducked down, stepped through the breach, and joined the others on the far side. When he cleared the borehole he stood up and shined his light around the massive room he found himself in. "My God."

The vault was *not* empty. The middle of the huge room was open, allowing even large trucks to enter. A turntable built into the floor would rotate them around so they could drive back out of the tunnel without having to back out. A dust-covered, eight-wheeled, seven-ton truck sat on the turntable, where it had been left more than a century before. Beyond it were stacks of shipping containers, neatly organized and arranged. The room was ten meters high, and the containers were stacked almost to the ceiling.

The four vault hunters, in awe, slowly moved deeper into the vast storage room, each wandering in a different direction. As before, the containers were marked and labeled with hard copy manifests of their contents. Cecil brushed the dust off of the clear plastic envelope and read the packing list. The artifact was given a serial number, and had been cataloged by when and where it had been found. The description itself was vague; Cecil didn't know what was meant by "anomalous materials," exactly. The thing that caught his attention was the last line, "ORIGIN": instead of "Native Zanzibari" like all of the stored artifacts they'd found before, this one was listed as "Unknown Extraterrestrial Antecedent Species."

It took Cecil a moment to process what he'd just read. *Antecedent species.* His heart dropped into his stomach. "Zak!" he shouted. "Zak, get over here!"

The historian, with Anna Kay and Aristotle Lang in tow, jogged over to Cecil, wondering what he was so upset about. Instead of explaining, Cecil merely shined his light on the container and pointed. Zak leaned forward and read the manifest, his mouth unconsciously moving as he did so. "Unknown extraterrestrial Antecedent...species..." he said, trailing off. He stood up slowly, eyes wide. "Cecil," he said, looking as if he'd seen a ghost. "This is it. This is the secret they were hiding. It wasn't just the Zanzibari artifacts. There...there was another species on this planet. Look at the date codes! It was from the same era as the Zanzibari civilization! Cecil, the natives, they were being visited by advanced aliens! My God, they found Antecessor artifacts... they...I don't..." Zak trailed off again, looking a little woozy.

He steadied himself on the massive storage shelf and breathed deeply through his mask for a moment. "Cecil, do you know what this means? Right here, in this room, are materials, artifacts left over from a species so advanced they were traveling the stars four *million* years ago. This is a priceless find...priceless."

In the depths of space, there had been found evidence of species older and more advanced than humankind. While humanity had encountered only one other spacefaring race, the aliens derisively known as the Maggots, the galaxy was nonetheless full of life. Most worlds that supported life had nothing akin to a sentient species; the few sentient races that *had* been encountered were all very primitive compared to humanity. Only the Maggots surpassed the human race in their technological capabilities, for they were far older. It was widely believed that the forces the Concordiat fought and defeated were the last remnants, the dying gasp of a once mighty, galaxy-spanning empire. The Maggots, it was believed, had been a spacefaring race for thousands of years before humanity ever left the Earth, but even they were young in a universe that was incredibly ancient. There had been scattered evidence of advanced, intelligent, spacefaring races far, far older than even the Maggots. Human scientists had no names for them, and knew nothing about them aside from what could be gleaned from the occasional bit of leftover material or fossilized biological matter. These multiple races were known collectively as Antecessors, and what little remained of them, after millions or even billions of years, was indeed priceless.

This fact was not lost on Aristotle Lang. He slowly ran a hand over the container, smudging the thick layer of dust with his gloved hand. The look on his face was one of awe, even lust. "Mr. Mesa," he said quietly. "You will be rewarded handsomely, you and your partner both. You cannot imagine how wealthy you just made me. You cannot imagine..."

Zak frowned. "All I want is to go home," he said ruefully.

Lang ignored his tone, still almost in shock. "Then go home you shall. You have earned it. I need...I need to get my men in here. I need to appraise these artifacts, find buyers...so much to do..."

Cecil, treading carefully, tried to caution the old warlord. "These anomalous materials could be toxic, radioactive, or dangerous in some other way. You must be careful. If the Zanzibaran colonists found prehistoric alien technology—"

"Then they have made me a very, *very* rich man, Mr. Blackwood," Lang interrupted. He turned to Cecil. "Zanzibar is my home. I was born here, in squalor. Every day is a struggle for survival on this Godforsaken planet. There is nothing here but chaos, violence, and suffering. This, this is the key, don't you see? By leveraging these natural resources, I can remake this miserable world into something fit to live on! Money, investment, research, all of these things will flow to Zanzibar now. The man who controls these resources controls the future of this world. *I* control these resources now, Mr. Blackwood. I'm going to make Zanzibar a better world."

And kill everyone who gets in your way, Cecil thought numbly. *Dear God, what have I done?*

A steady wind howled through Lang's Burg, blasting the east side of the settlement with dust and sand. Zak Mesa, huddled over his console, three separate displays up, paid the wind no mind. He was utterly lost in his work, and had been so for hours. It was only in the last hour or so, when he had gotten up to empty his bladder, that he realized that night had fallen. Cecil had staggered by sometime before that, guided by Bianca to his bed. He had gotten so drunk he could barely stand, and his Zanzibaran . . . girlfriend? Concubine? Zak had never really figured out their relationship. In any case, Bianca had been promising Cecil all sorts of intimate delights if he'd just stop drinking and come to bed.

The historian hadn't thought about it long enough to figure out what Cecil was on about. The Avalonian rich boy went through depressive mood swings like this from time to time, and the easiest thing to do was to just let him sort himself out. Bianca seemed to genuinely care about him, though, which puzzled Zak, but he had never been able to figure women out anyway.

Rubbing his eyes, Zak took another sip from an awful, probably unsafe, locally produced energy drink and focused on his reading. There had been so much information in the vault, saved on drives for long-term storage, that it had been utterly overwhelming. Lang had secured all of the found artifacts for himself, and had them under heavy guard. He was even now trying to find ships to take them off-world, buyers for the goods, and places to buy weapons from. Within a local year or two, Zak figured, his armies would overrun Freeport and he'd be the de facto dictator of the entire planet. The alien treasures, instead of being studied, cataloged, and put on display, would be hoarded away by greedy collectors, smuggled into private collections, or destructively exploited.

It sickened Zak. It sickened him that he'd uncovered one of the greatest xenoarchaeological finds in history, one that had been carefully and deliberately hidden before the Second Interstellar War, and it was all to the benefit of a violent megalomaniac like Aristotle Lang. He might end up in the history books, but he wondered what those books would say about him in the end. How many people were going to die because of Lang? What would become of the artifacts?

It was depressing to think about, so Zak tried not to think. At times, he thought he understood why Cecil drank so much. In any case, his ordeal was, hopefully, almost over. Cecil's sister was on her way; with luck, Zak and Anna would be off Zanzibar. He didn't know what would happen after that. He'd been too depressed, too overwhelmed, and too wrapped up in his work to broach the subject with her. That talk would have to come, sooner or later, and Zak found himself dreading it. She was a woman of wealth, education, and note. He had been barely making a living as an archivist, a minimum-wage historian, when Cecil had initially approached him. He had very little to go home to back on Columbia. Anna had everything she could possibly want on New Constantinople.

There you go again, damn it. Just focus. There was nothing to be gained from this speculation and brooding. He had in front of him a treasure trove of information, and Zak had long since learned that the best distraction from his troubles was to get lost in his reading. There had been more to this find than even the long-dead Dr. Loren had known. The Zanzibaran Colonial Government had kept the discovery of the Antecessor artifacts top secret. There was always the potential that alien discoveries could be dangerous, like a tribe of hunter-gatherers discovering a box of hand grenades. They kept everything as secret as they could, compartmentalized the project as much as possible.

Very little was known about the Antecessor species that had once walked on Zanzibar. It did seem that like the human scientists four million years later, they knew their end was coming. Everything that had been found of them had been located underground, discovered by a mining operation. Whereas some fossilized skeletons of the bipedal, three-eyed native species had been recovered, there was no leftover biological remnant of the Antecessors. All that was known of their makeup and appearance came from the artwork of the Zanzibari.

This Antecessor species looked nothing like a human, and the Zanzibari depictions of them were nebulous at best. So unfamiliar was their form that one didn't immediately recognize what one was seeing when studying a picture of them, though it reminded Zak of a mix of Earth sea creatures.

The trunks of their bodies were stalklike and resembled a sea cucumber standing on end, at least two meters tall, with different Zanzibari illustrations showing individuals with surface bumps and projecting spikes. At the bottom of the stalk there seemed to be an elastic pad, similar to a slug's, that was used for mobility. Halfway up the stalk, four tendril-like appendages emerged from their bodies, and the depictions by the natives indicated that these appendages could be extended or retracted as needed. Their bodies curved slightly forward and were crowned with what resembled a grotesque sea anemone. The tendrils and tissues on this structure were theorized to be sensory units, but that, too, was little more than speculation.

The xenobiologists who had studied this species theorized that this Antecessor species had aquatic origins. They called them *Pseudocaelus aquagrandis*. Like many of their theories, this was also speculation, as no biological remains of them had ever been found.

The ancient native Zanzibari hadn't known anything about the Antecessors, either. Everything the human scientists had learned of their arrival and presence on Zanzibar had come from a series of remarkably well-preserved etchings and sculptures, created by native artists millions of years before. The Antecessors were depicted coming down from the stars in great vessels. The Zanzibari believed that the Antecessors had found them as hunter-gatherers and had lifted them up, teaching them writing, farming, mining, and city-building. The native civilization flourished under the guidance of the aliens, and in turn, the Zanzibari seemed to have worshiped the Antecessors as gods. Great temples were built in their honor, orders and societies were dedicated to their devotion.

For thousands of local years, the Antecessors ruled over Zanzibar. They seemed to have been few in number, but their influence was great. They were depicted observing, or perhaps directing, the construction of great pentagonal pyramids that dwarfed the ones constructed by the Ancient Egyptians on Earth. They oversaw the digging of great canals to get fresh water from great northern glaciers to the equatorial cities. The Antecessors taught the Zanzibari to build ships and navigate the planet's shallow, salty seas. They were shown teaching astronomy and apparently medicine as well. They gave the natives alloys stronger and longer-lasting than anything they could have forged for themselves, which, Zak realized, probably explained the short sword Anna had been studying.

The advanced aliens' generosity came at a price, however. One of the murals, which Zak was presently studying, depicted a group of Zanzibari rebelling against the Antecessors, even slaying one with swords and spears. In turn, the aliens punished the natives cruelly. They obliterated one of the great cities they had helped the Zanzibari build, wiping it from the surface of the planet like Sodom and Gomorrah in the Old Testament. The wayward natives were slaughtered by the thousands, sacrificed as a penance for their uprising.

The Antecessors may have wielded godlike power and influence over the Zanzibari, but they were not gods. The scientists studying the artifacts had not ascertained what had happened to the planet four million years before, but it seemed the Antecessor beings knew the end was coming. Great murals, preserved for millions of years in the incredibly dry darkness of subterranean caves, depicted the Antecessors digging great underground structures, holdfasts against the coming doom. Others were shown fleeing back to the stars, leading to speculation that they might still be out there somewhere.

The Zanzibari, too, prepared for their end. They dug catacombs and tombs for themselves, but unlike the Antecessors, they seemed to hold out no hope for their survival. Interpreting the artwork of a long dead, nonhuman species involved a lot of guesswork and speculation, but in observing the murals, etchings, and sculptures, Zak came to the same conclusion as his predecessors: they had known that they were doomed. There was a fatalistic sadness to their art that transcended the gulf between human and inhuman intellects.

When the end came, it happened rapidly. The geological

record of the incident could be found all over the planet. The world was scorched, burned, cleansed in fire. The seas, indeed almost all water on Zanzibar, boiled away and were blown into space as the planet's magnetosphere dissipated. Solar winds did the rest, slowly thinning out the planet's atmosphere over the course of eons. Colossal upheavals shook the surface of the world, causing great quakes unlike anything ever seen on Earth. Mountains crumbled and fell, rifts kilometers wide opened up, and still scarred the surface of the barren world.

Everything the Zanzibari had built, all of their achievements, were rendered unto dust and carried away by the winds of time. Only fragments of their once mighty civilization remained, broken remnants buried between layers of silicate. Zanzibar, now a cold and dead world, wheeled quietly around Danzig-5012 for four million years before another living being set foot on it.

Conflicting theories as to the cause of Zanzibar's apocalypse abounded. Many believed it had been an unusually powerful solar flare, or even a discharge from Danzig-5012 striking and altering the planet's atmosphere. Some postulated the culprit might have been a nearby gamma ray burster. Others insisted that neither of these scenarios would have ended the planet's seismic and volcanic activity, but the counter for that argument was that it wasn't known when such activity stopped. It could have been millions of years earlier, as the geological evidence was inconclusive.

The most chilling theory, to Zak's mind, was the one that most of the scientists had dismissed. This theory held that Zanzibar was deliberately destroyed by other alien intelligences, greater than even the Antecessors. By what means they did this could only be guessed at. The thought of something capable of wielding such titanic power frightened Zak to his core. He looked up from the warm glow of his screens, listened to the howling wind buffeting the building, and felt very small in a dark and hostile universe.

Zak startled when a hand was lightly placed on his shoulder. He turned around to see Anna, looking concerned. "You should get some rest," she said softly. "Do you know what time it is?"

Zak blinked hard and looked at the chrono on one of his displays. "Oh man. It's late."

"You've been at this for more than a day straight," Anna said.

"I know. I'm just frustrated. Look at what we found, what we learned, and it's all going to Lang!"

"There's nothing we can do right now," she replied. She was right, of course. "Once we get off this planet and back to civilization, we'll have more options. Your message was sent out. You've done everything you can do, and risked your life in the process. Stop beating yourself up."

Zak closed his eyes as Anna rubbed his shoulders. "I know. Once I get back to Columbia I can get a hearing with Concordiat officials."

"I'll be there with you. I may be able to use my family connections to open some doors."

Zak opened his eyes again. "You're going back to Columbia? Why not go home to New Constantinople?" He immediately felt stupid for asking. *Are you trying to convince her to be on a different planet than you, idiot?*

Anna smiled, looking down at the historian. Her hair hung down in his face as he looked up into her eyes. "Because I don't *want* to go back to New Constantinople yet, Zachary. When I do go back, I'm taking my paramour home with me."

"Paramour?" Zak asked. "Is that what they—" Before he could finish, Anna leaned down and kissed him passionately.

She stood up after a long moment, gently stroking the top of his bald head. "Paramour, Zak. It's aristocratic-speak for boyfriend. Lover, if you will. Now come to bed. Those files will still be there tomorrow, and being the paramour of a woman in my position is a serious matter. I'm tired of going to bed alone. You've been derelict in your duties."

Zak blinked rapidly, and tried to think of something clever or charming to say, but he stammered out "I, uh, okay, sorry," instead. Anna just smiled at him one last time and turned for her room. Zak watched her leave, glanced back at his screens, then looked at the partially open door to her room. She was right: the long and tragic history of Zanzibar would wait a few more hours. Perhaps it was time to focus on something positive. The rather-less-dour historian stood up, kicked off his shoes, and followed Anna into her room. *Carpe diem, right?*

The Privateer Ship *Andromeda*
High Solar Orbit
Danzig-5012 System

It had taken over four thousand hours, according to the ship's internal clock, but the *Andromeda* winked into existence two hundred million kilometers from Danzig-5012. The orangeish Type G main sequence star was orbited by six planets: two gas giants, one ice giant, a scorched, barren world closest to the star, a tiny frozen planet furthest out, and one average-sized, terrestrial rock called Zanzibar.

As the ship's systems recovered from transit shock and came back online, Captain Catherine Blackwood recorded a message for Aristotle Lang. She informed the warlord that she had arrived in system, and would be planeting on Zanzibar within the next several local days. That gave her plenty of time, as the *Andromeda* slogged across space on her reaction engines, to prepare for the next stage of her mission: finding and recovering her brother.

There were other pressing matters to attend to, however, and Catherine left Wolfram von Spandau in command of the ship and headed down to the ship's security office. It was here that Mazer Broadbent had his office, as well as a tiny brig with one cell. The captain joined Mazer and Marcus Winchester in watching the security camera feed from the cell. There, the Orlov woman called Lana-90890 was being questioned by Randall Markgraf.

An intelligence officer by trade, Markgraf was in his element. Lana seemed scared and bewildered, so he was applying a softer, friendlier touch. She was beginning to trust him and was becoming very forthcoming with information. Little of it was of any use to the crew of the *Andromeda* at the moment, but everything was being carefully recorded. First-hand intelligence about the Orlov Combine was hard to come by; such information could likely be sold at a high price.

"He's good," Marcus remarked absentmindedly. Lana was sobbing again, and had her head buried in the mercenary's shoulder. He comforted her as if he were her father. "She's really warming up to him."

Catherine raised an eyebrow. "I don't suppose there's any chance he's just being decent to her?"

"Maybe. Either way, she's an asset now. She's been involved in the smuggling of refugees to Zanzibar before. She's heard of this Sanctuary place."

"Combine political refugees aren't my immediate concern," Catherine said, sounding colder than she would've liked. "We have a job to do."

Marcus nodded. "Yes, ma'am. But the only information we have about the situation on the ground on Zanzibar is what Halifax has told us, and that's years out of date. This woman has information that's more recent. If we deliver her to Sanctuary, perhaps they'll trust us enough to share some information on Aristotle Lang and his operation. It might give us a way in, an edge."

"I'm still planning on simply paying his ransom, you know," Catherine said.

"I understand, Captain, but I'm preparing for every contingency I can. If simply buying your brother back does the job, that's all well and good. Until then, I'm going to assume the worst-case scenario and plan for that."

The captain nodded thoughtfully. "I continue to get my money's worth out of you, Mr. Winchester."

On the screen, Markgraf was asking Lana about Sanctuary. "We don't know anything about it," he said calmly. "Your father told us to take you there. He said you'd know what that meant." Lana looked uncomfortable, as if she was afraid to reveal this secret, even after the crew of the *Andromeda* had saved her life. Markgraf pressed in on her. "Lana, listen to me," he said firmly. "You're safe from the Combine. We almost started a war with them to get you out. The crew of this ship risked their lives to save yours. We were told by your father to bring you to Sanctuary on Zanzibar, but none of us know where that is. Help us help you."

"My...my ECCOM is still active," she said, pointing to the device attached to the side of her head. "With...without my programs, I can't deactivate it or fool it. Everything we say is being recorded."

"I'm aware, Lana. It doesn't matter. You're outside of Combine space, on an independent privateer ship. Your electronic comrade has no one to talk to. It can record, but it can't upload. We can have the ship's flight surgeon look into removing it for you, if you like. After that, you can launch it out of the airlock, burn it up in the ship's exhaust. You're free now, Lana, but we need to know where to bring you. One way or another, we're going to Zanzibar. We're almost there."

Even in the face of overwhelming evidence, Lana was hesitant, as if she feared this whole thing was some kind of elaborate ruse. Catherine couldn't imagine the kind of living conditions, if you could even *call* it living, that could make a person so afraid to *think*.

"Lana, we need your help," Markgraf insisted. "Our mission on Zanzibar is not related to this Sanctuary place, but maybe they can help us. We need information about a dangerous warlord, if they have it. We need to know what the situation on the ground is, so we're not going in blind. If we can even find them, they're not going to talk to a bunch of off-worlders. But if we bring you to them, explain what happened, maybe they'll be willing to talk to us."

Lana, still sitting on the bunk, folded her hands in her lap and looked down. She seemed terrified. "This could be a trick," she managed after a moment. "InSec could've hired you people to find Sanctuary."

"Lana, you watched the video of your station being destroyed. You saw the message your father left for you."

"My father could be *in* on it!" she snapped, tears in her eyes. "Everything else could be faked!"

Catherine could see Markgraf's frustration, but he kept his professional demeanor and changed tactics. "Listen to me. If you really believed that, you wouldn't have come with us. Do you want to speak with the captain again?" Lana didn't answer. "Okay, I'll bring her in here." He looked up at the camera. "Captain Blackwood, would you be so kind as to step in here with us, ma'am? I think our guest would feel better hearing this from you."

Catherine's eyes went wide for a moment. Marcus shrugged.

"I didn't tell him you were here, if that's what you're wondering. He probably just assumed."

"Well then," Catherine said, smoothing the wrinkles out of her flight suit. "I suppose I ought to go talk to the woman. Excuse me." With the ship accelerating at 0.75 gravities, the captain was able to walk to the holding cell instead of pulling herself along by handholds. Markgraf nodded at the skipper and excused himself as she entered the tiny brig and sat on the bunk next to Lana. "Hello," she said, after a pause.

"Hello, Captain," Lana said quietly.

Catherine took a soft tone. "Listen to me, child. I know you're scared. I know your whole world was just turned upside down, but we need your help. We can't get you to Sanctuary if you don't tell us how to find it. It's okay if you don't know everything. Just tell us what you do know, and we'll go from there."

"Why are you going to Zanzibar?"

"I'm going there because a local warlord is holding my brother hostage. My father hired me to pay his ransom and bring him home. Our meeting you was completely unintentional, arranged by your father. He practically blackmailed us into it, as a matter of fact."

"And you're just going to let me go?" the young woman asked incredulously.

"Yes, dear. Unless you're interested in joining the crew, I've no cause to keep you on board. One way or another, after we make planetfall, you're free to go. Zanzibar is a dangerous place. We can help you get to Sanctuary safely, and maybe your compatriots there will be able to help us as well."

She absentmindedly touched the gray monitoring device attached to her head. "You can really take this off? It's . . . it's been on me since I was a girl."

"We have some time before we land. Doing the procedure in freefall isn't ideal, but my flight surgeon is very skilled. I'm sure he can remove it. I can take you right to him, if you like."

Her eyes teared up again. "Thank you," she said quietly. "Thank you, Captain. I know a way to contact Sanctuary, and an emergency code. It's old, but it should still be good. If you take this . . . this *thing* off of me, I'll take you to them when we land."

"You've got yourself a deal, Lana," Catherine said. "Come now, let's go see Dr. Emerson."

Zanzibar
Danzig-5012 Solar System
City of Freeport, Equatorial Region

It was still dark in Freeport when the *Andromeda* touched down. Given that most of the world was uninhabited, they didn't necessarily have to berth there, but Freeport contained the remote world's only operational spaceport, and the ship needed to be refueled and refitted for the long journey back to Avalon.

For Marcus Winchester and his Cowboys, things got busy as soon as the ship settled onto its landing jacks. Captain Blackwood and her crew would handle the negotiations with Aristotle Lang. It was Marcus' job to prepare an alternative plan, and that meant getting off the ship, scouting the city, and learning everything he could about the situation on the ground. The first order of business was to take Lana and make a connection with the denizens of this so-called Sanctuary on Zanzibar.

To that end, Marcus and Wade Bishop prepared to take the young lady wherever it was she needed to go to make contact with her brethren. Meanwhile, Benjamin Halifax and Randall Markgraf headed out into the city to gather intelligence on Lang and his operation. Ken Tanaka, Devree Starlighter, and Jeremiah Hondo were charged with unpacking all of the mercenaries' equipment and readying it for combat operations. They hated to be left behind, of course. None of them had been able to leave the ship since Opal, and they all wanted to be involved in the mission. But every task that Marcus assigned needed doing, and each member of the team understood that. *Besides,* the mercenary team leader thought grimly, *they'll get their chance.* He had a bad feeling that negotiations for Cecil Blackwood were not going to go as well as the captain was hoping.

The three mercenaries left behind weren't the only ones unhappy to remain with the ship. "No," Marcus said firmly, looking his daughter in the eye. "Absolutely not."

"But Dad!" Annie protested.

Marcus was having none of it. "This place is a shithole. You are not to leave the ship under any circumstances. Your mother is already going to kill me when she finds out about that Combine ship shooting at us, and now you want me to bring you out in to a place like this? No way. Besides, you're still a member of the crew. You've got work to do."

"I know," Annie pouted. "I just want to help you. You need somebody to watch your back, otherwise a crazy cyborg might choke you out again."

Marcus immediately regretted letting his daughter talk him into divulging the details of that incident. "Listen, darlin', I know you're worried, but I'll be okay. Believe it or not, I used to be pretty good at this kind of stuff. I'm in my element."

Annie stepped forward and squeezed her father tightly. "Just promise me you'll be careful."

"I promise," Marcus said, hugging his daughter.

"And look out for Wade," she said. "You know how he is. He'll get killed."

"I'm standing right here!" Wade protested. Marcus laughed.

Freeport was every bit as dirty, cluttered, and dangerous as Halifax had warned. The present city was built entirely too close to the spaceport, and every time a ship would lift off or land the foundations of every building would shake. Marcus wondered what the long-term effects of radiation exposure were like for the residents. Most ships had takeoff and landing modes for their engines which reduced the overall output and contained the radiation, but still, there was a reason spaceports weren't usually located next to residential areas.

The part of the city the trio of off-worlders were making their way through was actually the nicer part of town. Even though it was early in the morning, a few areas were busy and crowded with people. Bars, nightclubs, and drug dens lined the streets. There were arcades, brothels, souvenir shops, and casinos, every imaginable way of separating weary spacers from their money.

Yet aside from pickpockets and the occasional odd intoxicated belligerent, this part of Freeport was relatively safe. The city of Freeport and the spaceport were controlled and managed by a cabal of local elites called The Board, Halifax had explained. Their current chairman, a man named Frank DeWitt, was deadly serious about keeping peace and order in his city. There weren't a lot of rules, but it was best to abide by them. Security men known as Enforcers patrolled the streets in pairs, heavily armed and looking for trouble. If you caused problems, if you were bad for business, or if you committed fraud, it was as likely as not you'd end up buried in the desert with a bullet hole in your head.

Away from the spaceport, in the slums and shantytowns, it was another matter. There were places there that even the Enforcers wouldn't go, where violent street gangs fought for turf, resources, or merely because life on Zanzibar was cheap and generally short. Beyond the walls of the city, there was no law except for that which Aristotle Lang had imposed. There had once been more warlords, but he had eliminated all the competition. There were scattered, isolated independent settlements all across the planet, but many of them were under the thumb of Lang now. He'd been building his army for years, and it was no secret that he had his sights on Freeport. The city-dwellers had better access to off-world tech and weapons, but they were outnumbered by those living outside. People had taken to having large families to survive and to counter the high child mortality rate, and the population outside the city had been steadily growing for decades.

Marcus could see the writing on the wall. Sooner or later, Lang would attempt to take Freeport. If his forces got inside the walls, they'd sack the city and possibly burn it to the ground out of spite. There were plenty of criminals and degenerates, many of them fugitives from off-world, who'd be willing to fight for a man like Lang for the money and the chance to loot the city. It bothered Marcus that the ransom money the captain was paying would merely go to help the warlord buy weapons, but there was nothing he could do about that. He had a job to do, and saving Zanzibar from itself wasn't it.

The planetary network was patchy and unreliable, but Wade was able to get enough signal to locate the address of their present destination. Lana didn't know anything about the place other than its name: The Blue Manx. To Marcus, that sounded shady, like a nudie bar or a brothel. He wasn't surprised, then, when they turned down an alley and came to the entrance of the place. Prostitutes in outfits as revealing as the harsh wind would allow stood by the entrance. Some were men, most were women, and a few were indeterminate, especially with respirator masks on. They welcomed would-be patrons as they made their way down the alley, and bid those leaving a fond farewell. Thumping, harsh industrial music echoed down the alleyway like a shattering pane of glass. One side was flanked by a crumbling prewar ruin and on the other by a housing project. A huge, cracked screen over the door depicted the name of the place. Occasionally, a blue, tailless cartoon cat would chase an animated sex worker across the screen, tongue hanging out lustfully.

"Classy," Wade said, his voice muffled by his respirator. Marcus chuckled.

Lana didn't see the humor in the situation. "I don't understand. What... what is this place?"

"Seriously?" Wade asked. "It's a brothel."

"A what?"

"A whorehouse. A place where you can go pay people to have sex with you."

Lana's mouth was concealed behind her mask, but her eyes were wide. "*What?*" she asked incredulously. "That's... that's disgusting!"

"You need to lighten up, kiddo," Marcus suggested. "They say it's the world's oldest profession."

"There are no... no houses of *whores* on Orlov," she said. "They say that sex without reproduction is a waste of time. Sex is for expanding the population base. Having children serves the state. Such depravity is selfish, putting the individual before the society. It's something the Proles do."

"Jesus, what a drag," Wade said. "No wonder people want to leave so bad."

"Who's Jesus?"

"You're not on Orlov anymore, Lana," Marcus said, putting his hand on her shoulder. "I know it's a culture shock for you, but that's the way things are here. Try to focus on why we're here."

"Of course," she said. "You're right. It's just... I've never done sex before."

"Well, I'm sure you'll get your chance now," Marcus said, ushering her forward. "But worry about that later."

"Yes. I was told to go in here, and say a specific phrase to one of the workers."

"Which worker?"

"I don't know. I was told I'd know the person when I saw the person, and that's all they told me."

Marcus and Wade looked at each other knowingly. They were both thinking the same thing: the poor girl had been given bad information, and she was in for a serious disappointment. There was nothing to do but try, however, so they went inside.

As on Opal, the buildings on Zanzibar tended to be overpressurized. Not only did it keep out the fine dust, but Zanzibar's surface atmospheric pressure was as low as it was at five thousand meters above sea level on Earth. Travelers not used to the thin air suffered from dizziness, shortness of breath, headaches, and occasional blackouts. All of these things were unacceptable when you were trying to have sex, so the Blue Manx was pressurized to something much more comfortable for most people.

Marcus' ears popped as the airlock-like set of double doors cycled. Immediately inside was a dimly lit foyer, with glittering lights and mirrors on the walls. It seemed that on every world, houses of ill repute had the same décor. Two security guards, dressed in black and wearing respirators, glared at the trio as they entered. One, a large burly man, had a pistol holstered on each hip. The other, a rough-looking woman with short hair, carried a short-barreled flechette gun with an honest-to-goodness bayonet affixed under the barrel.

"Welcome to the Blue Manx!" said a slender young woman with a much more personable demeanor. She was in a booth behind armored glass. She had olive skin with intricate, colorful tattoos across it. Her long, dark hair and Asiatic features were accented by glittering jewelry hanging from her ears and belly button. She was topless, dressed only in what looked like short hot-pants and high-heeled boots. "Will that be three?"

Lana's eyes were wide. Her pale features deeply reddened around her respirator. *Who'd have thought the Orlov Combine was full of prudes,* Marcus thought. She tried to reply, but stammered something unintelligible, so Marcus stepped forward and removed his mask. "Yes," he said, turning on the charm and struggling to make eye contact with the woman. "That's three."

"Great!" the hostess said. "You can swipe your credit chit here.

We also accept hard currency from several sources. Prices and exchange rates are listed on the screen over there. No refunds. Were you three looking for a companion or two for a group activity, or did you just want to go to the bar? We usually recommend first-timers go to the bar."

Marcus caught his eyes wandering downward to the woman's ample bosom. He could hardly be blamed; he was a married man, but he wasn't dead, and she wasn't exactly being shy. "Yes," he said with a grin. "I think the bar will be best. We're first-timers."

"Great!" the hostess repeated. She pointed to a closet behind Marcus after scanning his credit card. "All patrons are required to remove hats, coats, respirators, goggles, and weapons before entering, for the safety of our staff and to keep the dust out." She slid him a small plastic card. "I've given you a large locker for your personal effects. It should be big enough for all three of you. If you need more space, come back and see me!"

"Will do, darlin'," Marcus said with a grin. "C'mon guys, let's put our stuff away and go inside."

Having left his hat, long duster coat, goggles, respirator, and sidearm in the locker, Marcus took his compatriots and entered the main part of the club. Inside, electronic music pulsed over a sound system. Naked women danced on one stage, and naked men danced on the other. In one corner, sex robots were available for rent. Marcus didn't say anything, only nodded at the robots and smiled at Wade.

"Screw you," Wade said. "Also . . . they don't even look human." It was true; the sex robots available were not designed to mimic the human form. They were angular and metallic, possessed of jointed, articulated arms and mechanical claws.

Marcus shrugged. "Robosexuals. I doubt it's the strangest thing going on in here." Scattered across the room were chairs, couches, and tables, all covered in plastic, where patrons sat and chatted with the staff before being led into the sex rooms.

At a nearby table, a man was getting a lapdance from a naked woman. Lana was aghast. "What a bunch of degenerates!" she sputtered. With her cloak and mask removed, her face was fully visible, even in the dim light. She self-consciously tried to adjust her hair to cover the gray synthetic plate on the left side of her head, where her electronic comrade had been. Her hair was short and it didn't fully hide the ugly blemish on the side of her face.

Lana gasped as a woman's arm reached over her shoulder,

around her face, and gently caressed the side of her head. One of the Blue Manx's staff had snuck up behind her and was now pressing her breasts into Lana's back. Her fingers gently ran across the spot where the ECCOM had been located.

"What's the matter, sweetheart?" she asked softly. "Is this your first time in a place like this?" The woman's pageboy haircut was a bright, metallic blue. Her fingernails were painted to match. She wore a very short, very tight evening dress, also a metallic blue, and matching high-heeled shoes. Glowing bracelets and earrings accented her style in the dim light. She spoke Commerce English with the same accent that Lana did, though it wasn't nearly so pronounced.

Wade leaned over to Marcus with a grin. "That's what I'm talking about!" Marcus elbowed his partner, but didn't disagree with his assessment: the woman was a *goddess*.

Poor Lana seemed too terrified to move. "I...I...I'm looking for someone!" she blurted out, pulling away from the blue woman's embrace. She turned to face her, then looked down. "I'm sorry. This is all new for me."

"Oh, sweetie," the blue woman said, "it's okay." She reached forward and caressed the side of Lana's head, again touching the plate where here ECCOM had been. "I know you're not from around here." With her left hand, she brushed back her own hair, revealing a synthetic plate of her own. "It's hard, getting used to life in the real world," she said. "I've been where you are. My name is Lucy."

Lana's eyes were wide. "The winds of time carry away all things," she said.

"And all things are dust in the wind," Lucy replied. "What's your name, child?"

"Lana Nine-Zero-Eight-Nine-Zero," Lana answered, looking up into Lucy's eyes, almost in shock.

"Not any more, honey. That was your slave designation. People have names, not numbers."

"Just Lana, then," she said quietly.

Lucy leaned in close to Lana, almost like she was going to kiss her, but stopped short. "Welcome home, sister," she said.

"My...my friends here helped me escape," she stammered, a tear rolling down her cheek.

"Ma'am," Marcus said professionally. "My name is Marcus Winchester. I need your help."

The Privateer Ship *Andromeda*
Freeport Spaceport, Equatorial Region
Zanzibar

Captain Catherine Blackwood checked herself on her screen one last time. Her sage green flight suit was crisp and fresh. She straightened her leather flight jacket, gold wings on her left breast and the four gold captain's bars on each shoulder. The peaked cap, the one she almost never wore, was sitting perfectly on her head, very slightly cocked to one side. Behind her command chair, Wolfram von Spandau stood quietly, striking an imposing figure with his shoulders squared and his hands folded behind his back.

On one of Catherine's screens, Mordecai Chang's face appeared. It took some prodding, but he, too, had cleaned up his normally disheveled appearance. Catherine wasn't able to coax him out of his tiny cabin, but there wasn't really any reason for the eccentric purser to be on the command deck anyway. She needed him to be on top of his game, and that meant keeping him in his comfort zone. Mordecai was not the social type, and he didn't like to deal with people face-to-face.

The command deck of the *Andromeda* was unusually quiet. Aside from Catherine and her exec, it was deserted, and the hatches were closed. For highly sensitive negotiations like this, she needed to be able to focus and not have any distractions.

"Are you ready, *Kapitänin*?" Wolfram asked.

She took a deep breath. "I am. Let's do this. Mordecai, make the call."

"Yes ma'am," Mordecai said. "Stand by."

Though outwardly she projected the perfectly calm demeanor of confident command, Catherine's heart was racing. She'd sent a message to Aristotle Lang upon arriving in-system, and again after landing. The only response was a terse text message telling her when to place a video call to begin negotiations. She didn't know what to expect when the call went through. *What if something happened to Cecil? What if he's been tortured?* It had taken her an awfully long time to get to Zanzibar.

Catherine's heart jumped up into her throat as Cecil's face appeared on the screen. Apart from dark circles under his eyes, and the facial lines of a man who drank too much, her brother looked no worse for wear. "Hello, Cat," he said with a weak smile. "It's...it's good to see you."

"Cecil..." she said, trailing off. She couldn't help but let her expression soften. She hadn't seen him in years, but he was still her baby brother. She had carried him around when he was an infant, played with him as a child, and hugged him as he cried after their mother passed away. "It's good to see you too, little brother."

"I was worried you wouldn't come."

"I'm sorry it took me so long to get here." Catherine took a deep breath. It was time to get down to business. "Tell me, Cecil, where was our secret hiding spot as children?"

"What?"

"Where was our secret hiding spot as children? The one we never told anyone about."

"Oh! My God, I can't believe you remember that. It was in that grove of trees on the northwest corner of the estate. We hid there for a day after you broke mother's Earth-native vase."

"*I* didn't break that vase, Cecil," Catherine said, unable to stop smiling. "*You* broke that vase and *I* got blamed for it." She was relieved. There's no way anyone but Cecil would know that. She'd just verified that it was him, and not a trick.

"That's not how I remember it, Cat," he said coyly. "It's good to see you. Thank you for coming all the way out here."

"It wouldn't be the first time I got you out of trouble, would it now? Are you well?"

"As well as can be expected," he said.

"He is *quite* well, I assure you, Captain!" Aristotle Lang said, stepping into view. He sounded pompous, overconfident, but

Catherine could tell he was not a man to take lightly. He was a stocky man with a bald head, dressed in a gaudy fur coat. "I am a businessman, not a monster. I have no interest in damaging the merchandise! As you can see, your brother is quite well. Once we've settled the small matter of payment, he's all yours, and you can be on your way home."

Mordecai Chang chimed in. "Our correspondence is all months out of date at this point, but I don't believe you have specified a price. I am sending you what I think you'll find is a very generous offer."

"All I want," the captain added, "is to bring my brother home safely. I would like this matter to be resolved as quickly and painlessly as possible."

"And my associates," Cecil interjected. "Zak Mesa and Anna Kay."

"Yes, yes," Lang said, silencing Cecil. He looked away from the screen, presumably at the offer Mordecai had sent, but seemed nonplussed. "Captain, that is indeed a generous offer, but I have more money than I can spend on Zanzibar as is."

Catherine's eyes narrowed. "Then what is it, exactly, you want?"

Lang leaned in toward the camera. "What I *want*, Captain, is *Freeport*. What I *need* in order to *get* what I want are *weapons*. Modern weapons, the kind you can't get on this world. Powered armor. Plasma weapons. Long-range missiles. This planet is nothing but chaos and squalor. I can change that. I have the will, and the loyal followers, but I need better tools to do the job. Once it is over, there will be peace, and I will bring to Zanzibar prosperity that it hasn't known in any of our lifetimes. With these weapons, I can not only take Freeport, but *hold* it. Defend it from off-world interlopers who come to steal our natural resources."

The captain kept her game face on, but a quiet rage was boiling inside her. "I have spent over four thousand hours in transit, operating under the assumption that the payment you sought was money. At no point did you specify specific goods in exchange for Cecil. As such, I didn't *bring* the specific goods you want. My cargo hold is full of the supplies I needed for this journey, not weapons for your army. What would you have me do, fly back to New Austin and buy the weapons you want?"

"No need for such hyperbole, Captain. I am not an unreasonable man, and I do not make unreasonable demands. Valuable trade goods have come into my possession. I have made deals for the tools that I need. However, because of Frank DeWitt's cowardly defamation of my character, none of the ships at the spaceport will let me hire them, and I'd be hesitant to trust them with this cargo in any case. You," he said, patting Cecil roughly on the shoulder, "you have cause to honor a deal."

It was all Catherine could do to stop her hands from shaking with anger. "Very well," she said calmly. "Send me the specifics of what you require."

Lang tapped his screen, sending Catherine the requested data packet. "Excellent! If you do this thing for me, you will have your brother back, no worse for wear." Cecil went to say something, but Lang hushed him. "I will demonstrate my sincerity. If nothing else, it will calm your brother down. I will send his assistants to Freeport to meet with you. Consider it a symbol of my good faith. They will carry with them the coordinates of where you will land your ship to collect my trade goods."

Cecil's mouth fell open. "My God, thank you. Thank you so much. I—"

Lang pushed him out of view of the camera, interrupting him. "Do not mistake my generosity for a lack of resolve, Captain. If you want your brother back, you will do as I ask."

"I understand," Catherine said, ice in her voice. "I need *you* to understand, Mr. Lang, that I *will* kill you if this is some kind of a trick."

Lang laughed. "Many have tried, my dear Captain, many have tried. But you needn't worry. Everything you need to know is in the packet I just sent. Your brother's associates will arrive in the city within a day, and I will leave them with instructions to contact you."

"I will have to come back to Freeport first," she said. "The port services here are slow. It will take a few days to get the ship refitted for a long flight."

From the look on his face, Catherine could tell that Lang didn't like that. She expected him to tell her to wait, to come get his trade goods when she was ready to lift off, but he surprised her by just shrugging it off. "Very well. You should know, Captain, that I have people everywhere in Freeport. If it is you who tries to trick me, your ship will never leave this world. I promise you that." The connection was cut.

"God *damn* it!" Catherine snarled, slamming a fist onto her armrest.

"Cap'n," Mordecai asked, "do you have any idea what these trade goods are?"

"No, Mordecai, I do not, and I don't care. Paying a ransom is one thing. I will be *damned* if I'm going to be an errand girl for that pompous ass, flying all over known space fetching weapons for his army!"

"There is another matter to consider, *Kapitänin*," Wolfram said. "If we do equip his forces with weapons, and our involvement in the matter becomes public knowledge, our license to operate in Concordiat space could be revoked. There is a clause in the interstellar trade laws regarding the arming of brigands and terrorist groups. Aristotle Lang almost certainly meets that definition."

"I'm aware, Wolfram. I'm not worried about the Concordiat. It's the principle of the matter."

Wolfram nodded. "We always knew this could happen."

"Indeed, Cap'n," Mordecai agreed. "He got greedy. He seems overconfident, though. Perhaps we can use this to our advantage?"

The captain sat quietly for a moment, brow furrowed in thought. "Perhaps we can, Mordecai," she said. "Perhaps we can. Is Marcus Winchester back yet?"

"Negative."

"Send him a message explaining everything that happened. Tell him I need him back here as soon as possible to begin contingency planning. Lang is in for a *very* rude surprise."

"I just received a message from him, *Kapitänin*. He says that he has made contact with the Orlov refugees. Lana is being delivered to Sanctuary."

Catherine rubbed her chin, thoughtfully. "Perhaps they can help us."

Dressed in a long brown cloak, respirator, and tinted goggles, Catherine was indistinguishable from anyone else on Zanzibar. Away from the security of the ship, discretion was a necessity. She didn't want to draw attention to herself, and the people she was meeting didn't want attention drawn to them, either.

Mazer Broadbent wanted to go along, to protect his captain if she insisted on leaving the ship, but Catherine had ordered him to stay behind. She didn't trust the security of the ramshackle spaceport and wanted him there to handle any problems that might arise. Escorting her were three of her hired mercenaries: Marcus Winchester, Randall Markgraf, and Benjamin Halifax. All were dressed in similar garb as they quietly moved through a bustling bazaar, trying not to draw attention to themselves. They were led by the blue-haired prostitute that Marcus had made contact with. She, apparently, was a point of contact for Sanctuary.

As Danzig-5012 sunk below the horizon, the woman with blue hair led the spacers away from the noise and crowds of the market, into the slums that surrounded it. She turned down a rapidly darkening alley and motioned for the off-worlders to stay behind. A lone figure was waiting for them. The man was also cloaked and masked, and was leaning against a wall. The woman, Lucy, went forward and spoke with him quietly. After a few moments, she motioned for Catherine and her men to approach.

"This is where I leave you," Lucy said. "This is Strelok. He will take you the rest of the way."

"Where are you taking us?" Catherine asked. She wanted these people's help, so she didn't want to sound too demanding, but the veteran spacer wasn't about to let herself get complacent, either.

"To a safe place," the man called Strelok responded, "where we can discuss matters."

"I must go," Lucy said. "Thank you for bringing Lana to us. She is among family here." Without another word, she turned down the alley and walked away.

"Are you taking us to Sanctuary?" Marcus asked.

"No," Strelok said. "We do not speak of that out here. We have a safe house nearby. Follow me, and do not draw attention to yourself. Aristotle Lang's spies do not go where I am taking you, but it is not a safe place for off-worlders. Come."

Forty-five minutes later, Catherine found herself inside a partially damaged building beneath the crumbling ruins of a highway overpass, on the very edge of Freeport. Her mercenary escorts had balked when Strelok insisted that they disarm and submit to a weapons scan, but she ordered them to comply. No one was waiting for them in the main room of the building, but it was stocked with provisions and beds. There were no guards, but the off-worlders were tracked by a ceiling-mounted turret as Strelok led them into the building. He pushed open an ancient, creaking door and motioned for them to follow him down a flight of stairs.

One floor below was a small room filled with a cluttered mishmash of computers and communication equipment. At least a dozen screens illuminated the otherwise darkened room, as did a holotank. At the center of it all was a pale, skinny man with a headset over his eyes and ears, and cables leading into the back of his neck. Standing next to him was an older, silver-haired woman with a weapon in her hands and an unhappy expression on her face.

"Ah...Captain Catherine Blackwood, of the privateer ship *Andromeda*," the wired man said, without turning his head in Catherine's direction. An unkempt mop of hair hung down over his face and headset. "I'm glad to meet you."

Strelok indicated the strange man plugged into his machines. "This is Piro, our—"

"Technomancer," Piro interrupted. "I am a Technomancer. I am connected to every network on Zanzibar, every satellite, every ship in orbit. I go everywhere and see everything."

Strelok sighed audibly through his mask. "No one actually calls him a *technomancer*." The woman didn't say anything, but she rolled her eyes.

"It'd catch on if you people would use it!" Piro protested.

"But he is very good at what he does," Strelok said. "The best, in fact."

"This is what I did for the Combine," Piro said sadly, slowly moving a hand over his banks of screens. "I was the omnipresent eye of the state, always watching, always listening, always judging. One of thousands, tens of thousands."

"That's...unsettling," Marcus said.

"You have no idea," Piro replied, a hollow grin splitting his face. "It's dehumanizing, even in a society that dehumanizes people as a matter of policy. But even the watchmen are watched in the Combine, and ultimately, all of us are guilty of crimes of thought in the eyes of the State. My new comrades here, they took me in, forgave my sins, gave me a home. So for them I do the only thing I know how to do. I watch over them, as I have been watching you."

"Enough," the woman said, slinging her weapon and stepping forward.

"This is Maggie," Strelok said.

"Thank you for meeting with us," Catherine said.

"We wouldn't have," Maggie admitted, "but you are not the only one to seek us out lately."

"And it's no coincidence," Piro said. Video footage of Cecil's assistant, Zak Mesa, appeared on one of his screens. "You are not the first to mention Cecil Blackwood."

"He's my brother," Catherine said. "I came here to pay Lang's ransom and take him home."

"What do you want from us, then?" Maggie asked coldly.

Catherine studied the three Orlov refugees carefully before speaking. "Lang doesn't want money," she said. "He wants weapons. In order to get my brother back, I am to take trade goods to a designated meeting point and exchange them for heavy weaponry."

"What kind of weaponry?" Maggie asked.

"Plasma weapons. Missiles. Powered armor."

"I see," she said.

"It is as we feared," Piro said. "Mr. Mesa was correct."

"Correct about what?" Catherine asked. "I don't know this Zak Mesa, but Lang is releasing him to my custody as a sign of good faith."

Strelok seemed pleased with that news, but didn't elaborate. "He suggested that Lang would try to acquire weapons."

"When was this Mesa fellow here?" Catherine asked. "And why?"

"That's not important now," Maggie said. "What is it that you want from us?"

"We need your help," Catherine said. "I have no intention of arming a petty warlord like Aristotle Lang so he can take over this planet. That's just what he means to do, too. He told me as much himself."

"You mean to recover your brother by force," Strelok said.

"I do," Catherine said. "I don't know where he's being held. I was hoping that your organization would be able to help me locate him. I had my security officer put in a query with the Enforcers of Freeport, but they were of no help."

"No, I do not expect they would be," Maggie said thoughtfully. "This is all as we feared."

"The weapons I'm to acquire are all coming from the Orlov Combine," Catherine said. "There's no one else in this sector of space to buy such weapons from."

"It is as we predicted," Piro said. "Mr. Mesa suggested as much himself. I know where your brother is being held, Captain. I must ask you, though . . . are you aware what these trade goods are?"

"No," Catherine admitted. "The information I was sent was vague. Prewar materials, was how he described it. The containers are to be delivered to the buyer, sealed."

"You need to watch this," Piro said.

A video recording of Cecil's assistant appeared on several of his screens at once. "My name is Zachary Dionysus Mesa," he began.

Catherine's eyes went wide as she listened to his message.

Zak Mesa nervously stuck his hands in his pockets as the elevator slowly climbed the skeletal docking tower. The huge cargo elevator had to be a hundred years old, and given that it was exposed to the elements, Zak was amazed it was still working. A cold, dry wind whipped fine dust through the safety cage as it slowly ascended, forcing the historian to tighten his goggles.

Zak and Anna looked up at the ship as the elevator slowly ascended the tower. It was big, probably seventy meters tall. Its fat, armored, gunmetal hull dully reflected the light of Danzig-5012 as the platform slowly lifted them above the city. It had a cluster of four engines at its tail, and four airfoils in between them. Each engine cowling had a radiator sticking out of it. As the elevator brought them level with the cargo bay doors, Zak caught a glimpse of nose art painted on the side of its hull; he recognized it as Princess Andromeda from Ancient Greek mythology.

"This is it," Zak said, as the elevator ground to a halt. The cage doors opened, allowing Zak and Anna to make their way across the bridge of the landing tower to the ship's open cargo bay doors. Like the rest of the structure, the bridge was skeletal, exposed to the elements, and harsh winds buffeted the pair as they approached. At the end of the bridge, Zak could see into the cargo bay. It was well-lit, clean, and a group of people were waiting for him.

The first person to approach was a short, stout man in a sage green coverall. "Greetings, gentlefolk," he said, crushing Zak's hand as he shook it. "I am Cargomaster Kimball. Welcome aboard the Privateer Ship *Andromeda*."

"Thank you," Zak replied nervously.

A tall woman in a leather flight jacket stepped forward. She had gold wings on her left breast, and four gold bars on each shoulder. "I am Catherine Blackwood. This is my ship."

"I recognized you from the message you sent your brother," Zak said. "I was there when he received it. I...I almost didn't want to believe it."

A tall, broad-shouldered man with dark skin and a cybernetic ocular implant scanned the two newcomers with a handheld device. "We're secure, Captain. No transmitters detected."

The captain nodded. "Thank you, Mr. Broadbent. Now," she turned her attention to the two young researchers, "did you bring the landing coordinates from Lang?"

Zak retrieved his handheld from his pocket. "I did. Captain, I...thank you. I don't know what else to say. Your brother is a good man. He secured our release, just like he said he would."

The spacer seemed pleased with Zak's praise of her brother. "Yes, well, we're not done yet," she said. She looked over Zak's shoulder. "Ah, there you are."

Zak turned and found his contact with the Orlov refugees standing behind him. "Strelok!" he said. "What are you doing here?"

He had removed his goggles and hood, but left his respirator on. "Zanzibar is a small world after all," he said. "The captain and her companions sought us out, just as you did. It seems that our Sanctuary isn't a secret any longer."

"But how...?"

"There'll be time to catch up later, Mr. Mesa," the captain said. She put her hand on the shoulder of a young girl, a teenager, who was wearing the green jumpsuit that her crew all wore. "Crewman Winchester here will take you and...Miss Kay, was it? Yes. She will take you up to the personnel deck and get you assigned berths. You will remain with us from now on, no matter what happens."

"What *is* happening, Captain?" Zak asked. "Lang gave me coordinates for a meeting point. I don't know what's going on, but I'm assuming he's using you to go buy his weapons for him. But why is Strelok here? Did he tell you what it is Lang has in his possession?"

"He did," the captain said. "And if Lang thinks I'm going to fly halfway back to Combine space, meet up with some unscrupulous arms dealer, and secure weapons for his army he's delusional. Trust me, Mr. Mesa, that son of a whore picked the wrong woman to try and strongarm."

"There's more than just Zanzibari artifacts," Zak said. On his handheld, he pulled up a picture of one of the mysterious aliens that had ruled over the Zanzibari natives eons before. "We found artifacts from an unknown Antecessor species."

Captain Blackwood turned and faced Zak again. "I'm sorry, what did you say?"

Marcus Winchester and his Cowboys stood around the holo-tank on the *Andromeda*'s Astrogation deck. Instead of 3D star charts, they had displayed before them a representation of the surface of Zanzibar.

"...so that's the long and short of it so far," Marcus said, having briefed the team on everything that had transpired. "The captain made it pretty clear she isn't going to go fetch weapons for Lang. Tomorrow morning, the ship is going to lift off from Freeport and land here," he said, pointing to the holographic map, "in order to take on the first batch of artifacts Lang intends to sell. He managed to set up a deal with a buyer, we don't know who, but that guy either can't or won't come to Zanzibar. So supposedly the captain is going to take the *Andromeda* through three systems, weeks of travel time, to meet with the buyer and secure the weapons. Then it's weeks of travel time back, hand over the weapons to Lang, and supposedly Cecil gets to come home."

"Bull-*shit*," Wade snorted.

"That's more or less what Captain Blackwood said. Lang seems overconfident, like letting the bald guy and his girlfriend come aboard as a sign of good faith."

"It is said that dealing with Antecessor species in any fashion drives men mad," Ken observed.

"I think Lang was a little crazy to begin with," Devree said.

"Oh he's crazy, all right. He straight up told the captain that he intends the use the weapons to overrun Freeport, become the dictator of this whole planet, and use the money from the sale of the artifacts to rebuild the colony the way he sees fit."

"A regular Napoleon," Randy said derisively.

"Who?" asked Wade. "Never mind. Where do we come in?"

"The Orlov refugees gave us good intel on Lang's operation, including where Cecil Blackwood is being held. This was confirmed by the two prisoners we took aboard. He's being held here," Marcus said, pointing to the holographic map, "in a town called Lang's Burg. It's got about five thousand residents and is the center of Lang's power base. It's walled off, nestled against these rocky hills, and is pretty well defended."

"And we're going to hit that with seven guys?" Wade asked.

"That's where our friends from Orlov come in. They've got a vested interest in seeing that Lang doesn't take over this whole planet, especially with Lang buying weapons from the Combine. When the ship lands here, at the pickup site, they're going to stage a diversionary attack on Lang's Burg. Most of Lang's army is spread out throughout all the towns in the wasteland. This will draw them in and give us the cover we need to get in and out."

"It's going to draw them right on top of us!"

"I didn't say it was going to be *easy*. This is our best bet for getting in there and getting Cecil out alive. If we try a diversionary attack someplace else, Lang will suspect he's being double-crossed, and will likely move or kill Cecil Blackwood. This way, we have the initiative, we catch Lang's army off guard, and we get in and out. Once we report that we've got our guy, we'll head back to here, Rally Point Alpha, or here, Rally Point Bravo, regroup, and head back to the ship at the best possible speed. The Orlov refugees have helped us acquire some ground vehicles to get us there, and have offered up some long-range fire support. We'll be leaving tonight, before the ship lifts off, to give us a good head start. Any questions?"

Wade shook his head. "Yeah, how the hell did I let you talk me into this again?"

Marcus laughed. "Listen, guys, joking aside, this is dangerous as hell. I want your input."

"I don't like it," Randy said, "but it's probably our best bet. You're right, I don't think a diversion anywhere else will work. Lang will know what we're doing as soon as we fire the first shot."

"Aye," Halifax agreed. "We're very lucky to have the Orlov people helping us. Lang is a lot better equipped than we thought."

Randy nodded. "Strelok gave me a ton of useful intel on Lang's overall operation. They've been worrying about his plans for a while now, and I guess recent events just confirmed their fears. Word is, he's trying to cobble together some attack aircraft and some artillery. Freeport is protected by walls and armed guards. If Lang can bring support weapons to bear, he'll have a huge advantage."

"I don't like trying to assault that town, Marcus," said Devree. "An Espatier Corps special ops team would have a hard time sneaking in there and getting him out without getting cut off."

"Our only other option would be to use the ship's weapons as fire support while we assaulted the town, and that puts the ship at risk. Captain Blackwood isn't willing to risk the lives of her crew for the sake of one man, not even her brother."

"I trust your judgment, Marcus," Hondo said. "We won't let you down."

Marcus nodded. "Very well then, people. We'll have to be fluid once we get on the ground, as the situation will change. Here's how I'm thinking we actually stage the assault..."

Lang's Burg

Cecil Blackwood let his empty flask fall to the floor. He was sitting in the common room of the old building he'd shared with Zak and Anna for so long, and without them it felt very empty. Slumped down in a low, cushy chair, he watched the screen on his handheld and wished he had more to drink.

This was supposed to be his moment of liberation. He'd done it, he thought. He'd *endured*. Now, his salvation was at hand! His sister Catherine, the great and mighty privateer, had arrived to rescue him from Aristotle Lang! It was the moment he'd dreamed of since the original ransom demand was sent more than local year before, even though he'd tried very hard not to cloud his mind with hope. Now, as he watched a video feed of the *Andromeda* conducting a short-hop atmospheric flight, he despaired. It would take his sister weeks to deliver the alien artifacts to Lang's buyer, and weeks more to return to Zanzibar. What then? Would he let Cecil go then, or would he have more demands? What would happen when Catherine became fed up with Lang?

As near as he'd been able to discern, the old warlord hadn't had much luck finding ships willing to haul his goods. Shooting down a damaged and off-course transport ship and picking the crash site for scrap is not a good way to endear yourself to spacers, and Lang's men had done just that several months before. Making matters worse for Lang was the fact that the board that ran Freeport had forbidden any ships using their services from doing business with him. Given that it was the only place in a very long way to buy reaction mass or resupply, there hadn't been any crews willing to risk defying Frank DeWitt's edict.

A ship conducting a surface-to-surface short hop is an odd thing to watch, Cecil thought drunkenly. A ship like the *Andromeda* probably had a maximum thrust-to-mass ratio of eight or ten to one, more than enough to allow it to hover over the surface with ease. It was still an odd thing to watch, this big, gray, ballistic shape, seventy meters tall, launching a few thousand meters into the air, tilting slightly and slewing sideways, then coming back down at the designated landing site. The ship disappeared in a massive cloud of dust and smoke as it neared the surface. The particulate cloud was all that could be seen when it touched down, and even with the Zanzibaran wind it took several minutes to clear up.

The video feed was coming from one of Lang's vehicles. Lang was letting Cecil watch as a courtesy, he said, to show him that he wasn't going to betray his sister. He didn't know where the landing site was, exactly, but he thought he recognized a terrain feature in the background. He hadn't heard the rumbling of the ship's engine, so it had to be far away. Too far away, at least, for Cecil to make a run for it, which is what he really wanted to do. He contemplated it briefly, his courage as enhanced by alcohol as his reflexes were inhibited by it. But what would it accomplish? Lang's Burg was on lockdown. His building was being watched, and there were guards at the door. He'd convinced the warlord to let Zak and Anna go, but the Avalonian aristocrat was worth a great deal more to Lang.

Despairing, Cecil briefly thought of just slitting his wrists and having done with it. *To hell with Lang, and to hell with this miserable, Godforsaken rock!* The thought of suicide was brief and unserious, though, and Cecil knew it. He didn't have the will to go through with it. He didn't want his sister to have come all this way, only for him to end his own life. He wasn't going to take the coward's way out, especially not as she was securing his release. As he observed the *Andromeda*, now barely visible through the cloud of dust, slowly open its cargo bay hatch, Cecil clung desperately to the hope that this would all work out somehow in the end. That hope was all he had.

"Whatsa matta, Mista Cecil?" Bianca said sweetly as she sauntered into the room. The dusky Zanzibaran woman was clothed only in a pair of very short shorts and a cropped, low-cut top that showed off a lot of cleavage and her midriff. She lowered herself to her knees behind the chair, wrapping her arms around Cecil and resting her chin on his shoulder. "Why so sad? You sista come to get you, neh? You leave soon. You leave poor Bianca behind forever." Her thick, guttural Zanzibaran accent made her sound unintelligent, but Bianca was anything but dumb. She played the fool, Cecil suspected, but she was a survivor.

As he studied her smooth brown skin, pouty lips, and dark eyes like deep pools of water, something stirred within Cecil, and it wasn't just in his pants. This woman's affection and companionship had carried him through the worst experiences of his life, through his seemingly endless captivity, and now? Was he really going to just leave her behind?

"Lang said that if we did all he asked, he'd let you come with me," he said slowly, trying not to slur his speech. Cecil was no stranger to alcohol, and even the thick local hooch would wear off before too long. He just needed to rest until then, and having Bianca's soft, warm body pressed against his was certainly relaxing. "Would you like that?"

"I neva been offa Zanzibar before," Bianca said. "I born here, I live here, I think I die here."

"Don't talk like that," Cecil said, squeezing her hand. "I want you to come with me."

"You take cara me, Mista Cecil?"

"I take care of you," he assured her. "I'm a nobody here, a prisoner, but back home, I'm well off. You'll never want for anything again. You'll never have to be afraid, or go hungry, or any of it, ever again."

"You . . . you promise?" she asked.

"Of course I promise, Bianca! Don't talk like that. You've been here—" before Cecil could finish, Bianca was kissing him passionately, hands running through his hair and unbuttoning his shirt from behind. She paused only to stand up, strip her insubstantial clothes off, straddle him, and lower herself back down. Her perfect breasts and shapely legs rubbed against him as she kissed him, filled with more passion and lust than she'd shown in a long time. It was as if she was freshly reunited with her lover after a long absence. Cecil had had *sex* with Bianca countless times, but as she arched her back in pleasure, hands on his shoulders, moaning his name, the Avalonian realized something: this was the first time she'd ever *made love* to him. It was different, she was different, and he found himself hoping, praying to the God he didn't really believe in that he'd find a way to take her with him like he promised. At that moment, all they had was each other, and he couldn't bear the thought of leaving her behind.

A few hours later, Cecil found himself sitting up in bed, lost in thought. According to his video feed, the *Andromeda* was finishing up loading Lang's cargo. It was slow going because they'd had to raise the containers one at a time via crane, but the ship would be lifting off again before first light. His passionate sex romp with Bianca had moved from the chair, to Zak and Anna's work table, to the kitchen counter, to finally the bedroom. He was tired, but the good kind of tired, and the physical effort had sobered him up some.

Bianca was asleep, naked, her black hair splashed over her pillow. She snored occasionally as she slept, which Cecil thought was adorable, and seemed to be completely at peace. He gently ran his hand across her back, feeling the smooth skin and noting the scars; he'd never asked where she'd gotten them, but her back and arms had several ugly scars that she was self-conscious about. He wondered if Lang would let her go with him. He wondered if she really *wanted* to. After all, she was a concubine, a *whore*. Would she not tell him anything he wanted to hear? Wasn't that her job? He knew damned well that she'd been spying on him for Lang the entire time, too.

The remarkable thing was that Cecil didn't care about any of that. He knew he was being a fool, but he didn't care. He'd bedded hundreds of women in his life, from bar girls to lofty aristocrats, but Bianca was the first woman he'd ever loved. He *had* to find a way to get her off of this rock, he just had to! Even if... even if she didn't really love him. Even if it was all an act. She deserved a better life than what fate had given her.

There was no way Cecil was going to be able to sneak her out, but maybe if he talked to Lang, pleaded with him, humbled himself and appealed to the old warlord's enormous ego, maybe then he'd really let her go. Cecil hated the thought of groveling in front of that son of a bitch. He hadn't lived the life of adventure his sister had, but he liked to think he wasn't a coward, and he certainly had his pride. Even still, for his sweet Bianca, he'd do whatever was necessary.

Quietly slipping out of bed, Cecil pulled on his pants and went to get cleaned up. He'd contact Lang tonight, as soon as he was finished. The bastard ought to be in a good mood, he reasoned, now that his first shipment of arms was going out.

He didn't get two steps before Lang's Burg was rocked by a huge explosion.

Concealed under a cloak of active thermoptic camouflage, some six-hundred and seventy-five meters away, Devree Starlighter watched the fireball erupt through the high-powered smart scope mounted atop her rifle. From her position on one of the rocky outcroppings overlooking Lang's Burg, she was able to see everything with little risk of being spotted.

"Holy shit," Randy Markgraf whispered. He lay next to her, also cloaked, once again serving as her spotter. He watched the fireworks through a pair of electronic binoculars. "Direct hit to their hydrogen tanks."

The Orlov refugees of Sanctuary had long been training a militia to defend their new home, and over the years had quietly amassed an impressive, if patchwork, arsenal of weaponry. A guided missile, launched from a truck kilometers away, had shrieked in from above, slamming into the hydrogen tank farm. Swiveling her rifle on its bipod, Devree found another target, and used the laser of her scope's rangefinder to designate it. She keyed her microphone. "This is Overwatch. Impact confirmed, target destroyed. Requesting fire for effect, three rounds, air burst, twenty meter spread. Area target, vehicle motorpool, designated now, how copy?"

One of the Sanctuary Militiamen responded in a thick, almost mechanical accent. "Roger. Firing now." Far to the south, a heavy-duty off-road truck with an improvised launcher sent three more missiles roaring into the night sky, in the direction of Lang's Burg. The truck immediately moved, tearing across the flat, rocky desert at high speed, staying mobile in case Lang's forces were able to get off counterbattery fire.

The missiles had no target, but were searching for the reflected laser that would tell them where they were needed. Devree watched a video feed from one of the weapons on her eyepiece, appearing black-and-white as its sensor scanned in the near-infrared. There was little to see until the glowing fires of the Lang's Burg tank farm appeared, as did her laser in the town's motorpool. A bracket appeared around the laser dot, and the missiles dove, screaming in from above, toward their designated target. They detonated in the air, sending lethal fragmentation tearing through the mostly unarmored vehicles and the men who had been running for them after the first explosion. At least a half-dozen of Lang's men died immediately, and several others were down and wounded.

"Good hit," Devree transmitted. "No sign of return fire. We caught 'em with their pants down." She adjusted her grip on the powerful, semiautomatic, 14.5mm heavy rifle in front of her, switched her smart scope to thermal, and scanned for targets. The particular barrel the weapon was presently using was wrapped with an integral sound suppressor. While it hardly made the powerful weapon silent, it was enough to hide her position from a distance, especially with the racket of explosions, alarms and the shouts of men in Lang's Burg.

"Cowboy-Six copies," Marcus Winchester said. "Fire Support," he said, addressing the missile truck, "hold fire for now. Overwatch, we're almost in position and will be entering the town soon. Stand by."

"Overwatch copies," Devree said, a predatory grin splitting her face beneath her respirator mask. "Gotcha covered, Boss."

Beneath the town of Lang's Burg was a network of access and service tunnels, meant to allow maintenance of the settlement's infrastructure and allow for disposal of its waste. Dating back to before the war, much of it had fallen into disrepair over the years, and aside from some easily disarmed alarm systems had been left unguarded.

It was through these tunnels that Marcus Winchester led his four-man team. The roar of the fires above could be heard even down there, in the darkness beneath the settlement. The mercenaries navigated via night vision googles, weapons at the ready. The only other thing moving down there was the occasional giant, mutated rat. Some of them were as big as dogs, and they were quite aggressive, but the heat and noise from the chaos above was driving them in fear from the tunnels. They ran past the team's feet, paying the human interlopers no mind.

Marcus paused, flipped up his goggles, and studied the tactical map on his handheld. His face was dimly illuminated by the screen. "This is it," he said, indicating a nearby ladder. "We'll surface in the southwest corner of the town, here," he indicated, pointing at the small screen. "The building Cecil Blackwood is staying in is here, not far away. Four stories, hard to miss. Tanaka, take point." Marcus flipped his goggles back down and pocketed his handheld.

Ken Tanaka nodded once and proceeded up the ladder, his short 5.8mm carbine slung behind his back. He disappeared up the manhole and his teammates moved in closer to keep eyes on him while maintaining security in the tunnels. At the top of the ladder, Ken tried, as quietly as he could, to undog the hatch. "It opens," he said quietly. He lifted the hatch only slightly, scanning the surface with a fiber-optic camera. "It comes out in an alley by the wall. It looks dark, no sign of movement. I'm going up."

"Be careful," Marcus warned. "Stack up on the ladder," he told his team. Ken quietly opened the hatch, the orange light of the fires burning in Lang's Burg pouring into the manhole, and disappeared from view. Marcus was next up the ladder. He peeked over the top of the hatch; Ken was crouched a few meters from the manhole, carbine shouldered, covering the alleyway. He lifted himself up onto the dusty street and took a knee beside Ken. Next was Hondo with his machine gun, and finally Wade, who had covered his teammates in the tunnels until they were all clear of the manhole.

Wade shot his team leader a thumbs-up. Marcus nodded, indicated forward with a hand signal, and the team of mercenaries was on the move.

Devree Starlighter's calm soprano voice crackled in Marcus' earpiece. "I'm scanning on thermal, can't see you."

"There are structures in the way. We came up behind the dome-shaped building. How's it look?"

"They're running around like crazy down there," Markgraf answered. "I'm watching through binos and the drone feed. Dozens of people running around, most of them armed—Lang's militia. All the noncombatants seem to be hunkering down inside. They're trying to put the fires out, treating the wounded. I count at least six guards around the target building."

"You want another volley?" Devree asked.

"Negative," Marcus said. "Not going to risk killing noncombatants if we don't have to. Stand by. Cowboy-Six out."

The team stacked up on Marcus as he peeked around a corner. In order to get to the building Cecil was in, they'd have to cross the main thoroughfare of Lang's Burg. "Shit," he snarled quietly.

"Mother-humping skags are everywhere," Wade agreed. "In the street, on the roof. How you wanna do this?"

"I'm calling in the heavy. War Wagon, this is Cowboy-Six, you copy?"

"Aye," Halifax said. "You ready for us?"

"Roger. We need to draw the crowd away from the target building."

"Understood. I'm ready."

"We'll cover you," Devree said.

"I appreciate that, lass," Halifax said. "The heavy is moving." Just outside the gates of Lang's Burg, a large cargo truck donated by the Orlov refugees was waiting. Hidden in its tall cargo bay was Benjamin Halifax in his powered armor suit, crouched down, with the primary engine turned off. The truck was self-piloting, so as not to risk any more people than necessary. Merchant vehicles, delivering goods and services, crisscrossed the wastelands of Zanzibar constantly, and did plenty of business with towns occupied by Lang's army. An unmanned truck would have raised suspicion, but its approach had been timed to coincide with the attack. The gates were locked down, and no one was paying attention to the lone truck stuck outside.

That is, until Halifax made himself known. Monitoring the feed from the aerial drone, Marcus watched as the hulking powered armor suit pushed itself off the bed of the truck and stood up, tearing through the nylon cover. The truck's suspension compressed as the armor stepped off and landed on the ground. Stepping around the vehicle, it fired off a pair of high explosive rockets at the main gate.

"I'm coming in," Halifax said tersely. Marcus acknowledged, watching the massive suit run toward the hole in the gate and use a manipulator claw to make the hole big enough for it to enter through. Once inside, it opened fire with its machine gun, rockets, and plasma gun, and hell came to Lang's Burg.

"He's through," Marcus said to his team. The guards on the target building kept to their posts despite Halifax's rampage.

Their funeral. "Wade, Ken, you two pop smoke to cover us. Then we'll move."

Wade nodded. He and Tanaka stepped forward, smoke grenades at the ready. It was easy to be sneaky amongst the chaos engulfing the town. Simultaneously, they tossed the grenades into the street ahead, filling the air with even more smoke than there had already been.

Marcus keyed his radio mic. "Overwatch, we're assaulting the building. Fire at will."

"Roger," Devree said. A few seconds later, the militiaman on the roof's chest burst open as a high explosive, armor piercing round tore through it. His mutilated body tumbled over the edge of the roof and plummeted to the street below.

The two men by the door looked stupidly at the corpse before them. Marcus snapped off a three-round burst, killing the one on the left while Wade fired a single, well-placed 8mm APHE round and dropped the one on the right. "Move, move, move!" Marcus ordered.

Halfway across the street, bullets began snapping through the smoke like angry hornets. "Contact left!" Hondo shouted, taking a knee and bringing up his 8mm machine gun. The heavy weapon roared in the narrow street, sending a stream of bullets in the direction of the incoming fire. Halifax's heavy armor suit rounded the corner, flanking the position the fire had been coming from. With a brilliant, blue-white *FWASH*, he fired his suit's plasma gun. Men screamed and metal burned as his weapon found its mark.

Marcus, Wade, and Ken scrambled to the front entrance to the structure, a metal door at street level. It was locked, but Wade was placing a breaching charge even before Marcus told him to. The demolitions expert snapped his head up in surprise when Tanaka fired off a burst from his carbine, but went right back to what he was doing. "Ready!" he said. "Get back!"

Confused and terrified, Cecil huddled against the wall of the upstairs common room, away from the windows, with Bianca in his arms. Out of nowhere, half of Lang's Burg had exploded and was on fire. Now there was gunfire coming from right outside, men were shouting, and it was chaos in the streets. Three of the men guarding him had rushed into the building and locked the doors behind him. They were downstairs, clutching their weapons nervously. Cecil was staying up on the fourth floor, where his living quarters were. Gunshots rang out from below. In their near-panic, convinced that someone was trying to get inside, the guards were firing through the walls of the ground level.

Cecil's handheld vibrated in his pocket. *What?* Keeping an arm around Bianca, who was squeezing him so tightly he could barely breathe, he retrieved his mobile device and tapped the screen. There was one text message from an unknown sender: *They're coming to take you to your sister. Get ready to move.*

Cecil's eyes went wide. "Bianca!" he said excitedly. "Get—" *BOOM!* Cecil's ears popped as something exploded downstairs. The whole building shook, showering him with dust.

"Cecil, what happening?" Bianca cried as gunfire echoed through the building.

"Get ready to run, love!" Cecil said, trying to sound courageous. "This is our chance!"

"I don't undastand!" she said. "Run where?"

"Away from here!" he shouted, standing up. He pulled the terrified woman to her feet. "Come on, this is our only chance! We've got to—" Cecil froze, looking down the barrel of a pistol.

"Oh no, rich boy," a burly militiaman said. "I think you go nowhere." He held a clunky weapon in his right hand. His left was covering a bleeding wound on his neck. His goggles were cracked. "You gon run? You gon run from Mista Lang?" He raised the weapon to eye level.

"No!" Bianca screamed, pulling away from Cecil. She flung herself at the guard. Cecil tried to stop her, but it was too late. She grabbed the gun, pulled downward, and a shot rang out. In shock, horrified, paralyzed, Cecil watched as Bianca fell, seemingly in slow motion. Her hands moved to cover the wound in her abdomen. She collapsed to the floor like a puppet with its strings cut, blood oozing out of the wound.

The militiaman gazed down at her for a second with a confused look on his face. His dark eyes met Cecil's, and he raised the gun again. Cecil was frozen, unable to move, staring helplessly at Bianca.

BRRAAP! A stream of bullets ripped through the guard from the side. He went limp and flopped to the floor, dropping the weapon with a clatter. Before Cecil could even react, a trio of armed men poured into the room, weapons raised, checking all the angles. They were dressed out in brownish-tan mottled camouflage fatigues, armor, helmets, respirators, and smart goggles.

"Clear!" the lead announced.

"Clear," the other said, checking to the right.

"Clear!" the third man, taller than the other two, agreed. He covered the doorway they'd come in from.

Ignoring the newcomers, Cecil regained control of his body and ran to Bianca. He dropped to his knees and slid to a stop at her side, eyes wide, staring helplessly at the wound. She was still conscious, still alive, and her dark eyes met his. Her lips moved as she tried to speak, but Cecil shushed her. "Don't talk!" he said. "I'm . . . I'm going to fix you! Just—"

"Cecil Blackwood?" one of the camouflaged men asked. Cecil looked up at him, in shock. The man had lowered his weapon, but still struck an imposing figure. "I'm here to take you home."

Cecil shook his head. "You've got to help her!" he shouted, placing his hands on Bianca's wound. There was so much blood! "Please, she's going to die!"

"We have to go, now!" the man said, looking around. "Come on!"

"I'm not leaving without her!" Cecil shouted, wondering just how much clout he had with the three armed men who had just killed all of his guards. "Please!"

The man swore aloud, then turned to the shorter of his two teammates. "Ken, help her. Stabilize her for transport. Halifax," he said, apparently talking into a radio, "Sitrep!"

As the team leader listened to his radio, the man named Ken slung his weapon behind his back and retrieved a medical kit. His face was hidden behind a respirator and goggles, but he sounded reassuring all the same. "Abdominal wound," he said, stating the obvious. He dug through his kit and retrieved an emergency wound seal. "Missed the spine. If I can stop the bleeding, we can move her. We'll treat her on the ship." He ripped open the package the seal came in. "Lift up her shirt."

Cecil did as he was told, lifting up Bianca's blood-soaked shirt to expose the wound. Ken wiped off the smeared blood with a sterile cloth, then placed the wound seal over the hole in Bianca's midsection. She cried out in agony as he pressed it against her, her eyes pleading with Cecil, but it needed to be done. "Hold here," Ken said, nodding at the seal. "Keep pressure on it. Make sure the seal is good." As Cecil kept pressure on his lover's wound, Ken retrieved an auto injector, pulled off the cap, and jammed it into Bianca's thigh. "This will help with the pain, keep her from going into hypovolemic shock. She won't be able to walk. Can you carry her?"

"How far?"

"As far as necessary! Can you carry her or not?"

"I can!" Cecil insisted. "I'll carry her! Thank...thank you."

"Is she ready to go?" the leader of the trio asked. Ken nodded in reply. "Good. We've been here too long. Come on, Mr. Blackwood, it's time to get the hell out of here."

"Bloody well don't have to tell me twice!" Cecil said, grunting as he picked Bianca up in his arms. "Let's go!"

"They're coming out," Markgraf said, watching the chaos below through his binoculars. Hondo and Halifax were covering the front entrance as the rest of the team came out. Much of the resistance had given up, afraid to tangle with the powered armor.

"Overwatch, Cowboy-Six," Marcus said over the radio. "Egressing now, package in tow. Cover us until we get to the truck if you can. Relay all to the ship. How copy?"

"Overwatch copies!" Devree said excitedly. "You need to hurry, Cowboy-Six. The drone has spotted a convoy of fourteen vehicles inbound from the south, ETA ten mikes."

"Understood. Can we get any more fire support from our friends?"

"Negative, they bugged out. They were too exposed where they were. We're on our—look out!" Devree snapped off a shot at a militiaman who had appeared on a rooftop with a shoulder-fired missile launcher. Even with its recoil stabilization, the powerful rifle bucked against her shoulder with a sound like the cracking of a whip as it sent a fat, armor-piercing slug downrange. The missile-carrier's head nearly separated from his neck as the round struck his spine, the impact looking like a hot splash on thermal. "He's down," she said coldly.

The sniper team had moved since the assault on Lang's Burg began. Devree had been a law enforcement sharpshooter, not a military scout sniper, but she knew better than to stay in one place for too long. Even with thermoptic camo and suppressed weapons, it was only a matter of time before they were spotted, so it was critical to stay mobile.

She watched Halifax engage a group of militiamen with the plasma weapon on his suit; its report was a white hot flash on thermal and a blue-white streak to the naked eye, a terrifying weapon that sent Lang's thugs fleeing for their lives.

"That's right, run along now!" he said, laughing over his suit's PA system. He followed up with a long burst from the armor's machine gun, and led the others toward the gate of Lang's Burg. The team was going to use the large truck the suit had arrived in as an escape vehicle.

Markgraf tapped Devree on the shoulder. "We need to go." Moving quickly in thermoptic camo could give your position away, so the sniper team had slowly stalked across the rocky hills above Lang's Burg. They had gone unnoticed so far, but with reinforcements on the way it was only a matter of time before their luck ran out, and the team was headed for the gate. It was definitely time to go.

Driving the point home, an indicator light flashed in Devree's goggles. "The proximity alarm!" Markgraf said. "Get down! Fire in the hole!" As the sniper team hit the dirt, he mashed the remote initiator. *BOOM!* The explosion echoed and rolled through hills, even over the roar of flames and sporadic gunfire coming from Lang's Burg. A couple hundred meters behind them, the sniper team had set up proximity warnings and remotely detonated directional fragmentation charges, just in case someone tried to sneak up on them. Their drone was now kilometers away, shadowing the incoming convoy, but the sensors had stopped their attackers from getting the drop on them.

"Come on, Devree," Markgraf said, "we need to get the hell out of here, *now!*"

She nodded jerkily, face hidden behind smart goggles and respirator mask. The two mercenaries low-crawled down the rocks until some solid cover was between them and Lang's Burg. Markgraf took a knee, shouldering his boxy 4.5mm caseless assault rifle, and covered Devree while she disassembled the huge antimateriel rifle. She removed the magazine from its well behind the grip, detached the scope, and pulled the barrel out. The whole thing broke down quickly, fitting into a more manageable carry case.

Far below, through more than a kilometer of rugged, rocky terrain, the sniper team had a parked their vehicle and concealed it. The plan was to make to it the vehicle and head straight to

the ship, linking up with the others if they were able to catch
up with them. It was an inelegant plan, but there weren't many
roads on Zanzibar and few places to hide on the open wastes.
Heading directly for the ship was the fastest, easiest, and least-
chance-of-going-south plan Marcus could come up with. As he
had explained to the team, he wasn't a fan of elaborate multistep
op plans. In his experience, he'd said, they usually went to shit
after the first shots were fired.

The key now was getting to the vehicle and escaping without
being cut off or surrounded by Lang's militia, who were converg-
ing on Lang's Burg with a vengeance.

The Privateer Ship *Andromeda*
183 kilometers northwest of Lang's Burg

Captain Catherine Blackwood stood sternly on the cargo deck, hands folded behind her back, as she watched her cargo handlers secure the last of Aristotle Lang's trade goods. Everything had to be logged, checked, fastened down, and symmetrically laid out so as not to unbalance the ship. Under Cargomaster Kimball's close supervision, the process was going as slowly as possible. The ship's cargo crane, they had insisted, could only handle one of the large boxes of stolen alien artifacts at a time. It could handle much more than that, but the illiterate fools delivering the goods to the *Andromeda* weren't in any position to argue. They stood around in a cluster at the base of the ship, with two dozen ground vehicles, watching stupidly as the cargo was loaded onto the ship at a snail's pace.

Catherine had very much hoped that Aristotle Lang would be so foolish, so arrogant as to want to oversee the transfer himself. Had that happened, she had fully intended on inviting him onto the ship for a tour, then holding *him* hostage until her brother was returned unharmed. If at all possible, she'd planned on keeping him until the *Andromeda* lifted off and personally flushing him out the airlock once they'd gotten into orbit. His frozen corpse could orbit Zanzibar for hundreds of years, a shining example of why brigandage was a poor career path.

The captain hadn't been surprised when Lang didn't oblige her personal vengeance fantasy, but she was disappointed. *Oh well,* she thought to herself, her face a mask. *He'll be surprised*

311

enough when I send him a farewell video with Cecil next to me on the command deck, his precious cargo still secured in my hold. The mask cracked a little, and she allowed herself an evil smile.

When the assault on Lang's Burg began, Catherine had feigned ignorance of it. Lang was suspicious of her, but since she was still over a hundred kilometers away, slowly and calmly loading his cargo, he hadn't done anything about it. She had warned Lang that if anything happened to her brother, even if it was the fault of whatever enemies he had, the deal was off and she'd be keeping his precious cargo. He hadn't liked that one bit, but her acting had been convincing.

Luis Azevedo's voice sounded over her earpiece. "Captain!" he said excitedly. "Incoming transmission from the ground team!" A tone sounded, and Azevedo's voice was replaced with that of Devree Starlighter. "*Andromeda*, this is Cowboy-Overwatch. Egressing from Lang's Burg now. Package in tow, I say again, the package is in tow. We are being pursued. Requesting pickup at extraction site Charlie, over."

Catherine's heart was in her throat. They'd *done* it. Marcus, that magnificent son of a bitch, had *done* it. "I'm monitoring the feed from the drone, Captain," Azevedo said, snapping her out of her elation. It wasn't over yet. "Lang's militia is on full alert. There's a convoy of vehicles arriving at Lang's Burg now. Sensors detect more coming in from nearby settlements. I've got eyes on our ground team. They're in a two vehicle convoy headed toward extraction site Charlie. The terrain is rough and they can't go that fast. Captain, they're being pursued. They're . . . stand by."

"Luis? What's happening?" Catherine asked, unable to hide the concern in her voice. Lang's men, gathered all around the *Andromeda*'s landing jacks, were either unaware of the firefight in Lang's Burg or didn't care about it.

"Captain, the ground team is in trouble. Their big truck, the one carrying the powered armor, is stopped. Something wrong with the wheel I think, I can't tell from the feed. The other truck isn't big enough to transport them all. Hostile vehicles are about to catch up with them. What are your orders?"

"Prep the ship for liftoff. Sound general quarters. I want a short-hop trajectory to get us to the ground team. High altitude, come straight down on top of them, as close as we can get without burning their hair off. Tell them to we're coming for them, and to hold on. I'll be on the command deck momentarily." She turned her attention to the crew on the cargo deck as the ship's general quarters klaxons began to sound. "Mr. Kimball, is the cargo secured?"

Kimball turned to Annabelle Winchester, who had been hustling through the cargo deck, doing final checks on everything. She flashed him a thumb's up. He nodded and answered the captain, "It is. We can lift off at any time."

"Very good. Secure the hatch. Get to your stations." Captain Blackwood turned for the ladder.

Azevedo piped up over her earpiece again. "Captain, what about the guys on the ground? External feed shows they're not moving. I don't know if they're waiting for orders, or if they thought we'd tell them when to clear out, or what, but if they're still there at ignition they *won't* be there a second later. What do you want me to do, ma'am?"

"Do nothing," Catherine said coldly. "They'll move when we start spinning up the engines. If they don't have the sense to do that, well... how unfortunate."

"Suppressing fire!" Marcus shouted, even though there was no need for him to do so with his helmet's communications suite. Jeremiah Hondo, covering behind a damaged heavy truck, ripped off a long burst from his machine gun. Benjamin Halifax's plasma gun lanced out into the dim light. The heavy truck, overloaded with the weight of the powered armor, had broken an axle on the rocky, uneven terrain. Devree and Randy's vehicle had been pursued by Lang's militia from the moment they'd left Lang's Burg, and now that the convoy was stopped, the pursuers had caught up. Now they were firing heavy weapons, mortars and rockets, at the mercenaries, pinning them down. Even Halifax, in his powered armor, had to make careful use of available cover. The heavy weapons were powerful enough to destroy his suit, and even enough concentrated small arms fire could damage it.

Covering behind a rocky outcrop in a pile of spent plastic cartridge cases, Marcus slammed a fresh magazine home and leaned out, looking for targets of opportunity. Beside him, Wade Bishop fired off two shots from his own rifle before ducking back down, barely avoiding a hail of incoming gunfire.

"They're pretty pissed off!" Wade said, reloading his rifle.

Marcus snapped off a controlled pair, dropping a rifle-wielding militiaman only two hundred meters away. "Lang must've figured out what we did!" he said. "Probably told them to get Cecil back or he'd kill them all!"

"Bloody hell!" Cecil exclaimed, rock chunks pelting him as bullets impacted all around. He was farther down the sloping rock formation the mercenaries were using for cover, tending to the Zanzibaran woman who'd taken a bullet for him. He'd been given a pistol, but hadn't yet fired it. Whenever an incoming missile or mortar detonated nearby, he'd shelter the unconscious woman with his own body. "I'll shoot myself before that bastard gets me back!"

An unguided rocket screeched overhead, grazed the roof of one of the disabled trucks, and veered off-course, exploding in midair. Ken Tanaka responded with a missile from a single-shot, disposable launcher. Unlike the crude munitions the militia were using, this rocket *was* guided. It impacted one of the militia gun trucks with a loud bang, knocking the vehicle on its side and leaving it burning.

Another gun truck rounded a rocky outcropping. In its bed was mounted a large caliber machine gun, blazing away at the mercenaries' position. These improvised gun trucks, called "technicals" for reasons that had been lost to history, were the mainstay of Lang's forces, and he seemed to have an endless supply of them.

Ken Tanaka was able to get a missile lock on the truck through the smart-link to Wade's rifle scope. He fired his last single-shot missile launcher upward, at an angle, without leaving cover. The rocket's engine kicked on with a roar an instant later. Thrust-vectoring paddles flipped the missile over in midair, sending it shrieking down on top of the technical. It detonated with a flash, engulfing the truck in a hydrogen and ammunition-fueled fireball.

Several of his Cowboys let out cries of victory, but Marcus knew they weren't in the clear yet. One more gun truck had been destroyed, but there were still probably three dozen gunmen and several more technicals out there. The team was running low on ammunition, were saddled with a wounded woman they couldn't move very quickly, and had no working vehicles. The *Andromeda* was inbound, but Lang's forces had reinforcements on the way, and the gunmen already on the ground kept pushing closer and closer.

There was only one thing to do: *attack*.

"Listen up!" Marcus said, speaking to the whole team on the radio. "Dev, Randy, you two move off our left, push forward, and find a position to fire on their right flank. Ken, Ben, same thing, but head right. Halifax, me and Wade will fall in behind you, using you for mobile cover. We're going to provide fire support for the flank elements until they get into position, then we're going down the center. Cover to cover, move fast, keep going forward. We gotta take 'em out before they regroup. Any questions?"

"Ah, yes!" someone said timidly. "What shall I do?" It was Cecil Blackwood.

"Mr. Blackwood, it's my job to get you back to your sister alive," Marcus said. "I'll do everything I can to keep them off you until the ship arrives, but I can't promise you anything. No matter what happens, stay here, and stay alive until then. Do you understand?"

"I do."

"Good. Alright, Cowboys, let's do this! Overwatch team, move, move, move!"

"Hey!" Cecil said, getting Marcus' attention. "Mr. Winchester? Thank you for this. I won't forget this. No matter what happens, you and all your families will be taken care of! I swear it!"

Marcus and Wade both nodded at Cecil. "Just stay alive, man," Wade said. "One thing at a time, yeah?"

Off on the left flank, Devree and Randy vaulted from one rocky outcrop to the next, bullets snapping overhead in the thin air. Randy went prone behind a windblown boulder and fired off several short bursts from his carbine, allowing Devree to leap to the next available cover.

"Gotcha covered!" she said, shouldering the little 5.45mm personal defense weapon she carried as a backup to her unwieldy rifle.

"Moving!" Randy said. He pushed himself off the hard ground, feet skidding in the dust, and ran for Devree's position as fast as he could. He dove down and slid to a stop next to her, grateful for the knee pads integrated into his trousers. "I gotcha covered! Put that rifle together!"

Devree nodded, took cover, stripped off her pack, and began assembling her rifle as Randy fired off single shots at the enemy's position. The militiamen were holed up behind a rocky terrain feature about two hundred meters from the mercenaries' position, and had taken enough casualties in their assaults that they were now mostly keeping their heads down, waiting for reinforcements of their own. Off in the distance, Hondo and Tanaka pushed forward, flanking them from the right.

Halifax was using his suit's plasma weapon sparingly, as he was running low on fuel cells and spare barrels for it, but the enemy militiamen seemed to be terrified of it. Even near-misses caused horrific burns. Direct hits caused the fluids in a human body to flash-evaporate, blowing the victim apart in a cloud of steam and boiling blood. Hits on solid objects like rock and stone caused explosive decoupling and dangerous secondary fragmentation. Plasma weapons were banned on most worlds, and were heavy, expensive, and maintenance-intensive on top of it. But a full-up plasma gun, mounted on powered armor, in the hands of an aggressive killer like Halifax, was a fearsome instrument. His voice boomed over the suit's PA system. "Cry some more, you sons of whores! I'm a comin' for ya! Ha ha ha!"

As Devree slid her rifle's barrel into place and locked it in, Captain Blackwood's commanding voice crackled over the teams' battle net. "Cowboy, this is the *Andromeda*," the captain said calmly. "We are on our way. ETA nine minutes."

"Cowboy-Six copies!" Marcus replied, breathing over the radio. "We're holding them off, but enemy reinforcements are en route. The package is still alive, but he has another person with him who's wounded. She's going to need immediate medical attention."

"Copy that. A med team will be standing by. We'll have to land at least five hundred meters from your position. Can you make it that far?"

"We'll hold our own, Captain, but sooner would be better. Cowboy-6 out."

Devree set the heavy sniper rifle down in front of her, pulling her thermoptic cloak down over her head. The rifle's bulky, camouflage-painted shape stuck out from under the active camouflage garment, which mimicked whatever colors were around it and masked (if only temporarily) a person's thermal signature. Using them was power intensive and had to be done sparingly.

A warning from their little recon drone flashed in the sniper team's smart goggles. "What's that?" Devree asked.

"Balls," Randy muttered, before transmitting over the battle net. "Cowboy-6, Overwatch! Be advised, incoming enemy aircraft, high rate of speed, ETA momentarily, how copy?"

Marcus sounded confused. "Say again?"

"Get down!" Randy shouted into his microphone. "Incoming gunships!"

A pair of ungainly looking aircraft came into view a moment later. The Orlov Combine refugees from Sanctuary had warned that Lang's forces were getting some attack aircraft put together, but they didn't know how far along they were. *Pretty goddamn far along,* Devree thought bitterly, as the armored VTOL roared at them forty meters off of the deck. It was an ugly thing, held aloft by two massive, screaming, ducted-fan engines and bristling with guns and rockets. It was headed right for the sniper team.

"Do you have a shot on that thing?"

"I think so!" Devree replied. "Hold on a sec!"

"We don't have a sec!" The gunship blasted off a volley of rockets that shrieked toward the sniper team at hundreds of meters per second. Randy barely had time to throw himself over Devree and push her head down before the first blast, and all was lost in darkness, dust, and the roar of explosions.

"Marcus!" Wade shouted. "They hit the sniper team!" The militia survivors on the ground were using the gunship attack as cover to flee. One slapped-together, blunt-nosed, armored beast slewed sideways, firing a pair of heavy machine guns in the direction of the mercenaries, kicking up dust and shattering rocks as it went. The other circled higher, firing at its leisure.

"Open fire!" Marcus ordered. "Everything you got! Shoot them down!" He tried to pop up, to fire off a burst at one of the marauding aircraft, but blast from twin machine guns kept him from getting a shot off. Only Halifax's suit weapons and maybe Hondo's machine gun were going to be effective against them. The aircraft hovered sideways again, circling like a hungry shark, firing burst after burst from its machine guns.

Halifax pivoted his suit from behind cover and tried to get a shot off, but the higher, circling gunship answered with a pair of rockets before he could fire. "Damn it," he snarled over the radio. "I'm hit. Stand by."

"What are you doing?" Marcus asked, but Halifax didn't answer. The powered armor took off at clunky run, back toward the destroyed vehicles. The higher of the two gunships broke off and followed, firing burst after burst. The aircraft's guns were inaccurate, and Halifax jinked side to side as best he could to avoid fire. After a few seconds, the suit slid to a stop, turned around, and ran back toward Marcus and Wade.

"What the hell is he doing?" Wade asked, but it became apparent a second later. The pursuing gunship overshot Halifax, allowing him just enough time to get a lock on it. He raised his left arm and fired streak after streak of white-hot plasma at the aircraft. One hit exploded an engine nacelle. The other punched a hole through the main fuselage. The mercenaries cheered as one gunship crashed to the rocky ground, but the other one turned on Halifax with a vengeance, firing a full volley of rockets at him. He tried to dodge, but was lost in cloud of dust and smoke as the rockets detonated.

"Goddamn it!" Wade snarled. He and Marcus both fired off shot after shot, but the damned thing kept jinking, slewing, and changing altitude while returning fire. The two mercenaries jumped to the other side of the rocks they'd been hiding behind, getting behind cover just as big-bore machine guns blew chunks off of boulders and turned rocks into dust. "Marcus, Halifax isn't answering his radio. It looks like the heavy is down. What are we gonna do?"

Marcus didn't have an answer. He'd failed his team. He didn't anticipate enemy aircraft. They were out of missiles, half his team was likely dead, their vehicles were disabled, and they were out of time. In desperation, Marcus keyed his mic. "*Andromeda*, Cowboy-6! I need fire support, now! Target the enemy aircraft and *shoot it down!*"

"Roger," Captain Blackwood said calmly. "Stand by."

Devree's ears were ringing when she opened her eyes. Face down in the dirt, she couldn't see anything, was having difficulty breathing, and couldn't remember where she was. A heavy weight rested upon her, and her head throbbed. She fumbled with her hand until she touched the stock of her rifle. It was lying on its side, covered in dirt, but the feel of it brought everything back to her. Her head shot up, but she could barely see anything and gasped for air. She pulled the no-longer-functioning thermoptic cloak off of her head, took off her helmet and goggles, and removed her respirator.

Panting and wheezing in the thin air, she tried to push herself up, but pain shot through her left arm. Her legs weren't responding as they should; she knew her prosthetics were damaged. She was able to leverage herself off of her artificial right arm, push, and roll out from under whatever was on top of her.

Randy Markgraf slumped to the ground, unmoving. Devree gasped when she realized that the weight had been him. "Randy!" she said, her voice weak in the thin air. She forced herself to sit up, panting, sweating, aching, her balance screwed up and her ears ringing, and pushed on his shoulder. "Randy!"

It was like pushing on a bag of sand. There was no response, no give, only dead weight. "Oh God, Randy," she cried. Devree pulled herself up to her knees, and examined her partner. Blood leaked from several wounds on his body. His armor had protected him some, but he was bleeding from every place the armor didn't cover. She grabbed the drag handle on his vest and grunted as she rolled him over on to his back.

Randy was dead. His smart goggles were cracked, his respirator clogged with dirt. Blood trickled from a head wound under his helmet. He wasn't breathing.

"Oh my God," Devree said quietly, her ears still ringing. As her hearing slowly came back, she was able to hear the roar of the remaining gunship's engines and the firing of weapons. There was no time to mourn! She had to get back in the fight and take that damned thing down! Scrambling back to where her rifle was, she lifted it up out of the dirt, checked to make sure it was locked and loaded, and settled down behind it. Her left arm was injured, throbbing with pain, but she didn't need it. The rifle's weight sat on its bipod and buttstock monopod. Her prosthetic right arm was functional enough for trigger control.

Fuck, she snarled quietly. The scope was smashed, nonfunctional. She hit the quick release and pulled it off, then flipped up the rifle's back-up sights. *Range ... about four hundred meters. Moving about fifty KPH. Winds, northwesterly, ten KPH. 0.95 gravities.* The open sights didn't correct for environmental conditions like the smart scope did, but she didn't need it. The rifle's powerful rounds were high enough velocity that very little correction would be needed at this range. It was just a matter of hitting a moving target. With no magnification, she couldn't be especially precise. She lined up the sights, waiting for the gunship to come to a hover. It stopped slewing momentarily, firing its machine guns, and became blurry as Devree focused on her front sight. She inhaled, exhaled partially, and squeezed the trigger.

CRACK! The suppressor had been damaged along with the scope, but the rifle was still comparatively quiet. The barrel recoiled smoothly into the action as it fired. The massive, explosive bullet struck the gunship's starboard-side engine cowling just as it was about to fire a volley of rockets. The impact and detonation threw it off enough that the rockets went wide.

Devree barely noticed another, louder roar coming from high above. She fired off a second shot, again with a muffled *CRACK*, but this one missed. The roar grew louder and she looked up. High above her, slowly descending on a magnificent, smoky plume of fire, the *Andromeda* was coming in for a landing. A brief flash from one of its weapons ports, the slightest shimmer in the air accompanied by an electric crack, and the hostile gunship exploded in midair. The ship's laser weapons were meant to destroy other ships or missiles thousands of kilometers away. At a range of less than a kilometer, they were devastating.

Devree stood up slowly, watching in awe as the ship approached the surface, balancing on its exhaust plume. As it neared the ground, a massive cloud of dust erupted from its landing site, obscuring the ship completely from view. The roar was amplified as the ship made its final descent, landing jacks extended, and was so loud that even as far away as Devree was, she covered her ears.

A few moments later the roar ceased, echoing through the rugged Zanzibaran mountains for a few seconds before fading away. Suddenly it was eerily quiet. There was no sound but the wind and the whine of the ship's engines as they spun down. The *Andromeda* became visible again as a breeze cleared away the dust cloud. Like a massive, finned bullet, the ship sat upright on the dusty brown wasteland. The light of Danzig-5012 reflected dully off the gunmetal hull as the sun finally cleared the distant mountains. It was morning, the fight was over, and she was still alive.

Her radio, somehow still functional, crackled to life. It was Marcus doing a status check. "Everyone check in!" he demanded, sounding pretty ragged.

"This is Halifax," the first response came. "I'm injured but I'm still here. Somebody come cut me out of this can. The heavy is down."

"Roger," Marcus said. "Wade is with me. I have eyes on Ken and Hondo. Overwatch, check in! What's your status?"

Devree removed her radio from its pouch, not having the microphone that was built into her helmet. "This is Overwatch," she said slowly, her own voice sounding unfamiliar. "I am injured. Markgraf is KIA. I say again, Markgraf is dead."

There was a long pause before Marcus spoke again. "Copy that," he said simply. "Med teams are on the way. Stay where you are."

"Overwatch copies," Devree acknowledged. She looked down at Randy's dust-covered body, then back out over the wastes of Zanzibar as the sun slowly rose. At that moment, she felt numb, detached, like she was still in mission mode. But later, she knew, later it would be different. She'd only known Markgraf for as long as they'd been on the ship together. He hadn't owed her anything, hadn't even known her that well, and he'd sacrificed his life for her. *Damn it,* she thought bitterly, lowering her head. *Damn it.*

The *Andromeda* stood like an obelisk, monolithic against the dry, rocky terrain of the Zanzibaran wastes, casting a long shadow as Danzig-5012 slowly rose over the horizon. Columns of smoke from destroyed militia vehicles rose into the pale sky, drifting southward on the wind. The ship's cargo bay doors were open, her crane outstretched, slowly raising a personnel cage. Inside, Cecil Blackwood knelt by his wounded lover's side, holding her hand, as a medical technician tended to her. Far below, a group of the ship's crew, armed with laser weapons, stood watch. Three of the six remaining mercenaries had been wounded, and the seventh had been killed; their mood was solemn and none of them felt like climbing up the access ladder to the interior of the ship. So they waited in silence for the cage, which could only hold four people at a time.

On the cargo deck, Captain Catherine Blackwood stood quietly, hands folded behind her back, as she waited for the cage to be hoisted aboard. Her leather flight jacket protected her from the impossibly dry, gusting winds; her peaked cap sat upon her head, very slightly cocked to one side. She struck the very image of the quintessential independent spacer, free-trader, and pirate hunter, yet for all that she was on edge. Her stomach fluttered as the cage was lifted into view. She hadn't seen her brother in so long, and had spent many nights wondering if he'd even be alive when she arrived on Zanzibar. Now there he was at last! She wanted to run to him, hug her little brother, then choke the life out of the damned fool. Yet she refrained; Catherine was not one to lose her composure in front of her crew, and Cecil seemed preoccupied with the injured woman before him. Catherine didn't know who she was, but she was obviously important to him, so she stood back and let Felicity Lowlander, the medical technician, raise the woman's gurney and rush her to the medical bay.

With the injured woman rushed off, and the cage already being lowered again, Cecil looked lost. In that moment, he very much resembled the shy young boy Catherine remembered, a gentle soul who was afraid of the dark, hated thunderstorms, and relied on his big sister to protect him after their mother passed away. Now, though, he had the look of a man who had been drinking too much for too long, and appeared to be almost in shock. His rescue and the ensuing gun battle must have been overwhelming for poor Cecil.

Catherine took off her cap and approached her brother. "Hello, Cecil," she said quietly.

His eyes met hers. Before saying anything, before Catherine knew what was happening, Cecil wrapped his arms around his sister and gave her a big hug. His voice wavered as the thanked her. "Thank you. Thank you for everything."

Catherine embraced her brother for a long moment, then stepped away rather awkwardly. "Yes, well...it's good to see you, Cecil. I'm glad to see you alive."

"I'm sorry about your crewman down there," he said. "What was his name?"

"Randall Markgraf. I hired him on New Austin. That will be one of our stops on the way home."

"The family fortune isn't what it used to be," Cecil said, "but I'll make sure his family is taken care of. They saved my life. They saved Bianca's life. I can't repay that debt."

"Bianca was the injured woman?"

"Yes. She's...well, it's complicated. I should go with her. Where did they take her?"

"Cecil, I know how you feel, but the medical bay isn't that big, and we've got wounded to treat. I'll have one of my crew take you down to the personnel quarters and find you a berth."

"I could really use a shower."

"Right now we've got to secure everything for liftoff. We're going to hop back to Freeport. Once we get there, you'll be able to get cleaned up. It'll only take a short while."

"What about Bianca?"

"My flight surgeon is one of the best. She's in good hands. Right now they're going to stabilize her for the boost. After we land, they'll begin whatever treatment is necessary."

He nodded shakily. "It means the world to me."

"After we land, and you get some rest, and Bianca is recovering, we need to sit down and have a talk, little brother."

"There is a lot to tell."

"We have a very long journey home. There will plenty of time."

"Are Zak and Anna still with you? Are they okay?"

"They're both on board, and yes, they're fine."

Cecil looked visibly relieved. "Thank you, Cat. My God, thank you so much." A crewman appeared to take him down to the crew deck.

Catherine touched her brother's arm as he was led off, then spoke into her headset. "Command deck, this is the captain. Any other hostiles detected?"

Luis Azevedo answered promptly. "Affirmative, Captain, but they're all keeping their distance. We've received no communications from Aristotle Lang, either."

"Very good. Begin preparations for liftoff. I want us airborne as soon as all personnel are aboard and accounted for." Even with its weapon systems, a ship like the *Andromeda* was vulnerable on the ground. "Get us back to our berth at Freeport. Out." The ship still needed to be resupplied and refitted for the long journey back to civilized space, and given the state of port services on Zanzibar, the process would take more than a day. In the meantime, she'd have to alert the Freeport Enforcers and have a constant watch rotation standing guard on the ship. Lang might have been bluffing about his influence inside the walls of Freeport, but Catherine didn't want to take any chances.

There was much to do, but Catherine paused. She gazed across the surface of Zanzibar, a brown, windblown, barren wasteland, and waited. She wanted to greet Marcus and his team personally when they came back aboard.

The Privateer Ship *Andromeda*
City of Freeport, Equatorial Region

The last two days had been a flurry of activity for Cecil. The *Andromeda* had flown back to Freeport, and was in the process of being refueled, refitted, and resupplied for the journey ahead, as rapidly as port facilities would allow. He had a bad feeling that Lang would try to come for him, and wanted to get off of Zanzibar as quickly as possible. His sister said they needed to do the refits and take on the supplies, though, or they wouldn't make the trip. Cecil had to wait, and he hated waiting. Worrying over Bianca had taken his mind off of things, though. He'd stayed by her side as she was wheeled into the med bay for treatment, and the ship's flight surgeon had had to practically throw him out of the room to stop him from hovering.

Bianca was resting quietly now, on a gurney in the medical bay. An IV fed fluids into her arm, and a tube supplied oxygen to her nose. The gunshot wound had been severe, given her slight frame, but it had missed her spine. Cecil thanked the God that he was no longer sure he didn't believe in that she had survived the ordeal. She'd saved his life. This woman, a slave, a concubine assigned to him by a vicious warlord, had taken a bullet for Cecil Blackwood. Cecil Blackwood the drunk. Cecil Blackwood the womanizer. Cecil Blackwood the playboy.

He sat in an uncomfortable folding chair next to her gurney, holding her hand, and was lost in thought. His little adventure on Zanzibar had cost much, not only in terms of money, but in lives. One of the mercenaries that had helped rescue him, Randall

Markgraf, had been killed. Several others were wounded, though their wounds were not severe. Dozens of Aristotle Lang's men had been killed, but Lang was still out there. Now, thanks to the unwilling efforts of Cecil and his employees, the old warlord had access to priceless alien artifacts with which to fund his army. Zanzibar would suffer even more, and it was all Cecil's fault. He hung his head in shame. How can a man come back when he'd made such terrible mistakes?

Cecil looked up at Bianca, who was still unconscious. Her breast rose and fell beneath the Mylar blanket as she breathed. "I've made a lot of mistakes," he told her, even though she couldn't hear. "Mistakes I can't forget, can't live down. But I can do some good, too. When we get home, I'll make sure you're taken care of, love. You'll have everything you could possibly desire. You'll see the best doctors, eat the best food, live the best life. You'll never want or fear again. I swear to you. I'll...I'll even quit drinking," he promised, wondering if he'd be able to live up to it. "I'll be a better man. For you."

Of all the women Cecil had wooed and bedded over the years, this Zanzibaran refugee was the only one that had ever loved him. All the others had wanted something from him—money, power, or access to both. But all she'd wanted was to be safe, and to be with him.

She squeezed his hand weakly. "You really gon' take care a' me, Mista Ceecil?"

Cecil leaned forward, clasping her hand in both of his. "Bianca! Yes, love. You don't have to worry about anything now. I'm going to take care of you. I promise you."

Bianca managed a slight smile. "I love you, Mista Ceecil." She then closed her eyes and drifted back to sleep.

"I...I love you too," he said quietly.

Cecil was startled when someone knocked on the hatch. Behind him was Felicity Lowlander, dressed in a green flight suit with her hair in a bun. "I'm sorry to disturb you, Mr. Blackwood, but the captain has requested that you join her in Astrogation. She wishes to debrief you before we lift off. Mr. Mesa and Ms. Kay are already there."

Cecil nodded. "Of...of course." He stood up, still holding Bianca's hand. "Will she be alright?"

"She has a long road ahead of her, but time in freefall will take the strain off of her heart and help her recover. I'll take good care of her."

"Thank you, love," he said. "Could someone show me the way?"

A short while later, Cecil found himself in Astrogation. Catherine and the leader of the mercenary team were waiting for him. Zak and Anna were using a large holotank to present their findings and brief the ship's crew on the alien artifacts.

"Thank you for coming, Cecil," Catherine said as he entered the room. "Please have a seat. Your employees were just filling us in on what they'd found, and their interaction with the Orlov refugees in Sanctuary."

"I'm afraid I was unaware of that last bit," Cecil said, sitting down.

"I'm sorry, Cecil," Zak said. "I didn't tell you for your own safety. If we got caught, we were dead. No sense getting you killed too."

"I appreciate that, mate," Cecil said. "I suspected something was going on, you know, but I didn't want to ask. Say . . . Mr. Winchester, right?"

Marcus Winchester nodded. "The same."

"Thank you, sir. I owe you and your team my life. I'm sorry for your loss."

Marcus nodded quietly. "Just doing what we were hired to do."

"Be that as it may," Cecil said, "if Mr. Markgraf had any family, I'll make sure they're taken care of. I promise you that."

"I appreciate the gesture, but he didn't have any family. His will stipulates that everything be left to a couple of different charities on New Austin."

Catherine sat down and crossed her legs. "Cecil, there are some things I need to ask you. Forgive me if I sound prying or suspicious, but I came a long way and endured a great deal of risk to find you."

"What did Father tell you?" Cecil asked.

"He didn't tell me about any alien artifacts. He said that you were off on Zanzibar on some kind of treasure hunt. I was told you'd chartered a ship and gallivanted off to the frontier, on what he described as a fool's errand. He said he heard nothing from you for months, until he received the ransom demand from Aristotle Lang."

"Fool's errand, eh?" Cecil shook his head in frustration. "It bloody well was. But Father is a fool, too, then. He knew what I was up to. He partially funded the expedition."

Catherine's eyebrows shot up. "He did, did he?"

"Indeed. He thought it was foolish, all right, but we were desperate."

"Cecil, just how desperate is the situation at home getting?"

"Father has been all but marginalized on the Council. Aberdeen Province has lost its prestige and much of its power."

"So you came up with this scheme to go hunting for alien artifacts?"

"Yes. And if not for Aristotle bloody Lang, it'd have worked beautifully, too. I had it all arranged. Once I secured the dig site, I was to send word home. Father would send Blackwood and Associates transport ships out to pick up the cargo, and we'd haul them back to Avalon."

"What?" Zak exclaimed. "*That* was your plan? You were going to loot Zanzibar?"

"Yes, damn it!" Cecil snarled. "And why not? Look at this place, man! Those artifacts were lost to history before we came along. What did you think we were going to do with them?"

"The Concordiat wouldn't have approved of Avalon trading in stolen alien artifacts," Catherine said coolly.

"The bloody Concordiat doesn't have a say in it," Cecil said. "Avalon is not a signatory to that treaty, and there are plenty of independent systems willing to trade in xenoarchaeological artifacts. There are Concordiat worlds willing to deal in them, too. How do you think the ones that have been found end up in museums and laboratories?"

"Okay, okay," Catherine said, "calm down. I'm not accusing, I just want to know what's going on. Cecil, if Aberdeen is in such hard times, surely even a large infusion of money wouldn't turn things around?"

"No, not by itself," Cecil admitted. "Father and I had bigger plans. Avalon is withering away, slowly, by being so isolationist. Our trade with the Concordiat and others is limited. Our economy is stagnant. We're hindered at every turn by protectionist trade laws. It's time to start looking at unorthodox strategies. We were also discussing trying to make inroads into the Orlov Combine, maybe even normalizing relations with them. And Zanzibar... Cat, this planet is a hellhole, but it's a practically *uninhabited* hellhole that's rich in resources. Right now, its resources aren't being tapped. If this all worked out the way we hoped, Zanzibar could have become a protectorate of Avalon, trading with the Orlov Combine and the Llewellyn Freehold alike. This place was once the crossroads of the frontier. It could have been again. Now? Well...I just want to get off this bloody rock."

Catherine pinched the bridge of her nose between a finger and thumb, the way she always did when she was frustrated. "Well, this is a fine thing. Why didn't Father just tell me all this?"

"He was probably afraid you wouldn't help if he did. It was easier to blame it all on me, I suppose. It always was easier to blame it on me."

Catherine's expression softened. Cecil had always been something of an embarrassment to the family, and everyone knew it. It was unfair, of course, one of the downsides to Avalon's stodgy culture. He'd always been different, never quite the heir their father had wanted him to be. He'd had something to prove his entire life, and when he'd tried to prove it, it had all blown up in his face. "This does beg the question of what is to be done with the artifacts in my cargo hold."

"They're not ours to take," Zak protested.

"Mr. Mesa," Catherine said firmly, "I appreciate your passion for the matter, and I assure you, I'm no grave robber. But the fact of the matter is they're in my possession and I need to figure out what to do with them. If I don't sell them they're extra mass I don't need, and you and I both know what will happen to them if I leave them here."

"I'll buy them from you!" Cecil said. "Or rather, Blackwood and Associates will."

Catherine raised an eyebrow. "Are you sure Father would approve?"

"Father can piss off," Cecil said. "I'm still the CEO of the company, assuming he hasn't written me off for dead, and I still get to make the decisions. I'll buy them from you." Before Zak could say anything, Cecil turned to his partner. "No worries, Zak. I'll arrange to sell them to legitimate scientific establishments, where they'll be properly researched and documented and whatnot. If you still wish to be in my employ, you can supervise the whole thing, vet the potential buyers."

Anna Kay, who had been quiet, tapped the side of her head

with her finger. "I may be able to help you with that, Cecil," she said.

"Oh?"

"The University Byzantium has a very well-funded xenoarchaeology department. Ancient Antecessor artifacts have been found on my homeworld as well, and researching them is one of the colonial government's top priorities. We may be able to work out a trade agreement."

"Anna, love, I appreciate that, but how do you propose to do all this?"

The archaeologist smiled. "As Zak would say, I'm kind of a big deal on my homeworld. The New Constantinople government has a policy of buying any and all artifacts from Antecedent Species, no questions asked, even if the prices are inflated. It's one way of cracking down on the black market: they simply buy it out."

Cecil looked confused. "Yes, but how do you propose to arrange this?"

"I'll explain later," Zak said.

"Yes, well, let's focus on the matter at hand," Catherine said. "Cecil, you've got yourself a deal. I'll have you work out the details with the ship's purser at your leisure. There is also one other thing you may be interested in. Again, it's worth nothing to me if I can't sell it to someone who can exploit it, and...to be honest, I'd like to show Father that I'm still willing to put my homeworld first, even if I don't live there anymore."

"Right. What is it?"

Catherine tapped her handheld a couple of times. A detailed, 3D image of a massive ship appeared in the holotank. "She's called the *Agamemnon,* and she dates back to the Second Federation. She's mostly intact, though we were unable to ascertain what happened to her crew. We found her adrift by chance. It's possible someone else will find her before you can get there, and it's doubtful anyone will respect the salvage claim beacon we left. But she's out there, waiting for someone to uncover her secrets. I'll sell the info to the company for a fraction of what I could get for it on the open market."

Cecil, Zak, and Anna all stared at the holotank, fascinated. Zak shook his head. "What a find!"

"You've got yourself a deal," Cecil said, not taking his eyes off of the hologram.

Catherine touched her ear for a moment, as if listening to her headset. "I see. Stand by." She tapped the controls, and the hologram of the *Agamemnon* was replaced with the face of Aristotle Lang.

"...citizens of Freeport, for too long you have lived in squalor, forgotten about by your self-appointed masters who sit comfortably behind walls and fences. Now is your moment! Rise up! Throw off the yoke of oppression and join me! I have in my possession a wealth of ancient alien artifacts, and I will use them to rebuild Zanzibar! Our home will know the glory it once did, but only if you fight by my side! Join me! Rise up! Kill the Enforcers, take their weapons! All of you who are forced to scratch a living from this desolate world, while Frank DeWitt and his board sit fat and happy, not wanting for anything, rise up! Ninety-nine percent of this world's inhabitants live in squalor, while the elite one percent have everything! I say no more! I say it's time for the revolution! Join me, and take back what is rightfully yours!"

Cecil felt sick. "My God."

Lang wasn't done yet. An image of Catherine, Cecil, and the *Andromeda* herself appeared on the screen. The warlord's expression darkened. "These two people are brother and sister by the name of Blackwood. The woman is the captain of this ship, which is now berthed in Freeport. Bring me their heads, and I will make you wealthy beyond your wildest dreams. Deliver me the ship intact, and I'll reward you just as generously. To the spaceport controllers, I say, I will pay you ten times your yearly salary if you don't release that ship from the landing tower. You will be rewarded. Aristotle Lang always keeps his word. These people are off-worlders who've come to loot this world to steal our precious resources and sell them elsewhere."

He looked right at the screen, as if speaking directly to Catherine and Cecil. "You thought you could betray me, Captain? You think I am some uneducated fool? You think you can back out of a deal, kill my men, and steal my property without consequence? I will take your ship, Captain, and it will be *my* ship. Surrender now and I'll let your crew live. Resist and I'll kill every last one of them. The choice is yours." The message ended.

"Wolfram says that the message has been looping over and over," Catherine said. "Our watch-standers are reporting gunfire at the spaceport." Cecil turned green and looked as if he was going to throw up. Ignoring her brother, the she spoke into her headset. "Can we launch? How long? Damn it. Any response? Understood. Get every spare crewman on it." She looked at the others in Astrogation. "The situation is quickly deteriorating in Freeport. When Lang's message went out, riots began in the slums almost immediately. We have reports of actual street fighting going on downtown. He may have been planning something like this for a while, and it would appear that he's successfully infiltrated Freeport."

"How is this possible?" Zak asked.

"There's no way this is spontaneous," Marcus Winchester answered. "Outside the walls of Freeport are the ruins of Nova Prospect, the former capital city of Zanzibar."

"The locals call it the Dead City," Cecil said.

"It'd be a good place to prestage materiel and weapons for just such a day, too," Marcus said. "No, this is a contingency plan. The bastard's probably had it for a long time. He just wasn't ready to make his move."

"What . . . what shall we do?" Cecil asked.

His sister looked thoughtful and fell silent, mind racing, eyes darting back and forth. "Mr. Mesa. I want you to contact our friends in Sanctuary. They undoubtedly know about it already, but just in case, give them a call. Ask for help, see if they can spare anyone to defend the spaceport until we can leave. Any help at all would be appreciated."

"Uh, yes, ma'am," Zak said.

"We're still locked into the landing tower. The spaceport controllers aren't responding, and it seems they've fled as well. We called for help from the Freeport Enforcers, but got no response from them, either. I was assured that they could protect the city, damn it all. I even paid some extra bribes for them to keep watch over our ship, for all the good it did. It's possible that Lang's men are overrunning spaceport control even as we speak. Marcus, I'm afraid I have to ask for your help one last time."

"Understood, Captain," the mercenary said. "Damned shame we lost the heavy. We could really use it right now. I'll get my team together, pull up the spaceport plans, and come up with a strategy."

Cecil's sister nodded. "Quickly, please, we don't have much time." She tapped her headset, activating the ship's internal PA system. "This is the captain speaking," she said, her voice echoing throughout the ship. "Go to general quarters. We are presently locked into the landing tower and are unable to lift off. As I'm sure you've all heard by now, the natives are restless and should be presumed to be hostile. All available crew, draw weapons and stand by to repel boarders. This is not a drill. That is all."

Cecil was unable to take anymore; he turned and threw up. His sister sighed. "And can we get that cleaned up, please?"

"Sorry," Cecil said, meekly.

Annabelle Winchester was hurriedly making sure all shipping containers on the cargo deck were lashed down and secured properly. The word had come down that as soon as the ship was free of the landing tower, they'd be lifting off, and they needed to be ready to go at any time. When the work was finished, she was to report to the arms locker to draw weapons. *This is not a drill.* Annie was scared, and kept hoping she'd wake up from this nightmare, but it never seemed to end.

She perked up when her father slid down the ladder to the cargo deck. "Dad!" she said, running over to him. "What's going on?"

Her father directed his team to get their weapons and gear out from where they were stored. "You heard the captain's announcement, Annie."

"Oh my God," she said, unable to hide the fear in her voice. "What's going to happen?"

Her father put a hand on Annie's shoulder. "Nothing bad's going to happen, baby. The guys and me are gonna go over to the spaceport control office, release the landing tower, then come back. As soon as that's done we'll be on our way home."

"But she said to prepare to repel boarders!"

"The locals are having some problems right now, that's all. Listen to me. Honey? Look at me. I'm not going to let anything happen to you, or to the ship. Okay? Stay calm. You have to stay calm. If you panic, you've already lost. Do you understand?"

Annie nodded. "Okay. Yeah, I'm okay. I can do this."

"I know you can, baby. Look, I haven't said this enough, but I'm so goddamn proud of you I could bust. Look at you! I know you'll be fine, no matter what."

"You'll be fine too, Dad," Annie insisted. "Promise me!"

"I swear, Annie. I'll come back to you. We'll be back in a few minutes. I have to go now, okay? The sooner we get this done the sooner we can go."

"Okay, Daddy." Annie hugged her father tightly. "I love you. Please be careful."

"I love you too, Annie."

"Crewman Winchester!" Kimball said, jogging up to her. "Are all containers secured?"

"They are, Mr. Kimball," Annie said. "We're ready to lift off at any time."

"Excellent," Kimball said. "Now come with me, quickly, to the arms locker. Can you shoot?"

Annie's father interjected. "She's a better shot than anyone else on your crew," he said proudly. "But you keep her down here, okay? Kimball, please, she's my daughter. She's sixteen."

"Dad, I can fight!" Annie protested.

"No worries, Mercenary Winchester," Kimball said. "It was my intention to have her stay here with me. I won't let her out of my sight. I promise you, as long as I'm still breathing, no harm will come to your daughter. She's my shipmate."

Marcus nodded, leaned down, and stuck out his hand. Kimball took it, and the two men exchanged an Earth-style handshake. Annie's father turned and went to put on his gear with the rest of his team. Kimball turned to Annie, "We'll be fine. I'll be here with you. Come with me, now. We need to draw weapons."

Annie nodded and followed Kimball up the ladder.

In the bowels of the ship, Marcus Winchester led his team down toward the personnel hatch. Like most ships of her class, the *Andromeda* was designed to be serviced from a landing tower at a spaceport. She did, however, have access ladders so that crew could come and go in the event a landing tower was unavailable. A narrow passageway, squeezed between the main propellant tank and the outer hull, led to a vertical shaft with a lift large enough to move only two people at a time. Rather than use the lift, Marcus asked the ship's crew to disable it so that he and his team could access the ladder. It was a long climb down, but it would be a lot faster that way.

The Freeport Spaceport was in chaos. Lang's call to arms had caused an uprising in the slums and shantytowns; thousands of dissatisfied locals, living in squalor, were rioting, burning, looting, and stealing whatever they could. Rival gangs were shooting it out in the streets, and Freeport's Enforcers were under siege everywhere. The spaceport itself was being mobbed, as thousands tried to flee the carnage for the perceived safety of the ships. There were only four ships at the Spaceport, and none of the locals tried to get on board the *Andromeda*. The other ships, also unable to take off, were fending off the locals by force of arms.

Lang's army had infiltrated the city well in advance, and reinforcements were on the way. The Enforcers were losing the fight, and had seemingly abandoned the spaceport. Marcus estimated that within a day or so, Lang would be in control of Freeport, and his army would sack the city, raping, looting, and killing as they pleased. From a professional standpoint, Marcus couldn't help but admire Lang's tactics. The decision to attack was undoubtedly made in a fit of rage, but it was working, because he'd planned ahead. The defenders had grossly underestimated how powerful Lang's forces had become, hadn't been aware of how successful their infiltration efforts were, and had been caught off-guard. If the mercenaries couldn't free the ship, he very much doubted any of them would make it out of this alive, including his daughter.

"Alright, listen up," Marcus said, addressing his team in the cramped passageway. "I'm going down first. The ladder comes out by the landing jacks. It's going to be wide open out there, so we're going to have to move quickly. Wade, I want you right behind me, and have your breaching charges ready. I'm going to try to pop the hatch to the service tunnels that run under the spaceport. If I can't get them open, you'll have to blow them."

"I'll get the sumbitch open," Wade said.

Marcus keyed his radio. "Overwatch, this is Cowboy-6. You in position?"

"Roger that, Boss," Devree replied. She was on the bridge that connected the landing tower to the ship's cargo bay. It was exposed on all sides but the bottom, but it gave her a good vantage point. "I've got you covered."

"You okay up there?"

"Affirmative. I've got security from the ship's crew watching my back." Crewmembers had drawn lasers and rocket guns from the ship's armory, and Devree had a three-man team, led by Mazer Broadbent, protecting her.

"Understood. If the hostiles start coming up the tower, you

fall back into the ship. Don't be a hero." As Devree acknowledged, Marcus turned his attention back to his team. "The rest of you, hold here until we give you the signal. No sense in all of us milling around down there while we're dickering with the hatch. I only want one man on the ladder at a time. Move fast, but for hell's sake don't fall. The ship will cover us with its lasers as much as it can, but they weren't designed to fire at stuff on the ground, beneath its own fins. There are big blind spots, and the captain is hesitant to use ship weapons when there are so many civilians running around. On that note, check your shots! There are a lot of bad guys down there, and none of them are wearing uniforms, but there are a lot of innocent people out there too. Let's not make this shithole any worse than it is, yeah?"

The team acknowledged. Marcus turned to Wade. "You ready, partner?"

The explosives expert grinned. "Are you?"

"Hell no," Marcus said. He reached around to the back of Wade's head and pulled their heads together so their helmets collided with a hollow *THOCK!* "Let's do it." He slung his weapon and descended down the ladder.

After a few meters, the vertical shaft opened up to daylight. Scrambling down the ladder as fast as he could safely go, Marcus took in the insanity all around him. Hundreds of people were running around the launch pads, stealing whatever wasn't bolted down. Gunfire echoed across the spaceport, and columns of acrid smoke rose from the city beyond. Lang's plan had been executed brilliantly, and Marcus was impressed with how quickly the city had gone to hell. As an irregular warfare veteran, he could appreciate beautifully executed chaos on a professional level. After a few moments, he was on the ground. He radioed Wade to come on down, took a knee, and readied his weapon.

"Contact," Devree said calmly. "Armed men coming in from the south side." Her rifle roared as it launched a huge APHE slug downrange. The suppressed barrel had been damaged in the rocket barrage that had killed Markgraf, and she'd had to use her spare. "One down," she said coldly. The rifle roared again. "Two down. The rest are retreating."

Marcus acknowledged her as Wade landed on the launch pad. "Come on," he said to his partner. "Hatch is this way." The two mercenaries moved quickly, breathing heavily through their respirators, trying to maintain a low profile as they made their way to the hatch. The launch pad was huge, and the access hatch was over the edge. At the edge of the pad, there was a short two-meter ladder that led down to ground level. In between the launch pads was nothing but rocky, barren, exhaust-blasted ground.

"Cowboy-6, this is the *Andromeda*," Captain Blackwood said, over the radio. "Be advised, vehicles are inbound, presumed hostile. We can see armed individuals in them. They just crashed the gate on the north end of the spaceport and have entered the underground vehicle tunnels. The tunnels open up to the surface about a hundred meters from the launch pad. There is presently a battle going on at the city gates. Lang's reinforcements are here. Please hurry."

"Understood," Marcus said. "I see the tunnel entrance." He turned to Wade. "Get down!" The partners dropped into the prone, weapons leveled, just as a trio of 4×4 trucks came roaring out of the underground tunnels. They each had heavy weapons, machine guns or rocket launchers, mounted in their beds, and began firing wildly at the *Andromeda*.

"Rocket launcher!" Wade shouted. He ripped off shot after shot at the lead truck, which was fitted with piecemeal, bolted-on armor plating, and had an improvised rocket launcher in its bed. Horizontal metal slats covered the windows, protecting the driver somewhat. Marcus opened fire on it a second later. Bullets snapped overhead as the other trucks shot back, circling the ship like sharks in the water, looking for a weak point to attack. The machine guns were no threat to the ship's armored hull, but the rocket launcher was.

"Take that thing out!" Marcus said, broadcasting the order to everyone that could hear.

"I'm coming down!" Halifax said. He had a man-portable plasma carbine that would certainly do the job.

"Negative!" Marcus shouted, flinching as bullets impacted the edge of the launch pad, spraying him with debris. "It's too hot! Stand by!"

"How the hell did he get technicals here so fast?" Wade asked in frustration. Marcus wasn't sure. They had to have been staged somewhere ahead of time.

"I've got it!" an unfamiliar voice said. It was Luis Azevedo, one of the ship's junior officers. The ship shuddered and let out a mechanical groan as large doors on one side opened, revealing the powerful manipulator arm hidden within the *Andromeda*'s belly. The arm unfolded itself smoothly, its huge claw opened wide. As the three gun trucks circled, the arm came smashing down, plowing into the bare Zanzibaran soil. The driver hit the brakes and tried to turn, but it was too late. The rocket technical slid sideways, crashing into the manipulator arm and coming to a halt. Before the gunner could get his bearings and react, the claw ripped out of the ground in an explosion of dry soil, moved over the top of the truck, and clamped down on it. Powerful hydraulics groaned, metal twisted, and improvised armor buckled as the claw crushed the vehicle in its powerful grip, hoisting it into the air as it did so. Marcus could hear the truck's occupants screaming as the claw dropped them from thirty meters, sending them plunging to their deaths.

"That was awesome!" Wade said, pushing himself up.

"Nice work, kid," Marcus told Azevedo over the radio. "The other trucks are running off to the north."

"We're tracking them," Azevedo replied. Marcus watched them leave plumes of dust in their wake as they fled. "Okay, Wade, get that hatch open!"

"Already on it!" Wade said. He had dropped down to ground level and found the access door that led under the launch pad. "It's a blast door, heavy alloy, but not meant as a security door. Prepping a shaped charge." Marcus provided cover as Wade worked, expertly placing the charge and priming the initiator. He came scrambling up the short ladder a few moments later. He and Marcus both retreated so they were well away from the edge. "Fire in the hole!" Wade said, and mashed the trigger.

BOOM! With a single blast and a puff of dust and smoke, the door was open. Marcus and Wade provided cover as the rest of the team made their way down the ladder, one at a time.

Hot air hit Marcus in the face as Halifax fired several shots from his plasma carbine. The heat and flash were searing in the close confines of the tunnel, but the terrifying weapon did the trick. The squad of Lang's militiamen heading the other way up the tunnel didn't even fire back as they broke and fled. Lights flickered and the air stank of ozone and burnt skin.

"God damn, I love this weapon," Halifax said.

"Let's move!" Marcus ordered. "Tight stack, guns up!" There was no cover in the tunnel, nowhere to hide. The mercenaries had to be careful not to be surprised by a shooter or a grenade. The service tunnels were run down, poorly lit and poorly maintained, little more than ceramicrete tubes with a metal walkway at the bottom. The mercenaries, with their vision-enhancing smart goggles, had the advantage, but they were badly outnumbered. You didn't have to be good to win a firefight in a narrow tunnel, you just had to be lucky.

It was a long walk from the launch pad to the spaceport control center, almost six hundred meters, and apart from a couple of doglegs in the tunnel most of it was a straight shot. Advancing as quickly as possible, breathing hard through respirators, boots clanking on a metal walkway, the team made it to the end of the corridor without encountering any more hostiles.

Their destination was the spaceport control center. It was the only thing keeping the *Andromeda* from lifting off. The spaceport controllers had apparently fled, leaving the ship locked in to the landing tower, and spaceport control was where the landing towers were operated from. They'd already encountered Lang's men, so Marcus was assuming the control center would be guarded. Moving through the service entrance, the team entered the basement of the control building, weapons up, trying to cover all the angles. Up a flight of stairs, around the corner, and they were on the first floor. The building was in the same dilapidated shape as everything else on Zanzibar. The walls were cracked, the lights flickered, and the air stank of dust and garbage. Nerves were on edge as the team moved through the building, checking every doorway, trying to watch every direction. Men could be heard shouting somewhere in the building.

"Contact front!" Hondo shouted, and opened up with his machine gun. The weapon's roar was deafening inside the hallway. Three long bursts scattered the enemy squad while the mercenaries found cover behind corners and in doorways.

Ken Tanaka kicked in a door, trying to get out of the fatal funnel of the hallway, only to crash into a pair of militiamen inside the room. He shot one at point-blank range with his carbine, dropping the man, but the other tackled him and dragged him to the ground. The Nipponese mercenary struggled with the man, who seemed under the influence of drugs and was screaming incoherently. Ken was outweighed by the militiaman, who was trying to plunge a large knife into his throat. Gunfire echoed throughout the building, bullets zipped up and down the corridor, and Ken was effectively alone. At the last instant, he was able to get his sidearm clear of its holster. He stuck the muzzle of his 9mm pistol under the thug's chin and pulled the trigger, splattering his brains on the ceiling. The dead man slumped down on top of Tanaka, leaking blood onto his gear.

Hondo appeared in the doorway a moment later, machine gun at the ready. "Are you alright?"

"I'm fine," Tanaka said.

Hondo rolled the body off of him and helped him up. "I'm sorry, we were pinned down in the hallway."

Gunfire echoed throughout the building. Men shouted, and a fire alarm screamed. "Let's keep moving."

Marcus rallied the team. "On me, let's move!" The control room was up another flight of stairs and at the end of the corridor.

The second floor was even more heavily defended. The team encountered resistance even before they got up the stairs, exchanging fire with Lang's men at the top of the stairwell. The hostiles fell back when Halifax brought his plasma carbine to bear. White-hot plasma flashed in the confines of the building, burning men to ash and terrifying those who were lucky enough to get out of the way.

Once at the top, Marcus and Wade both tossed grenades around the corner before exiting the stairwell. The double concussion made their ears pop, and the team was moving before the dust had even settled. Gunfire ripped through the defending militiamen, most of whom wore no body armor. Wade snarled and fell to the floor. Hondo stepped forward, cutting down his attacker with his machine gun, while Marcus checked his partner. His vest had stopped two bullets. Marcus helped Wade to his feet and they pressed on.

The corridor stank of ozone, propellant, smoke, dust, and death when it finally fell silent. It was so smoky that it was difficult to see, even with smart goggles. At the end of the hall was a bullet-riddled security door that led to the control room. It was locked.

"Wade, prep a breaching charge," Marcus ordered.

"Hold up a second, lad," Halifax said, leveling his plasma carbine.

Marcus couldn't see his team member's evil smile, but knew it was there. He nodded, and the rest of the team retreated behind Halifax. The bearded, stocky mercenary shouldered the weapon and fired off a bolt. The weapon sounded like a tiny electric thunderclap

in the confines of the hall, and the blue-white flash would've left
them seeing stars if not for their smart goggles. The top of the door
evaporated in a blast of searing heat; a second shot burned away
the bottom. He raised the muzzle of the weapon and stepped back
to cover the hall.

"Grenade out!" Wade said, throwing the frag through the
doorway. *BOOM!* They flooded the control room, weapons firing, not giving the defenders a chance to recover. There was no
cover, nowhere to hide. Doorways were lethal in a gunfight, and
the only thing to do was to press through. Hondo fell with a
pained grunt; Halifax dragged him back out of the room as the
remaining three kept shooting.

"Clear!" Marcus said, carbine shouldered, breathing hard.

"Clear!" Wade agreed. His rifle was slung across his chest,
the bolt locked back on an empty magazine. He had his revolver
drawn and ready.

"Clear!" said Ken Tanaka, who held his carbine shakily in
one hand while covering a bleeding wound on his neck with
the other. The control room was large and open, and eight dead
militiamen littered the floor.

"Wade, Ken, find the landing tower controls," Marcus ordered.
"Halifax! How's Hondo doing?"

"Rifle round to the leg, chief," Halifax shouted from the
corridor. "Hit the bone. I stopped the bleeding but his leg is
shattered. He can't walk."

"Leave me!" Hondo said. "Get back to the ship!"

"Horseshit, lad," Halifax said. "No one is getting left behind."

"You're damn right we're not leaving anyone behind," Marcus
agreed. "Wade! What's the status on those controls?"

"I'm working on it!" he said. "I'm an explosive ordnance tech,
not a goddamn space traffic controller!"

"Here!" Tanaka said. "I think it's this ... yes, that was it!"
Warning lights flashed. A computerized voice announced that
the emergency lockdown had been lifted. The screens had mostly
been smashed in the firefight, but the computer confirmed it: all
landing towers were being retracted.

"Outstanding!" Marcus said. "How can we rig it so they can't
lock us back in after we leave the room?"

Halifax raised his plasma weapon. "Will burning the controls
work?"

Marcus looked at Wade. Wade just shrugged. "It's worth a shot. It might buy us time," Marcus said. "Everyone clear out. Halifax, burn it all down." As Halifax used his powerful weapon to destroy the spaceport control stations, Marcus stepped out into the hall and radioed the ship. "*Andromeda*, this is Cowboy-6."

"*Andromeda* standing by," Captain Blackwood replied. "What's your status?"

"Landing towers are unlocked. They'll begin retracting momentarily. We're headed back to the ship, over."

"Any injuries?"

"Affirmative, two injuries, no KIA. Hondo can't walk, though."

"Be advised, more enemy forces are arriving at the spaceport control center from the city. The Enforcers are holding several key structures, like the power plant, but no help is coming to the spaceport. The Orlov refugees are unable to provide assistance. You need to get out of there ASAP or you'll be cut off!"

"Understood. Cowboy-6 out." Marcus turned to his team. "Alright gentlemen, you heard the lady. Somebody help Hondo up. We're getting the hell off this rock!"

Devree Starlighter, from her vantage point on the bridge between the landing tower and the ship, had a wide view of the north side of the spaceport. A pile of spent plastic cases rolled around beneath her, as she'd been firing at targets of opportunity the entire time. The panicked civilians had cleared out once the shooting started. Devree had lost count of how many men she'd killed.

"Overwatch, Cowboy-6," Marcus said over the radio.

"Send it!" Devree replied.

"Be advised, we're coming out the front. We've got wounded. Cover us, over!"

"What? Negative, there are bad guys all over the place up here. Go back through the tunnel!"

"We can't!" Marcus insisted. "We're cut off. We're taking one of the service vehicles. Watch for us!"

A warning light on the scaffolding began flashing, as did an annoying beeping alarm. "Understood," Devree said. "I'll cover as long as I can!"

Mazer Broadbent was at her side, slapping a new magazine into his 20mm rocket gun. "Devree, that landing tower will retract any moment now. We've got to get back to the ship!"

"I'm not leaving until they're back!" she insisted.

Mazer sighed. "Damn it, girl. You two," he said, pointing at Techs Oswald and Daye. "Get back on board. I'm staying with her!"

Daye protested. "But sir!"

"Go, damn it!" he snarled.

"You should go with them," Devree said, looking through her scope as the crewman hustled back to the ship.

"You should too," Mazer said. "I guess we're both fools. I'll spot for you."

"Here they come!" Devree said. Hundreds of meters away, the door to a service garage opened up, and out rolled a six-wheeled utility vehicle. Marcus was driving, while Wade sat next to him, rifle at the ready. Behind them, Ken Tanaka had his carbine up, while Halifax sat in the bed with Hondo. They opened fire on militiamen in the garage as they sped off toward the *Andromeda*. Hondo's machine gun roared across the spaceport, and the blue-white streaks from Halifax's plasma carbine were impossible to miss.

"Top floor," Mazer said. "Rocket launcher!"

"On him!" Devree replied. Her rifle bucked against her shoulder. An instant later, the round hit the man in the chest, blowing open his insides. "He's down!"

"Garage entrance!" Mazer said. He fired off two rounds in rapid succession; the laser-guided rockets shrieked downrange, accelerating as they went, and detonated in clouds of dust and fragmentation when they hit. Devree followed up with a pair of shots of her own.

"All down," she said. "Nice shooting."

As the utility cart rolled across the spaceport, kicking up a plume of dust in its wake, another gun truck appeared from the far side of the control building. "Where the hell do they keep coming from?" Devree snarled, lining up a shot. She missed. The thing was swerving so badly, trying to avoid the fire from the mercs in the cart, that even her scope's auto tracking was having a hard time compensating. Mazer fired off a couple more rocket rounds, both of which detonated just behind the truck, but it kept rolling on, its gunner firing wildly.

A moment later, the mercs' cart swerved and slowed down. It had been hit! It came to a stop, and Ben Halifax jumped out, rolling on the rocky ground and coming up on one knee. He cut loose an fusillade from his plasma carbine, protecting his teammates, firing as rapidly as the weapon was capable of. The first shot missed the truck, the second hit it dead on. Its bolted-on, improvised armor plating was no match for the searing heat of a direct plasma blast. Halifax kept firing as the truck swerved off. It rolled to the side, burning as it came to a stop. Through her scope, Devree could see Halifax shaking a fist victoriously, before yanking the red-hot barrel out of his weapon. He didn't seem to have any more spares.

The annoying beeping turned into a loud klaxon. Devree realized she was moving to the side.

"The tower is retracting!" Mazer said. "Come on, we have to go!"

"No! They're not back yet!" She watched as Marcus and Ken each threw one of Hondo's arms over their shoulders, helping the big man hop and hobble back toward the ship as fast as they could go. Halifax switched to a pistol while Wade fired off burst after burst from Hondo's machine gun, retreating as he did so. Devree fired off another shot, then another, then another. Mazer stayed by her side, squeezing off rockets as fast as he could accurately place them. It seemed like there were dozens of militiamen swarming the spaceport now, using every available piece of cover to fire at the fleeing mercenaries and the ship itself.

"Mercenary Starlighter, come on!" Kimball shouted, motioning for Devree to come inside.

Annabelle Winchester was at his side, clutching a laser carbine nervously. "Devree, hurry!"

The tower was retracting slowly, but there was already a meter-wide gap between the bridge and the cargo bay. Marcus was hit in the back and fell, dragging Hondo and Tanaka down with him. Devree killed the shooter as Wade pulled his team leader to his feet, his vest having stopped the bullet. They dragged Hondo back to his feet and pressed on.

The landing tower continued to retract. Mazer stood up, grabbed Devree's arm, and yanked her to her feet. "We have to go!" He turned and ran for the cargo bay.

Devree was on his heels, but stopped when she spotted a pair of militiamen setting up a tripod-mounted heavy rocket launcher by the control building. She dropped to her knee, rested the heavy sniper rifle on the scaffolding, and lined up the shot. *Lase. Range. Correct. Exhale. Squeeze.* The rifle roared again. The explosive-tipped bullet struck one of the rockets the militiamen were loading into the launcher. It detonated, and the targets disappeared in a cloud of dust and smoke.

"Damn it, girl, come *on!*" Mazer shouted. Devree looked up and realized there was now a two-meter gap between the tower and the ship, and it was widening by the second. She left the rifle where it was, stood up, and ran for it, limping as fast as her damaged prosthetic legs would allow.

"Jump for it!"

Coming to the edge, Devree jumped. She floated in space for what seemed like a long time, arms outstretched, straining to reach Mazer on the other side. She realized in that instant just how high up she was, and that she would surely fall to her death if she missed.

She missed. Her hands fell a few centimeters short of Mazer's, but smacked down onto the lip of the open cargo bay. Her shoulders wrenched as she dangled in space, legs kicking against the hull of the ship, so high up in the air. A second later, two pairs of hands grabbed her arms and pulled her up, into the safety of the cargo deck. She crawled clear as the bay doors began to close.

Up on the command deck, Captain Blackwood tried to watch five screens at once to stay on top of the chaos all around her ship. Marcus' team had done it. The landing tower was retracting. The fuel and power lines to the launch pad were severed, the manipulator arm was stowed, and the ship was spooling up for liftoff. Her crew had performed phenomenally defending the ship. Kimball, Broadbent, and the Winchester girl were firing out of the cargo bay doors right up until the moment they sealed. Now all personnel were on board and accounted for, and were heading to launch stations as rapidly as possible. This was when the ship was most vulnerable, and a bead of sweat trickled down the Catherine's face as she reclined her seat into the takeoff position.

"Captain, incoming transmission from . . . from Aristotle Lang!" Azevedo said.

"Send it to my screen."

A truck rolled to a stop at the base of the ship, observed from a camera high above. Mounted in its bed was a large, multi-barreled rocket launcher, probably a 90mm bore diameter or larger. Lang appeared on the screen as his militiamen brought the weapon to bear. Catherine had no idea where he was transmitting from. "This is the end, Captain!" he announced, his voice raspy as if he'd been shouting. "You think you can double-cross me? You think you can rob me and run away? This is *my* planet, you bitch, *my planet!* Power down your ship, now, or my men will destroy it!"

"Captain, we're ready for liftoff!"

"Colin, punch it!" Catherine said. Her pilot pushed the throttle up. The four engines roared to life, sending a cloud of dust and smoke across the spaceport, followed by the heat of the exhaust.

The rocket launcher, the militiamen, and the not-fully-retracted landing tower were all blasted by the exhaust of the ship. The ship rumbled off of the ground, vibrating as it slowly accelerated. At two thousand meters, Colin throttled up, and Catherine was mashed into her chair as the ship made for the safety of orbit. Lang's ranting transmission faded to static as the *Andromeda* left Zanzibar behind.

Never in all her years as a spacer had Catherine been so relieved to make it into space. The brown sphere of Zanzibar was far below the ship now, and though she was still under multi-G acceleration, Catherine was at ease for the first time since this journey had begun.

Wolfram sent her a private text message. *Congratulations, Kapitänin,* he said. *You've done it. Mission accomplished.*

Catherine smiled. *I couldn't have done it without you,* she wrote back. *When we get back to Heinlein, I want the whole crew to take some well-deserved vacation. We'll stay planeted for a few months this time. We've earned enough money on this run that we can afford it.*

The ship will need a refit anyway, Wolfram pointed out.

I know you had your doubts about this mission, Wolfram. So did I. Thank you for expressing them, and thank you for backing me up when I made my decision.

There is no need to thank me for doing my job, Kapitänin. This what an executive officer does. It is I who owes you a great deal. You know what happened to my career with the Fleet.

Catherine was well aware of it. A substance abuse problem, an addiction to stims, had cost Wolfram a promising career in the Concordiat Defense Force. It was unusual of him to talk about it.

You gave me a second chance. For that, I am forever in your debt, and you will always be my Kapitänin.

Catherine could not help but smile, mashed into her acceleration chair though she was.

"Captain?" Luis Azevedo said, getting Catherine's attention. He sounded concerned.

"What's the matter?"

"Ma'am, I've got an unidentified contact bearing down on us. They just came over the planetary horizon. I'll send it to your screen."

A moment later, a projection of the orbital system of Zanzibar appeared on one of Catherine's displays. It showed the *Andromeda* and her trajectory to the jump point. Coming from the other side of Zanzibar was the bogey Azevedo was talking about. Whatever it was, it was big. Its exhaust signature indicated that it was a small capital ship of some sort. Catherine's heart dropped into her stomach.

"Captain!" Azevedo exclaimed. "Telemetry says it's a *Conan-Delta* class cruiser. Orlov Combine fleet! It's on an intercept course, and we're being targeted! Incoming transmission!"

Catherine, for a very brief moment, closed her eyes, and took a deep breath. "Play it."

A Combine fleet officer appeared on her screen, looking pale and barely human. "Pirate ship *Andromeda*, this is Cruiser-Two-Four-Seven of the People's Combined Collective. You are wanted for collusion with anticitizen militants, kidnapping, bribery, and the destruction of a peaceful space station. Power down your engines and stand by to be boarded."

"That'll be the day," Catherine said firmly. "Luis, send a reply, tell them to piss off. Sound general quarters." She touched the intercom control. "Attention all hands, this is the captain speaking. Battle stations, battle stations, this is not a drill. We've got an incoming bandit from the Orlov Combine, looks like a light cruiser. All personnel suit up as quickly as possible. Damage control parties stand by. That is all."

Wolfram von Spandau appeared on her screen from his station below decks. "What are your orders?"

"We can't outrun them," she said, "and I don't want to leave them here to blast Sanctuary from orbit in any case. Colin, turn us around. Get me weapons lock. Target their propulsion system first. Retract the radiators. Engage ECM. I want a high speed pass, throwing everything we have at them."

"It's risky, *Kapitänin*," her exec said.

"We're not going to survive a long-range slug-match with that cruiser," Catherine said. "Colin, bring us right down their throats! Fire everything we have, then get us below the planetary horizon again!"

"Yes, ma'am," the pilot said, as the two officers on the command deck began targeting and electronic defenses. "Stand by for maneuvers!"

Nattaya Tantirangsi reported from her station. "Skipper, we're being scanned. She's locked on! Missile launch! Volley Alpha, six warheads, closing fast!"

"Targeting!" Azevedo said.

Catherine grimaced. "Engage ECM. Nuchy, empty the missile racks, rapid fire! Luis, shoot down the incoming! Target their propulsion system with the gauss gun and fire at will!"

"Splash one!" Azevedo cried. "Splash two!"

"Firing!" Nattaya said. "Missiles away!" The *Andromeda* ripple-fired her two rotary missile launchers. Ten missiles all screamed toward the Combine cruiser. "Our racks are depleted!"

"I know. When we get to knife-fight range, divert lasers to targeting the enemy ship. We're only going to get one pass. We won't have time to reload the magazines."

"Hang on!" Colin said, grunting as G-forces crushed him into his seat. The two ships, the seventy-meter-long *Andromeda* and the hundred and twenty-meter-long Combine cruiser, closed on each other in silence, at a blistering speed.

"Another volley inbound!" Azevedo said. "Six more missiles, Salvo-Bravo!"

"Target with lasers and engage, fire at will!"

Nuchy cried out excitedly. "Skipper! Two of our gauss slugs got through! Bandit is damaged! Her acceleration is dropping rapidly!"

"Excellent, keep up the—"

"Third volley inbound, Salvo-Charlie! Jesus, eight missiles!"

"Remain calm, Mr. Azevedo," Catherine warned. "Divert the gauss gun to targeting the incoming warheads. Don't let anything get through! Keep firing our missiles! Deploy all countermeasures, and try to fry the missiles' targeting with our radar! Now, people!"

Luis and Nuchy focused on their duties, mashed into their chairs by the acceleration, their hands nonetheless flying across their consoles. The missiles were destroyed, spoofed, or lost their lock, one after another. One of the Combine missiles, however, had a surprise. It missed on the first past, flipped around to pursue the *Andromeda* from behind. "Skipper!" Nuchy said. "Missile on our six! It was hidden behind our exhaust plume!"

"Shoot it down!" Catherine ordered. It was too late. The ship shuddered violently, a sickening groan of twisting metal echoing through her corridors.

"We're hit!" Nuchy said. An alarm sounded and warnings lit up her screens.

"No detonation!" Luis added. "It's a dud."

Wolfram von Spandau appeared on her screen. "*Kapitänin*, I will go assess the damage."

"We're still under acceleration!" Catherine said. The ship was accelerating at four times the force of gravity. "We're about to make the pass! Target the bandit with everything we have left! Fire at will!" Zanzibar hung far below them as the two ships passed each other in a flash, exchanging fire and carving into each other with lasers. After the pass, the *Andromeda* kept going, racing to put Zanzibar between itself and the Combine ship. Klaxons and alarms screamed throughout the ship as weapons continued to fire. She'd been hit, but damage control parties couldn't begin their work until she stopped maneuvering. Until the fight was over, Catherine didn't even know how bad the damage was.

A few agonizing seconds later, the impossible happened: the Combine cruiser, trailing atmosphere and no longer accelerating, began to break up. She then vanished in a flash as her reactor exploded.

"Captain," Nuchy said, almost in shock, "we . . . splash one bandit. We did it."

"Congratulations, ma'am," Luis Azevedo said, breathing heavily.

A cheer echoed throughout the ship. Crewmembers banged on bulkheads and shouted victoriously as they learned of the cruiser's destruction. Just like that, it was over. Space combat tended to be a long, slow-paced affair, and it was very rare that ships could surprise each other at such close range. But when it did happen, combat tended to be short and violent. Whoever got the first good hit usually won, and somehow, the *Andromeda* had gotten lucky and scored a critical hit on the Combine cruiser.

"Wolfram, give me a damage report," Catherine said. Her screens were lit up with red, but her exec was below decks and would have a better assessment.

There was no response.

"Wolfram, this is the captain, damage report!" Catherine was unable to hide the concern in her voice.

There was no response for a long moment. Then, "Captain, this is Tech Oswald. The first officer is dead. We've got a hull breach. Looks like one of their lasers hit the passageway he was in, just below the cargo deck. I'm ... I'm sorry, ma'am. I don't know what he was doing out of his compartment. Damage control parties are responding."

Catherine's heart fell into her stomach again. She sat in silence, barely listening as Engineering, Astrogation, and other critical systems were checked by their respective damage control teams. The *Andromeda* was hit, but she had prevailed, and she wasn't crippled. There had been a high price, though, and the butcher's bill kept climbing as casualty reports came in. She rubbed her face with her hands and struggled to keep her composure.

"Uh, Captain, I'm sorry to disturb you," Azevedo said quietly, "but we've got another problem. There's ... there's an unexploded missile stuck in our hull."

Catherine nodded. In the intensity of combat she'd almost forgotten about it. "Show me." A second later, the feed from an external camera, looking down the *Andromeda*'s hull, appeared on her screen. It zoomed in and focused on what was very clearly the rear-end of a missile, embedded in the honeycomb energy absorber layer.

"I can pull it out with the manipulator arm, Captain," Azevedo suggested.

"No. Leave it be. Get me Wade Bishop."

"There's good news and bad news," Wade Bishop said, studying a 3D representation of the embedded missile in the holotank. He had a tablet computer in his hands, and was reading a military ordnance publication of some sort. "Actually, the bad news is there *is* no good news."

"That's ... just lovely," Captain Blackwood said resignedly. "Please explain."

"Well, according to my pubs, that's a Combine Type-2404 anti-ship missile."

"Are those military ordnance publications you've got there?" Marcus asked. "Aren't those classified?"

"Yup," Wade said. "Anyway, the 2404 is about the most vindictive missile ever fielded. It's not designed to detonate upon impact. It's got an armored penetrator nose and a long-delay, anti-removal, anti-disturbance fuze. It's intended to embed itself in any enemy ship, like us, for example, and sit there being a pain in the ass. If we try to pull it out, it'll probably detonate. If we accelerate too much, try to land, or transit with it still embedded in the hull, it'll probably detonate. If we just wait and do nothing, eventually the timer will run down and it'll detonate. The warhead is three hundred kilograms of high explosive, more than enough to tear the ship in half."

"How much time do we have?" Chief Engineer Nair asked. She looked tired, disheveled, even. Her normally cool composure had cracked. Her assistant engineer, Love, who had entered the *Agamemnon* with Wade, had been killed in the battle. There was no time for mourning now.

"I don't know," Wade answered. "The timer is randomized. It could be a matter of minutes, it could be days or weeks. Eventually, though, the battery will bleed down and it'll detonate."

Kel Morrow, the Astrogator, spoke up. "Why would anyone design such a weapon?"

Wade shrugged. "It ties up resources. A ship lost in battle is lost. A ship that's damaged can limp home. A ship with this thing stuck in it? It's not going anywhere. Even if you try to abandon ship, there's a chance the missile will detonate during the evacuation. It was designed with the Concordiat Fleet in mind, I suspect. The Combine fleet isn't so concerned with losses, doctrinally."

"Can you disarm it?" the captain asked.

"I don't know, ma'am," Wade said honestly. "There are procedures for it, but they've never been tested. I can't do it from here. Unless you have a military-grade manipulator robot handy, I'm going to have to suit up, go outside, and go hands-on. The missile has anti-tampering features, but their software is pretty crude, I'm pretty sure I can get around it. But the only way to actually disarm it is to take it apart and remove the detonator assembly. It doesn't have an off-switch."

"Will you try?" the captain asked. "It's a lot to ask."

"No, it's not," Wade disagreed. "If we don't do something, we're all dead anyway. Bearing in mind that my Fleet Nuclear/ Explosive Ordnance Disposal certifications have been expired for a few years, I'll give it my best shot. I believe I can disarm it, but I can't make a positive statement. It's gonna be dicey."

"I understand, Mr. Bishop," the captain said. "Thank you. I know you'll do your best."

A short while later, Wade and Cargomaster Kimball were suiting up in the ship's docking bay. Kimball was quite insistent that Wade not go on his spacewalk alone, and the mercenary didn't argue; he needed help with all of the tools and equipment, as well as a safety backup. Kimball was the most experienced EVA operator by far. Annie was helping him into his suit.

Devree Starlighter joined them in the docking bay, and helped Wade get into his own spacesuit. "You be careful out there," she said firmly "Nobody else is going to die, you hear me?"

Wade looked at her as he sealed the suit's gloves. "If we go, we're all going together. But listen, I wouldn't be doing this if I didn't think it was going to work. No worries, hey?"

Devree shook her head. "You're an idiot." She moved forward, kissed him on the cheek, then pulled the helmet down over his head. "You're sealed."

Marcus was there too. "Wade," he said, looking over at Annie. "My daughter is on this ship."

"I know, Boss. I've got this." Wade checked his suit's systems. "Boards are green. Comms are good. O2 is good. Heating and cooling are good. Devree? Can I buy you dinner when we get back to New Austin?"

Devree raised an eyebrow. "You mean like a date?"

"Something like that."

She smiled. "We'll see. Focus on not killing us all and we'll go from there."

Wade chuckled inside his helmet. He watched Devree, Marcus, and Annie leave the docking bay, and the room fell silent as it slowly depressurized.

"Are you ready, Mercenary Bishop?" Kimball asked.

"As ready as I'm going to get," Wade said. "Let's go."

The brown ball of Zanzibar hung far below the *Andromeda* as Cargomaster Kimball and Wade Bishop emerged from the docking port in the nose. Catherine, along with everyone else on board, monitored the ship's external camera feeds as the two men made the long spacewalk down to where the missile was embedded. On the dark side of the ship, away from the sun, Wade pulled out a flashlight to examine the missile. Tethered to the ship for safety, he moved forward to do so while Kimball hung back.

"Definitely a Type-2404," Wade said. His communications were being relayed to the command deck. "She's stuck in there good, too. Kimball, bring the laser cutter up. We're going to need to take off a section of the hull so I can get to the internals."

Catherine watched in silence as Wade and Kimball used the laser to cut away a section of the honeycomb energy absorber. The chunk was sent spinning off into the darkness and Wade moved in, tools in hand. He removed a small panel on the outer section of the hull, plugged a cable into the computer mounted on the wrist of his spacesuit, and attached an adapter to the end of the cable. He then connected it to a port in the missile.

"Running diagnostics now," he said. "It's not letting me in, but let me try...." He trailed off momentarily as he tapped the screen of the computer on his wrist. "That did it. Their software is outdated as hell. I think I spoofed it. Okay, the anti-tampering mechanism should be disabled."

"Should be?" Catherine asked.

Wade didn't exactly shrug inside his spacesuit, but tried. "Best I can do, Captain. Okay, I'm going to remove this panel now and get at the internals. If it doesn't detonate, we'll know the anti-tamper is disabled." He chuckled humorlessly, hovering just above the missile in the blackness of space. Using a power tool, he removed a series of screws, pulled a computer board out, held his breath, and snipped the cable.

"Nothing happened," Kimball pointed out. On the command deck, Captain Blackwood exhaled heavily.

"Okay, next step," Wade said, reading his screen. "Damn it. I've got to get through this mass of cables and shit and get at the detonator. Some of them I can cut, some of them I can't, and they're not marked or anything. This will take a while. Stand by."

Everyone on the command deck watched nervously as Wade slowly navigated the tangled mess of cables, connectors, and circuit boards, occasionally cutting something when the publications told him it was safe to do so. The younger officers whispered to each other, but no one else said anything. After a few minutes, Wade brought the power tool back in and began to remove screws and fasteners from the detonator assembly.

"Okay," he said over the radio, sounding tired, "I've reached the detonator assembly. I'm going to remove it and disrupt the firing train." Bracing with one hand, he reached into the guts of the missile and withdrew a cylindrical piece about thirty centimeters long. It remained connected to the rest of the missile by an umbilical cable. "When I cut this cable, there's a chance the detonator assembly will explode. It's only got about half a kilogram of explosives in it. It won't set off the missile now that I've removed it. Stand by."

He retracted the detonator assembly until its umbilical cable was taut, then clamped a cutter onto it. Turning in his suit so his helmet visor was facing away from the detonator, he cut the cable. The cylinder exploded, popping in a silent flash and peppering the hull with fragmentation. Wade went tumbling away from the hull, bouncing back when he hit the end of his tether.

"Mr. Bishop!" Kimball said. He vaulted forward, as graceful in zero gravity as ever, and grabbed Wade. "He's alive!"

"My arm hurts," Wade Bishop said.

"You've got a suit tear," Kimball said. "I can patch it. *Andromeda*, this is Kimball, have the med tech standing by when we get back in. He's got a few minor suit tears. I'm patching now."

"I got fragged," Wade said.

"Mr. Bishop, this is the captain," Catherine said. "Is it safe for us to remove the missile now?"

He grunted as Kimball applied a second patch to his suit. "Affirmative. I've disrupted the firing train. Bring the claw down and yank it out. Gingerly, please, it's still full of high explosives." As Wade supervised, the *Andromeda*'s manipulator arm unfolded itself and came around. The claw clamped down onto the expended rocket motor of the missile. Everyone on the command deck cringed and the hull vibrated as the massive, one-ton missile was pulled out of the ship's skin. Once clear, it the claw released it, sending the Combine warhead tumbling off into the night.

Wade keyed his microphone one last time. "This is Bishop. Scene clear. Coming back aboard. Out." Wade couldn't hear the relieved cheers of the ship's crew. Catherine exhaled heavily.

The Privateer Ship *Andromeda*
Deep Space
Danzig-5012 System

It was somber on the cargo deck of the *Andromeda* as the crew stood in a tight formation, hands folded behind their backs, flight suits pressed and cleaned. The ship accelerated toward the transit point at a steady one G. The *Andromeda* didn't have a chaplain, and her crew held widely varied belief systems, but burial in space was a tradition dating back over a thousand years. All present paid their respects in their own way.

Annie stood quietly in the ranks as Captain Blackwood presided over the ceremony. Her father and his mercenary team were standing in the back, missing Randy Markgraf. The captain's brother and his two friends were there as well. Cecil Blackwood, in particular, looked a mess. He had dark circles under his eyes, as if he hadn't slept in quite some time.

Captain Blackwood's voice was solemn and clear as she read an invocation. In her hands was a gold-inlaid, bound-leather Spacer's Bible, one that was well over a century old. "In the ancient tradition of our forebearers, we will now commit the bodies of the fallen to the stars. Ashes to ashes, dust to dust, all things must pass, for even the stars themselves are not eternal. We all share the same origin. We all come from the stars, and to the stars we all must return, one way or another. It is the way of things, and it is the way it has ever been. Only God is eternal, only God is universal, and we now ask that He shepherd the souls of the fallen to their well-earned, eternal rest."

The captain closed the Bible, and looked up at her crew. "I have asked much of you on this tour. You have not once disappointed me, not once let me or your shipmates down. A captain could not ask for a finer crew, and serving with you has been my honor. We are fewer in number today, but we accomplished our mission, we rescued the hostages, and we defeated an enemy cruiser well above our throw weight. You all performed phenomenally. You all have much to be proud of. Most of all, let us be proud of our fallen shipmates. They sacrificed everything so that the rest of us might live. They died fighting for their comrades. Please take a moment to reflect, pray, and remember the dead. Thank them for their sacrifice, and bid them farewell. We depart without them now, for they must walk a different road. Mourn the dead, but do not despair; theirs is the road we all must walk, in time. Let us be comforted in the belief that we will see them again, before the end of all things."

The cargo deck was as silent as a ship under acceleration could be as the crew took a moment to reflect and, in most cases, pray. Some bowed their heads, others whispered prayers, some quietly wept, but all remained in formation together. Many of them were injured. Some could barely stand, but they stood anyway. Even Mordecai Chang, who hated to leave his personal compartment for any reason, made a rare public appearance, though he wore a surgical mask to protect him from germs. The only one not present was Luis Azevedo, who was manning the command deck alone.

This hadn't been at all like Annie had imagined it would be. She had read of the dangers of space travel, of course, but they had always seemed so distant to her. Three people had died on this voyage, and more were injured. The captain's face revealed little, but Annie thought she looked as if she'd been crying. She had been close to the executive officer.

Annie thought back to the things that had bothered her before, the things she had considered to be problems, and felt small and petty because of it. *You didn't get to see your friends enough,* she thought bitterly. *Life was boring. You wanted to meet a cute boy. You wanted to ride in the rodeo.* Those things had defined her life before leaving New Austin, but now? None of it seemed to matter. Annie's heart still ached over poor Sparkles, but she wasn't even angry with Victoria Alexander anymore. She was just a stupid rich girl, a child, too fried on drugs to even know what she was doing. Annie actually felt *bad* for her. How screwed up was her home life that that was how she acted?

Looking around at her shipmates, Annie knew that she was where she belonged. Maybe one ship in a great big universe didn't make much difference, but it could make *a* difference. The *Andromeda* had changed the course of history for an entire world! Maybe that wasn't normal, maybe that was an exceptional experience, but Annie had had a part in it, and she was proud. The troubles of her old life seemed so small in comparison.

After a long moment, the captain looked up. "Crew, atten-*HUT!*" Annie snapped to attention with the rest of the crew. "I will now read the names of the fallen before committing their bodies to the stars." The bodies of the dead were carefully wrapped in Mylar blankets and secured. One by one, they would be lowered into the ship's casualty chute, which would drop them out the bottom of the ship. In an instant, they'd be vaporized in the ship's exhaust plume. Mazer Broadbent stood at attention, sending the bodies off, as Cargomaster Kimball played "Amazing Grace" on a set of old Avalonian bagpipes. "Randall Markgraf, of New Austin. Wolfram von Spandau, First Officer, of Heinlein." A single tear trickled down the captain's cheek as her friend, adviser, and second-in-command was laid to rest, but she maintained her reserve. "Charity Delacroix, Assistant Engineer, of Heinlein." Indira Nair openly wept as her assistant's body was sent down the chute. One of her shipmates placed a hand on her shoulder to comfort her.

Annie had never seen her so emotional before. From what she'd heard, the engineer was going to do a damage assessment with First Officer von Spandau, but Charity Delacroix had insisted that she go instead. The chief engineer was more important, she'd supposedly said. She was killed by the same laser strike that had taken the first officer. Annie couldn't imagine the pain, what it was like to have someone die for you.

When the bagpipes fell silent, and the casualty chute secured, the captain told the crew to stand at ease. "It has been a long journey, and I'm afraid it's not over yet. We've taken damage and circumstances necessitate that we take the long way home. Our trip back to New Austin will be substantially longer than the one from there, and we will need to stop at the Llewellyn Freehold for repairs. Until then, we're limited in how much acceleration we can maintain, and it will be slow going. When we get back to New Austin, we'll stay planetside for a local week, and everyone will get some well-deserved R&R. I wish I could give you more time, but the mission isn't over until we return to the Arthurian System. After that, we will head home, to Heinlein, and the ship will remain grounded for some time while she's refitted and overhauled. Spend time with your families. Live your lives. Make the most of the time you have. If any of you wishes to remain grounded after we return, you can come see me privately and we'll discuss the matter. There's no shame in staying home for a while, not after we've been out so long and endured so much. Until then, I ask that you all stay focused on your jobs, and don't let complacency get the better of you. Complacency kills, and we've had enough death on this tour."

The captain thanked her crew one last time, called them to attention, then dismissed them back to their duty stations. Annie turned and saw her father comforting Devree Starlighter. She wanted to talk to him, tell him she wanted to stay on the *Andromeda*, but now was not the time. She quietly left the cargo deck. She had a lot to think about.

New Austin
Capitol Starport, Aterrizaje
Lone Star System
Five Thousand Hours Later

Marcus Winchester waited anxiously in the cargo bay as the landing tower locked into place. The rest of his team was with him, and all were excited to be home, but Marcus was particularly so: he was going to meet his *son*.

He'd been gone from home for well over a New Austin year at this point, and sending messages to his family had been next to impossible until they'd gotten to the Llewellyn Freehold. As soon as the *Andromeda* had arrived in the Lone Star system, he sent word to his wife that he was on his way home, and found himself trying to will the ship to go faster. Now, he could barely contain his excitement.

Wade laughed at him. "Fidget a little more, Boss," he said with a grin. "It'll make the tower go faster."

Marcus laughed.

"Shut up, Wade," Annie said. "You just want to get back to your gross sexbot." Wade made a face at her.

Marcus noticed that Wade and Devree were holding hands. He was glad of that. Devree was a nice girl, and seemed every bit as crazy as Wade. Wade needed a good woman in his life, and to get rid of that ridiculous sexbot he denied ever having used. Jeremiah Hondo had a huge smile on his dark face, so happy was he to see his wife and kids again. Ken Tanaka had no family, but had confessed to his teammates that now that he had the funds,

358

he was going to return to Nippon to find himself a Japanese wife. Benjamin Halifax was grinning like a fool, though no one really knew why; as far as his teammates knew, he had no family, and apart from crudely bragging about his sexual exploits he didn't talk much about his personal life.

Then there was Annie. Looking at his daughter, proudly wearing her green flight suit, Marcus knew that she was a woman now. If he had known the tribulations the *Andromeda* was to face, he would have left her at home, juvenile detention or not. She had seen too much in too short a time. She'd seen combat. She'd seen death. He was so proud of how she handled it, how she carried herself. Wade was right: she was just like him. But he also knew that she hadn't processed some of the things she'd seen yet, and that they might yet come back to haunt her.

He just hoped his wife would forgive him. He knew that she'd be proud of what their daughter had become.

A klaxon sounded, a warning light flashed, and the cargo doors slid open. As the gap between them widened, the mercenaries saw their loved ones waiting for them on the other side.

Eleanor Winchester stepped forward, and was nearly tackled by Annie. "Mom!"

"Baby, look at you!" Ellie said. She started to cry. "You've grown. You're all grown up."

"Ellie," Marcus said, embracing his wife. He looked down at the baby in her arms.

"Marcus, I'd like you to meet your son, David Andrew Winchester."

"Hey, buddy," Marcus said to the child, choking up as he spoke. Little David clutched his father's finger in his tiny hand. "It's good to finally meet you. I'm sorry I was gone, but I'm home now."

Annie was crying now too. "He's so beautiful! Mom, can I hold him?"

"Of course you can, Annie. Here."

Marcus and Ellie held each other as their daughter held their young son in her arms, rocking him gently and smiling ear to ear. For all the horrors he'd seen, Marcus couldn't remember being this happy. Behind him, Wade was grinning ear to ear. Devree, at his side, covered her mouth with her hands and was unable to keep from crying. After Marcus introduced her to his wife, she asked if she could hold the baby. Annie obliged, and Devree carried little David in her arms while Marcus, his wife, and his daughter all hugged. Wade, seeing Devree with the baby in her arms, had a slightly concerned look on his face. Marcus winked at him.

Meanwhile, as the crew of the *Andromeda* disembarked to get some much-needed dirtside leave, Jeremiah Hondo was mobbed by his half-dozen kids. His booming, raucous laugh echoed throughout the cargo deck as they pulled him to the floor, laughing and crying at the same time. His wife, a heavy-set but nonetheless beautiful woman, with skin as dark as midnight, cried as she joined in on the group hug of her husband.

Then there was Ben Halifax. Two women were waiting for him when the doors opened. They came trotting through in very tall high heels. One, a tall blonde with fair skin, wore a slinky red dress that left little to the imagination. The other, a shorter, raven-haired woman of Asiatic descent, was dressed in booty shorts and a halter top. One kissed him passionately, then the other kissed him, while he grabbed both of their butts. The two women then kissed each other before leading Halifax off to whatever debauchery they had in mind. Mrs. Hondo covered the eyes of one of her sons, who had been gawking at the two women.

Marcus couldn't help but laugh. He only wished Randy was here with them. One more thing to feel guilty about, he supposed. One more name to remember. But that would come later. For now, he let himself enjoy the moment, his long-awaited reunion with his wife and son.

Captain Blackwood surprised him when she spoke up. He hadn't seen her approach. "Mrs. Winchester, I'm sorry it took me so long to get your husband and daughter back," she said. "Thank you for your patience and understanding. It couldn't have been easy on you, but I can honestly say I wouldn't have been able to do this without Marcus. He saved my brother's life, and indeed my entire ship. I am eternally grateful, and he'll be rewarded accordingly."

"I didn't do it by myself," Marcus protested.

"Of course not. We didn't spend Cecil's ransom money on Zanzibar, so I had planned to break a portion of it up and pay your team a generous operational bonus. Unfortunately, I spent most of it getting repairs on the Llewellyn Freehold."

"Nothing in the Freehold comes cheap," Marcus said.

"Nonetheless, Cecil has promised pay your team from the holdings of Blackwood and Associates. You will all be handsomely rewarded." She looked back at Marcus' wife. "Mrs. Winchester, I need to say something about Crewman Winchester here," she said, putting a hand on Annie's shoulder. "This young woman is a phenomenal spacer. She's bright, she learns quickly, and she kept her head on during stressful situations. She's an exemplary young woman and, if she likes, she's welcome to become a permanent member of my crew."

Annie's eyes went wide. "Mom? Dad? Can I?"

Eleanor frowned. "Absolutely not, young lady. You're behind on your school, but I'm not going to let you just quit."

Marcus was about to step in and say something, seeing the crushed look on his daughter's face, but Captain Blackwood beat him to it. "Annie, listen to me," she said. "You did very well, and you're always welcome on this ship, but you need to listen to your parents."

"But Captain, didn't you run away to be a spacer?"

"I did, but I was rather older than you. More importantly, I'd already finished my education. You were a valued crewmember, but you'd be more valuable to the ship with some formal technical training."

Annie looked less like she was going to cry, and Eleanor didn't look angry anymore. Marcus was pleased, but Captain Blackwood wasn't finished yet. "I'll make a deal with you, Annie," she said. "If you stay home and stay in school, I promise you that you'll have a place on my ship when you're ready. I'll send messages via courier once in a while to check up on you. It doesn't matter if it takes you one year or five, I'll find a place for you as long as I'm the captain of this ship. Your family has done a great deal to help mine, and returning the favor is the least I can do. Right now, though, you need to spend time with your family. You've got a baby brother to raise. Your mother will need your help. You also need to study."

"Yes, ma'am," Annie said. She seemed satisfied.

"Thank you, Captain Blackwood," Eleanor said, also looking satisfied. "I'm glad she was able to be of service. I like to think we raised her right." As anxious about losing her daughter to a career in space as she was, Marcus could see the pride on Eleanor's face. He'd told her how Randy had been killed as soon as the *Andromeda* arrived in system, but hadn't gotten into details of the battle, and how close the ship had come to being destroyed. There would be time for that later. Right now, he just wanted to enjoy a moment of happiness with his family.

"You most certainly did," the captain said. She nodded and left the Winchester family to their reunion. Marcus was grateful for the mentorship she'd given his daughter. Maybe she'd try harder in school, now that she had a goal she cared about to work for.

There would be time enough to worry about that later. Right now, he just wanted to be with his family.

The Blackwood & Associates ship *Highlander II*
Deep Space
Baker-3E871 System
Eight Months Later . . .

The *Highlander II* was a huge transport ship, an aeroballistic cone one hundred meters tall from nose to tail. She was the largest ship in the Blackwood & Associates fleet, and yet she alone would not be enough for this operation. She was joined by half a dozen others, including an armed escort from the Avalon Space Force. This find was worth protecting.

Cecil Blackwood studied a 3D representation of the derelict ship *Agamemnon*. Amazingly, no one else had come across it, though it had been more than a standard year since his sister had found it. It made a sort of sense, though—it had drifted out here undisturbed for something like eight hundred years. One more year wasn't so much in comparison.

Zak Mesa and Anna Komnene were with him, and were excitedly taking in every detail of the ship that the sensors could provide. Zak had read up on the entire history of the ship, the Cosmic Odyssey VI program, and knowing him, the entire history of the Second Federation while he was at it. Anna, who it turned out *was* something of a "big deal" on her homeworld, had worked out a data-sharing program with the University Byzantium in exchange for a substantial donation to the recovery effort (including a research ship). Between that and the influx in funds from the sale of the Zanzibari artifacts, Blackwood and Associates was doing quite well. They were excited by the find,

363

despite the gruesome description of what Catherine's crew had found on board.

Cecil's father hadn't been thrilled with it all, of course. He'd bellowed at Cecil for screwing things up so royally, and even bellowed at Catherine when she'd stepped in to defend her little brother. Cat, being Cat, bellowed right back, and the whole affair turned into one of those infamous Blackwood family shouting matches. As usual, it had ended with the vintage brandy and scotch being poured, and things calmed down afterward.

Augustus Blackwood had actually offered Catherine his legacy. He offered to let her be the elder heir instead of Cecil. Cecil might have taken that as an insult, but he knew that she'd run things better than he could have, especially since it entailed eventually taking her father's seat on the Council. That would have certainly shaken up those stodgy old goats, he thought, and the image of them *harrumph*-ing and pouting about it tickled him so much he wished his sister had taken their father up on his offer.

But Catherine, like their mother, was a free spirit. She had a life of her own, a tall ship, and a star to steer by. That was, she explained, all she wanted in life. Cecil certainly couldn't fault her for that.

His father also hadn't been happy about Bianca. He'd been even less happy when Cecil confessed that he'd married her on New Austin. The Church of Avalon officially recognized marriages from outside the faith, even secular ones (Cecil and Bianca had a civil union at a municipal courthouse in Aterrizaje), so there was nothing Augustus could do but drink and fume.

Cecil, for his part, had been sober for a year now, and staying dry was getting easier every day. Bianca constantly encouraged him, and rewarded his progress with every decadent bout of bedroom gymnastics her devious mind would come up with. She was, as he'd once surmised, a better Avalonian wife than any of the stodgy, inhibited Avalonian women he'd ever met. She had no patience for the gossip and politics of Avalonian high society, however; upon hearing that a council member's wife had referred to her as a whore, she'd punched the woman in the mouth, right in the middle of a garden party for charity. It had been quite the scandal, and had made all the celebrity gossip media. Fortunately, they'd left for their current mission shortly after that. Even Bianca could only get into so much trouble in deep space.

Despite the hell Cecil had gone through on Zanzibar, he had to admit a lot of good had come of it. He was still haunted by the deaths of the people who had helped rescue him. Randall Markgraf, Wolfram von Spandau, and Charity Delacroix were their names, and Cecil would never forget them. He'd given half his share of the family fortune to a trust fund for the families of the New Austin mercenaries and the crew of the *Andromeda*. Blood money to be sure, but money was the only thing Cecil had left to give. Fortunately, thanks largely to his sister, Zak, and Anna, he had a lot of it.

As for Zanzibar . . . Cecil took a deep breath as he recalled that awful place. The message Zak had sent out so long ago had definitely gotten the attention of the mass media on a dozen Concordiat worlds. The excitement reached a fever pitch when word of ancient Antecessor artifacts located there had gotten out later on. Even as Cecil was focusing on the salvage of the *Agamemnon,* the Concordiat government was about to pass a motion to officially annex Zanzibar and send in a peacekeeping force. When word had gotten out about the conditions there, the suffering, and the possibility of ancient alien technology falling into the hands of a man like Aristotle Lang, the constituency on a dozen worlds had demanded that their leaders *do something*.

Cecil wasn't sure the *something* in this case was a good idea. According to the various political punditry, it was expected that the annexation and stabilization of Zanzibar would be a quick and easy affair. The bloody fools had no idea what they were getting into. Lang wouldn't give up so easily.

Still, none of that was Cecil's problem. His mind boggled at the role he'd played in, essentially, altering the course of the history of a world, but he desired no fame or recognition for it. Too many people had died. Too many had suffered. Maybe some good would come of it, but he wanted nothing to do with any of it. Cecil was happy where he was, with Bianca at his side, Zak and Anna excitedly scanning their new prize.

That, he thought with a smile, was how things should be.